Weekend Experience

Experiences: Book 3

*Exploration of Fetishes by an Unlikely Couple,
and the Blossoming of Love*

Simone Freier

OTK Publications
www.OTKPublications.com

Weekend Experience

EXPERIENCES: BOOK 3

By Simone Freier

Published by OTK Publications
http://otkpublications.com

ISBN: 978-1-942054-06-1
v1.5

Manufactured in the United States of America

COVER DESIGN BY OTK PUBLICATIONS

This is a work of fiction. All names, characters, and incidents in this work are fictitious. Any resemblance to actual events or to real persons is purely coincidental. No humans or animals were harmed during the creation of this work.

Caution: This work contains mature content, including graphic sexual descriptions and scenes, and is provided for adults only. Neither the author nor the publisher intends to encourage or promote any of the activities depicted in this work. Many of the specific activities and scenarios described in this work can potentially be dangerous, and should not be attempted without special knowledge or training and, as appropriate, use of sterile single-use supplies. No information contained herein is intended to constitute advice or serve as instructional material, and this work should not be relied upon to ensure safe practices in real life.

Table of Contents

CHAPTER 1: REFLECTIONS

I drove from Sam's house wondering whether the previous 24 hours had actually occurred. But I knew in my heart that the experience had not only been real – in an unreal, or surreal, sort of way – but that I had been profoundly affected by it.

I had expected an amusing but relatively tame experience. Simple things like undressing for Sam and letting him put me over his knee for a hand spanking. The experience over the past day – and night – had been anything but tame: It had evolved into much more than a fun, if not bizarre, one-time lark with this older guy.

In fact, it had *started* with more than I had expected: More seriousness, more discussion and intellectual interest, more kindness and compassion. And, yet, it also involved more pain – and not just the physical pain of being spanked (or paddled, strapped, or switched), but also the psychological aspects of Sam's fetishes. Perhaps Sam had been correct, when he said that it takes a strong person to complete – let alone enjoy – this type of experience?

And that brought another flood of thoughts into my head. Why *did* I enjoy being spanked by Sam? I really didn't think it was my adoptive father's lack of caring or sole focus on his sons and sports. I also didn't think it was just due to my bland male friends and their immature sexual approach. I realized that over the past 24 hours, this man had brought me to orgasm more times than I had experienced in the rest of my life. And, these orgasms were *hot*.

In a stream-of-consciousness flow of thoughts, I realized that a wide range of things now excited me. From Sam's introduction of spanking and discipline, to medical fetish, my imagination was boggled, and Sam had clearly delivered on his promise to introduce me to new things.

Had these been just described to me, I doubt that I would have seen them as a turn-on. But Sam's approach combined his weirdly interesting ideas, a deep compassion and sensitivity that I had not expected, and the capability to allow the tables to turn and let me be the 'top'.

In fact, I now realized that I had been more turned on by taking the dominant role than by being submissive. And, yet, I felt a deep-seated need to please Sam – and, yes, even to *submit* to him, to any of his desires. As Sam had told me, it takes a lot of trust to agree to submit without knowing exactly what you will be submitting to.

Sam had stressed that the source of his turn-on was more about the gratification of seeing someone voluntarily submit, than actually causing pain or discomfort. He had said that despite making my bottom sore, he wanted me to be comfortable. And, from the beginning, he had taken the responsibility for my well-being, so that I wasn't really being harmed.

And, he was a good host. He made sure that I had plenty to eat and drink ... and even anticipated my need to use the bathroom before he punished me. We had indulged in wine, and he had taken me to that French restaurant, but he had also prepared a nice lunch for me, and even dessert – which we never got to, or needed, after the dessert we shared at the restaurant.

Despite his predilection for spanking, Sam was a very kind and caring person. When he was in control, he focused intensely on my needs and feelings. And, even though he made my bum sore, he followed-up the spankings by expertly getting me 'excited', and then satisfying my need for release. I thought about those orgasms again; especially when Sam went down on me in the sauna.

I had told Sam yesterday that my strong emotional feelings were not about him, but about me. I now realized that had been only partially true. I may have come to terms with being taken from my original parents ... but something in the way Sam treated me had brought back indistinct memories – no, really more of innate feelings – of my childhood, and the protection and love of my parents.

Again, my thoughts jumped – this time, to the irony of experiencing these caring and loving feelings, as Sam spanked me until my bottom was stinging. I didn't recall my birth parents spanking me, or causing any physical pain. I had lived a perfect childhood ... until that day in the parking lot when I was taken away and told that my parents were bad people for leaving me alone in the car.

Sam had talked about the closeness of opposites – hot and cold, love and hate, pleasure and pain. I had never believed in the 'starving artist' theory – where one must experience pain to be able to experience pleasure.

And I still have no idea where the pain from being spanked fit in; perhaps it was only the endorphins producing a natural high that might be mistaken for 'pleasure'? I had definitely been turned on yesterday – many times throughout the day, including immediately after Sam had spanked me. But I wasn't sure that was due to pain.

It may have been that I had begun thinking of myself in the dominant role. Just as Sam had suggested was the case for him. Although for me, it was more the taking of control (or being allowed to take control) – the exchange of power. Ultimately, it was a turn-on to see someone submit to me. That Sam allowed me to spank him (as well as doing other things) after his *faux pas* at lunch had been a huge turn-on for me.

At the time, I probably did want to cause him pain for his comment about my age. But as he put himself into position and took the punishment that I gave him, it somehow became more than play. This was when I began to have real feelings for this 'older' man, and realize that he was the main focus of my turn-on.

In fact, I now saw him as much younger than his fiftyish chronological age, despite his wide experience, and his mature perspective. Sam was a 'hunk', several inches taller than me, with a tan and muscled body, wavy hair, and aquamarine eyes. He was 'built' down there, too. And, while some of my prior male friends could probably best Sam in a direct competition of strength, they couldn't come close to Sam's sexual stamina ... or prowess.

I thought again about some of the explosive orgasms that I had experienced yesterday by Sam's hand, and I realized that I was unconsciously clenching my pelvic muscles. Perhaps there *was* something to be said for the experience of an 'older man'?

As my stream-of-consciousness road trip continued, I couldn't help but face the question that Sam had now raised several times – infuriating me each time: What was I doing playing around with an older man? I had told Sam that it was a reaction to the lackluster dating – and sex – experiences I'd had with guys my own age. I had developed that impression based on the dozen or so males with whom I'd had intimate relationships.

But, in another context, I'd also had good experiences with males – teachers and professors, my brothers, and my parents' friends. (I had to remind myself, that's what Sam was!) Although I doubt that Sam could have ever been close to my father, as they are nearly 180-degrees apart in perspective. My dad was always the macho-type.

As sensitive and caring as Sam had been, I could not deny that there was a 'macho' element to him; in a good sense, and without his 'acting' macho. Sam was a strong person, obviously very experienced with women and with life, and very self-confident. He was comfortable to be with.

I briefly wondered if my comfort yesterday had anything to do with Sam's bizarre definition of 'sex', and insistence that we didn't have sex during my first punishment experience. If Sam's demarcation of sex was not bizarre, it was at least nerdy ... almost sophomoric. But sex had not been a concern for me: Either I would be getting out of there as soon as possible or, I assumed, we would be having sex. Not a big deal.

I pulled into the driveway of my parents' home, and drove around behind the detached garage. Grabbing the beach tote filled with a mess of clothes, I ran up the steps, opened the door of my 'apartment', and flopped down on the bed.

During the drive, my brain had been awash with memories of and thoughts about my incredible experience with Sam. Now, as I relaxed into the softness and familiarity of my own bed, I considered what all this meant. Where would it lead? What did I want from the relationship, and what would I put into it? But I already knew that I would be willing to put more into the relationship with Sam than I had been motivated to do any time previously in my life.

I was not naïve, and certainly could see Sam's point – that I might get hurt, when I realized that I didn't really want an older man, or when Sam decided he didn't want to be with me, after I was emotionally invested in the relationship.

On the other hand, I had not been looking for a relationship, only for a little spice and some companionship. With someone who I respected, and who respected me. With someone interesting, intelligent, tall, dark and handsome. Well, Sam was taller than me, has a nice tan and only a touch of silver around the sides of his head of thick hair, and he was very good looking ... for his age. That stopped me: Maybe I shouldn't have been so hard on Sam for his age-based generalities?

I would have to talk to my friends about Sam – not that I often agreed with their opinions or followed their suggestions. Julie and Linda's brief meeting with Sam in the restaurant had been strange; Sam and I had been preoccupied, and they had been on their way to a movie for Linda's birthday. And, I'd had that silly remote-controlled vibrator inside me. And Sam had insisted on 'pushing my button' several times while I spoke with Julie and Linda. I would need to explain my strange behavior, not to mention Sam's smirk, when I saw them next.

Even sillier was Sam's invitation to give Linda a 'birthday spanking'! Oh, my – this might be more difficult to explain than I had thought. There was Sam's suggestion of introducing him as a 'professional spanker'. But that was a crazy idea (who'd ever heard of a professional spanker, anyway?). An honest approach might be the best: Sam was helping me with my career, and also teaching me about the fetish world. That sounded ridiculous, also; but I had approached Sam with only my career in mind. We *had* discussed my career ... and oh, so much more!

Sam may have been correct when he had suggested that having an intense experience like we'd had yesterday brings people closer together, and develops emotional bonds. But even 'the morning after', in my own room, I could not escape the fact that I had strong feelings for Sam. I was actually sad that I had to leave this morning. Not that Sam had kicked me out of his house, exactly ...

I couldn't help but wonder again what I was finding so alluring, so inescapable about this man. I remembered what I had thought yesterday afternoon – that my eyes had been opened, and I was attracted to the higher standards lived by Sam: More openness, honesty, intelligence, consideration, intimacy, enthusiasm and excitement than I had ever experienced before with anyone.

I got up from the bed and reached down into the tote bag, pulling out my very conventional PJs. I smiled, remembering how Sam – rather than being disappointed that I hadn't donned a negligee – had told me how cute I looked in the pajamas. My emotions hit me again: Sam was a really nice guy.

As I was about to correct myself about the 'nice guy' thought, I reached into the bag and brought out some of the sexy bras and underwear from my 'fashion show' for Sam. No, not a 'nice guy' in that way! I then thought about Sam consoling me after my tawsing at the foot of the bed ... and those incredible beads! Sam was not 'nice', but he was very caring and considerate.

The image of Sam in the 'chair position', awaiting his spanking, suddenly appeared in my mind's eye. And then I recalled the discussion we'd had – just this morning – about my being a 'sex slave'.

I dropped the clothes on the floor, and lay back on the bed. As my mind wandered, so did my hand, making its way under my pants and underwear to my throbbing clit. I tightened my pelvic muscles rhythmically, as I remembered: Sticking needles in Sam's bottom; our time in the jacuzzi ... and in the sauna, when Sam went down on me; bending over for the belt in his closet ... and masturbating on top of his blindfolded but unrestrained body.

My mind was flooded with images, thoughts, and feelings that couldn't be unraveled – no more than the currents in the ocean could be unraveled; yet blending together to create the ultimate natural high ... of being in love.

I reflected on the past 24 hours, as I finished cleaning up around the house. On the one hand, my creation of a unique experience with a twenties-something young woman had been successful – in fact, more incredible than I could have imagined (and I'd had a lot of practice 'imagining'). The scene with Kelly had included many of my fetish interests, such as spanking and 'medical sex'.

And Kelly had performed wonderfully, being extremely open with her body and her thoughts, taking her punishments well, and even getting turned-on in both 'top' and 'bottom' roles. While I had tried to surprise her with new experiences, she also had surprised me at every step along the way – with her directness, openness, enthusiasm, and raw sensuality.

We had done a lot of things very intimately together without transferring body fluids ... until our water glasses from the sauna had gotten mixed up. It would be quite simple to 'redefine' sex to not include eating or drinking after each other ... or kissing. But Kelly and I were developing real feelings for each other. Kelly had expected sex. And I realized that, being widowed, I had no responsibility to anyone else; it was solely up to me. And an opportunity like this may never come again (in a manner of speaking). Kelly had not informed me of any sexually transmitted diseases. And, I trusted her.

On the other hand, this had become more than roleplay. I had deep feelings for Kelly – on many levels. In her parents' kitchen, I had been attracted to a beautiful woman. Kelly really was a knockout, with her long auburn hair, trim but muscular body, generous but firm breasts, and ample bottom! Her hazel eyes sparkled, and her smile was captivating.

As we began our experience yesterday (could it only have been *yesterday*?), I had been impressed that she had actually shown up on time, and prepared for an unknown experience with an only slightly better-known man. By lunch, Kelly had demonstrated her enthusiasm, good humor, openness, strong will, and self-confidence.

My suggestion that she punish me for misspeaking at lunch opened new possibilities, as Kelly connected with the role of the 'top'. I was very pleased that she was a 'switch', and what excited her quite compatible with my own fantasies.

Then an image of Kelly, 'Sex Slave', passed through my head. The idea was an incredible turn-on, even though had I been asked what this would entail, I could not have answered at this moment. As Kelly had already found, I would not be interested in any type of 'slave' in the conventional sense. And I didn't want to hurt her – I was not a sadist. But she would require training, and it would be challenging for her, from both a physical and a psychological perspective.

I thought of '*The Story of O*', but had no intention of doing anything degrading to Kelly, or sharing her with another man. Perhaps another woman, though ...

I wondered again whether I would be able to get turned-on as easily as before yesterday, now that I had lived many of my active fantasies? Perhaps this was why my thoughts this morning involved Kelly's friends? It certainly would be fun to 'play' with them. What could be better than a sexy play partner ... except several sexy play partners? Yes, it could be fun, and yes, I would want Kelly to agree to it. In fact, my hope was that Kelly would see this as an opportunity to show off her dominant side.

But the realization that Kelly was – and would be – more than a 'play partner', had not only dawned, but was becoming rooted in my soul. I wanted to be with her. After a 24-hour marathon experience, we had grown together, become a part of each other. Of course, this was ridiculous! We hardly knew each other.

Well, I guess in certain ways we knew each other very well ... But it seemed too good to be true. Kelly and I had meshed perfectly, in terms of our energy levels, thought processes, and even sexual fantasies and turn-ons. I could only hope that her feelings for me mirrored mine for her – at least in some small way.

I would likely be the one hurt, if our relationship ended. After all, Kelly was a beautiful young woman, and had the world at her feet, while I was a widower with an interest in a never-ending list of sexual fetishes and perversions. But I didn't care. Kelly had been the brightest light in my life since Sarah passed.

I was getting turned-on just thinking about Kelly. I plopped down on the playroom couch, and closed my eyes. A series of images appeared in my mind's eye: Kelly standing in front of the desk; Kelly sitting on my lap; Kelly lying on the exam table; and Kelly masturbating on top of me.

I had no excuse: I was too old (or, at least, 'mature') to wonder what was happening to me. It was obvious. Despite the best-laid plans, and the best of intentions, Kelly had possessed me. I had no idea where this would lead, but I knew now that it was not simple infatuation: I was in love.

CHAPTER 2: DISCUSSION WITH FRIENDS

I still could not stop thinking about my 'first experience' with Sam, several days after our get together. Visions from that day filled my mind, and became fodder for new fantasies. I couldn't remember the last time before this that something had turned me on enough to fantasize about it. The summer had begun, and I thought about what I wanted to do before school resumed in the fall. Certainly Sam would be part of these plans.

I had planned to call Julie to explain the evening when Julie and Linda had met Sam and I in the restaurant – me squirming as Sam activated the small remote-controlled vibrator that had been inside me. But it would probably be best to meet with both Julie and Linda in person to talk about things; to explain what I saw in Sam, and perhaps give my friends a glimpse into the D/s – dominance and submission – experience I'd had during that incredible day with Sam.

But how could I explain these things? I wasn't worried what my friends thought ... exactly ... but I didn't want this to come across as merely an infatuation with an older guy, or some dangerous kink that they could not relate to.

The subject had been broached with Sam's mention of a birthday spanking for Linda; and with the brief discussion of Julie's and Linda's southern upbringing that included corporal punishment in the schools. They never wanted their punisher – usually the Girls Vice Principal –

to know that the paddling really hurt, and it was a demonstration of strength to not cry or otherwise show emotion during the school punishments. My friends might view spanking as an evil, or perhaps as a game. I really didn't know.

I had mixed feelings about discussing these things with my friends: It could be embarrassing to admit that I was turned-on by some of the things Sam and I had done ... but Sam had planted the seed of fantasy when he suggested that perhaps introducing my friends to spanking and submission would be a way for me to 'get back' at my friends for always getting me into trouble in school.

The more I thought about it, the more I realized that it really could be a turn-on, seeing my friends squirm while they voluntarily took a thrashing on their fannies.

Julie was certainly proud enough, self-confident enough, and competitive enough to take a spanking as a dare. But would she really continue to submit after she found out how much a real spanking hurt? Could she be expected to continue after a simple over-the-knee hand spanking ... to the tawse, hairbrush, or cane?

Although it wasn't part of Sam's fantasy, perhaps my friends – if they agreed to try this scene at all – should be bound into position, so that they would have to suffer an entire punishment session. As I pondered this, I felt a stirring below, and realized that maybe Sam and I could design an introductory experience for my friends that would be a huge turn-on to me.

Normally, the 'gang' would include Kathy – and I would really like to hear Kathy's views on these things, as she always had a positive and enthusiastic outlook on new adventures, and was the most open of all my friends. But Kathy was still somewhere on the Mexican Riviera with her parents, and wouldn't be back for a couple of weeks. I had already asked my friends to come to my birthday party, and it would be fun to have the four of us together again. Then I thought about celebrating my birthday with my friends at Sam's house ...

I could not argue that the concept of watching my friends take a spanking was becoming a turn-on. Julie, especially, had been the ringleader on so many occasions ... with some of them resulting in me getting into trouble.

In my younger years, I had not been concerned about trouble at school, or even with the police (although it had never come to that) ... but now, with 20:20 hindsight, I could see that Julie and Linda had caused problems that may have resulted in my not being invited to take some honors classes in high school. I had never been physically punished for any of the shenanigans that my friends had gotten me into, but I now realized that their influence had probably reduced some of my academic and social opportunities.

In trying to visualize my friends 'submitting' to Sam, I realized that I would need to talk Linda – and probably Kathy – into doing this. I felt certain that – with a little prodding, Linda would probably go along with some things – like her birthday spanking. While Linda was an open person, I doubted that she would agree to anything else (Sam's exam room came to mind).

Julie, however, would probably take anything thrown at her as a challenge, and as a joke ... or as a dare. I didn't think much of Sam's suggestion to purposely get my friends into trouble and then blackmail them into taking a spanking from Sam. But, I thought, there might be other ways to arrive at the same outcome.

One small challenge that I realized I would face included getting my friends to be comfortable nude with Sam – as he had said he didn't usually allow bathing suits in the pool (skinny dipping, only), and I had visualized my birthday party as an outdoor pool party in Sam's beautiful park-like backyard.

A much bigger challenge would be coming up with an excuse or rationale for my friends to try a submission experience with Sam. I was not at all concerned about sharing Sam with my friends – they could all have a lot of fun, and I was confident that Julie, Linda and Kathy would not try to hit on Sam, primarily due to his age, and because of his interest in bizarre fetishes.

I remembered the question Sam had asked, in the context of my being a 'sex slave': Could I submit to Sam (and perhaps take a hard spanking) in front of other people? Ironically, I thought, I would probably be more comfortable in front of a stranger (even a male), than doing these things in front of my female friends.

I wasn't too concerned about being embarrassed (for example, by getting into various positions and allowing Sam to spank me). But I was worried that my friends would not understand the turn-on in this, and would ridicule me for submitting in these ways; especially, to an older man.

On the other hand, as I visualized myself bent over, being watched by my friends as Sam spanked me or did other things to me (now, a memory of the anal beads flashed through my mind), I could not help but get turned on.

Perhaps I was really more of an exhibitionist than I had thought? I realized now that, in fact, I had never thought about 'performing' in front of others in an intimate way – except for a boyfriend, of course. But, could I go through with something like that, and still speak to my friends afterward ... without blushing? How could I possibly explain the turn-on that could be experienced by submitting? Would my friends understand that this was something more than (and different from) Sam being sadistic? Or, me being masochistic?

I would take the 'honest' approach with my friends: Simply tell them that Sam was teaching me about discipline, submission and other kinky things, and that I had begun getting turned-on by some of these experiences. I couldn't hope that my friends would really understand. After all, I had not expected, myself, to be turned-on, even (especially) after I had received the first few spankings from Sam.

And, I could not expect my friends to agree to take enough pain to get them to the point of a sexual response. While I could probably avoid a detailed discussion of submission and fetishes, I was actually looking forward to hearing my friends' thoughts, and wanted to share my newfound turn-on with them. And, maybe even get them involved in some way.

After pondering the possibilities, I decided that I would have lunch with my friends and broach the subject of Sam — at least to explain my squeals and jumps when Sam and I had met them briefly in the restaurant on Linda's birthday.

A second step might be to invite Julie and Linda over to Sam's house during the upcoming long weekend that was planned for a week from Friday. They could get comfortable with Sam, and I could prepare them for some fun at my 'skinny dipping' birthday party at Sam's house. Whether or not they would actually do any submitting was questionable.

On Tuesday, I met Julie and Linda at a nearby mall, where we perused the clothing stores, before stopping for lunch at a Mexican restaurant near one end of the shopping center, next to a large department store. We sat in the bar, which was quieter this time of day (with most of the moms and their screaming children eating in the main part of the restaurant).

After we had ordered our food, and our drinks had been brought to the table, I sat back in my chair, wondering how the discussion would go in the next few minutes. It was Julie, however, after taking a long sip of her margarita and licking some salt off the rim of the glass, who broached the delicate subject of Sam. "So, who is this 'masked man' that we met at the restaurant, and who you've been so cryptic about?" Julie said, to open the conversation.

I briefly had a vision of Sam wearing the blindfold that I'd had put on him – not exactly a mask ... and images of Sam in a Zorro mask, with sword and cape flew through my head. Then, unbidden, came the image of Sam as pirate, and the next flood of thoughts included enough of my fantasy that my face turned red before I had said the first word to Julie and Linda. I calmed herself, and took a sip of my drink before answering Julie.

Finally, I began, "Sam is a nice guy." When Julie gave me a questioning look, I continued, "He's actually a friend of the family. His sons played soccer with my brothers when they were in middle school. I sort-of knew Sam and his wife, but didn't hang around my brothers or my parents, for that matter, so only saw them a few times. My parents recently had a party, and invited Sam over ... and that's where we re-met and started talking."

I took another sip of my drink and continued, "Sam was a pharmaceutical researcher, and I asked him for some career advice, as that's very close to the biotech field that I'm studying. We had lunch a couple of times, and he helped me to better understand what companies are looking for, and how I might best steer my career."

Julie gave me a look that said, 'That can't be all there is to it!'.

I sat back and looked at Julie and Linda; they really did seem intrigued, so I continued, "Sam's wife died a few years ago, and Sam has been trying to decide what he will do with his life – now that he's retired, and free to do anything he wants." The food came, and the three of us dug in.

I wasn't sure how this was going to come out, as I hadn't prepared a speech, but my 'honest' approach guided me, and I opened up to my friends. "Sam is an incredible person, with lots of interests, and very high standards."

Linda looked up, her fork filled with lettuce and meat from her tostada, "You mean high living standards?" I smiled, "Well, yes, but also high standards regarding everything else. Sam has a high standard of ethics and morality..."

My friends hadn't expected this, and scrunched their faces. I pretended not to notice. My gaze was distant, as I considered how I would explain this.

"Sam has very strong beliefs, and holds everyone to high standards: In terms of honesty, in terms of respect, in terms of openness, and in terms of communicating. He believes that everyone should act this way. I guess he's a little idealistic, but I can see in the way he has acted with me that he truly believes that everyone can attain high standards ... if they recognize them, and if they try."

I ate a few bites, and put my fork down. "In some ways he seems immature – holding onto values that we might have had in college and being so unwavering. But he actually lives his life that way, so maybe it isn't just idealism. And, in almost every other way, he is anything but immature!"

Julie was getting frustrated with this cryptic conversation, but I jumped in before Julie could comment. "OK. I'll get to the part you guys want to hear. Sam is a very sexual being."

Julie just rolled her eyes, and Linda kept eating, as I finally let the cat out of the bag. "He has a lot of fantasies." Now, Linda put her fork down, and Julie raised her eyebrows, both of them leaning toward me, anxious to hear the details.

I continued, "And, he is interested in many fetishes."

Julie couldn't help but chuckle, and said, "What kind of fetishes? Like licking women's feet? Or, having you pee on him?"

At that, Linda said "Uggh!" and continued eating her lunch.

I smiled, wondering what Sam would think about these ideas. Actually, they sounded like something that I might imagine requiring of Sam, in the role of domme. At least Julie was heading in the right direction with her interpretation of 'fetishes'.

"As he explains it, his turn-ons are mainly based on his childhood memories. Simple things like watching someone undress. Or bending over the Vice Principal's desk for a paddling. Or getting a shot at the doctor's office." Julie and Linda were silent, waiting for further clarification.

"Sam is turned-on by the idea of submission: Someone doing something that is usually embarrassing or painful, that they are willing to do for him. Just to make him happy. As I said, many of these seem like quite immature things for an 'older man' to be interested in.

"But it isn't really just seeing a nude body or even spanking a girl's bottom that excites him; his fascination is with the person's reactions and thoughts. Their ability to be open, and have the self-control to take a spanking, or maybe masturbate in front of him."

Linda had finished her plate, and sat back. "That sounds pretty perverted. What's 'in it' for you? Or any other partner that he has?"

I responded immediately, "Well, for one thing, he – and his repertoire of fetishes – is very interesting. I've learned a lot, just being with him a short time. He is turned on by submission, but he's very kind; he's not sadistic. And he's very intellectual, very *creative*."

I wondered how far I should go, but realized that this was my chance to explain my yelps and squeals when my friends had stopped by our table at the restaurant. I couldn't help but think, 'that *was* perverted'... although it was also very creative.

I cleared my throat. "I'm going to share some things with you guys. Things you probably won't understand. And I'll probably be very embarrassed. But, in the spirit of Sam's concept of openness and honesty, I'm going to be strong, and tell you some details. If you're interested ..."

Not a word was said around the table, but Linda's and Julie's mouths dropped open, and they leaned still closer to the table, although I had not been whispering or making any effort to hide the conversation.

Finally, Julie put her arms out with her palms up, and said, "Well?"

I closed my eyes. This seemed wrong – talking in such sexual detail with my friends, but somehow it was also right. I also thought briefly of the non-disclosure agreement I had signed; but Sam had suggested that I tell my friends some details, to gauge their possible interest.

I wiped my lips with the napkin. "Do you remember, when you surprised us, stopping by our table at the restaurant, that I couldn't concentrate?   I might have squealed a few times."

Julie chortled, "Of course. That's *all* we noticed. We were getting worried about you: Maybe this old guy was abducting you. But you didn't seem worried or unhappy, and it was a pretty nice restaurant to be abducted-to. We really couldn't figure it out."

Linda was nodding, and chimed in, "Kelly, you were acting pretty strange."

I smiled, and explained, "I told you that Sam was very creative. He's also a 'tinkerer' – he builds high tech stuff. So, he was trying out ... or, *I* was trying out ... one of his inventions: A radio-controlled vibrator capsule that goes in like a tampon."

I was already thinking I had gone too far.

But I felt compelled to explain. "And, just as you guys arrived, he decided to have a little fun, 'pushing my button'." At that, both Linda and Julie cracked up, shaking the table so hard that the glasses nearly fell over. Julie screamed, "That's funny!" Linda covered her face with her hands, but her whole body was racking in laughter.

I chuckled, "And I had forgotten that it was even in me. When Sam pressed the button I jumped. But I didn't realize that there were 3 buttons, and Sam just sat there, and enjoyed escalating the vibrations as I was talking with you guys. There wasn't much I could do ..."

Julie and Linda laughed even harder. There weren't many people in the bar area, but everyone suddenly turned to see what the commotion was all about at the table with the three girls.

I continued, "Sam likes to surprise me. Even though I expected some of the things he's come up with, others are just 'out there' – I could never have imagined them. And just when I think I have experienced everything he has to offer, Sam surprises me again."

The table quieted down, and I became more serious. "Linda, you asked earlier what's in it for me. After Sam and I had a couple of lunches with some interesting conversation – including sharing some of our fantasies – I spent a day with him – what he calls my 'first experience' with fetishes. I thought it would be an interesting one-time thing. A fling that meant nothing, but brought me closer to this man who could really help me chart my career.

"Sam had told me that he wanted to spank me; and I pictured having my pants pulled down, and going over his lap for an old-fashioned hand spanking. Big deal! If I could help a nice guy get off, that would be fine." I gulped the last of my drink.

"But Sam was very serious. He spanked me, and strapped me, and paddled me!" Julie's and Linda's mouths dropped open again. I was not going to let myself be hampered by my friends' reactions. "I had to hold myself in position. And my bottom got really sore. I was OK with giving him his fantasy, but really wasn't enjoying the pain; until something happened." I shook my head.

After another sip of my Margarita, I continued, "Sam says that pain and pleasure are very close emotions, and that pain can become pleasure. I'm not sure that occurred with me, but along with the pain came an incredible release of tension, allowing me to lose control, and ... along with Sam's expert stroking ... have some of the best orgasms I've ever experienced. Now you guys are probably thinking that *I'm* the one who's perverted!"

Julie and Linda were quiet, trying to assimilate more information than they had needed. Linda finally mumbled something, and when both Julie and I turned to her, she opened up, "Actually, I can understand that. Julie doesn't know this,"

Julie indignantly put her hands on her hips, and said, "I thought I knew everything about you!"

Linda smiled, and continued, "But when we lived in the South and were paddled in school, it was a turn-on for me."

Now, Julie's mouth dropped open, and so did mine. Linda had a far-off glaze in her eyes, as she remembered, "I didn't like getting swats, but Julie and I took it as a game – to show the Girls Vice Principal that she wasn't going to 'break' us. But afterwards, when I got home from school and went to my room, I almost always masturbated, while thinking about getting paddled."

Julie just chuckled, but I was shocked. I had thought that my friends would never understand my interest in Sam, and that they could never understand being turned-on by a spanking ... but Linda had proven me wrong. Maybe Sam's idea of 'playing' with all of us was not so farfetched. And, I knew now that Linda would be taking a belated birthday spanking from Sam.

I had to go the next step. "I've had fantasies about being ravaged, and someone controlling me, but I never imagined being turned on by pain. And I don't think it's the pain that is a turn-on for me now. Something happened during our day together that convinced me that my real turn-on is being the one in control, having someone else submit to me."

Julie looked at me, both seriously and sensually, and said, "That's hot!" Linda was nodding, and she brought her hand up to the table after she realized that it had been in the crotch of her jeans.

I explained, "Sam sometimes says things that get me really upset. He knows better, but during our day together he said something that almost made me leave. He knew that, and offered himself for punishment – allowing me to spank him (and do other things) until he was nearly in tears. Somehow, the power of being the 'top' intoxicated me."

I smiled at my friends, and gave them the details, "It was an incredible turn-on to see him pull down his pants and bend over, his package hanging down and his butt quivering, and tell me 'I'm ready for my spanking now, Ma'am'.

"Sam is as open as he wants others to be, and he can be turned-on being either the dominant or the submissive: He's a 'switch'. Sam is the polar opposite of Tom, or some of my other bland hook-ups. Sam and I did quite a few things I've never done with a man before ... or anyone, for that matter."

Linda said, "That's incredible. It sounds like he's quite an experience."

Julie couldn't help but ask, "Like what?"

I looked at her questioningly, and then said, "Oh. Like having anal beads inserted into me and then being masturbated. Is that too shocking?" The table was quiet again, and Julie was slowly shaking her head 'no'. But it looked like they had both just come from a weekend at the beach ... as their faces were flushed. We had discussed sex many times over the years, but somehow this conversation was far beyond our normal social limits – even as close friends.

I felt more relaxed, and picked up a few tortilla chips, which I started nibbling. I had just eaten lunch, but somehow felt hungry again. And, not just for food. "I would really like you guys to come to my birthday party – which I'm planning on having in Sam's backyard. He has a great house, with a sauna, swimming pool and jacuzzi, and park-like grounds." My friends were nodding.

Then, I added, "He is hoping that you would be willing to come without bringing a boyfriend. And, that you will be open enough to go skinny-dipping. After what I've told you, you can see that nudity is not a big deal for Sam ... but openness is. I don't know exactly what he has planned, but I'm sure it will be interesting. And he would never force you guys to do something you didn't want to do. It's never about forcing someone ... it's about voluntary submission." I looked at Linda and then Julie, "I think we'll have a really fun time."

Julie immediately rejoined, "Of course we'd like to come to your party! And skinny-dipping will be fun! I'm sure you remember some of our skinny-dipping parties at your parents' house. Like the time when your dad yelled at us ... but wasn't going to leave until we got out of the pool naked?"

I tried to remember. "Is that what he was doing? That makes sense, but I didn't get it at the time." We all laughed, remembering some of the wild times of our youth.

The three of us left the restaurant, and wandered down the mall back toward our cars. I said, "And, of course, I want Kathy to be there. I know she's open – she's probably lying topless on a Mexican beach right now!"

Linda laughed, "Julie makes sure she's known as the 'wild' one, but Kathy is probably more open – about nudity, sex, and her body – than any of us."

Julie reminded us, unnecessarily, "Her parents were Hippies ... maybe still are. Kathy was brought up in a very open household – not quite a commune, but I know she and her brother are very open with each other, and the whole family went to nude beaches together."

I smiled, "I know – I went with them, once. So at least two of our dads have seen some of us nude!"

I had almost forgotten. "Would you guys like to come over to Sam's house a week from this weekend? Just for a quick visit. You could properly meet Sam – not like in the restaurant! – and I can show you around. I'll be staying there over the weekend. I don't know what Sam has planned, but I'm sure he would be happy to have you guys over. Maybe on Saturday afternoon?"

Julie and Linda nodded, and Julie spoke up, "Sure, that would be great."

Linda stopped walking suddenly, and turned to me, "Will he want to give me a 'birthday' spanking?"

I chuckled, "Probably." I added, "But you won't have to do anything you don't want to." My friends laughed, and waved as they went in separate directions to their cars.

As I drove home, I realized that I was breathing heavily. It was a relief to have told Julie and Linda about Sam. But I was also getting nervous about actually having my friends over to Sam's house. He had already asked me if I would let him spank me in front of others.

And I knew that he would want to get my friends involved in a 'scene'. It *would* be fun to see my trouble-causing friends go over Sam's knee for a hard spanking. I became more nervous. I hadn't mentioned the 'corner time' to my friends. Or the 'corrective' punishment. I wondered whether my friends would see the 'exam room'.

After parking and running up the stairs to my apartment, I flopped on the bed, and started imagining the upcoming weekend with Sam. How he would treat my friends. And I thought about my birthday party, which was a month away.

I hadn't masturbated since the morning I had come back from Sam's house. My fears in sharing Sam's fetishes with Julie and Linda had evidently been unwarranted. I could relax and again think about Sam. I would be having lunch with him on Thursday – and perhaps eating more than food. Then, another week and another lunch, before our long weekend together.

Unbuttoning my jeans, I turned onto my stomach. I let both hands slide underneath my body, across my lean stomach, through the dark triangle formed by my extended bikini wax, and between my legs. Flicking my clit in an unconsciously rhythmic pattern, and cupping my vulva with other hand, I put a finger on my anus.

I hadn't done this while masturbating before, but it brought back a rush of sensations and experiences: Sensations and experiences that Sam had introduced me to only recently; during that incredible day when I'd had my 'first experience' with him.

CHAPTER 3: LUNCHTIME TASTING MENU

I had been working hard during the past week since my experience with Kelly, getting the house ready both for the long weekend and for Kelly's birthday party – which required some unique preparations. The playroom, exam room, and downstairs bathroom/sauna were cleaned and ready. The main and upper floors were usually kept neat and clean, so only minor dusting was required.

But for the birthday party, I would need to get the 'pool room' into shape. This was a large room and connected half-bath that was accessed from the kitchen and from the outside deck. At one time, I'd had a Ping Pong table in the room. The bathroom was usually used by pool guests. But in the past few years, the pool room had been used for storage – with chaises, cushions, pool supplies, and a variety of other 'junk' filling it, and making it unusable for anything else.

I labored to clean the room, moving a lot of stuff into the garage. I also washed the patio and pool furniture, including fashionable umbrellas and several chaise lounges, and placed it on the aggregate deck bordering the beautiful expanse of grass.

The long weekend was coming up in a little over a week, but I couldn't stop thinking about Kelly's birthday. I had many things planned – for Kelly, and for her friends. I had been so busy and tired over the past week, I'd only masturbated a few times. But now, thinking about the plans for Kelly's birthday, I was retiring to the playroom couch every few hours, as I fantasized about new possibilities.

While many of my fantasies would undoubtedly never come to fruition, I wanted to be prepared. I built several items that necessitated trips to the hardware store to pick up lumber and fittings. I ordered some supplies from Internet stores, and reminded myself to visit a costume shop in the next week.

It was Wednesday night. I had done all I could for the day, and I looked forward to having lunch with Kelly tomorrow. I sent a quick e-mail, suggesting that we meet at another local restaurant for lunch. Then I lowered the huge screen in the playroom, and put on an old movie, as I relaxed on the couch with a nice glass of wine. My mind wandered, as I thought again about Kelly's birthday party.

I didn't know if her friends would even attend ... and, if they did, whether they would be open to skinny-dipping ... or maybe a lot more. And, would Kelly be open to what I was planning? It would be a 'scene' in front of her friends, something that would take courage and extreme openness to do. I had considered doing the scene with Kelly during the impending long weekend, but decided that a surprise experience on her birthday would be more special.

And I had a few more 'special' activities planned for her birthday. I had been making a list of the things that I still needed to buy for the party, and realized I had to add the party favors. I had ideas for two different 'favors' that would be appreciated by my guests.

If Kelly's friends were really as wild as she claimed, then maybe we could do a few things 'more' than skinny-dipping? I was not seeing the movie on the screen of my playroom, but visions in my mind's eye of the possibilities of playing with Kelly and her friends.

I began to masturbate, and my visions focused on Kelly: Her smile, her energy and enthusiasm; the sparkle in her hazel eyes, her blushing cheeks (both the ones on her face, and her rear), her pert little nose, and her long auburn hair that glinted gold flecks in the overhead lighting of the playroom; and this beautiful woman sitting on my lap, in my arms, in the shower ... and in the sauna; going down on her ... and, her going down on me.

I came without even realizing I was that turned on. Once again, I was amazed that I had experienced an orgasm, not by fantasizing about spanking or medical experiences, but just by thinking of Kelly.

I woke up Thursday morning thinking about the lunch I was going to have with Kelly; and our joking that perhaps we would be 'eating' more than our lunch. Lying in bed, only half awake, my fantasizing took over. I thought about eating Kelly for dessert. And, where we could do this: In the van that my wife had driven, which was still in the garage – and which I only used for trips to the market or the hardware store, when I had to carry a big load.

Then, my thoughts turned to another way of 'eating' Kelly. But that would require cleaning her up. Which meant I had to pack certain items in the van ...

On the way to lunch, I stopped at a market to pick up a few things. Actually, I walked out with several bags of food and supplies, which I put in the back of the van in the large plastic tub that was at the foot of the air mattress now covering most of the floor space where I had removed the seats. I had also picked up a small bag of ice, which I put in the cooler. A few items from the bags also had to be moved to the cooler.

By the time everything was ready, I knew that I would be late arriving to the restaurant; but only by a few minutes. Hopefully, my tardiness would be compensated-for after lunch by my preparations in the van for a unique experience with Kelly.

When I walked into the funky bar-restaurant, Kelly was sitting at a corner table, looking toward the front door. As she saw me, a big smile formed on her beautiful face and, I was sure, on mine as well. We hugged, and gave each other a peck on the lips before sitting down.

After gawking at her startling beauty for a few seconds, I pulled my chair to hers, leaned over, and gave her a long, deep kiss. I smiled at her and said, "I would like to straddle you and sit in your lap to hug and kiss you, but considering this is a public place, I'll try to restrain myself."

Kelly laughed easily, and then frowned, and gave me a stern look. "You were late, mister! At least six minutes. I may need to punish you later."

I smiled, and said, "OK. But you might want to see what I brought for dessert before you make your decision; my preparations took longer than expected."

Kelly raised her eyebrows, and said, "I was hoping that we would eat more than restaurant fare, today. Actually, I'm a little surprised that you didn't invite me over, and cook lunch for me."

Now, I frowned, "That would have been a great idea," and I said under my breath, "and much more practical for the dessert I have planned." I looked at Kelly, and explained, "But I wanted to make our long weekend special, and knew we would get carried away if you came over. The weekend would probably have started with a week-long orgy, as I might not have let you go home."

Kelly laughed, "And I probably wouldn't have left! I missed you, and didn't want to wait another whole week to come over and have some fun at your place." Kelly gave me a pouting look. "Why can't I just go home with you today, and start our long weekend immediately?"

I thought about it. It wasn't a bad idea. I was ready for the weekend, but still had some errands to do before Kelly's birthday party. But that was still three weeks away.

And, it wasn't as if my calendar was full: Just about all I was doing these days was thinking about Kelly, and preparing for our next two get-togethers. So, in the spirit of being spontaneous, I nodded, "I've missed you, too. And there's really no need to wait another week."

Kelly's eyes sparkled like diamonds, reflecting the lights from the bar around us, and her smooth skin glowed. I was sure I was seeing an aura of color around Kelly, or perhaps it was my emotions ...

"But, we both still have a few preparations, so why don't we start our weekend 24 hours from now?"

Kelly gave a mock pout, but quickly brightened, popping out of her chair, and putting her arms around me, hugging me tightly and then giving me a short, but ardent kiss, before sitting back down. "That would be great! Oh, Sam, I've really missed you!" It had been less than a week since our day together, but seemed like at least a month to me, too.

Our lunch was fine, but I don't think either of us was concentrating on the food. Kelly updated me on her school plans for the fall (taking a couple of seminar classes, but mainly working on her doctoral dissertation), and said she was looking forward to spending more time with me during the summer.

Then, Kelly suddenly yelped, "Oh! I nearly forgot to tell you!" I looked at her expectantly, and she continued, "I had lunch with Julie and Linda a couple of days ago. It was pretty interesting; I think it went well." Kelly smiled at me, drawing out the obvious suspense, and I realized that I was holding my breath.

"First, they will come to my birthday party ... and they've agreed that skinny-dipping would be fun. Second, I invited them to come over to your house for a short visit – just to meet you under better circumstances. Oh! I have to remember to call and let them know that it will be *this* Saturday, not a week from now! My other friend, Kathy, is still out of the country, but I know she'll come to the birthday party, also. I'm sure you'll like Kathy."

I was delighted, and a little surprised, that it had gone so well. I was now really curious what Kelly had said to them. "I'm almost afraid to ask ... what did you tell them – about me, what happened in the restaurant, and about your interest in submission?" Now, I was sorry that we hadn't strategized Kelly's meeting with her friends, and set some boundaries. If they were ever to 'play' with us, it would be better if there were some surprises left; I hoped Kelly hadn't spilled all the beans ...

Kelly looked brightly at me, and her smile grew. "So, I told them the truth – that you were an old (but not that old) friend, helping me with my career. And, that you were interested in some fetishes, and had shared them with me. And, that I got turned on by some of them."

I stammered, "But what about the specifics? I hope you didn't tell them everything, or it will be difficult to have some surprises for them ... if they ever decide to play with us."

Kelly shook her head, "I didn't say much. Mainly about voluntary submission, spankings, and that you helped me masturbate. I did explain my squeals in the restaurant when we played with that stupid remote-controlled vibrator. And, I guess I mentioned the anal beads. Oh," Kelly smiled, "and I also told them that you let me spank you."

Kelly was looking through me, either trying to remember what she had told Julie and Linda, or remembering our day together. I couldn't tell, and it didn't matter. She continued, "I didn't tell them about the corner times, or corrective punishment. And I don't think I mentioned the medical stuff at all."

I was relieved to hear this, and it brought a flood of visions into my mind; visions of giving these girls pelvic exams, sticking needles into their bottoms, and introducing them to a variety of anal play. I saw the three – or four – girls lying on chaises, their bottoms all presented in a line ...

I blinked, and realized that I had to calm down, as these things would probably never happen, anyway. Looking at Kelly, I said, "So I guess they didn't ridicule or mock you? They were comfortable with the things you said turned you on?"

Kelly nodded, "I think so. They were hysterical hearing about the vibrator. And Linda admitted that she actually got turned on thinking about school paddlings, when she got home from school after being punished. I told you Julie and Linda were pretty wild, so they weren't too shocked to hear what I told them."

Kelly smiled, and looked up at the ceiling, then back into my eyes, "But they may be shocked, if they see – or experience – your exam room!" We laughed, and I tried to restrain my fantasized thoughts.

Kelly then gave me an affectionate look that melted my heart again: Sparkling eyes, glowing cheeks, and a beautiful smile; with her waist-length hair flowing down behind her, a backdrop for her innocent, yet sensual, face.

I paid the bill, and we left the restaurant, walking down the sidewalk, holding hands, until we got to a large parking lot bordering a park. Only a few cars were there, in addition to my wife's van. I had taped black felt to the insides of the back windows, but it looked like a normal, family van, of the type in which many of the moms at the park brought their children.

I had parked in a corner of the lot that was more remote, near a hiking trail that wasn't getting much use on a weekday. We cut toward the van on one of the park trails, passing some ponds with ducks, and winding back toward the parking lot. I turned to Kelly, and looked into her eyes. My emotions overcame me, and I hugged her tightly, and then we kissed; long, languorously, lovingly.

When we came up for air, Kelly gave me a slightly strange look (curiosity? fear? excitement?) and asked, "Are we going to have sex in public?" I laughed – that wasn't a bad idea, at least for some future time. We hadn't made love at all up to this point – only gone down on each other.

I looked down at Kelly's jeans, and said, "Well, perhaps if you had worn a skirt, you could have sat on a bench, with my head in your lap ..." Kelly laughed. I decided to fill her in on my plan for the afternoon. "But I had a more interesting idea, after I thought about your suggestion of 'eating' after lunch, and then decided that we should make it a real 'dessert'."

Kelly gave me a confused look, and said, "I have no idea what you're talking about."

I laughed again, and responded, "Yes, Kelly. I have tried to be creative, to introduce you to new experiences, and to surprise you ..."

Kelly gasped, "Oh, no. Now, what?"

I hugged her again, saying, "I think you'll like it. Just dessert."

As I led her across the parking lot to the van, I heard her mutter, "Oh sure. No spanking, no needles, no butt plugs ..." She was obviously expecting more than I had planned, but would just have to find out – in a few minutes – what I was 'up' to.

We reached the van, and Kelly gave me a curious look; she hadn't been in my garage, so hadn't seen it. I opened the sliding door, and Kelly looked in, but didn't have an immediate reaction. The only thing visible was the air mattress, with a beige sheet covering it and folded underneath ... and a bunch of junk in the back that included a large plastic tub, large jug of water, and a few bags from the supermarket, plus the cooler.

Kelly looked at me, and I nodded for her to get in. We climbed into the back of the van, and sat on the mattress that covered the entire width, and nearly the entire length of the van, with just the tub, water cooler jug and supplies between the end of the mattress and the rear window.

I slid the door shut, and we sat cross-legged facing each other in the dark cave of the van, the only light coming through the front windows and windshield, although I had opened a heat protector across the windshield that reduced the light (and increased the privacy) still further. Kelly looked around, as her eyes became used to the dark, but didn't see anything of obvious interest.

"Kelly, I want this to be a 'fun' experience. No punishment. But you *will* have to submit." Kelly rolled her eyes, and I continued, "Submit to something I'm sure you will enjoy. We're going to eat our dessert ... and I'm going to eat you." Kelly was still giving me a confused look.

I laughed, "It's going to be very messy! And I'm going to have to clean you up afterward." Kelly now had a blank look on her face; she had no idea what to expect. Just the way I liked it! "Please take off your clothes, now. You can put them on the front seat, where they won't get soiled."

Kelly immediately began undressing. "Thank you, Sir, for blacking-out the windows. That was considerate of you." She folded her jeans and top, and put them on the front passenger seat. Kelly looked beautiful in her bra and panties – both black – the bra lacy, and the underwear simple bikinis with a thin lace waistband. She unhooked her bra, and swung it around to the front seat, then scooted herself toward the rear of the van, and lay back, lifting her legs, pulling off her panties and handing them to me.

I crawled over her and dropped them onto her bra in the front seat, then lowered myself to her, giving her a brief kiss before sitting up between her legs. I smiled at her, and again she gave me a questioning look.

Now, I undressed, folding my slacks and shirt, and dropping them over the driver's seatback. I finished undressing, as Kelly watched ... and then I put on a pair of running shorts and tank top. Kelly said, "You're not going to be undressed, too?"

I had thought about our bodies sliding along each other, with gooey and sticky dessert sauces between us. It would have been hot, and maybe we would try that another time. But today, I was the one eating, and Kelly was the one being eaten alive – along with various toppings and accompaniments.

I leaned toward the back of the van, and took the grocery bags out of the tub, laying them alongside us. A large water bottle – of the type used in office water coolers – could be seen sitting at the very rear of the van. I looked back at Kelly; she had lifted her head to see what I was doing, still confused. With the water and the tub, perhaps she thought I would be giving her an enema – here in the park.

But I was much more interested in doing something loving with Kelly than anything that challenged her, or tested her willingness to submit. I already knew that she would do anything I asked. But I also knew she would be at least a little surprised with this afternoon's fare.

I began unloading the grocery bags: Fresh fruit, chocolate and caramel sauces in squeeze bottles, shaved dark chocolate, cans of whipped cream, and some miniatures of liqueurs – including Kahlua and Grand Marnier.

I also took out of the shopping bags a small bag of brown sugar, a pint of sour cream, some Florentine cookies, a squeeze bottle of honey, some 100% pure maple syrup, and a few jars of jam. I had reached the bottom of both bags, and there were only a few non-food items left. I glanced back at Kelly; her head was still up, and her eyes were now wide, a smile growing on her face.

"Yes, Kelly, we're going to have dessert. More specifically, *I'm* going to have dessert – served off of you: You will both be the dessert platter and part of the dessert. I'm planning on eating my fill today, and you will need to remain very still, so the dessert doesn't fall off the platter."

Kelly started giggling, her flat stomach moving in jerks up and down, as her giggles became a laugh. She put her head back down, and I remembered to pull out the small pillow from another bag that I had brought from home, putting it gently under her head and giving her another peck on the lips. Also in that bag were a few spoons and Tupperware containers.

I pulled out a small spoon, and opened a jar of blueberry jam, taking a small amount in the spoon and feeding it to Kelly. "Yum!" she announced, and put her head back down. I then put a spoonful of the jam in my own mouth, and swirled it – as I might when tasting a fine wine. I leaned over Kelly, and lowered my head to kiss her – an open-mouth, tongue-swirling, experience that was sweetened by the jam. Kelly continued to kiss me long after we had swallowed the jam.

I then sat back up and reached for another jar, taking a spoonful of the green jelly. I told Kelly, "This will be a little different. You told me you wanted more spice in your life."

After putting the jelly into my mouth, I again leaned over Kelly, and her head lifted up to meet mine, as our lips joined. It didn't take more than a moment after our mouths had joined before Kelly gave a little squeal, and said through the kiss something that sounded like "That's hot!"

I smiled, and said, "Yes, that's what *I* thought." I knew she meant the Jalapeño jelly, but the romantic kiss was also very hot.

I grabbed the honey, and began to squeeze a line of the thick, sweet viscous liquid along her neck, zigzagging across her chest, and down to her breasts, then squeezing a blob of honey over each nipple. Kelly squealed, and then giggled, as she felt the honey drip over her skin. Finally, I moved back up to her face, and squeezed some honey up her neck, over her chin, around her cheeks, and then a large blob across her lips.

I began licking her, as a dog would, lapping up the sweet liquid ravenously. First her cheeks, and then down to her chin, working my way to her honey-glazed lips, which were open and awaiting my mouth. We kissed again, long and passionately – literally, one of the sweetest kisses I had ever experienced!

I continued licking – down her neck, across her chest, and over her breasts to her nipples. I spent several minutes licking, sucking, and gently biting each of her nipples in turn, and both were as erect as I had ever seen them. I looked into Kelly's eyes, from only a few inches away, and they seemed to be emitting their own glow in the darkness of the van.

I could tell that Kelly was quite turned-on already, but she would have to wait a bit longer for the release that she needed. I chuckled, and said to Kelly, "I licked my plate clean! But I'm still hungry. I'm going to make a nice dessert on this flat platter here," patting her stomach. Kelly's head was on the pillow, and her eyes were closed.

For a change of pace, I grabbed the sour cream, and a wooden spatula that I had brought, and began spreading a thin layer of sour cream over Kelly's abdomen – from her navel to just below her breasts, and from side to side. Kelly shrieked once, as the cold sour cream first contacted her skin, and she giggled, making a very nice scene of the rippling white landscape that followed the contours of her body.

Once she was coated with sour cream, I reached for the brown sugar, and began crumbling it over her – covering the sour cream with a thin layer of crunchy sweetness. Then, I opened a box of blueberries and dropped them, one-by-one, onto the sour cream and brown sugar mixture. Her stomach now looked like a pie, dotted with fresh blueberries.

Kelly couldn't stop giggling, and her stomach was jiggling, but the 'pie' was holding together. I arched my eyebrows and gave her a quick smile, then lowered my head, licking and slurping up the sweet mixture. It was a bit too much, and I scraped a portion off with the spatula, and put it directly into Kelly's mouth, so she could taste it. I then continued to lick Kelly's stomach until she was clean. Before I ventured lower, I decided to 'decorate' Kelly's body.

I sprayed whipped cream on her nipples, and drew a line of white around her breasts, and down her middle, to her dark triangle. Then, I took the chocolate sauce, and squirted it over her pubic hair, retaining the color contrast, but making a gooey mess. Finally, I added some decorations, including writing "I love you" using the squeeze bottle of caramel.

I put a raspberry on top of the mounds of whipped cream covering each of Kelly's nipples, and arranged a few strawberries and grapes on her now-sticky body. I gave Kelly credit for not complaining about the mess. She must have been wondering how she was going to get cleaned up enough to drive home. Or, perhaps not.

I picked up one of the raspberries, dipped it in the whipped cream from Kelly's right breast, and put it into her mouth. She propped herself up, both to eat the fruit, and to see the 'food art' I had created on her body. Taking my time, I selected fruit, dipped it in the chocolate or caramel sauce (or both), and used it to scoop up some whipped cream. It was delicious, and a nice way to eat dessert: From a submissive's body.

I had put too much chocolate sauce on Kelly's pubes, so started smearing it around using my fingers – like finger-painting – over her hips, down her thighs, and to the insides of her legs, working my way back up to her genitals. I licked chocolate, sucked up whipped cream, and generally had a great feast, while Kelly held still, and experienced the gooey, sticky, but sweet mess that now covered her body; and the wet, hungry tongue that was lapping it up.

I held myself over her – trying not to get my own clothes sticky – and kissed her softly. I whispered, "Are you OK? Enjoying your dessert?"

Kelly opened her eyes, and smiled at me. "Oh, yes, Sir. I'm enjoying *your* dessert."

I laughed, and said, "OK. If you're willing to wait a while longer for the '*pièce de résistance*', let me help you sit up, so you can enjoy some of this dessert, also."

I sat back, taking Kelly's hands in mine, and pulling her up to a sitting position. The remaining fruit on her tumbled into her lap and onto the mattress, while the various sauces and whipped cream flowed slowly down her body. It was sexy, and I did a little more 'finger painting' as she looked down at the mess. Then, I opened the cooler, and brought out a half-bottle of sparkling wine, which I poured into plastic champagne glasses, handing her one, and toasting to our new culinary experience in the van.

I gave Kelly a couple of the Florentine cookies and, as she chewed one, squirted some whipped cream into her mouth. She grabbed the whipped cream from my hands, and squirted at my mouth – getting more on my face than in my mouth. I considered again taking my clothes off, and pulling Kelly into my lap, holding her closely, and feeling the sticky sauces flow down our bodies between us. But I decided that we would do that another time – perhaps a full food-fight and orgy!

Kelly sipped the bubbly wine, and shook her head in disbelief at what I had created for our post-lunch enjoyment. We sat there for a while, feeding each other fruit with sauces and whipped cream, eating cookies, and drinking the wine. We enjoyed each other's company – just *being* with each other.

I picked grapes from a large bunch, and dropped them into a Tupperware. I used water from a small bottle in the cooler to wash the grapes, and then dumped the water into a second Tupperware. Then, I opened the miniature of Grand Marnier, and poured it over the grapes, covering them, and providing at least a bit of disinfection – and a nice flavor. After a few minutes, I dumped the Grand Marnier into the other Tupperware, and dried the grapes with a paper towel.

When we had finished the wine, and made a general mess of ourselves, I helped Kelly lay back on the mattress. I grabbed the little bottle of Kahlua, and poured a small amount over Kelly's clit, letting it drip down across her vulva. I separated Kelly's labia with one hand, continuing to pour, the Kahlua now flowing into Kelly's vagina.

I then took the can of whipped cream, and used the last of it to fill the rest of her dark, sweet (and now, sweeter) cave. Finally, I sprinkled dark chocolate shavings over Kelly's lower portions – covering the chocolate pool on her pubic triangle, her clit, and her labia. Now, it was time.

I lifted my head, and looked at Kelly, who – with her head on the pillow – glanced down at me, smiled, and gave a big nod. My head went down, ravaging Kelly with my tongue, licking the chocolate sauce, sucking the Kahlua, lapping up the whipped cream and chocolate shavings. What a dessert!

Kelly began to move her hips rhythmically, and I tended to her needs, swirling my tongue across and around her clit, down her labia, and deeply into her, slurping the whipped cream out of her, and lapping up the Kahlua. My tongue licked her, moving up her labia, and under her hood, remaining there, while I swirled and flicked her hardening button. Kelly was progressing nicely, but I had to surprise her once more.

I sat up, Kelly exclaiming "Wha ..!" as the stimulation from my tongue stopped. I told her that I would get back to work momentarily, and grabbed the Tupperware of Grand Marnier marinated grapes. I picked up a grape, and slid it deep into Kelly's vagina. Her eyes suddenly opened, and she said "Ow! That burns." Perhaps I didn't dry the grapes enough, but that was better than causing a yeast infection. Kelly calmed, and I continued to slip grapes into her vagina, as I went down on her, and continued working on her clit.

Kelly was now gyrating her hips, her pelvis thrusting up to meet my tongue, as I continued to stuff grapes into her. I don't know how many there were, but a lot of grapes fit inside her. When I could see the last grapes through her separated labia, I put my hand on her, letting a finger slip between her labia, and putting some pressure on her vulva, while I moved my hand and fingers slightly. The grapes inside her were moving around and, hopefully, creating their own pressure, as they rolled against Kelly's G-spot.

Kelly started bucking, and I knew she was in the initial throes of her orgasm. I held my tongue against her clit, lessening the pressure, as Kelly's natural response took over. Suddenly, Kelly stiffened, her clit throbbed, and she let out a shrill scream. I had never heard Kelly scream this loud during an orgasm before, and I hoped that there was nobody near the van; I was sure the sound must have carried at least a block.

I crawled up beside Kelly on the narrow mattress, and gave her a nice, but short, kiss, while my hand caressed her body, still sticky from all of the sauces and fruit. We lay there for several minutes, and Kelly finally said, "That was nice. And pretty creative. Yes, I was surprised at what you planned for dessert! Now, how am I going to get cleaned up enough to get back in my car and drive home? This was a pretty messy experience!"

I laughed, and pointed to the large plastic tub, "I'm going to *bathe* you, of course! But haven't you forgotten something?" Kelly just shrugged her shoulders, but I could see the gleam appear in her eyes, when she realized that I might be 'up' to something again.

I reached down, and slipped a finger into Kelly, pulling out ... not a plum, but a grape. Steeped in Grand Marnier, and Kelly's sex juices. I held it up for Kelly to see, and popped it into my mouth. I guess I *had* gotten the chance to taste Kelly, after all.

Then, I pulled out another grape, and held it in front of her. I wasn't going to force her, but Kelly needed no prodding; she knew what I wanted. She lifted her head, and took the grape from my fingers into her mouth. We both swallowed, and I leaned down to kiss Kelly again, a swirl of exotic flavors on our tongues.

"Do you want to take out the rest of the grapes, or shall I?" Kelly gave me a 'look', and reached down, pulling grape after grape out of herself, like a magic act. I helped Kelly sit up, and cleaned up all the leftover grocery products, which I stuffed into the empty bag. I opened the valve on the air mattress, as I knew that the tub wouldn't balance well on top of it.

Finally, I put the tub on the air mattress, and helped Kelly get into it. The tub was perfectly sized to fit her sitting cross-legged, her knees resting on its rounded rim. I lifted the large water bottle, and set it down on the deflated mattress next to the tub; it had been sitting in my garage, and summer was here, so the water was nicely warmed. I took a sponge from the other grocery bag, on which I squeezed a little body wash, and tilted the water bottle over the tub, soaking the sponge.

Kelly sat there, amazed at what we were doing in this van, sitting in the parking lot of a public park. Now, I was giving her a sponge bath!

I began by softly washing her face, removing the sticky stuff with the sponge, and re-soaking it from the water cooler bottle, as the tub filled a little more with not-so-clean, but at least warm, water. I guided the sponge around Kelly's neck, and over her shoulders. Then, across her chest, and down to her breasts, where I spent time cleaning her nipples, and then moved it under her breasts, gently stroking her soft tissues with the now soapy sponge.

I bathed Kelly's stomach, and hips, and it took quite some time to get all of the chocolate sauce out of Kelly's pubic hair. Finally, I slipped the sponge downward, and washed some very sticky genitals. Kelly seemed contented. She looked up, and said, "Please wash my underneath, sir, as all that stuff dripped down there." Kelly lifted herself up a few inches, and I washed her perineum.

Then, I grabbed one more item I had bought at the market – without having gotten a second look from the female cashier. I opened the box, and showed Kelly. "I don't want you to get an infection from the grapes and whipped cream, so let's use this douche – it might provide some additional protection." Kelly guided the nozzle into her and I squeezed the bottle, until all the liquid had gone into her and come out into the tub.

I crawled next to her, and looked around at her back, but it seemed to have kept mostly clean. I used the sponge, and did some 'touch ups', making sure that Kelly was as clean as possible using this primitive set-up. I gave Kelly a large, fluffy, towel, and she started to dry herself, top down. She would still need a shower, and her hair was wild, but Kelly was as beautiful as always.

As Kelly held the towel around her, I slid open the van door, and climbed out. Kelly took one foot and then the other out of the tub, as she balanced herself in the confines of the van. I slid the tub to the door, and then picked it up, and dumped the bathwater, along with some random uneaten fruit, in the grass. There were still no cars near us in the parking lot, and nobody in the nearby portions of the park.

I stood outside the van, with the door slid partially open, while I watched Kelly finish drying off. She reached over to the front seat, and grabbed her clothes, putting them on slowly as I looked into her eyes. "Kelly, I hope this was fun for you. Something a little 'different'."

Kelly smiled, as she finished buttoning her jeans and fastening her belt, "Yes, Sir. Sam. Again, you seem to have gone beyond my 'wildest' imagination. We had talked about 'eating' each other after lunch, but I couldn't figure out where we would be able to do it. I guess you came up with a pretty creative answer to that!"

Kelly looked down, in thought, "I told Julie and Linda about your high standards ... and this is one more example. Other guys might have brought a van to have sex in, but I doubt they would have thought of the dessert, and the nice sponge bath afterward! This has been a lovely experience." Kelly chuckled, "But I didn't get to eat *you*. You would have been so tasty with caramel sauce."

We both laughed. Kelly was right, "Yes, next time we'll have to have a food orgy and eat each other. Or, a food fight and then an orgy with each other." I helped Kelly out of the van, and we walked slowly back toward the restaurant, where she had parked. "Go home and get packed for the weekend. You don't have to bring anything special. But maybe you could bring different bras and panties to model. And any 'toys' you might have that you think we should play with."

Kelly laughed. "And, Kelly ..." She looked up at me seriously, but then batted her eyes. "You won't have to worry about any preparations, or rules, this time. We're beyond contracts and testing openness. I would just like to have a nice, romantic, weekend with you. And, I would like, finally, to make passionate love to you."

Kelly stopped and looked down. She finally looked back up at me and said, "Romantic? You mean you won't be spanking me?" I didn't know if she was serious, but then she laughed, and said, "I still need to finish the level-100 that we started last time!"

I laughed too, and said, "Well, I never said there wouldn't be spankings ... or other things you might have to submit to. Maybe even a few things that will be new to you. You *know* I love to surprise you!"

I thought about all of the ideas I had for the long weekend ... and Kelly's birthday party. It would be a combination of romance and 'intrigue', passion and pain. Well, at least a little pain. Then I had another idea, "Kelly, if you have some clothes that will make you a 'schoolgirl' – like pleated skirt, white blouse and shoes, and bobbysocks – that might be fun. Otherwise, you can pick your own wardrobe. Maybe, you can surprise me with something interesting?"

Kelly nodded. "I'll try, Sir. Shall I come over around one o'clock?"

"That sounds fine. I need to do some more marketing tomorrow morning, but the house is in good shape, and I'm really looking forward to being with you the whole weekend. Oh! Don't forget to call your friends, and let them know you'll be at my house *this* Saturday." Kelly nodded, and bit her lip, the suggestion obviously causing her to think of something, but I had no idea what.

We hugged and kissed; and kissed again. I was glad that we would be starting our long weekend tomorrow. I wasn't sure that either of us could have waited another week. Kelly seemed to have enjoyed our lunch and the dessert tasting afterward; she was a very sensual woman, and it took little to bring her to an orgasmic state.

I was glad that we were 'saving' our first lovemaking experience for the weekend – tomorrow – and hadn't given in to having a food and sex orgy in the van. Kelly was a very special person. And, I wanted to treat her that way.

CHAPTER 4: LONG WEEKEND BEGINS

Preparations for the long weekend were mostly done, but there were a few things that I could not plan; just be prepared for. Kelly was more than a play partner to me, although our stated relationship was still on a casual level. I decided that tomorrow afternoon and evening would be a surprise – a nice one – for Kelly.

I planned the menus and marketed for the fresh vegetables and fresh bakery items on Friday morning. I would be cooking an Italian dinner for Kelly, but didn't need to do much preparation. And lunch tomorrow would be casual. I wasn't sure what we would do for dinner Saturday night, and decided to leave it open – we could go out or stay at home, depending what Kelly was up for.

I took the Brunello that we would be having with dinner out of the wine cellar, and put a White Zinfandel and a Rosé in the fridge. I looked across the playroom to the bed, wondering whether we would have our first 'real' lovemaking experience on this bed, or the one in the master bedroom upstairs. I decided that it would be this bed, as I had some ideas for playing afterward, and it would be more convenient down here in the playroom.

I spent nearly an hour 'decorating' the bed area of the playroom – suitable for a romantic experience. When I decided everything was ready, I lowered the motorized screen, which had the effect of closing off the bed area from casual view.

I had already cued-up a video that I would start, using a small remote that I put on the granite playroom bar top. But I didn't bother to set-up the video recording capability of the room. Today – and tonight – would be a casual experience for the two of us, not a submission challenge.

I did prepare a few special items that we would 'play' with before we came down to the playroom for our romantic experience – including something new, as I had promised Kelly. I dressed, again in running shorts and a tank top, as I would be doing some enervating work this afternoon.

Around noon, I made some fresh iced tea, and put several snacks into bowls and on a plate: Some yogurt-covered pretzels, roasted cashews, and slices of banana nut bread. I also made a small antipasto platter, with some good meats, cheeses and olives. After our 'dessert' in the van, I decided that we'd had enough fruit for a while!

I went out to the patio, turned on the pump for the pool waterfall, opened the umbrellas, and set the table for our snack. The backyard was 100% private, the house sitting on a large lot, and the property bordering forest behind the back wall.

It was a beautiful early summer day: Brilliant blue sky, trees covered with leaves, flowers in full bloom, and birds chirping. A couple of hummingbirds sucked the sweet nectar of the agapanthas, now a deep purple on their long stalks.

I sat on one of the deck chairs, and gazed over the idyllic setting, my thoughts turning once again to Kelly's birthday party. I envisioned the girls frolicking in the yard … and fantasized about some of the things we might do. I looked beyond the pool, to the right, where a series of large boulders created the border between a winding path next to the grass and, on the other side of the boulders, the flowerbed and trees at the back of the lot. I pictured the four girls on the rocks, their bottoms high in the air.

I shook my head, and decided not to overthink what might – or might not – happen. Then, I thought about my special birthday surprise for Kelly, and the construction that I still had to do alongside the pool. I had bought the materials, which were being stored next to the garage out of sight. And I had designed what I wanted to build, mostly.

But whether I could really pull this off was still questionable. It was a challenge. Just as it would be for Kelly – not so much the activities themselves, but doing them in front of her friends.

I shook my head again, still amazed that my relationship with Kelly had progressed so quickly; and that she was so open and enthusiastic about playing with me. I had mixed feelings – on the one hand, wanting to develop the romantic aspect of our relationship with tender, loving, kindness.

But, on the other hand, continuing to give Kelly more tastes of the submissive life – including pain – about which I had fantasized, and which Kelly seemed to crave. I had both types of activities cued-up for the weekend, but would just have to wing-it. I was certain that Kelly would make her wishes known, and give me sufficient feedback to adjust the experience to her satisfaction.

I packed my things – all pretty casual, but including a few outfits that Sam had not seen, some sexy thongs and panties (although I didn't usually buy underwear based on how sexy they would be to a man seeing them, but on how comfortable they were). I didn't wear the thongs often, but thought that they would give Sam some good spanking access, in conjunction with a short skirt that I had also packed.

I would have to buy some stiletto heels – something I had never thought of, previously. In fact, I was now thinking of a whole new range of clothing; I had looked on the internet, and had seen latex rubber bodysuits, corsets, and many other sexy possibilities for future consideration.

I didn't really know what Sam had planned for the long weekend, but I was sure we would be making love for the first time. And, Sam would undoubtedly surprise me with some new sensual – and possibly painful – experiences. I smiled, realizing now that I didn't care; Sam could do to me whatever he liked, and I was confident that I could not only handle it, but would enjoy it, too.

My thoughts drifted, and I tried to picture what I expected the weekend to hold. Including the completion of my level-100 punishment. I knew it would hurt, but I also knew that it would turn me on. In fact, I was already feeling a stirring below, and I clenched my PC muscle.

Despite Sam's casualness, I had prepared for my visit by observing most of the rules that Sam had outlined for our first experience – even sipping a laxative tea before I went to bed last night. I felt good, and prepared for anything that Sam might 'throw' at me today. I was looking forward to the experience; and to being with Sam.

I closed my eyes, and saw myself with Sam, on the playroom floor, making wild, passionate love. Being spanked, ravaged, taken to my limits – and beyond. I was becoming wet, and knew that if I continued any more of these thoughts, I would need to take a break. But I wanted to get to Sam's place, and decided to finish packing and let the weekend begin.

As I drove over to Sam's house, I told myself to remain calm; but I could feel my pulse racing, my chest pounding, as I anticipated the afternoon. I was determined to not only take, but also enjoy, what Sam had planned – no matter what it entailed.

I was nervous, but excited; prepared, but not sure what to expect. I had eaten only toast for breakfast, but was too anxious to think about being hungry, and I squirmed in the driver's seat, fully expecting my bottom to be very sore in just a few hours. Or less.

I rang Sam's doorbell ('pushed his button'), and made a decision at that moment to address Sam as 'Sir'. It wasn't necessarily for Sam's benefit, but for mine. I had worn a pair of stylish jeans, with one of my thongs, and a simple silk blouse with nothing underneath. I was too big on top to go braless, usually, but was just firm enough to pull this off. I didn't think I looked very good, this way, but thought Sam would appreciate it. I doubted that my clothes would be staying on very long, anyway.

The top three buttons of my blouse were undone, but I still felt like I was overheated; maybe it was just the warm weather, or perhaps it was my expectations of what I was 'in for' today. The door opened, and I looked down at Sam's bare feet. "Hello, Sir. I'm here to complete my punishment. And to enjoy the weekend with you." I couldn't help smiling, but continued to keep my eyes down.

Sam smiled, also. He put his hand under my chin, and – with a single finger – lifted my head so that we were looking into each other's eyes. We spontaneously hugged each other, and then kissed, eyes closing, mouths opening, and tongues swirling.

Sam let his right hand slide down my back, and into my jeans, cupping and gently squeezing my bare bottom below my thong. He opened his eyes and, looking into mine, said, "Ummm! I'm getting excited already." As he pressed against me, his eyes widened slightly, and he brought his hand back up to cup and gently squeeze one breast, and then the other, through the thin material of my blouse.

I smiled, my hand caressing the front of Sam's running shorts, "I hope so!" We both laughed, and Sam ushered me into the house, taking the rolling suitcase that I had brought this time, and closing the front door behind us.

We walked downstairs to the playroom, and Sam put the suitcase on the floor next to the desk in the L-shaped section of the room designated as his 'office'. Sam then turned to me, and put his hands on my shoulders, looking at me seriously for a long moment, and finally asked, "Kelly, will you submit to me, today?"

I chuckled, and said, under my breath, "That's getting down to business fast!" Then I looked at Sam seriously, and said, "Of course, Sir. I am your 'sex slave' for the weekend." I decided that I really was prepared to do anything that Sam asked, to take whatever pain he deemed appropriate, to satisfy his every desire.

My question had been intended only to prepare Kelly psychologically, as my real intentions were to please Kelly, to morph the relationship from primarily dominant-submissive, to more feeling ... more romantic. And to satisfy Kelly's every desire.

I knew that she was turned-on by our prior experience, but I didn't know whether she really wanted a hard spanking this weekend (and, if so, it would be a challenge – the completion of her level-100 punishment) ... or if she desired a more romantic experience.

Well, I had planned both. But we were going to start with a more casual experience – to lighten things up, so Kelly and I could talk, *and* play, a little. Then, when she had gotten comfortable and relaxed, I would have a few surprises for her.

"OK, Kelly, then let's go sit out on the patio for a while. And maybe take a dip in the pool. You're welcome to bring a bathing suit to change into, if you like. As you know, I normally don't allow bathing suits in the pool, but this can be a special exception."

Kelly grinned, "That's not necessary, Sir. Unless you want me to?"

It didn't really matter, but might be fun, "Why don't you pick out a suit, and bring it up with you. Then we can decide."

Kelly unzipped the rolling case, and lifted a few things, pulling out a bright red suit made of so little fabric it could easily be balled up into one hand. Kelly stood and looked at me brightly. I gave her a quick peck on the lips, and took her hand, leading her upstairs.

I opened the fridge and handed Kelly the pitcher of iced tea, and then grabbed the several plates and dishes of snacks I had prepared, balancing them, as Kelly held the door open for me. We arranged everything on the umbrella-covered patio table, and Kelly poured the iced tea. I had used the pink tablecloth and napkins, again.

Kelly took a sip of her tea, and exclaimed, "I didn't know you were making lunch! I didn't eat much this morning, and I guess I am a little hungry."

We each took a small plate and a few of the snacks. I sat back in wonder at the beauty of Kelly sitting in my backyard. What masterpieces of nature! The sun was past the meridian, and highlighted the contour of Kelly's firm breasts under her stylish blouse. As my eyes fell lower, I was again impressed with her athletic build – her flat stomach, small waist, and strong but shapely legs.

Her hips and bottom were larger, in a slightly Rubenesque way – entirely apropos to my fetishes, most of which focus on a beautiful woman's rear (or a woman's beautiful rear). Kelly's legs were muscular, and the jeans were incredibly sexy on her. She was wearing simple sandals with a natural, woven material between her toes.

I guess I had been once again staring – reviewing her body – and Kelly once again asked, "Do you like what you see, Mister?"

She laughed, but I didn't: This was no laughing matter: Kelly was the most beautiful woman I had ever seen. Even ignoring the incredible curves of her body (which, of course, would be difficult for any heterosexual male to do), Kelly was stunning – with rosy cheeks of smooth skin, just a hint of dimples, a pert nose, a gorgeous full-mouth smile and gleaming teeth, and those mesmerizing hazel eyes; and, of course, her amazing waist-length auburn hair.

Once again, I considered canceling the events I had planned for the day, and doing an impromptu photo session with Kelly. I envisioned portraits, fashion shots, semi-nudes, and nudes; in the backyard, in the pool, and in the playroom bed. But, once again, I decided to stick to the plan I had made for our first long weekend.

"You know I do, Kelly. You are the most beautiful woman in the world!"

Kelly beamed, but then put on a mock pout and said, "I'm not! My neck is too long. And, my breasts and butt are too big. My right foot is curled in. And, I have some fat under my arms."

I jumped out of my chair, and started tickling Kelly – in all the places she had just mentioned. I kissed her neck, and bit her ear lobes, then unbuttoned two more buttons of her blouse, and kissed her breasts. I reached around her with both arms, and squeezed her bottom hard, and then surprised Kelly by immediately tickling her under both of her arms.

She squealed and shrieked, but I kept up the tickling until we were both out of breath. I stood up and stepped back, "Kelly, I'd love to have a *real* tickling wrestle with you sometime. Whoever can pin the other down, can tickle them. But let's hold that thought for later."

Kelly shrugged her shoulders. "OK, Sir. Do you want to spank me, now?" Her head was down, but she was looking up at me with those big eyes, batting her eyelashes suggestively."

I laughed. I had not planned on spanking Kelly at all today ... but this was just too good to pass up. I said, "OK, if you're asking for it; and, since you wore that thong." I saw Kelly's eyes widen; perhaps she had just been joking, and didn't expect me to really spank her? But I continued, "Come over here, young lady!"

Kelly got up and walked over to me. I slid the chair back, and sat on the edge of it, hoping that it wouldn't suddenly tip forward with Kelly's additional weight suspended on my legs. "Pull your pants down and get over my knee!" Kelly quickly obliged. I watched her face, and saw a flush of dark red, as she undid and lowered her pants. She promptly got herself in the over-the-knee (OTK) position, and turned her head to look back up at me.

"I'm ready for my spanking, now, Sir."

I smiled, and told her, "Kelly, I'm only doing this because you asked for it. I think I'll show you how I plan give Linda her birthday spanking. She's now 25 years old?"

Kelly gasped slightly, stammered, and said, "Yes, Sir, 25. Plus the other three: One for health, one for wealth, and one to grow on. Not that Linda needs to grow any more." She giggled, and lightly pushed her head down, facing the variegated flagstone surface of the patio.

"OK, Kelly. We'll do the first 25 quickly, and then the last three harder." I didn't delay, and began her spanking immediately with a sound slap on her right butt cheek. I spanked her continuously, alternating sides, about one spank every second. The 25 spanks took only half a minute to complete, but Kelly's bottom was already nicely pink, and slightly wobbling. "You held your position well, young lady. Let me know when you're ready for your three hard spanks."

I saw Kelly's head bob. Her hair had flowed entirely around her, and down to the ground, so her head and face were nowhere to be seen. Kelly took a couple of deep breaths, and said, "OK, Sir. I'm ready."

I was not going to spank Kelly again today, and decided to give her some zingers – about the hardest hand spanks that I could give. They would sting for a few seconds, and she may feel them for a few minutes, but they were nowhere near the level she had experienced when she had been here last time. I started with a smack on her left side. Kelly jumped a little, and an 'Ow!' came unbidden from her throat. I waited a few seconds, and then gave her just as hard a smack on the right side … and immediately, a second swat on the same side.

Kelly cried out, "Oh! Ow! Oooh," and then, "Sorry, Sir." She took a few more deep breaths, wiggled her bottom, and said, "Thank you, Sir."

I laughed, and helped Kelly get off my lap. She stood in front of me, with her pants down to her knees. Still sitting, I put my arms around her waist, and turned my head, resting it on her stomach. My hands slid over her bottom, and Kelly only slightly flinched as I lightly stroked and rubbed her reddened globes.

Kelly put her arms around my neck, and kissed the top of my head. We held each other like that for a long time; well, at least a couple of minutes. Then, I looked up at her, and said, "As long as you're half undressed anyway, why don't you put that suit on, and we'll go in the pool for a while?"

Kelly said, "OK, Sir." And then giggled.

She stayed exactly in the same position. Actually, looking up, I realized that she was in the standing position, waiting for me to undress her. I chuckled, and lowered her jeans, taking them off one foot, then the other, as Kelly put a hand on my head for balance.

Then, I unbuttoned the last couple of buttons on her blouse, and helped her take that off. I reached over and dropped the blouse over the back of the other chair. I looked up and said, "Actually, Kelly, I would like to see more of this thong from behind. Why don't you model it for me?"

Kelly immediately took a couple of steps to the side of the table, and began doing a slow, soundless dance for me. She moved her arms fluidly, and began to turn slowly from side to side, increasing her turns until she suddenly turned around completely, displaying her beautiful now-pink mounds and the 'T' of the thong.

She continued to turn back and forth, at the same time bending over and widening her stance, until her back was horizontal, and I was looking between her legs at her hair falling to the ground, her full breasts hanging down, and the skimpy thong retaining her womanly topography. Kelly was a sexy creature!

"If you've seen enough of the thong Sir, maybe I could take it off now? It's getting a little tight and uncomfortable." She couldn't help laughing, and neither could I.

"Sure, Kelly. That's a nice thong. Thank you for wearing it today." It had been worn less than an hour so far, but she had other attire to exhibit – including her bathing suit ... and her birthday suit.

Kelly continued her slow dance, now obviously a strip tease. She lowered the thong slowly, one side more than the other, alternately, until it was around her ankles, and she stepped out of it. Her stance then widened, and she bent over as before, now exposing herself openly, the way she knew I liked to see her.

She reached down and separated her labia, and her hands went around and held her buttocks, which she pulled to each side, separating them, and exposing her rosebud. If I'd had the thermometer handy, I would have inserted it. But I was content to watch Kelly finish her striptease, which I was finding incredibly sensual.

Kelly slowly raised herself up, and danced her way over to me, finishing the show, and sitting on my lap, straddling me, with her arms around my back. We kissed, and then I kissed her nose, then her cheeks, then her forehead, and then all over her face, her neck, her chest – as far down as I could go with us in this position. I looked at Kelly, and she had a curious expression.

"Aren't you going to help me get off, now that I've performed for you?" She laughed, but I could tell that she was at least half-serious; probably at least 80% serious.

I told her, "I am trying to slow-down our experience a little today. Let us just be with each other, nothing too challenging. But I plan to make passionate love to you later – at the right time and the right place."

Kelly just shook her head, "You're strange, Sir ... if you don't mind me saying so. You always make me wait to be satisfied."

I didn't think this was true. "Always?" Now I shook my head at this self-assured woman, who knew what she wanted. And was going to get it. Of course she was. I was going to give it to her. "Kelly, take this leg and put it between us." Kelly did so. Now, she was straddling just my left leg.

"Good girl. Now, you may satisfy yourself." I held Kelly, and we rocked back and forth, as I slightly lifted her, in time with the rocking, lowering her onto my thigh each time she rocked forward. It didn't take long for her to understand, and soon she was in control of the rocking and the up-down movements herself – like horseback riding. I pulled her close to me, so that we were pressed together, rocking as one.

Kelly leaned forward, pushing me into the back of the chair, and began humping (how else can I describe it?) my leg – like riding one of those electric bulls in a bar – her head thrown back, and her hair a shimmering backdrop to her beautiful face. Then, Kelly moaned, her head turning back and forth, hair flying out to the sides. Her breasts were pressed against my chest, and our upper bodies were still ... but her lower body continued to work itself against my leg.

I had expected Kelly to use at least one of her hands – I was holding her firmly – but she ended-up coming solely by doing her own 'lap dance' (actually, 'thigh' dance). We hugged tightly, and eventually Kelly leaned back, as I held her, and we smiled at each other. She kissed my nose, and said, "Thank you, Sir. That was nice." And then, "Even if I did have to do most of the work myself."

I laughed, "Well, this is how I reward a 'sex slave' for a fine performance. I allowed you to have an orgasm. You don't expect me to do the work all the time, do you?" We both laughed.

Of course, I was more than willing to 'do the work', any time that Kelly wanted. But it was fun watching her – feeling her – get herself off, using part of my body. Not so different from her incredible masturbation on top of me before we went to dinner last time.

It was very pleasing to me – and still a great turn on – to see a woman so open, self-confident, able to satisfy herself. "How about getting that bathing suit on now, so we can go in the pool? It's getting hot out here!" In more ways than one!

Kelly got up and grabbed the bathing suit. She dropped the top over her head, and then took the strings from each side and pulled them around back, tying a nice bow, and then adjusting her breasts so they were comfortable in the too small and unsupportive cups. Then, she put on the thong bottom, pulling it up, and smoothing the portion that ran under her, between her buttocks, and up to her trim waist. Kelly smiled at me, and did a few 'poses'.

I had to comment, "A few more spanks, and I think we could have gotten your bottom to match the bathing suit! That's really hot! I must take some photographs of you sometime." I was already thinking ahead: Perhaps an afternoon photo session next Thursday, instead of a 'normal' lunch? Maybe, with a happy ending? For both of us.

I got up and took off my shorts and tank top, and we got into the pool, which was slightly cool, but perfect once we were in. The day was hot, with a brilliant blue sky and not a breath of wind. We floated around, occasionally passing each other and sliding a hand over the other's body. We went to the deep end, and Kelly put her legs around my waist, her arms around my neck, as I treaded water.

It hadn't been planned – I was just trying something – but it turned out to be a great turn-on, as Kelly's front was now doing a different type of 'lap dance' on my groin. Unfortunately, I didn't have the strength to keep treading water, *and* continue to get turned on. I would have to work on that.

We swam over to the jacuzzi, and walked up the stones of the waterfall. As soon as we were in the hot, swirling, water, Kelly removed her suit. "No need for this!"

I laughed, "Yes, I agree. You seemed a bit over-dressed. Or, perhaps I was a bit *under-dressed*?"

Kelly said, seriously, "Oh, no, Sir. You're perfectly dressed!"

"You, too, Kelly. I like you the way you are – naturally. I don't think the suit adds much beauty – just takes away. Your birthday suit is the best suit of all." Then I added, "I'm glad your friends are comfortable in their birthday suits, too. I think we'll all have fun at your birthday party!"

I was picturing Kelly's birthday much as today – a beautiful blue-sky day. It was always possible that we would have rain, as this area gets some serious thunderstorms in the summer. But, hopefully, we would enjoy a nice, hot, day by the pool.

Kelly responded, "I'm sure we will. My friends are pretty open – skinny-dipping is no big deal to them. Being with a strange older man, and not bringing their boyfriends, were probably bigger considerations. But after what I told them about you, they were curious enough to agree to whatever I asked of them."

I gasped, hopeful, "Really! *Whatever* you asked? Now, we're getting somewhere!"

Kelly laughed, "Don't get too excited. I never said they would do anything but go skinny-dipping with us and have some birthday cake."

Shit. I had forgotten to order the cake ... it wasn't even on my list! What else had I forgotten? I had a brief mental flash on the three girls punishing me, under Kelly's supervision, if I had screwed-up and not gotten a nice cake! I had better do a little more planning, and a little less fantasizing.

Kelly continued, "Except I know that Linda is expecting her birthday spanking when she comes over tomorrow. But I never said anything about pulling her pants down. We'll just have to see." Kelly looked at me and smiled, "I agree: It should be interesting – both tomorrow, and on my birthday!"

We were getting very relaxed, and it was time for some different kinds of activities. "Kelly, let's get out of the pool and dried off. I'd like to introduce you to another experience."

Kelly looked at me, wondering what was in store for her in just a few minutes. "OK, Sir."

It would be a unique experience – something very different, and hopefully stimulating for Kelly. Perhaps it would be a little uncomfortable, but certainly not painful. At least, not in the usual sense of the word.

CHAPTER 5: VIOLET WAND, SENSUAL MASSAGE

We got out of the pool, and dried off – which didn't take long, as the sun did most of the drying for us. We had a few more nibbles of the snacks, and another glass of iced tea, and then took everything back to the kitchen. We were both nude, and completely comfortable with each other.

I put everything in the fridge, and led Kelly through the door to the pool room. Interestingly, although the pool room's sliding doors opened to the patio and pool area, Kelly had not previously noticed this room. I had kept the window coverings drawn, and our focus was usually out to the backyard, not back to the house. As we walked into the pool room, Kelly exclaimed, "I never saw *this* room! Wow, this is pretty nice!"

The room was quite large, paneled with light wood, and mostly empty (now that I had cleaned it out), containing only a massage table that was placed alongside the sliding doors. I had covered the table with a sheet, and positioned next to it a small rolling stand that carried various oils and lotions.

A second rolling stand held a strange-looking instrument, with knobs and meters, and wires emanating from it. A box on the stand held something else entirely. It would be only a first introduction for Kelly, but hopefully she would find it interesting, if not sexually stimulating. The room had a heavy-duty Berber carpet installed; it was thin, but would hold-up well to some of the activities for which the room was used. At the far end of the room was a small half-bath.

I waved my arm around, presenting the room, "This is the 'pool room', where our pool guests can change. I have a Ping Pong table in the garage that can be rolled in here. Or, I can use the room as a photo studio. The bathroom is handy for people who are wet from the pool."

I walked over to the near-end of the sliding doors, and pulled the cord to slide open the verticals, opening one entire wall of the room to the pool and backyard. Then, I opened both sliding doors, which slid from the middle, opening the room entirely to the outside. The massage table was centered on the wide opening; moved a foot further toward the backyard, the table would be on the patio.

"Kelly, I'm going to have you get up on this table." Then I remembered, "Oh! First, Kelly, please use the bathroom, if you need to, before we get started." Of course, I hadn't elaborated on exactly what we would get started doing.

Kelly walked over to the bathroom in the far corner, looking around at the room and out to the backyard. She sat on the toilet, not bothering to swing the door closed. That bathroom door is louvered, giving people plenty of visual privacy, but not privacy from sound, even when closed. When Kelly was finished, she washed her hands quickly and skipped back to the massage table.

Kelly hopped up onto the table, swung around, and lay down on her back. Her hair was all pulled to her left, and fell over the side of the table. Kelly lifted her head slightly, and looked at the various items on the rolling metal tables, then put her head back down and stared at the ceiling.

"Kelly, my plan today is to do things that make you happy; to satisfy you; and to romance you – culminating in our first time making love to each other. So I was not planning to spank you or punish you. Unless you asked me – like a few minutes ago." I smiled, wondering what else Kelly might ask for.

"I would like to start by giving you a sensual full-body massage. It should be relaxing, and stimulating – and your skin should be tingling afterward." I hadn't thought to ask earlier, "Have you had a professional massage before?"

Kelly looked at me from her lying position, and said, sheepishly, "No. Not really. I had a boyfriend who tried to massage me, but we didn't have oil, and he didn't know what he was doing, so it didn't feel very good." Kelly lifted her head a bit and smiled at me, "But a massage right now sounds nice."

I was amazed, as I had assumed that Kelly had experienced a good massage before. I am not a professional, but Liz had taught me quite a bit, and I had both received and given many massages. "I will massage you. But, as you know, I like to surprise you – especially, with new things – and I have some new toys that I think will be something interesting for both of us. I would like you to experience a little before your massage, while your skin is dry, and then we'll have a different experience after the massage, when your skin is covered with oil.

Kelly had put her head back down, and her eyes were closed, "I know I shouldn't ask ... but, what kind of toys are they?"

I laughed, "In general, it's called electrical stimulation." Now Kelly's head was up, giving me a concerned look.

I explained, "It's sometimes called 'e-stim' for short. You may have heard of TENS? That is transcutaneous electrical nerve stimulation – it can help relieve pain, and something very similar is used in sports medicine, to exercise and relax muscles. In fact, it's also used medically – for example, to help a woman exercise her pelvic muscles to improve symptoms of urinary incontinence."

Kelly said, "What?" I laughed, realizing again how relatively young she was.

"Kelly, many women – more than 40 million in the U.S. alone – have some amount of urine leakage at various times. One type is called 'stress incontinence', which occurs when your urethral sphincter (valve) cannot hold the pressure – because you are laughing, coughing, riding a horse, or jumping, and so on.

"The other type is called 'urge incontinence', where you don't realize you have to pee until the last moment, and then you have a great urge to go – and you may or may not make it to the bathroom in time. That's more related to your bladder (it's sometimes called 'overactive bladder'), where the detrusor muscle of your bladder squeezes too often and too much. Both of these conditions have been treated with electrical stimulation."

I opened the box on one of the carts, lifted up a black cylinder, and snapped onto it a long glass tube, with a mushroom-shaped tip. Holding it up for Kelly to see, I continued, "And, then we have the 'Violet Wand'. This is a device made especially for sex – and BDSM. It uses static electricity, and it lights up this tube of gas, which I can then put next to your skin, and you'll feel a 'tingling'."

Kelly looked up and asked, "*Only*, a tingling?"

I laughed, "Actually, you may feel a variety of things, from a pulsing of your muscles, to mild shocks, to a feeling of 'fuzziness' along your skin. It just depends where we put the electrodes, the settings on the instrument, and how your skin is prepared. That's why I'd like you to try it, and tell me what the sensation is like before your massage, and then after. For the 'after' part, I have a variation on this that I think will intrigue you. None of this should hurt – it should be fun, and ... *stimulating*."

Kelly laughed. "OK. What do you want me to do? "

"That's what I like to hear!" I kept laughing, "Why don't we try the medical version of this first?" I reached behind the box, and lifted up a long, phallic-shaped device, quite similar to a large vibrator, with two metal bands surrounding it, and a wire coming out the end. I held it up and showed Kelly, while I lubricated it with a thin layer of KY, "This is a 'vaginal probe', used to treat incontinence in females. It's hooked up to this generator," pointing to the box with the dials and gauges on the cart, "and is supposed to exercise your pelvic muscles."

I set the probe down on the paper covering the rolling table, and opened a small bag. I took out two 'ground pad' electrodes, each about two inches square, and took off the adhesive backing. I reached around Kelly, lifting her bottom slightly, and placing one of the ground pads on her upper hip. I did the same on the other side, and then connected the ground pads to the leads on the generator.

I then asked Kelly to lift her knees and put her feet on the table, and she let her knees fall apart, as I slowly inserted the vaginal probe. Then, I helped Kelly lower her legs again. I turned on the generator, and adjusted several settings.

"Kelly, let me know what you feel."

As I slowly turned up the intensity of the stimulation, Kelly stared at the ceiling. Finally, Kelly said, "Mmmm, I can feel that." As I increased the intensity still further, Kelly made some 'Aaah's' and 'Oooh's', and I could see the flesh near her hip rippling. I got to about 2/3 of the maximum intensity before Kelly looked over at me and commented, "That feels really strange. I do feel my pelvic muscles tightening and relaxing all by themselves. It's not painful, but I wouldn't say it was an enjoyable sensation."

I said, "OK. Let me change the frequency." I slowly increased the frequency, and Kelly produced a succession of primal sounds. I set the generator to alternate frequencies, and let it run for a couple of minutes, while I slowly moved the probe slightly out and then back in a few times. Kelly wasn't impressed.

I turned the intensity all the way down and the generator off, and then extracted the vaginal probe, but left the ground pads on Kelly's hips. I picked up the Violet wand, leaving the mushroom electrode in place, and turned it on. Kelly's eyes darted to the device, as the tube lit up with an eerie purplish-blue glow, and emitted a low hum and occasional crackling sound.

I lowered the mushroom tip to just above Kelly's stomach, and then gradually lowered it further, as I glided over her skin. When it was a few millimeters from her skin, a series of sparks began to connect the glass of the mushroom to Kelly's stomach, and Kelly emitted a few more 'Ooooh's' and 'Aaaah's'.

I floated the Violet Wand over Kelly, moving between her breasts and up to her nipples. When the sparks crackled from her pert pink protrusions, Kelly screeched, and then started giggling. "That felt like a bunch of rubber bands snapping me!" Kelly exclaimed.

Kelly's oil-covered body would probably react better, with less resistance, and not as intense sparks. I moved the wand down, through her dark triangle, and between her legs. I lifted Kelly's legs up, and she put her feet back on the table, and let her knees fall apart in the 'butterfly' position. I slowly lowered the wand, and moved it slowly over and around her clit, down her labia, and then back up while slightly parting her labia with the fingers of one hand. Kelly jumped a few times, and continued to make small sounds. She seemed to find it amusing, but was not getting turned on.

I turned off the Violet Wand, took off the mushroom tip, and put everything back into the box. I turned to Kelly, and bent down, kissing her tenderly on both nipples, and then on her mouth. "I guess you can see why that's usually used for BDSM. But I'd still like us to try it again after your massage. If that's OK with you."

Kelly smiled, and nodded. "It was different! Maybe I should try it on *your* genitals?"

Laughing, I told Kelly, "Well, you'll get your chance after the massage, because we will both be getting electrical stimulation together. Just wait." I pulled off the ground pads from each of Kelly's hips, and put them on the rolling table.

Kelly said, earnestly, "I can wait."

I ignored her comment, and said, "OK, Kelly. Now, why don't you roll over onto your stomach, scoot up on the table, and put your head in the hole near the end." As Kelly did this, I helped lay her arms by her sides, palms up. I grabbed a tie from the rolling table and tied her hair into a ponytail, laying it to one side.

I squeezed some oil into my palms, and rubbed them together vigorously to warm the oil and my hands. Stepping around to the head of the table, I leaned over Kelly, placing my hands at the top of her upper back, and then gradually applying more weight, as my hands slid slowly down her muscular body. I repeated this maneuver several times, starting at her shoulders or at her neck, and then increasing pressure, as my hands slid downward to her waist.

I worked from the outside of Kelly's back inward to her spine, using my fingers to gently work down her vertebrae to the small of her back. I did several more 'back strokes', starting lower, and continuing across her waist, and over her buttocks. I moved to one side of the table, and squirted more oil into my left hand, while my right continued to put pressure on Kelly, moving back and forth around her waist.

I let the oil drizzle out of my hand onto Kelly's bottom, making a looping pattern of oil and letting some drip between her buttocks. I immediately slid my finger down her butt crack to rub the oil along her, from her tailbone to just above her anus. Kelly moaned, and I spent time stroking and kneading her buttocks.

I squirted more oil along the back of her right leg, as I used my other hand to make an even coating over her skin, and then massaged her leg with long strokes, from her hip down to her ankle. I put both hands around her thigh, as high up as possible, and squeezed, as I slid my hands down to the back of her knee.

I continued from knee to ankle, then swirled my hands around her right foot, putting pressure with my thumbs on her sole, and moving the tips of my fingers between each of her toes. I repeated the same process on her left leg and foot. Finally, I lifted both feet, and gently bent her legs back, until her heels were touching her bottom. I held them there for a few moments, and then slowly unbent them, until they were flat on the table.

Using a little more oil, I stroked the insides of Kelly's thighs, working my way up to her crotch, and doing some teasing flicks of her genitals before starting the next stroke. I heard Kelly chuckle for a moment, but otherwise she was silent, and very relaxed. With her entire backside well oiled from neck to toes, I went over some areas again – this time with my arms instead of my hands; and with my chin.

And, finally I used my chest, leaning over, and putting pressure on Kelly's back, bottom and legs, as I moved my chest over her. With my chest nearly flat on her back, I circled her neck with my oily hands, and stroked under her hair, and then rubbed her ear lobes with the thumb and first finger of each hand. Kelly purred.

I wiped my hands on myself to get most of the oil off, and then put my hands through Kelly's hair, and slowly massaged Kelly's scalp. I could not imagine what Kelly might be thinking right now, but hoped it wasn't more than a Zen blankness, and the good physical feeling that I was trying to give her. For me, this was hard work, and my back was starting to feel the strain of leaning over the massage table. But my love for Kelly was becoming more certain now, and I was determined to show her, this weekend, how I felt about her.

Kelly 'Mmmm'd', and I leaned down and whispered in her ear, "I hope this feels good to you, Kelly. I want you to feel good." I kissed her ear.

"Are you ready to turn over, now?" Kelly nodded, and I helped her to roll over and get comfortable on her back. I put some oil into my hands and rubbed them together, then put my palms on Kelly's forehead, moving them very slightly in a circular pattern. The fingers of both of my hands then caressed her cheeks, and I slid my hands down her face, over the precipice of her chin, and down her long neck to her chest.

While keeping my hand on her chest, I walked around the table to face her, and I put both thumbs on the soft tissue below her ears, moving them in a spiral pattern, with only the slightest of pressure. I again massaged her forehead, with my thumbs starting together in the middle, and sliding outward, stretching her thin scalp.

Moving back to Kelly's chest, I drizzled more oil in a snake pattern, and then made circles around her breasts, spiraling the oil in, and letting it drip onto her nipples until there were streams of oil slowly running down, like ice cream melting down the sides of a cone. Kelly giggled.

I massaged her chest, and then gently spread the oil over each of her breasts, in turn. I then drizzled more oil over Kelly's flat stomach – from about two feet over her. The sudden drips caused Kelly's body to convulse, her abdominal tissues rippling; Kelly giggled again. Her eyes had been closed since she had turned onto her back; her face was relaxed, and she looked contented.

I moved up to the head of the table and, leaning far over Kelly (my stomach was touching the top of her head), I used both hands to make long strokes from her collarbone, down her chest, and between her breasts, continuing down her stomach as far as I could reach. I did these one-way strokes several times, and then changed to a stroke where my hands separated and came underneath and around her breasts, and back up to her chest.

Moving back around to the side of the table, I massaged her middle lightly, my hands moving in opposing circles, and down her sides to the table, where my hands slid under her, down to her hips, and then – lifting them – sliding back up to her stomach.

I used long strokes to massage each leg, this time from the top, from Kelly's thighs down to her ankles. After I had massaged both of her legs, I stood at Kelly's feet, and took her toes in my hands, wiggling them, kissing them, and sucking them. Kelly opened her eyes and lifted her head, realizing that this was the beginning of a new – more playful – phase of the massage.

I used a little more oil, and slid my hands up the insides of her legs to her crotch, and then up her inner thighs to her navel. Then, I stroked downward in the same way. Then, upward; but, each time, avoiding any sensitive areas, my hands detouring around them. Finally, I did a 'once-over lightly' on her genitals, lubricating exterior and interior portions, ending at Kelly's anus, where I swirled my fingers around, and then deeply inserted my middle finger. Kelly relaxed herself well, and the insertion of my finger rectally was smooth; Kelly showed little reaction.

From the e-stim box, I took out two anal probes. These were similar in size and shape to small butt plugs, so they were not too uncomfortable, and would be easily held in place by our bodies. After I had lubricated each of the probes with KY, I set them down on the paper covering the surface of the rolling table.

I walked over to the half-bath, and washed my hands with warm water, and then opened the small fridge in the corner of the room and took out a couple of ice cubes from the freezer section. I returned to the massage table, where Kelly lay on her back, her body relaxed, and her eyes closed.

I had brought the ice for something else, but as I looked over Kelly's beautiful body, I couldn't resist. I took an ice cube in each hand, and slowly leaned over Kelly, bringing the cold cubes down to just above her nipples. Then, I lowered them further, so that they contacted Kelly's nipples simultaneously. I did not press them down, but let them float on Kelly's tissues with the slightest of force and then, very slowly, moved them around her areolas, gliding alongside her nipples, which were already in an enlarged and hardened state.

Kelly moaned and made a few brief sounds when the ice touched her nipples, but otherwise remained still and quiet. I moved the ice slowly down her body, leaving trails of water droplets across Kelly's slick oiled skin.

"Kelly, we're not quite finished with your massage, but let's try a little more electrical stimulation, now that you're oiled. This should feel very different."

Kelly left her head on the table, and her eyes closed, as she said, "The massage felt really good! My body is already tingling. I'm not sure any more 'stimulation' is required." She laughed, and I saw her open one eye and look at me. I leaned over the table and kissed her oily lips.

I pulled the rolling cart closer and, assuming that this 'professional' massage table would hold both of us, I climbed carefully onto the it, facing Kelly's feet, and managed to get into a knee-chest position, with my butt somewhere above Kelly's stomach, and my forearms on the edge of the table, just outside of Kelly's legs. I managed to reach over and take one of the anal probes from the cart and hand it to Kelly, "Here: Go ahead and insert this into me. Carefully. For what we're going to try, we'll both have to have anal probes in place."

I felt Kelly reach up and fondle my 'package', and then hold my stiffening member in the fingers of her left hand while, with her right hand, she leveled the probe behind me and touched the lubricated tip to my anus. I took a breath, and tried to relax, allowing my sphincter to take in the probe. Kelly was getting very good at these kinds of insertions, not going too fast, using back-and-forth movements, and advancing the probe smoothly.

Then she giggled and moved the probe around in circles, and brought the end she was holding in an upward direction, so that the probe tip would press against my prostate. Kelly moved the probe tip around expertly, providing a very stimulating prostate massage.

Finally, she put some pressure on the end of the probe, and pushed it in slowly, until the steep slope just before the electrode pulled the probe further into my rectum, ensuring that my anus was tightly positioned around the metallic ring on the probe.

I had thought I might be able to insert Kelly's probe from this position, but it just wasn't physically possible, so – somewhat to Kelly's dismay, I crawled over her, and got off the table. It *would* have been a good '69' position, and it would be very interesting engaging in mutual oral-genital stimulation along with the electrical stimulation.

I asked Kelly to lift her legs, and she brought her knees to her chest, her arms clasped around them, holding them in place. I inserted the anal probe without ceremony, and adjusted it to make sure that the electrode was properly positioned. I helped Kelly put her legs back down on the table, and then connected the cable from her probe to the 'ground' connector on the generator.

I attached the cable from the anal probe that was inside me to a special accessory that is usually used to connect a body to the Violet Wand. Then, the person can touch the 'grounded' person, yielding an incredible variety of stimulating feelings (depending which parts of each body are touching) without having to use the 'mushroom' probe of the Violet Wand. By using the anal probe to attach my body to the Violet Wand, it would stimulate Kelly and I at the same time.

We were now ready – or at least, 'all wired up'. I turned on the Violet Wand and adjusted the intensity to medium. Kelly was fully oiled from head to toes – some droplets of water snaking their path over her breasts and down her stomach ('over the hills and through the vale ...'). My hands were oily and, at some point, I might have to oil portions of my own body in order to be a good 'electrode' for stimulating Kelly.

"Kelly, we're going to try the Violet Wand again, but in a slightly different way. Before, we used the 'direct' approach – where I touched you with the wand, and the current went through you. This time, I'm using an 'indirect' approach – where the wand is connected to me through the anal probe, and then my fingers and any other part of my body will act as the Violet Wand electrode. I can electrically stimulate you with my nose, or all of my fingers at once.

"Too bad it isn't dark – if we did this at night, the room would light up with all of the sparks and glows between our two bodies. That would be neat! In addition to 'indirect' approach, we'll try the 'reverse' approach, where current flows from you to me, as well as the other way around."

Kelly looked like she had fallen asleep. Two seconds later, I heard some rather loud 'snores'. I didn't believe it for one minute! She was just bored by all my technobabble. It didn't matter: Kelly would be wide-awake as soon as my body contacted hers.

Not wanting to start out too 'shocking' (in a manner of speaking), I separated the fingers of each of my hands, and slowly lowered them to the sides of Kelly's stomach. We both felt a slight 'buzzing' or 'tingling' as I slid my fingers along Kelly's body, up each side, across her chest, and around her breasts, culminating with several of my fingers emitting sparks directly to Kelly's nipples. What a great photo this would make: A macro close-up shot of Kelly's erect nipple, emitting sparks, like the top of a skyscraper attracting lightning.

I would need to remember to tell Kelly, when I taught her how to use this equipment, that stimulation from the medical system should never be used around the heart (meaning the chest and breasts) without special knowledge and precautions. The Violet Wand uses high voltage (thousands of volts) but extremely low current, to achieve its action, so is a safer device to use on the upper body, assuming neither person has a pacemaker implanted.

Many of the things I had done with Kelly would not normally be considered 'safe' sex play for the average person. However, I was in the healthcare field, had access to sterile devices and supplies, and knowledge from decades of working with medical equipment and procedures.

I slid my hands down Kelly's breasts and off to the side, as I lowered my head over her, and moved the tip of my nose into close proximity with Kelly's right nipple. At some small distance, a spark, then a series of sparks, and then a 'fuzz' of electrical energy passed between us. I did the same with Kelly's left nipple, and then moved toward her head, where I ran my nose along her chin.

I wasn't sure what would happen, but I stuck out my tongue – and Kelly mirrored my actions – until sparks were flying between our tongues. Our mouths came together, and the stimulation lessened as we kissed deeply … but as we moved our arms and fingers to hold each other, we gave each other a series of electrical tinglings wherever we touched. The feeling was very mild, having several points of contact, and it wasn't painful at all.

Kelly started giggling, and said, "Sometimes it feels like Champagne bubbles are breaking all over my skin. Between the tingling from the massage and the electrical stimulation, my body feels like it's in another dimension." Kelly lifted up a hand, and caressed my face, a long line of tiny sparks stimulating us along each finger and facial feature.

I wasn't sure whether Kelly would get turned-on by the electrical stimulation, but it was time to see. I moved alongside the table to Kelly's thighs, and put my hands first on the tops of her thighs, and then slid them down the insides of her legs, and to her perineum. I tried using a single finger to stimulate her, and found that if this finger were pushed too far into her, the stimulation would be lessened. So I held her labia apart with my other hand, and then ran a single finger along the insides of her moist lips. Kelly jumped once, and there were a few 'Oooh's' and 'Aaaah's' from the other end of the table; I was learning what would be stimulating, and what would be too much.

While keeping my palm on Kelly's pelvis, I used two fingers to swirl her clit. By having less or more of my palm on her, I could control the intensity of the stimulation to Kelly's clit. Kelly was letting me do this, but didn't seem to be responding sexually, as I had hoped.

I decided on another tack: My hands went around Kelly's thighs to the top of her hips, and I 'played' her, as I would play a piano, fingers moving so that they were tapping patterns across her hips, each time connecting with Kelly via a series of small sparks. We could smell the Ozone being produced by the sparks (not entirely safe to breathe, but there was only a tiny amount and it did have an interesting smell – like the freshness after a rain storm).

As I tapped my fingers rhythmically on Kelly's hips, I lowered my head and went down on Kelly. Her clit was already enlarged, and my tongue licked up under the hood, over the small button at the top, and then to each side. I flicked my tongue, very lightly bit her clit through the hood, and then sucked under the hood, with Kelly's clit between my lips.

I then started humming loudly – and making 'buzzing' sounds with my lips, vibrations that were instantly felt by the bundle of nerves in Kelly's most sensitive area. Kelly thrust her pelvis upwards, arching her back, and tensing her entire body. I softened my licks of her clit – more like lapping it up, as a cat would sweet milk, but in slow-motion – and Kelly emitted a long, low-pitched "Oooooohh!" Kelly bucked several times, and then her body relaxed on the table.

I lifted Kelly's bottom, and stuck a large (several inch round) ground pad onto her, connecting the other end to the medical stimulation generator. I did the same thing to myself. I rewired the cables from our anal probes to Channel 1 and Channel 2 of the generator, set a ramping frequency, and turned up the intensity to about 1/3.

Kelly and I both felt contractions in our pelvic area, in my case, providing some stimulation to my prostate. It wasn't as much as I would have liked, and I would have to work on other ways of electrically stimulating the prostate – perhaps with an electrode ring near the tip of the anal probe. What a fun way of doing 'medical research'!

Then, I carefully climbed back up onto the table, this time facing Kelly, and slowly crawled over and across her body, so that I could lie on top of her. Our bodies were both oily, and it felt good to slide my body over Kelly's, providing a sensual massage for both of us. I tried to make a mental note to give Kelly her next massage 'Thai' style, using much more of my body than my hands to stretch her muscles and mold her tissues.

I thought we were both ready for some proper lovemaking, but it wasn't going to happen on this narrow table, with both of us wired up. I was still holding out for a romantic first lovemaking session – on a real bed – before the afternoon was over.

As our oily bodies glided over each other, Kelly and I hugged, and I slid up so that I could kiss her. The stimulation from the anal probe was very mild, and I reached across to the rolling cart, and increased the intensity on both channels.

Kelly thrust herself against me, and we could feel our own, and each other's pelvic muscles contracting and releasing. Kelly slipped her hands between us and slid them down to my waiting manhood. Kelly used all of her techniques, and I was fully erect within moments. It felt wonderful.

As Kelly 'did' me, using her manual skills, my arms around her shoulders, our eyes looking into each other's, and both of us breathing heavily. I put my cheek on Kelly's, and we lay on the massage table, nearly as one, my body still moving slightly along Kelly's, with some additional 'movement' going on between us with her hands down below.

I lifted my head and looked into Kelly's eyes; she knew that I was nearly ready to come. She gave me a slightly expectant look, and I nodded imperceptibly and closed my eyes. Kelly's stroking was masterful, and as she took me in one of her hands, fingers curled around my shaft, tightening her hold and sliding towards the base, I came intensely, my hot fluid spurting to our chests, and Kelly continuing to stroke, now with both hands.

Kelly was not at all squeamish, and her eyes twinkled as she looked into mine again and giggled. I was already thinking that there was quite a mess between us, when Kelly's hands started 'finger painting' on my stomach, the 'paint' consisting of massage oil and semen.

I didn't usually play with bodily fluids, but Kelly was determined to smear the semen-oil mixture around both of us. Then, she took her hands out, and put them around me, and smearing the rest of the goop from her hands onto my back. Our bodies were now in total contact, and we both slithered and squirmed, ensuring that the sticky and oily liquids were spread in a thin layer between us. Almost like glue, holding us together. It was sensual – reminiscent of the movies of 'hot sex' in the South on some sweltering evening, sweat glistening, and running down conjoined bodies that were silhouetted in moonlight.

Kelly smiled, and said, "Can we please get down from here, now? I have an urge to pee again, and you still have to get that *thing* out of my butt." I laughed, and carefully slid across Kelly, and over the side of the table onto the ground. It was amazing that the massage table hadn't collapsed, or one of us fallen to the ground, with all these maneuvers.

"OK. Lift your legs, and I'll take the probe out." Kelly complied, and I slowly pulled the anal electrode out of her, and put it on a paper towel on the rolling cart. I told Kelly, "Now, you can get off the table, and take my probe out." I bent over and held my buttocks apart, as she pulled the probe out and set it next to the other one on the cart. We stood up, facing each other, and looked at the sticky, goopy mess covering my stomach and chest, and Kelly's chest and breasts. It had felt better then, than it looked now.

Kelly skipped over to the bathroom and sat on the toilet. I unhooked all the cables, and brought the anal and vaginal probes into the bathroom, putting them into the sink, and washing them with soap, as Kelly finished up.

We washed our hands together in the small sink, and I was about to wet a hand towel to clean off our fronts, when Kelly suggested, "Let's take a shower downstairs ... and maybe go in the sauna!" That sounded like a nice idea. It seemed like the weather was too warm for a sauna, but the house was nicely air conditioned, and we could cool off under a cold shower. And, it was about time for me to complete the preparations for some romantic lovemaking.

We walked downstairs, both of us still nude, and went into the large bathroom. There was only a toilet and small vanity with sink in the first room, but the sidewall opened into a very large shower area, with closets and racks for shoes between the first room and the shower room. Across from the shower was a tiled area with chaise lounges and a small round table. The far end of the shower room was wooden tongue-in-groove cedar paneling, with a smoked glass door – the entry to the sauna.

The sauna was large, for a home, with an L-shaped seating arrangement on low and high wood-slat benches. I had suspected that we would be using sauna at some time today, so the thermostat was already turned up to 175 degrees Fahrenheit – not quite hot enough, but a good starting temperature, and it would get close to 190 degrees within ten minutes after I turned it up as we entered it.

I got the showers going – including the overhead rain shower and the jets that we could aim toward our legs. We grabbed a couple of washcloths from the shelves next to the shower, and stepped under the warm water that was falling in huge drops.

We bathed each other lovingly, and I rinsed Kelly and then soaped her a second time with the washcloth, going over her entire body to remove the massage oil … and semen. I then took out a Loufah and scrubbed her soaped-up body until her skin glowed. Then, Kelly did another 'once-over' of my body – with a strange amalgamation of intensity and tenderness.

We rinsed off, with the rain shower temperature down to about 90 degrees, and the leg jets to about 75 degrees, so that we would slowly cool down. Finally, we turned off the water and grabbed a couple of sauna towels. Then we walked though the smoked glass door into the warm, dark cavern of the sauna.

CHAPTER 6: FIRST LOVEMAKING EXPERIENCE

The scent was cedar, with a hint of pine. A single dim red light provided the only illumination, the atmosphere intimate, without being cloistering. Kelly laid the short end of her towel on the top bench, and let the rest hang down, straightening the bottom on the lower bench to put her feet, as I had instructed her.

It was still only 180 degrees, so I used a wooden ladle to pour some water from a matching wooden bucket over the hot rocks of the heater. Steam billowed up to the ceiling of the sauna, and spread out, dramatically increasing the feeling of the heat on the top bench.

I sat next to Kelly, and we began to relax, as the heat floated over and around us. I reached over and turned the wood and glass sand dial that was mounted on the back wall, and had markings every minute for 15 minutes. Kelly looked at me, smiled, and shook her head.

"What?" I asked.

"I knew I wouldn't be disappointed, spending the weekend with you. I've been here less than 3 hours, and you've already spanked me, tickled me, electrified me, massaged me, and given me a nice orgasm. Now, you've bathed me, and we're sitting in the sauna. I really didn't expect any of this. Except the spanking."

I replied, "And that was the one thing I *hadn't* planned for today."

In the shadowed red light of the sauna, I saw Kelly's big smile. I don't think she had been disappointed in the experience, so far. She hadn't mentioned the 'dessert' we'd had 24 hours ago.

I put on my mock pout now, and said, "You didn't think that was a *real* spanking, did you? I just gave you a few pops to simulate what Linda will feel tomorrow, and just because you (literally) asked for it." Then it was my turn to smile, "And, I haven't forgotten: You will receive the rest of your level-100 punishment this weekend. Then, your bottom will *know* it's been spanked!"

Kelly looked down, and she was no longer smiling; she fidgeted with her fingers, and appeared nearly as nervous as she had been when we were on the couch discussing the rules for our previous experience. I had to soften this, in preparation for a much more romantic experience in just a little while.

"Kelly, let's not talk about spanking, now. And don't get too nervous about your hard punishment: I'm sure you'll do fine, just as you did last time. As I said before, I want to please you today. But still give you some new experiences that might be a bit painful ... I mean *sensual*."

Kelly looked up, and chuckled, then looked nervous again. "Sir, I am here voluntarily. And I know that you will be giving me some pain. You already know that I'm OK with that. I want to be here ... and to experience whatever you think is appropriate."

Kelly laughed, "No, not 'appropriate', but whatever you would like to do to me ... or with me ... or anything you would like me to experience. Just the expectation of what you might do is a turn-on to me." Kelly smiled; and I smiled. Then, Kelly admitted, "Although I wasn't too crazy about the electrical stimulation."

I looked over at the sand dial: We had been in the sauna for only 6 minutes, but were both dripping already. I had to take a few minutes to 'prepare' things in the playroom, and I knew we were both getting dehydrated, so I told Kelly, "In a few minutes, we'll get into the shower. We should do at least one more sauna cycle after that. But I know we'll be thirsty, so let me run over to the playroom bar and fix us some ice water, and then I'll come back and get warmed up again Then we'll get out, drink some water, and cool off in the shower. How does that sound?"

Kelly smiled, "That sounds fine. I'm starting to get hot in here. Ice water sounds like a good idea. I'll try to stick-it-out in here until you come back." I hoped she would, or a nice surprise might be ruined.

We both stood up. I put my towel over my arm, and Kelly took hers and laid it out lengthwise on the lower bench. She grabbed a wooden triangle for under her head, and lay down on her back, with her knees up and feet on the bottom edge of the towel.

I exited the sauna, quickly re-closing the glass door, and hung my towel from a hook. I turned on the shower and rinsed off quickly, then toweled mostly dry, and walked, nude, into the playroom. I took a large plastic pitcher of water with a lime slice from the bar fridge, and put it on a tray with a couple of glasses that I filled with ice. I left the tray on the edge of the bar, while I tended to the 'real' reason for my slipping out of the sauna.

I ran to the far end of the room, and ducked around the side of the huge projection screen. I opened a drawer by the bed, and took out a lighter shaped like a gun, with the trigger initiating a flame at the end of a narrow barrel, so that fires could be lit from a distance. I circled the room, lighting all of the candles that I had set out earlier. The bedspread had already been folded and placed on a small bench along one wall, and the satin sheets turned down crisply.

The rose petals that I had scattered over the bed and pillows gave this entire end of the room a fragrant aroma. Hopefully, Kelly wasn't allergic to roses; I would find out soon. I picked up a wooden pail next to the bench on the wall, and ducked back around the screen, leaving a trail of rose petals from near the center of the screen, in a meandering path, nearly to the entrance of the playroom.

I then walked to the bar, and pushed the 'play' button on the remote control. I picked up the water tray and retraced my steps to the bathroom, placing the tray on a small circular table between two small chaise lounges in the open shower area, just outside the sauna.

I entered the sauna, and Kelly looked well-done: Flesh red and juices flowing, her body glistened. The 'juices' were sweat, which puddled in Kelly's navel, dripped from her breasts, and soaked her dark triangle.

Kelly opened her eyes, and looked up at me. "I hope you can get warmed up quickly, because I'm ready to get out of here." She sat up, cross-legged on her towel. I put my towel down, and sat cross-legged facing her. She had made a good decision to move to the lower bench; the sauna thermometer now read 189 degrees Fahrenheit.

Kelly and I leaned toward each other, our knees touching, and kissed. I ran my hand down her hair, which fell to the sauna bench. Then, I ran my hand *through* her hair, but less than 1/3 of the way down, my fingers were stopped by knots. Kelly let out a quick 'Ow!' and then she laughed, "You haven't pulled my hair, yet. Not that I would like it much ... but it's one of the details in my pirate fantasy."

I laughed, telling her, "Hair pulling seems a bit demeaning ... unless you ask for it. But I would have fun combing it out after our shower."

Of course, my entire brain was focused at that moment on the mention of the pirate scenario that Kelly had disclosed to me when we had shared some of our fantasies – and we first realized that they might actually be compatible. Much of my efforts in preparing for Kelly's birthday party – and most of the remaining tasks – were directed toward an enactment of Kelly's fantasy. I hoped that I could keep it a surprise until the big day.

I was certain that Kelly – and her friends – would be amazed at what I had planned; I just hoped that it would also be a huge turn-on for Kelly. And, that she wouldn't balk at doing a few things ... OK, more than a few things ... in front of her friends.

Kelly uncrossed her legs and swung them off the bench onto the tile floor. "I'm overheated. Let's get cooled off!" And then she batted her eyes, "Please, Sir?"

We exited the sauna, and I started a lukewarm rain shower. Kelly and I lightly soaped each other and – using our hands – bathed each other's sweaty bodies. I then turned the rain shower to a cool setting, and fired-up the leg jets: There were 4 vertical rows of three jets (ankle, knee, hip) that could be individually aimed. I often set these for 'cold', and the rain shower for warm, and then gradually decrease the rain shower temperature.

I have tried 'cold pools' (dunking quickly into near-freezing water immediately after coming out of the sauna) ... but it doesn't seem they could be good for the heart. At least the 'pins and needles' aren't as bad as when going from a hot tub – naked, of course – and rolling around in the snow, then hopping back into the tub. That can be painful! But, perhaps, not a bad 'new experience' for a sex slave in training?

We showered together for several minutes, mostly turning around in the cool-cold water, and letting the huge drops hit us in the face and cascade down our bodies. Finally, we turned off the water, and toweled off, wrapping the towels around us.

I then went into the bathroom and found the coarse men's comb that was in the drawer, picked up another towel, and walked back into the shower room. We sat on the small chaises sideways, facing each other, and I poured waters. We both finished our glasses, and I refilled them. I turned Kelly around, facing away from me, and brought the chaises closer together. It was a perfect position from which to comb Kelly's hair.

I've had some experience with knotted hair, and worked with only a couple of inches at a time, from the bottom, up. Kelly's hair was the longest I'd ever combed, and it took quite a while. But we were both very content to sit quietly, enjoying the feeling of our bodies – skin tingling, neither hot nor cold, but *alive.*

When Kelly's hair was done, I could run the comb through it from the top of her head down to her waist, the dark strands of hair combining into a shimmering curtain – almost mesmerizing. Kelly had not asked, but I decided to go one more step, and braid her hair with French braids. I had learned this from Liz, during our many outings to the stream and pond.

I would have to take Kelly there sometime – it was only a short bike ride away. As I thought about it, I realized that the pond might be a nice outing later this weekend.

I separated Kelly's hair into bunches, and separated the bunches, braiding, and swapping bundles of hair in my hands. I pulled hair from the sides of her head, and incorporated every hair into the braid, which continued to nearly the middle of Kelly's back, where I finished with a ponytail. I hadn't practiced this in a while, but it came out nice, although a bit looser on the top than I would have liked.

We both lay back in the chaises, sipped water, and enjoyed each other's company. I wondered how Kelly would react to the surprise in the playroom. I would still need to go to the bar for the remote control ... but she would see the path of rose petals and the beautiful scenes on the video. I had considered showing erotic images, but decided on a *'Planet Earth'* video that featured beautiful scenes of mountains, streams, flowers, trees, and clouds. I was getting excited with anticipation ... fortunately not physically, yet.

Kelly turned to me, and asked, "Do we have to get back in the sauna? It's very hot, and I'm pretty mellowed-out right now." Then she turned her head down, with her bewitching hazel eyes raised up at me, batting her long eyelashes, and said, "But, I'll do anything you ask me to, Sir. I won't complain. I am your sex slave."

This was perfect! I thought a moment of how I would phrase this, and then said, "Kelly, I want you to be happy. You don't have to do anything you don't want, especially today. I'm really glad to hear that you'll do anything I ask. And about 'sex slave' ..." Kelly looked at me curiously. "You will never be my 'slave'. But I'll take the sex!"

Kelly looked at me: Her head was cocked, and her eyes slightly wide. I continued, "In fact, I don't really want sex, either. At least not right now." Kelly's eyes fell, and she started shaking her head, barely perceptible, but she was probably wondering whether we would *ever* have sex

... or maybe that I was secretly gay? But I would quickly dispel any of her wayward thoughts.

"Kelly, please stand up." Kelly put down her glass of water, and stood at the foot of the chaise. I gave her a bear hug ... and didn't let go. I rubbed her back, under her braid, and put my arms around her, cupping her buttocks in my hands. I looked into Kelly's eyes, and told her, "Kelly. You might not have wanted to hear this. It wasn't my idea when we met, or when we had lunch together. In fact, I wouldn't have believed that I was capable of this ..."

A cloud crossed over Kelly's face, but I continued before she could say a word. "Kelly, I love you." I hugged her again, and then took her by the shoulders, and looked back into her eyes. "Kelly, I *do* want sex. But what I want more is to make *love* to you."

Kelly's eyes were wide, and her smile wider. She was fairly bubbling with energy. I continued, "I've gone through a lot of phases. We can talk about that later. But I've realized that I want you. I need you. I'm in love with you." Kelly's mouth dropped open, and I took the opportunity to give her a long, hard kiss. Well, it was a *soft* kiss, but as passionate as I could imagine.

I held Kelly's shoulders again, and said, "Kelly, I have a little surprise for you. It might be easier without your towel." Kelly looked into my eyes, trying to fathom what crazy new idea I had come up with this time, and she dropped her towel on the chaise. I gave her an enigmatic smile, then lifted her up, her feet kicking up and down in a mock-feminine way, as I carried her into the playroom, setting her down just inside the door.

I stood motionless and stared into the room. The indirect lighting had been dimmed, the video screen that stretched nearly across the width of the room and to the floor was showing a pan shot of wildflowers on a blue-sky day in the mountains, and soft music was coming from the multi-channel sound system – seemingly coming from everywhere, but being so soft that it took a few moments to realize that it was the beginning of Ravel's *'Bolero'*. And, there was a path of rose petals on the floor! The room was fragrant, matching the flower scenes in the video.

I had not moved a muscle, but jumped as I heard a loud 'POP!' I looked over to the bar, and saw Sam standing there smiling, and pouring two glasses of Champagne.

I slowly walked towards the bar, and Sam walked around to the couch, putting the fluted crystal Champagne glasses on the coffee table, and taking the towel from around his waist and spreading it on the couch.

Sam and I sat on the towel, and Sam kissed me again. Then, he reached for the Champagne, and we toasted with a clink of the glasses. We sat there, totally relaxed from the sauna, and becoming more relaxed sipping the bubbly, and listening to the increasingly persistent music.

When we had finished the few ounces of Champagne in our glasses, Sam stood, taking me by the hand. We walked by the corner of the bar, where Sam pushed a button on the remote; the video stopped and motorized screen rose silently. *Bolero* was just getting going.

I wondered if Sam had envisioned his coupling with me as the lovemaking scene in the movie '*10*' that I'd seen one night on TV; hopefully, our lovemaking would go better than in the movie!

I stopped in my tracks – on the rose petal path – and stared, awestruck, at the flickering candles – in holders on the wall, on the bedside dressers, and in holders mounted to the headboard, far above the pillows. The rest of the playroom lights were dimmed, making the bed the focus of the room. I walked slowly along the flowered path, and turned to Sam.

Sam smiled, "You're beautiful, Kelly. Your body is reflecting the flickering candles in a reddened glow, your hair looks iridescent, your curves and recesses are accentuated in deep shadows. Sparkles are flickering from your eyes. And, I think I can see an aura surrounding you."

I couldn't believe what I was seeing ... what was happening. As in a dream, I continued slowly down the rose petal path towards the bed. I couldn't help but look at the variety of candles around the bed, providing their dim flickering light as an alternative to the modern electronic world. The room smelled wonderful. How had Sam done this? Just an hour before, I was on a massage table, and an hour before that, in the swimming pool. I'd had no idea that this romantic dream world had awaited me downstairs.

I also couldn't help but wonder where the relationship with Sam would lead – I had hoped he wasn't already looking for commitment. On the other hand, I was ready to commit – more than I ever had before. Not to being a housewife (nothing wrong with that, but it wasn't my current idea of excitement and a future with opportunity), nor to being a mother. That wasn't a consideration with Sam, as his vasectomy would limit such an 'opportunity'.

I'd been expecting Sam to make love to me since an hour or two after I arrived at his house last time. Sam had this strange definition of 'sex', and insisted that our first experience be based on submission, openness, cooperation, and self-control, rather than as just a prelude to sex.

Not that I would have minded sex, also. Sam was very experienced, and had brought me to orgasm numerous times already; I was truly curious to see how he would handle 'straight' sex. But it was clear that he was looking at this experience as more than 'sex' – just as he had said. The strange thing was ... so was I.

Sam led me to the bed, and hugged and kissed me again, our bodies tightly pulled together by both our efforts – communicating to each other silently, but clearly, that we did not want to lose each other.

We got into the bed, but the rose petals were a bit much ... I had to brush them from the pillows, and several stuck to my back and hips. They were romantic, perhaps, but not really practical. But how could I complain? Here was a man who was focused solely on me. A man able to give me incredible experiences – including wonderful orgasms. A man out of the ordinary ... truly 'extraordinary'.

Sam was sometimes too intense, and maybe even overly creative, but he certainly knew how to treat a woman with respect ... even while he 'had his way' with her in some bizarre and possibly perverted ways.

Now, Sam was kissing my body ... from my neck, down. He put his hands under my bottom, and lifted, while going down on me ... licking and sucking my clit, swirling and flicking his tongue. I was already turned-on, and wanted to be sure that we really made love this time ... not just help each other masturbate. I reached down, and grabbed his hair, pulling gently.

Sam got the message, and crawled up my body, once again giving me a deep, long kiss. He held my face, and looked into my eyes. I gave a tiny nod, and Sam took his position between my legs. I reached down and guided his already-stiff cock into my cunt ... savoring a feeling that I had not experienced in a while. I was so wet that he easily slid into me, and we both moaned.

Sam was elevated above me, on his knees and elbows, and moved his body with long, slow strokes, as he looked into my eyes. He lowered his head and kissed me again:

Delicious. What a contrast to yesterday's food-sex experience! Both were a turn-on, but this was truly romantic. I still couldn't believe the candles, the rose petals, the music. *Bolero* was in full swing now, and the continuous pounding of its rhythms were really sexy. I expected Sam to come any time.

I was surprised when Sam stopped his motion, and asked me to put my legs around his waist, but – of course – I did so immediately. Sam thrust a few more times, pushing deeply into me; I was certain he was against my cervix. Then, Sam reached around my shoulders, and rocked us. I put my arms around his neck, and our rocking motions increased ... until he was in a cross-legged sitting position, and had pulled me up into his lap, while still being deep inside me.

We rocked gently back and forth, holding each other, although there was little movement of him inside me. I realized that Sam had brought us to this position in order to experience *less* sensation, and last longer. He cupped my bottom in his hands and lifted me toward him as he rocked forward, so we were both still feeling his shaft – sliding, and throbbing. I thrust my pelvis against his movements, and was sure that another minute of this, and Sam would come. And, so would I.

But Sam surprised me again. He stopped his motion, and took my head in his hands, looking deeply into my eyes. And then we kissed: Our lips sealing our open mouths, tongues swirling; two bodies joined, above and below. As we kissed, Sam put his arms around me, and rocked forward, gently laying me back down on the bed. His legs straightened, and he stopped kissing long enough to ask me to straighten my own legs, and hold on to him. Before I knew what we were going to do, Sam had rolled us over, with me on top.

Then, he smiled at me, and asked, very sincerely, "Kelly, will you make love to me, now?"

That was funny – I guess he'd considered everything up to this point to only be foreplay. I nodded and closed my eyes. Straddling Sam, I lowered myself until we were nearly touching, and started a slow movement of my body along his. Sam put his hands on my bottom, pulling on the up-strokes, thrusting his pelvis at the end of each down-stroke.

I opened my eyes briefly, and saw that his eyes were closed. I closed my eyes again, and lowered myself further onto Sam, now taking full responsibility for the motions that were about to bring us both to climax. I was in the moment, oblivious of everything around me ... except Sam.

My orgasm exploded, and Sam's followed within a few seconds. I came, and came, as Sam continued his thrusting and squeezed my bum. My energy was spent, and I left Sam impaled on me as I lowered my entire weight onto Sam's body. Our legs intertwined, and I kissed Sam as I ran my fingers through his thick hair. The room was silent, except for our heavy breathing; *Bolero* had finished. We lay joined together, Sam still inside me.

When I could think again, I realized that this lovemaking experience had been very different: Different from our mutual masturbation, and different from my prior sexual experiences. It was sex, but it was also much more than that. It was love.

CHAPTER 7: NEEDLE PLAY, CANDLE WAX

Sam and I held each other for a long time. Eventually, I lifted my head from his chest, and looked into his eyes. "That was nice. Both the lovemaking, and all the preparations you made. Very romantic!" I really did appreciate Sam's efforts ... but would have been delighted even without the candles, roses, and Champagne. On an intellectual level, I still wondered about the relationship that was developing with Sam. But on an emotional level, I was enthralled ... and in love.

Sam smiled, "I love you, Kelly." And, as an afterthought, "I hope that doesn't frighten you."

I laughed – that was a good one! But then I thought about it. "It does frighten me, a little. It frightens me more ... that I think I'm falling in love with *you*."

Sam had become flaccid, and was now coming out of me. We sat up and hugged again. Sam hopped off the bed, and I watched his naked body, as he headed toward the bathroom.

Sam was a handsome man, and he was fit – he really was a 'hunk', if you didn't dwell on his age. I knew that he was intelligent and creative, and that he held high ideals, but I had not really known how romantic he could be.

I enjoyed Sam's company, and playing with him: I could probably have been satisfied by fulfilling Sam's (and my) spanking fantasies, and having casual sex. But Sam, as usual, went far beyond my expectations, opening my eyes to a new and different 'level' of experience.

I walked slowly, my bare feet treading on rose petals, as I crossed the darkened playroom, the walls flickering with light from the many candles. When I got to the bathroom, I looked in the mirror, as Sam finished peeing. The woman staring back at me somehow looked younger, and had a more contented smile, than I could recall seeing in a long time.

Sam stood next to me and washed his hands, giving me a quizzical look in the mirror. It seemed like I had been in a trance. I shrugged my shoulders, and then leaned over and gave Sam a kiss on the cheek, before sitting down on the toilet. As Sam exited the bathroom, he told me to meet him back at the bed, when I was ready.

I put the crystal glasses and the still mostly-full Champagne bottle on an inlaid wooden tray, and set it next to the bed. Then, I quickly straightened the sheets, and collected rose petals from the bed, dropping them into the wooden pail sitting near one wall. Going back to the office area, I took a shoebox from the credenza, and brought it back to the bed, putting it next to the drink tray.

Sitting, cross-legged, on the bed, I contemplated our lovemaking experience. Perhaps I had over-done the romantic flair? But this was how I *felt*. The romance was only partly for Kelly.

Kelly re-entered the playroom, carefully following the curving path of the rose petals on the carpeted floor. We had been nude most of the afternoon and, of course, I had seen every millimeter of her body the last time she had come over (in a manner of speaking), but I still marveled at her beauty.

Her long, French-braided hair fell behind her, to where her rounded hips extended from her narrow waist. Her long, athletic legs carried her with poise; even her breasts had 'poise' – being firm enough to stand from her body in double convex curves, despite their size.

The long neck, that Kelly considered a fault, led to a perfect face, framed by her thick hair, and featuring large, hazel eyes that scintillated, as they reflected the multitude of flickering candles. Kelly's sincere, natural smile – without the benefit of any makeup – exuded sensuality, while commanding attention.

Kelly climbed onto the bed, and we sat cross-legged, with our knees almost touching. I leaned over and poured two glasses of Champagne, handing one to Kelly, and toasting to the next phase of our relationship. "Kelly, I wanted to make you happy today. Are you happy?" I smiled at the obviously relaxed and contented woman in front of me.

Kelly chuckled, "You know I am. And you know that I want to make you happy, too. I realize you wanted to make our lovemaking romantic ... but I'm a little surprised that you didn't want me to have a sore bottom first. I think you know that I will submit to anything you ask of me ... *Sir*."

Kelly looked down at her lap, and chuckled again. I awaited her comment. Finally, she looked up, and said, "I don't know. Maybe I'm becoming an endorphin junkie. I almost crave having you spank me." Kelly was now laughing, "Or, me spank you."

I laughed too. "Kelly, you may spank me if you want. But I didn't want to spank you today ... and I've already given you a sample of what I'm planning for Linda. But if it's endorphins that you're craving, I do have another 'new experience' that I would like to share with you."

Kelly rolled her eyes exaggeratedly, then looked at me seriously, and said, "I guess I asked for it." Then, she smiled and gave me a mock salute. "Yes, Sir. Would you like to tell me what my next new experience will be?" Then, as an afterthought, she added, "Not that it matters. My body is yours, Sir. At least for this weekend." We both laughed, and I was pleased that Kelly was still willing to take the role of the 'sub'.

I then had to consider how to best introduce Kelly to a combination of new sensory challenges. "Some of what I would like to share is from the BDSM world. But the main event is usually considered in the same vein as 'body modification', and mostly done for the endorphins and for its artistic value."

Kelly inclined her head, mockingly, "*Art*, Sir?"

I wasn't sure if today's experience would qualify as art, but a simple Internet search shows a bewildering variety of patterns, images, and even something that I was planning for Kelly's birthday: The corset. "Kelly, I'm going to teach you a little about 'needle play'. I'll show you the basic idea, and then a few images of what some people have done."

Kelly frowned, "You're going to stick me with needles, again, Sir?"

"Yes, but this will be different. I'll use the same small needles that we used before, but instead of sticking them into your muscle, they will be stuck through a pinch of skin, and back out. I'll show you some pictures and then demonstrate it for you."

I thought about the intramuscular needle insertions and shots that we had done previously, which was more of a turn-on for me than conventional 'needle play'. Perhaps I shouldn't limit our activity? "And, yes, Kelly I may also stick some needles in you like we did last time. But we will only continue if you are comfortable with it."

Kelly laughed (which was better than crying), and responded, "Well, Sir, I don't think you can call those big needles 'comfortable'. But, as I said, Sir, I am yours. I'm looking forward to any perverted new experiences you would like to share with me." She batted her eyes at me again.

I decided to take advantage of her comment, "Good, because this experience will also entail a couple of other sensual – or at least sensory – experiences." I looked around the room, "I noticed that you liked the candles."

Kelly nodded, "Yeah, I think they're great. I love candles."

I smiled inwardly, and probably outwardly, as I continued, "That's good, Kelly, because I will be using candles to drop hot wax on you!" Kelly's mouth fell open, and her eyes grew wide.

I nodded. "Actually, we'll be using special candles that have lower-temperature wax. But it would still burn you, if I let the wax fall from too low above your skin. Many people combine needle and wax play ... although I don't like the idea of the wax coming in contact with the needles or the breaks in your skin ... so I'll keep the wax areas and needle areas separated."

Kelly scrunched her face, "That's very considerate of you, Sir." She shook her head, and looked at me, "How do you come up with all these things, anyway?"

I laughed, "It's amazing – the range of things some people are turned-on by ... and it's all on the 'net. There are hundreds of fetishes. I can't relate to most of them, and some are downright nasty ... but others seem interesting, especially from the perspective of someone submitting to pain. And, I did promise you that I would come up with new experiences for us to try."

"Us, Sir?" Then Kelly laughed, "Can I still spank you first? Sir? You might need a small reminder of what a sore butt is like, before you start sticking me with needles. And, there should be a corner time to go with the spanking!"

Again, I thought 'what kind of monster have I created?'. And, again, I said to myself, 'fair is fair'. I knew that in Kelly's exploration of discipline and submission, she had found that she was a 'switch': She could be turned on as a sub or a domme. Perhaps she was more turned-on in the role of a dominatrix, I was now starting to discover.

"Yes, Kelly, you may spank me. But I hope it's not for doing something wrong. And maybe you'll first let me get my computer and show you the pictures of needle play art? Perhaps you'll be easier on my spanking, when you see how creative it is."

Kelly harrumphed, "You'll get the spanking I think you deserve, young man. But you may get your laptop, and we can look at some pictures while we have a little more Champagne."

I arched my brows at Kelly, and she arched her brows at me. I got off the bed, and ran over to the office area, fetching my laptop, and running back to the bed. I was halfway back before I realized that my semi-erect penis was bouncing up and down as I ran. I looked up, and Kelly had a big smile on her face, keeping her eyes on the bouncing balls.

I climbed onto the bed, and refilled our Champagne glasses, which were fluted Baccarat crystal that my wife and I had bought in Paris years ago. I opened the laptop, and Kelly scooted around next to me, as I typed in a URL, and a body modification website popped onto the screen. There were images of male and female genital piercings, bizarre tattoos, labial weights, and a guy hanging from two hooks.

I clicked, and images appeared of intricate patterns on a girl's back, on a guy's arm, and many more – all created using needles slipped through the skin, with a pinch of skin 'skewered' on the needle, and the tip of the needle coming back out through the skin on the other side of the pinch of tissue.

Zooming in, I scrolled around one of the more complex patterns, and Kelly gasped when she realized what she was looking at: Literally hundreds of needles – of different sizes, colored hubs, and orientations – making spiraling patterns across a girl's backside – from neck to ankles. Other images showed similar patterns on women's breasts, and still others displayed multiple needles through a woman's labia.

I was still as shocked, seeing some of these images, as I had been when I had first been introduced to needle play; some went beyond 'art', and far into the S&M realm.

Kelly took a couple of gulps of Champagne, and said, "It looks pretty painful, Sir." And then, "But I know I can take it, Sir. And some of them actually do look very artistic." Then Kelly laughed, "We could do some body painting, instead. It probably wouldn't hurt, as much."

I exclaimed melodramatically, "I thought you wanted some pain?" I pointed to the image of a woman's labia being pierced by a half-dozen needles, "But I agree: Some of these are pretty extreme – we won't do anything like that, today. And body painting sounds like fun – some other time."

I closed the laptop, and put it on the dresser, then I grabbed the shoebox. Opening the top, I saw Kelly's eyes focus on the items inside. "I have some of the 25-gauge, 1.5-inch needles, that didn't bother you much last time. And, I have some larger needles (each size has a particular color hub). And some acupuncture needles, which are solid, but much thinner – and much longer – than the hypodermic needles." Then, I showed Kelly the special candles. Finally, at the bottom of the shoebox were a couple of other long, thin objects, which Kelly recognized immediately.

"Sparklers? Sir?"

I laughed, "Yes, Kelly. It will give the room even more flickering light ... and your back even more sensations." I didn't bother mentioning that, once again, I would need to be careful – holding the sparkler a certain distance from her skin, so that she would feel the 'pinpricks' of the hot metallic particles, but not be burned by them. I continued, "Before we use all this stuff, I'll give you a demonstration of how the needles look – and feel – in 'needle play'."

Now, Kelly laughed. I didn't know what was so funny, until she informed me, "Well, Sir, before you give me that demonstration, I intend to spank your bottom."

We sat there laughing, and finished our Champagne. I put everything back into the box, and put it and the glasses on the dresser. I got off the bed, and into the 'standing position' – my feet about shoulder-width apart, and my hands on my head. Down below, I was still somewhat hard, but pointing in a downward direction.

I was nervous, as I didn't know what to expect from Kelly. I trusted her, and would submit to whatever she asked, which I knew would be a turn-on for her. And, hopefully, for me ... assuming I could think about things other than the pain. I looked up at Kelly, and earnestly, "I'm ready for my spanking now, Miss."

Kelly smiled, and signaled 'come here' with the curled pointer finger of her right hand. I got on the bed, and crawled over to her, lying across her lap, as she put a pillow behind her against the headboard, and adjusted herself under me. Kelly hadn't asked me to bring any 'implements', and I hadn't offered to; she could easily have decided to blister my bottom with the hairbrush, sting it with the small strap, or even use the 'slipper'.

I waited patiently, across her lap, with my re-hardening member between my stomach and her left thigh. Kelly was lightly stroking my back, sliding her hand over my bottom, squeezing a handful of flesh, and then repeating the process. She was helping me to relax, and it was working.

Suddenly, her open hand came down with great force on my right buttock, and I involuntarily yelped, but managed to stay in place. A harsh series of spanks rained down on my butt, one after the other, alternating sides, and – I'm sure – reddening my rear.

Just as suddenly, Kelly stopped, and lightly rubbed my bottom. She said, brightly, "I'm not as mathematical as you, Sir. So, I'm not counting the strokes ... and I don't care for you to, either. The number doesn't matter: I'm going to spank you until your bottom is a nice bright red."

With that, the spanking continued, never letting up with the hard spanks, and surprising me with the force that this young woman could muster. Finally, the spanking stopped again, and Kelly rubbed each of my buttocks in a circular pattern.

"You're getting me wet again, young man! We'll have to do something about that. But your spanking isn't finished." My bottom was already sore, but Kelly continued spanking me, harder still; it was really hurting now.

I knew better than to reach behind me, and concentrated on keeping my hands and feet still ... but I realized that I was rocking from side-to-side on Kelly's thigh, which was keeping me hard, despite the hard spanking. Kelly stopped once more, and rubbed my bottom – which I'm not sure helped or hurt at this point.

Kelly asked, "Have you had enough, young man? I planned to give you at least another ten minutes worth," I groaned, "but I think your bum is ready for a corner time now." I nodded, relieved, as I wasn't sure how much more spanking I could have taken ... although I was sure that, someday, Kelly would make me find out.

As I was pondering this, Kelly said, "OK, young man. Get off me, and bring me a towel to wipe up the mess on my leg. And, the red butt plug." It was the biggest one I had.

I was shocked, and still wasn't sure what I had heard. Actually, I *was* sure, but didn't want to accept it. But Kelly had asked, and I would oblige ... *submit* ... even though I knew that this would be an uncomfortable, if not painful experience.

While many of the vibrators and butt plugs provide great stimulation to the prostate, this particular one was just too wide – at its widest point – for comfort. I had inserted it into Kelly during our last experience, and she had held it while we gave each other 'practice' shots – intramuscular injections of sterile saline. But, still, that butt plug hurt when going in, unless significant time was taken to dilate the anal sphincter.

I brought the towel – moistened with warm water at one end – as well as the red butt plug and a small tube of KY. Kelly cleaned her thigh, and handed me the towel to clean myself. I gave her the butt plug and KY, and she told me to get in a knee-chest position on the bed. Kelly first lubed my anus, and then inserted a finger into me deeply, moving it around and lubricating my rectum.

It felt good but, too soon, she took her finger out, and I felt the tip of the butt plug pressing against my anus. Kelly knew that this had to be done slowly, and she gradually advanced the butt plug, moving it in and out slightly before advancing it further. It only took a few minutes for most of the butt plug to enter me. But it was the wide portion still outside me that I was worried about.

Kelly held the butt plug up against my anus, while I consciously tried to relax my sphincter. The pressure being applied by Kelly was starting to hurt, but at that moment, Kelly slid the butt plug mostly out of me, and then back as far as it would go. She slid the butt plug out again, and held it there.

Then, she said, "OK. Now!" Kelly pushed the butt plug against my anus, and continued to push; there was a moment of sharp pain, but the butt plug was suddenly past the widest point, and immediately 'sucked in', so that only the thin red disc was outside of me. I had stayed silent, but realized that I was now panting. The butt plug didn't hurt much, now that it was in me, but I was still feeling the pain of that final push.

Then, Kelly had her hand under me, taking hold of my erection, wrapping her fingers around me, and stroking slowly. I was close to coming, when Kelly's hand left me, and she said sternly, "Back over my lap, young man!" Oh no ... I didn't want more spankings. I had thought there would be *no* spanking today ... especially not on *my* bottom!

However, I knew that Kelly was testing my submission – just as I had done with her many times. I crawled over and got over her lap – which, this time, was covered by the towel. My hard-on was throbbing, and I assumed that either Kelly would spank me hard, and I would get turned-off, or Kelly would get me off in the towel.

Kelly put her hand on my bottom, and said, "Now, we will complete your spanking!" I groaned, not realizing it until I heard it, as if coming from somewhere else. Kelly had not been trained as a domme, yet, but I was sure she could see how sore my bottom must already be.

Kelly said sternly, "Are you ready for the rest of your spanking, now, young man?" I coughed, and said, "Yes, Ma'am. I mean, Yes, Miss." I was flustered, and my mind was becoming a blank. I felt a searing smack on my left buttock. Then another on my right side. I wondered whether I would be able to finish this spanking without crying.

But no more spanks came.

Kelly chuckled above me, and said, "Thank you for cooperating. I guess that will be enough spanking, for one day."

I'm sure Kelly heard me let out a breath. "Thank you, Miss." Kelly rubbed my bottom, and said, "You did well, Sam, Sir. Sir Sam." We laughed, and Kelly offered, "I'm ready to make love again, if you are ..."

That was all the encouragement I needed. I got off Kelly's lap, and back into a knee chest position. I waited. Kelly asked, "What are you doing?"

I replied, "Aren't you going to take the butt plug out, now?"

Kelly laughed, "No. I wasn't planning to. I thought you could keep it in this time, while we make love."

Now, my face was scrunched. "Kelly ..." I was still in the knee chest position, with Kelly behind me.

"Yes, young man?" Kelly asked. Then, she said softly, "If you don't want to make love ..."

That's all it took. I crawled over to Kelly, who was now lying on the bed, her knees up, feet on the bed, and legs widely separated – ready for me to take my position. A thought entered my head, and I asked Kelly, "May I prepare a couple of needles? I'd like to see the response inserting them while I'm in you."

There was a few-second delay, and then I was surprised to hear Kelly say, "That's a great idea! You can get them ready." So I did.

I unpackaged two of the 25 gauge needles, and put them, and an alcohol swab, on the second pillow, within reach. Then, I crawled between Kelly's legs, and entered her. The butt plug was uncomfortable, but more annoying than painful, and it was a small price to pay for a chance to make love again to Kelly.

I hugged Kelly, and we kissed. I rolled us over so that she was on top again, and then told her, "I don't think it's going to take very long for either of us ... so I'll insert the needles now – one on each side. Just try to relax."

Kelly's eyes flew open, "Oh, no, young man. The needles are for *you*! It sounds like you're going to be sticking me with a lot of needles, so I thought we would follow your suggestion, and see *your* response as I insert them while you're in me."

That *hadn't* been what I'd meant ... and I was fairly sure that Kelly knew that. I would have to watch out, with Kelly, as her dominant side was emerging, and I could be in for more pain than I wanted, if I wasn't careful. I would, of course, let Kelly do what she had asked; in fact, I probably would let Kelly do anything she wanted. But I wasn't prepared to make that offer to her. Not at the moment, at least.

I could also tell Kelly that we were going to do as I had planned ... and I was 'supposed' to be the top, anyway. But I wouldn't deny Kelly something that was sure to turn her on. I had wondered what it would feel like to make love with a butt plug in me ... and now I was getting that opportunity ... along with two big needles.

I couldn't help but groan a little, and Kelly and I rolled over again, so that I was on top. Kelly reached over and picked up the needles and alcohol swab, and I lowered myself to her, and made one last thrust, so that I was as deep as possible inside her.

"Hold still now," Kelly said, as she opened the swab and rubbed it high up on my left hip. I heard her uncap the needle, and felt Kelly lift her head slightly and reach her arm down my left side. The needle went in quickly, and I stayed relaxed. It hurt a little, but Kelly could not have done any better. Then, I felt the cold swab on my right hip, and Kelly readying the needle.

She said, "I don't think I can do it quickly with my left hand ... so I'll have to push it in slowly." I was also right-handed, and – without practice – am uncoordinated in using my left hand to insert a needle; pushing it in slowly was an appropriate solution, but Kelly knew that it would be more painful for me that way. I felt the needle on my skin, and then a second of pain, until the needle broke the skin and slipped into my hip.

Kelly said, "Continue on, young man." I did not get back up on my knees and arms, but stayed on top of Kelly, and we moved our lower bodies in counterpoint, savoring the pleasure of long, slow strokes. As I had expected, it took only a couple of minutes for both of us to reach an orgasmic state, and we came together, holding each other tightly.

The needles then started to hurt more, and I realized that Kelly was holding and wiggling them. As our motion slowed, I felt Kelly pull the needles out slightly, and then push them both back in. Both the needles and the butt plug were now hurting. Perhaps I had not created this monster, but unleashed her? In any case, Kelly was really getting it on as the 'top'.

I realized that I would have to get up on my knees to get off Kelly, and the tensing of muscles made the needles in my bottom hurt even more. I swung my upper body around, and put my hands on the bed, letting Kelly get out from under me, while I remained in a knee chest position. Kelly slid out, sat up, and slowly pulled each needle out of me, dropping it on the dresser. Then, she asked, "How do we get this butt plug out of you?"

I was really ready for it to come out. I instructed Kelly, "just grab the red disc, and while I push you can pull, and it should pop out." I knew it wouldn't be painless, but it should hurt less than when it went in. I wasn't psyched up yet, but heard Kelly count, "3, 2, 1, push!" I pushed, and the butt plug came out, with a brief moment of pain, as the widest point passed through my anal sphincter.

I stayed in position as Kelly wrapped the butt plug in tissue and put it on the dresser. I was still in position only because I wasn't sure I could get up ... but Kelly took the opportunity to wipe the excess KY off my peri-anal area with a tissue. I finally got up, and carried the needles to the sharps container on the credenza, while Kelly took the butt plug and tissues into the bathroom.

When I entered the bathroom, Kelly was washing the butt plug. "Shall we take another quick shower before you stick me with needles, Sir?" That wasn't something that I would turn down, so I stepped into the shower room, and got all the jets going. A moment later, Kelly stepped in, and we bathed each other wordlessly. Then we toweled off, hanging the towels by the sauna, and walked back into the playroom.

I made a detour to the bar, and asked Kelly whether she would like water, iced tea, lemonade, or Diet Coke to keep her hydrated, perhaps along with the Champagne. I didn't have orange juice, or would have offered to make a Mimosa for her. I made another detour, this time to the office, and grabbed the sharps container, bringing it and our drinks to the bed, and putting everything on the dresser.

We sat cross-legged again on the bed, facing each other, with me closer to the side of the bed with the dresser. I handed Kelly her Diet Coke; she took a few swallows, and handed it back to me. I set it on the dresser, and reached for the shoebox and sharps container, setting both on the bed.

I prepared a needle and alcohol swab, and asked Kelly, "Are you ready for a demonstration of 'needle play'?"

Kelly gulped, and said, "I guess so. Sir."

I swabbed the inside of my right thigh and pinched some skin with my left hand. With my right, I uncapped the needle and positioned it next to the pinched skin. I think Kelly was surprised that the first demonstration would be on me, but she was watching intently, as I pushed the needle through the skin on one side, through the thin layer of flesh, and out the skin on the other side.

I pushed the needle up to the hub, and let go with my left hand. The needle was horizontal to my skin – almost laying flat on the skin of my thigh – but going through a pinch of tissue. I decided to insert three more needles, parallel to the first, going up my thigh.

As I inserted the next needle, I told Kelly, "Going through the skin from the outside doesn't hurt much – you've already felt plenty of needles being inserted. But, coming out through the skin from the inside *does* hurt, especially if you're pushing the needle slowly."

When the four needles were in, they formed neat parallel lines on my thigh, with the blue-colored hubs on one side and the needle tips on the other side of the pinches of skin. I asked Kelly, "What do you think?"

Kelly nodded, and said, "It's pretty neat. I don't know if it will hurt more or less than sticking the needles straight in, but I'm still afraid of the pain."

I laughed, "After all you've been through? Yes, they will hurt a little, but you certainly won't have a problem taking it. The reward – hopefully – will be a flood of endorphins through your bloodstream, and a pretty design on your body – which we can photograph. You can be proud to wear needle play artwork, in the same way as wearing a tattoo – everyone knows that you had to put up with pain to get it; but needle play art is only temporary – maybe an hour or so at most. Let's give you a taste for how it feels. Do you want to insert a needle in your own thigh, like I did?"

Kelly scrunched her face, "No, not really, Sir. I will do it if you ask me, but I'd prefer that you do it."

"OK, Kelly." I swabbed her left thigh, and uncapped a new needle. Taking a small pinch of skin, I positioned the needle. "You should have the bevel of the needle up, so that it goes through only a thin layer of tissue." I then quickly shoved it through the tissues, until the tip re-emerged on the other side of the pinch of skin. I heard an 'Ooooh!' from Kelly, but she did just fine, even watching while the needle popped through her skin. "That didn't hurt too much, did it?"

Kelly chortled, "Well, I guess not, Sir. It only hurts a little now ... but I'm not sure what 50 of those things will feel like!"

I then proceeded to insert another three needles, just as I had done on my own thigh. Kelly watched, but was silent, save for a couple of small grunts, when the needles came back out through her skin. "I would like you to try it now. You may do it on your right thigh, or on my left thigh, if you prefer."

Kelly sighed, and opened an alcohol swab. She glanced up at me with a coy expression, and then swabbed the inner portion of my left thigh. Again, I realized that I should be careful what I offer Kelly. Kelly took a needle, and then, with her other hand, pinched my skin. "Like this?" she asked.

Now, I sighed, "Yes, Kelly." I prepared myself for another needle stick (actually two sticks – one going in, and one coming out). Kelly giggled, but I wasn't sure what was so funny; I wasn't laughing.

Then, Kelly surprised me ... again. She picked up the alcohol swab, and scrubbed her own right inner thigh, dropped the swab and pinched some tissue, and – before I even realized that she was going to do it, Kelly pushed the needle through her own flesh. She was silent as the needle went through, and she took another few seconds to make sure the needle was pushed all the way to the hub.

Kelly then looked up, and asked, "How'd I do?" I leaned over and kissed Kelly, and she smiled at me, batting her eyes in mock flirtation. Well, maybe not so 'mock'.

I picked up another needle and new swab, and said, "Now, Kelly, I'll give you a simple example of needle play 'art'." I thought a moment, looking down at our legs, and asked, "Kelly, would it be OK if I took out all of the needles that are in us now?"

Kelly nodded, "Sure, that would be fine with me, Sir. I think I've gotten the 'feel' of those needles."

I proceeded to pull each of the needles out of her thighs, and then my thigh, dropping them all into the sharps container that was sitting next to the pillow on the bed. I then unpackaged another 8 needles, dropping them into a small blue Tupperware bowl. Kelly's eyes were a bit wider, when all the needles were in the bowl and I grabbed another swab. We were still sitting cross-legged on the bed, with our knees touching.

I reached over and swirled my hand lightly over Kelly's right breast, and then swabbed in a circular pattern around her nipple. I took a small pinch of skin just to the left of her areola. With the other hand, I picked up and uncapped a needle, then smiled at Kelly as I reached over and quickly stuck the needle through the pinch of skin. The hub was about half an inch from her nipple with the needle facing outward. Kelly gasped quietly as the needle went through.

Kelly sat there, very cooperatively holding still and not making a sound, as I inserted another three needles; now there were needles facing left, right, up and down around her right breast. I looked at Kelly, but she just nodded and looked down at her breast. Then, I repeated the process on her left side, ending up with needles surrounding both of her breasts.

I smiled as I remembered that I had put a few more things into the shoebox, and I rummaged through the supplies until I found two small nipple clamps. Kelly watched closely, and then gave me a questioning look, as I held them up for her to see. I proceeded to clamp each of her nipples – tightening them until Kelly winced, and then a half-turn more. I took Kelly by the shoulders, and held her back from me, so that I could admire my work.

"Would you like me to take a picture of it, Kelly?" I realized that I should have brought a small camera – or phone – over to the bed before we started.

Kelly replied, "That's not necessary, Sir. Unless you really want to."

I was going to forget it, but then had an idea. "Kelly, I think we should document your first needle play experience. I have a small camera on the desk, just to the left of the In-Box. Would you please get it for me?" I realized that having Kelly move – and even walk around – with the needles in her would give her another new experience.

Kelly started to crawl off the bed, and immediately emitted a low 'Oooooh', and finally an 'Ow!' when she finally stood up next to the bed. She did not complain, but slowly walked to the office area, and returned with the camera.

I smiled, "Kelly, I can take the pictures while you're standing." I took some snapshots, a couple of close-up shots, and turned Kelly slightly one way and then the other, so that I could get a few side-looking and angled shots of her breasts, together and each one separately, with the needles and nipple clamps in place. Kelly was doing very well, though I knew that she was feeling some pain from the needles.

When I had finished taking the pictures, I asked Kelly, "Would you like me to take these needles out, now?" I gave her a smile, and continued, "Or, we could keep these in, while I do some *real* needle play art on your behind."

Kelly smiled also, but declined the offer to keep the needles in. I had her get into the standing position in front of me, and I slowly pulled each needle out, and dropped it into the sharps container. Kelly winced a few times, and we locked eyes at one point, but she was mainly looking down, watching, seemingly detached, as each needle was removed. There were a couple of tiny dots of blood, so I took a 2x2" gauze pad and held it on each of them for a few seconds. Then I stood up and took Kelly in my arms, hugging her, and ending with a passionate kiss.

This had been a good introduction to needle play for Kelly, but I wanted to try something more complex, more artistic – something that would challenge Kelly and, hopefully, culminate (climax?) with a 'happy ending' for

Kelly, as she lay there with an artistic pattern of needles on her backside. I looked at Kelly, trying to gauge her emotions, and whether she would be interested in one more needle play experience this afternoon.

I kissed her on the nose, and decided to just ask her. "Kelly, now that you've done so well with your needle play introduction, would you allow me to turn your bottom into needle play art? This isn't a test of submission: We don't have to do this; only if you're interested."

Kelly smiled and put her arms around me. "Yes, Sir. I would be OK with having another a needle art experience. You are allowed, Sir." Kelly stepped back, and asked, "What would you like me to do?"

After I retrieved more supplies from the office area, we got back on the bed, and sat facing each other. I put a small Tupperware bowl and a box of 100 thin 25-gauge hypodermic needles in front of us, and told Kelly that we would need to unpackage the needles and put them into the bowl. As Kelly got started with the box of needles, I unpackaged a dozen or so needles of larger sizes. Kelly asked, "Are you going to use *all* of these needles, Sir?"

I laughed, and answered honestly, "I don't know, Kelly. I only have a rough idea for the design. But, yes – you might end-up with 100 needles in your bottom. Does that scare you?"

Kelly dropped an unpackaged (but still capped) needle into the blue bowl, and swallowed hard. "Yes, Sir. I know you've stuck me with these needles before, but this sure looks like a lot of them, Sir. My bottom is hurting, already."

I laughed, thinking about the spanking I had just received and the needles that Kelly had stuck in me as we made love. "Actually, it's *my* bottom that's hurting, at the moment." Kelly chuckled, and we continued preparing the supplies.

I suggested that Kelly make herself comfortable on the bed, lying on her stomach with her head on the pillow. I sat next to Kelly's left hip, and used a skin-marking pen to carefully mark tiny points along a spiraling 'S' pattern on her left buttock, swirling around her hip to the back of her leg. Then, I moved to her right side, and marked a mirror image of the spiraling 'S'. I told Kelly, "This is your last chance to get up – if you need to pee, or drink something, whatever ..."

Kelly's head was on the pillow, facing right, and, with her eyes closed, said, "No, Sir. I'm OK. You may start inserting the needles now."

I smiled. Kelly was a natural submissive. Not necessarily a submissive person, but easily able to get into the bottom's role – asking me and thanking me for each new challenge.

I began inserting the needles, starting near the center of her left buttock, taking a pinch of skin, inserting a needle, and moving to the next 'dot' that I had marked. Kelly was quiet, making only a few 'Ummm's' and 'Aaaah's' as I continued the pattern around her buttock, over her hip, and down the top of her leg. The needles weren't as close together as I had originally planned, but when I completed the pattern on her left side, 33 needles had been placed.

"How are you doing, Kelly?" I asked, although she appeared to be quite relaxed, lying on the bed with her eyes closed.

Kelly responded, "I'm OK Sir. It does hurt. But it's not that bad. This time, maybe you should take a picture of the finished art, Sir."

I nodded, "Yes, Kelly, I plan to photograph you when it's done." I then proceeded to work on Kelly's right side, again inserting needle after needle through her pinched skin, making a spiraling pattern that mirrored the other side.

When another 33 needles had been inserted, I photographed Kelly's backside, as it was at this point ... but I wasn't finished, yet. "Kelly, you're almost done, but I need to add a few 'decorations' with the bigger needles. Some of those will be stuck directly into your bottom, as we've done before. Then, I'll make a few more decorations with the acupuncture needles."

Kelly sighed, but didn't complain. I inserted a 21-gauge needle straight in – like giving an intramuscular shot – at the center of each of the spirals, and I inserted a few 23-gauge needles to make 'points' at various positions on the spirals – each side mirroring the other.

Then, I opened a package of acupuncture needles, and inserted several by first tapping the needle with the guard in place, then removing the guard, and slowly twisting the needle until it was nearly an inch into Kelly's bottom.

I put the acupuncture needles mainly in Kelly's upper hips, angling out and making a 3-dimensional needle artwork. I considered lighting moxibustion wads on top of each of the needles, but decided that we still had the candles to play with. And the sparklers.

The artwork was finished, and I thought it looked amazing, with spirals of needles, a few hubs showing from needles inserted straight into Kelly's bottom, and the acupuncture needles standing up above it all. I picked up the camera, and took photos from various angles, using various types of flash, and then with a macro lens, focusing on small sections of the needle pattern.

I then lay down next to Kelly, and showed the images to her on the camera's small LCD display. Kelly looked at the images, while I zoomed in to show her detail, and out to show her the overall view. I wanted to give Kelly the final statistics, so I sat up and counted the needles: There were now 80 needles of various types in Kelly's rear.

"Kelly, you now have an 80-needle artwork on your backside! How do you like the design I've created?" I preferred to start with that, rather than ask her about the pain that she must be feeling.

Kelly replied, "It's beautiful. Too bad nobody else will see it ... except in the pictures." I thought about my needle art plans for Kelly's birthday – something that I was keeping as a surprise, but something that her friends would certainly see.

I had to ask. "So, how are you feeling with all those needles in you?"

Kelly chuckled – which was a good sign. "Well, I guess there's pain. But it's a unique feeling – the pain both at particular points but distributed over a large area. I'm pretty comfortable with it ..."

I was delighted to hear this. Nobody had ever made needle play art on me, and I'd probably never had more than half a dozen needles in me at one time. Obviously, the endorphins had kicked in, and Kelly was, as they say, 'feeling no pain'; or at least minimal pain, considering that there were 80 needles in her.

In fact, I realized that, as each of the spiral needles was put through a pinch of skin, there were actually *two* needle sticks per needle. So, thinking about it another way, Kelly had endured nearly 150 needle sticks in total. She was being incredibly calm, and hadn't complained at all. "Kelly, I'm so proud of you. First, for trying this experience; and, second, for taking it so well."

"Well, Sir, I'm pretty mellow from the champagne. And, I still have a 'glow' just thinking about our lovemaking amid the rose petals. And, you've trained me to accept some pain, and relax. I'm pretty relaxed now, Sir." Kelly chuckled, and then closed her eyes.

I was laughing inside, but tried to say seriously, "That's great, Kelly. It will really help tomorrow if you can relax and accept the pain of your caning ... and the rest of your level-100 punishment." Kelly's eyes opened, but instead of a look of horror – or even a scrunched face, she smiled at me. My heart warmed.

It was already late in the afternoon, and I still had the dinner to make, so we needed to finish this scene ... with another new experience that Kelly would remember. "OK, Kelly, it's time for you to feel a little hot wax."

Kelly was so relaxed that she appeared to be nearly asleep ... but the wax would probably wake her quickly. I took one of the low-temperature candles and lit it from one of the large candles on the dresser that was still illuminating the room in flickering golden light.

I tested the temperature of the wax – as with baby food – by letting some drop onto my wrist from about two feet; the farther the wax had to drop, the cooler it would be when landing on the skin. The wax was tolerable, but a bit too hot (at least, for my wrist), so I decided to start with the candle about 30 inches above Kelly. I held the candle at an angle, and let the hot wax fall in large drops onto Kelly's back.

Kelly jumped when the first drop landed, her eyes now wide open, a small yelp indicating that the hot wax was doing its job. I slowly moved the candle above Kelly's back, making a Rorschach pattern of wax from her shoulder blades to her waist. I continued dripping wax, on her upper hips, and then down to her upper legs, carefully avoiding the spiral of needles. Kelly yelped a few more times, as I lowered the candle to about 20 inches above her hips. Finally, I let the wax fall in a long waving line down the backs of Kelly's legs.

It was time for the finale, so I lit the sparkler, and moved it up and down the length of Kelly's body, holding it higher or lower based on Kelly's response. At first, Kelly jumped, feeling the hot metallic particles that flew off the sparkler. Then, she settled down again, and I only heard a few 'Ooooh's' and 'Aaaaah's', as the sparkler burned down to its base.

I took a few more photos of Kelly's backside, this time including her entire body from head to toes. I asked Kelly, "How are you doing, young lady? We're about done with this experience."

Kelly yawned, "I'm OK, Sir. The wax was interesting, but not too exciting. And I guess I've gotten used to the needles, although my entire bottom and upper legs are feeling them as just one continuous pain in the ass. It's not too bad, but I don't think I could fall asleep like this."

I was pleased to hear that Kelly had not found this experience too intense. I asked, "Kelly, I can start taking the needles out now ... but would you like me to help you get off once more, before we get cleaned up and start dinner preparations?"

Kelly, her head still turned sideways on the pillow, looked at me, and smiled. "That would be OK, Sir. Maybe you can 'do me' and take the needles out at the same time?"

I thought that was a good idea, as Kelly would feel new sensations as I slowly pulled each of the needles out of her. I moved the sharps container next to Kelly's right hip, and put my left hand under her, as I began pulling out the needles with my right hand, starting at the tops of her legs, and moving up the spiral to her bottom. I slowly moved my left hand along her genitals, from above her clit to her perineum, while I continued to pull the needles out and drop them into the sharps container with my right.

When there was only a single partial spiral of needles on each of Kelly's buttocks, I began rubbing her more seriously down below. My fingers moved along each side of her clit, squeezing occasionally – in synchrony with each needle coming out. I removed the acupuncture needles, and all of the larger-gauge needles, except the ones in the exact center of each buttock.

Kelly was now moving her body against my hand, as I intensified the strokes and the squeezes of her clit. I gently slid two fingers under her hood, and held her now-hardened clit, as I removed the 21-gauge needle on the left side, and then quickly inserted it half a dozen times around her left butt cheek. I did the same on the right ... and Kelly climaxed when the needle had been re-inserted into her right buttock 3 or 4 times. I pulled out the needles and disposed of them, as I held my hand against her sex with the slightest pressure, not moving it.

Kelly came, and then came again, her body convulsing, a hot wetness exploding outward from her core. When her movements finally slowed, and she was relaxed again on the bed, I took an alcohol swab and 2x2 gauze pad, and removed tiny dots of blood along the spiral path. Then, I began picking the splatters of wax from her back, hips, and legs, and dropped them into the sharps container, also.

"So that was your needle play and hot candle wax experience for today. When you're ready to get up, you can get cleaned up and dressed for dinner. I'll go upstairs and get the cooking started."

Kelly smiled and said, "Can you stay for a few more minutes, Sir?"

I laughed, and said, "Of course, Kelly." I lay down alongside Kelly, with both of our heads on the pillow, and my arm around Kelly's waist. We smiled at each other, our faces just a few inches apart, and I kissed her on the nose. Kelly closed her eyes, and so did I.

When I opened them and glanced at the clock on the bedside dresser, I was surprised to see how much time had elapsed. I stroked the braids of Kelly's hair, and eventually got myself off the bed. Kelly was dozing, a smile still detectable, her lips moist, and her breathing slow. I pulled out the sheet and blanket on one side of the bed, and flipped it over, covering Kelly. I tucked her in, and kissed her forehead.

After cleaning up all of the supplies, and the nearly-empty Champagne bottle and glasses, I grabbed a robe from the downstairs bathroom closet and went upstairs to the kitchen, where I began taking vegetables out of the refrigerator and started heating olive oil in one of the sauté pans.

CHAPTER 8: EAT, SLEEP, DREAM

I had planned a simple dinner, just a traditional Caesar salad, made tableside, and my own version of penne al'arrabiata, with sun-dried tomatoes and Kalamata olives. I had considered spaghetti Putanesca, but wasn't sure that Kelly liked anchovies. Then I realized that she would be getting them in the salad ...

I had considered making a fancier dinner – such as veal Marsala, fresh vegetables, and home-baked bread – but that wasn't consistent with being together with Kelly as much as I knew we would want in the afternoon. I also had given in, and bought cannoli from a local Italian market, rather than making a dessert.

I opened the wine and set the table, putting out a modern candle centerpiece. About thirty minutes had elapsed, and the dinner was mostly prepared – with just the salad to be mixed and the pasta to be boiled (no, I didn't make fresh pasta, either). It was time to check on Kelly. I hoped that the combination of Champagne, and the endorphins hadn't wiped her out for the evening.

As I reached the bottom of the stairs, I heard the shower going. At least she was awake! I stuck my head in and asked, "How are you doing? You slept for quite a while."

Kelly smiled at me and yawned involuntarily. "I'm good." She smiled again, and stopped bathing herself. "Actually, I'm more than good. I wasn't so sure about the needle-play experience as it was happening, but it has left me with an incredible high. Or, maybe it's from our lovemaking ..." She started bathing again. "Do you want to get in with me?"

I chuckled, and shook my head, "I have to finish the dinner, and get myself dressed. Take your time. I'll meet you in the kitchen whenever you're ready." I went upstairs and put on a nice casual pair of slacks and dress shirt. I had no idea how Kelly would be dressed, and it really didn't matter, as she looked beautiful in just about anything; or nothing.

I finished the dinner preparations and poured a glass of Brunello di Montalcino, taking it out to the patio table, where I sat looking out at the backyard, now lit by colorful outdoor lighting, the pool glowing blue and sending dancing reflections of light onto the house.

It had been a strange afternoon – with Kelly doing a striptease, although I had seen her body many times; Kelly wearing a bathing suit in the pool, that was usually reserved for skinny-dipping; the bizarre electrical stimulation experience – that neither of us felt was a turn-on; the quiet togetherness as I combed and braided Kelly's hair; our lovemaking – the first real 'sex' that we had shared; and the needle play experience that had once again demonstrated Kelly's capacity to submit and accept pain.

It seemed like a jumble of unrelated experiences, but each further developed our trust in each other, and continued the flow of surprises and the sensuality of being together.

The wine was delicious, but I too had been slowed by the Champagne, and now felt very mellow, looking out into the beauty of the backyard setting, and watching the last of the summer day's sunset. I heard a sound coming from the kitchen, and called to Kelly; she walked out onto the patio, holding her own glass of the deep red wine, and looking like she was ready for a hot night in the big city. She wore a sleeveless, pleated, V-neck silk dress in apricot with a subtle floral print. A narrow satin tie defined her waist, bowed in the front, with the two ends hanging down nearly to the short hem.

Kelly stood there, in the half-light of the patio, poised and self-confident. She walked over to the table and put her wine down, then did a quick pirouette, smiled, and asked, "Do you like it?"

I stood up and took Kelly in my arms, letting them drop down her back and cupping her bottom, as I looked into her eyes. "It's beautiful, Kelly. You're a sexy woman, and this dress certainly accentuates your sensuality and your great body."

We kissed, deeply and passionately, and Kelly put her arms around my neck and pulled me to her, seeming almost desperate for our mouths to remain together. When we came up for air, I chuckled, "Now that we're both dressed to go out to a club, it's almost too bad we're staying home for dinner."

I didn't mean it: It was great to be able to have a private, romantic dinner together, keeping Kelly all to myself, not having to bear the looks that every male gave her when they first saw her.

I handed Kelly her wine glass, and we sat at the table, quietly contemplating the beauty around us – the reds and purples of the darkening sky, crickets chirping softly, and even a few fireflies glittering around some of the trees, their blinking lights turning the backyard into a scene reminiscent of the 'blue bayou' at Disneyland. The only sound was the gurgle of water tumbling down the rock waterfall into the pool. Kelly and I smiled at each other, and sipped the luscious wine.

Our glasses empty, and the brightest stars now appearing overhead, we finally strolled back into the house. I brought Kelly into the dining room, where I lit the candles, our settings across from each other at one end of the long table, and a large bowl of flowers that I had cut from the yard near the other end.

I pulled out a chair for Kelly, and she sat down, putting her empty wine glass in its place, and surveying the room. The table was covered by an antique, beige, lace tablecloth, and I had used the 'good' crystal and silver place settings. A simple breakfront that held some glass sculptures graced one wall, while original artwork – now barely visible by the dim light of the candles – hung on the wall that Kelly faced.

I quickly retrieved the bottle of wine and returned to the dining room, refilling our glasses, and placing the wine on a silver base on the table. I went back into the kitchen and assembled the salad fixings on a large black lacquer tray, which I carried into the dining room, setting it at the end of the table, next to Kelly.

"Madame," I began with flair, of course realizing that this was no 'Madame', but a 'Mademoiselle'. "Zee Caesar salade!" Quite a mix of cultures: My originally-Swedish background, Kelly's Irish heritage, the Caesar salad which, I had heard, originated in Tijuana, Mexico, just across the border from San Diego, and my mock-French accent.

I proceeded to make the salad, first rubbing a large clove of garlic on the huge wooden bowl, then crushing the rest for the dressing. I used a small strainer to lower an egg into a measuring cup of boiling water, while I squeezed the juice of a large, fresh lemon into the wooden bowl through cheesecloth to catch the seeds.

As Kelly observed closely, transfixed by my quick but smooth mechanical motions, I added the Tabasco, crushed garlic, a dash of Worcestershire, and dry mustard. I took the egg from the water at exactly one minute, and broke it into the bowl, stirring furiously as I began drizzling fine Italian extra virgin olive oil into the mixture. I took all but two of the anchovies and put them in the bowl, and then mashed them with a fork, into a thick, aromatic paste.

I stirred the dressing to incorporate all of the ingredients, and then mixed it with hand-broken romaine that I had placed in the bowl. I tossed in a Tupperware of croutons that I had made this morning, and another Tupperware of grated Parmesano-Reggiano cheese. I then tossed the salad with style, using long wooden utensils that matched the bowl, and finishing with a curt bow to Kelly.

"Wow," Kelly exclaimed, as I stood there, having done nothing more than I would have had I been making dinner for myself ... except the bow, of course. Before Kelly could say anything else, I placed the bowl between our places, leaving the wooden fork and spoon, and putting the two whole anchovies on top, but taking everything else back into the kitchen.

Finally, I returned, closing the door to the kitchen, and lowering the dining room lights to minimum, allowing the candlelight to set the mood.

I sat down and raised my wine glass, Kelly mirroring my motions. "Here's to a nice 'weekend experience'. I hope it will become more than that, Kelly. As much as I thought I could – or should – resist, I am compelled to give in to my emotions. But it's *not* just my emotions! I love you, Kelly."

It was incredible, maybe a little over-the-top. It felt like a dream world. Lying on the bed after Sam went upstairs, an unbelievable – almost psychedelic – euphoria came over me ... a feeling of intense, paralyzing pleasure. I couldn't get up and didn't want to: I didn't want anything to spoil that feeling, that moment.

But it hadn't been just a moment; that feeling had begun when Sam carried me into his playroom, and set me down on the rose petal path. It was the slow rhythmic beat of the music, the flickering of the candles, the fragrance of roses, mitigated by the pungent smell of the wax.

The wax! And the 'needle play'. It had hurt a little, but it felt like the needles were going into someone else; I was just an observer. Maybe it was the Champagne? I'd probably had more than I should have, to prepare for a 'hundred-needle' experience.

The *lovemaking*! Not the second time, but the first. I had already been stunned by the environment that Sam had created. Not just the rose petals and candles, but the large-screen video (I had never seen something that big and clear, except in the IMAX theaters). Then toasting with Champagne ... and following the petals to the huge bed. Our first coupling: The glorious feeling of having Sam inside me; the wondrous feeling of having Sam. I wanted to submit to him, to make him happy. But it was obvious that Sam also wanted to please me.

I realized that it hadn't just been Sam's slow and considerate manner, making sure that I was being stimulated and taking the time to feel my excitement – the hardness of my nipples, the wetness of my cunt. I have never been with someone so focused ... on me; it was an incredible feeling. The highlight had been when Sam rolled us over with me on top, and asked if I would make love to him. I was again getting wet, just sitting here at the dining room table.

Sam was running back and forth: Pouring the wine, making the salad. He now focused on what he was doing – his obvious skill, deftness, but still casual mien was intoxicating to watch. As the candles flickered, my mind flashed back a few minutes to sitting together on the patio, as the sun set and the pool shimmered. What a beautiful scene.

Suddenly, I realized that *everything* was beautiful; my attitude had changed – if just for the moment. Or the evening. I was no longer sleepy, but in an incredibly relaxed state. My eyes refocused, Sam having finished making the salad, and taking an exaggerated bow.

I heard myself say 'Wow', but could not have explained at that moment whether it was for Sam's performance, the overall evening, or just the way I felt – not unlike being heavily stoned, and moving like molasses, one's thoughts flitting from one vision to another, ideas rambling. Sam was running back-and-forth again; finally, he sat down, and lifted his wine glass. Mechanically, I did the same. Then Sam's words floated to my ears. He was toasting a nice weekend experience.

We had already *had* an incredible weekend's worth of experiences, and it was still Friday. I had never before met someone with Sam's energy, the ability to meet – and exceed – my own energy and enthusiasm. Especially, my need for the new, the unexpected, the *special*. And Sam was so romantic …

"I love you Kelly," Sam said, and suddenly my eyes cleared, a wave of reality washing over my body. Was it reality? I hoped it was. I think. But I knew the feelings I had for Sam; they were not just in my heart, but also in my brain.

"I love you, too, Sam. Sir." We laughed, and – after taking a sip of wine (I hoped that what we'd had on the patio hadn't already been too much) – we picked up our forks and tasted the salad. *Wow*, again! I was glad – with the flavor of the garlic, and the cheese, and the lemon –

that we were *both* eating this. "This is great!" I had to say. I tasted a crouton, and realized I'd never had anything like it. The bread (what kind had he used?), olive oil, a touch of spices ... perfect!

Sam said, "I'm glad you like it. I wasn't sure if you ate anchovies."

Anchovies? "Well, I don't eat anchovies ... themselves. But they sure taste good mixed in here." Then, I noticed the single anchovy topping the salad that, I guess, had fallen behind a piece of romaine. I decided to try it. Salty, and a little fishy for my taste, but I now realized that it was a stronger version of the salad dressing. Maybe I did like anchovies, at least in moderation.

It was very salty. I reached for some water, but realized that there was only wine ... and I'd had enough. I then noticed the empty crystal water glass next to my wine glass.

Sam had been tracking my look, and he suddenly hopped up and ran to the kitchen, returning with a clear plastic pitcher of water with a few lime slices near the bottom. He poured our waters, smiling obliquely at me.

I smiled, as I wondered whether Sam would – could – ever become *my* sex slave? Having made a mistake such as this (not filling the water glasses) could result in a bare-bottom spanking. It was more exciting a prospect than I had ever imagined ... before Sam had opened my eyes.

He was *still* opening my eyes. How could I explain it? It was *more*: More intensity, more tenderness and loving, more thoughtfulness and creativity. As I had said to Julie, it was a 'higher standard', beyond my expectations. Beyond what I was used to, what I had ever experienced.

Maybe it *was* my age? But I don't think so. I knew my parents weren't like this, nor was anybody else I knew. And then there was the comfort level: I was more comfortable with Sam – whatever we did – than I had ever been with another person, even my girlfriends. I had certainly done more with Sam than with anyone else, at least regarding intimate experiences, but I don't think it was that, either.

Somehow, it was just the match in outlook, energy level, thought processes and, yes, in our sexual orientation. I don't know how many more fetishes Sam could introduce me to, nor how many I would ever want to do again. This made me think, once again, of the possibility of doing these things to Sam. Giving him some of his own 'medicine'.

"What's so funny?" Sam said.

I must have been smiling. Now, I pictured something funny: Sam serving me in this formal dining room, wearing nothing but an apron. As I thought this, I envisioned the apron beginning to bulge out in the center. I smiled again. "Oh, nothing. Sir." When Sam arched his eyebrows, I decided not to arch mine, but be serious, for a change. "I was thinking of you as my sex slave, serving me dinner dressed in nothing but an apron."

Sam laughed, "Well, I'm not sure about the sex slave part, but I'll serve you the pasta in nothing but an apron, if you like?"

He finished his salad, probably thinking I had only been joking. I decided to surprise him, as he had been doing to me all day ... and throughout our relationship. "That would be nice," I smiled, while holding up a few pieces of romaine on the tines of my fork.

Sam looked up, a worried expression quickly turning to a smile, as he contemplated the situation. "Sure. I'll be happy to serve you in an apron." We laughed again, and I finished the last morsel of the best salad I had ever eaten.

Sam quickly got up and swept the plates off the table. I heard a rustling in the kitchen, a pot lid being set down, the clanging of a spoon against a pot as Sam stirred something. I took another small sip of wine: It was really delicious. I noticed that the bottle was already half empty. Or half full.

My mind drifted into another stream-of-consciousness flow of thoughts. Pain and pleasure, firm control and caring, even macho'ness and tenderness; perhaps even a touch of femininity (something I hadn't recognized previously) – the opposites of which Sam had spoken.

I was a little startled, my rambling train of thought broken by Sam's entrance to the dining room ... wearing just an apron, as I had requested. While I had pictured a waist-down apron, Sam had donned a neck-down version, evidently made for barbequing – black, with some red-colored images of grills and flames. That was *hot* (Sam would say, 'in a manner of speaking'). Sam stood at attention next to me.

"Zee pasta will be ready in a few moments, Mademoiselle. May I refill your cup ... I mean, get you anything? My mistress?" Sam's eyes went down to the ground, in a subservient pose ... but I could see that he was beginning to crack a smile.

As was I. "Yes, young man. Would you please turn around, so I can see your punished ass?"

Sam looked up at me, and a large smile burst upon his face; he spun around one hundred eighty degrees, putting his bum at my face level. A nice view of his backside – from head to toe, with only a strap around his neck, and the tie at his waist, knotted into a bow. A summer 'Christmas present', all wrapped up for me.

I briefly envisioned Sam – or more accurately, Sam's bottom, with him curled in a fetal position – under the Christmas tree. Something clicked again inside me, bringing me slightly back to reality. That was perverted!

What had Sam done to me? Or, maybe, he had just unbridled something that had always been there? As I stared at Sam's butt, I asked myself, 'Had it?!!?'.

"Your bottom doesn't look very 'well done' to me: Perhaps you should bring the proper 'kitchen utensil', and I can warm it up?" I wondered what Sam would do, but he immediately pranced straight away from me, through the door, and back into the kitchen. I heard a drawer open and some rattling sounds.

Sam then reappeared, bending at the waist, and presenting a very long, wooden, cooking spoon, in two hands, the way, for example, Japanese present their 'meishi', or business cards. I took the spoon, and slapped the convex part against my left palm a few times. It stung.

With his eyes to the floor again, Sam said, "What position would you like me to assume, Miss?"

There was suddenly a wetness between my legs, and my right hand involuntarily flew down there, frantically pulling up the hem of my dress and pressing my fingers where they needed to be, through my underwear. I let Sam sweat a few moments, as I kept the pressure up (do I dare say it again? 'in a manner of speaking'), and I realized that this would be the ultimate turn-on for me.

I straightened my dress and brought my hand into my lap, as I wondered how this would affect our relationship: I knew that Sam considered himself the 'top', a dom. Even though he may also be a 'switch', I couldn't help fearing that my aggressiveness could sour our relationship.

But if I had learned anything from Sam, it was to be open and honest. That's how our relationship had begun, and was the foundation upon which it was based. I put the wooden spoon down on the table, next to my knife. "You've done very well so-far with the dinner, young man, so I don't think you deserve to be punished ... yet."

I smiled.   And then, "Sam, please sit down for a minute. I would like to say something to you." This came out much more seriously than I had intended. I saw a very worried look on Sam's face, and – once again – he ran out of the dining room, and back into the kitchen. A minute later, Sam returned, carrying a dishtowel. He pulled out the end seat, and placed the towel over it, before sitting down and looking at me with a darker-than-usual complexion.

"What is it, Kelly?" Sam's voice broke, and it appeared that he could cry at any moment. This was a man of deep emotions and, evidently, I had triggered them by my seriousness. Sam's full attention was on me, awaiting something that I had to say that was undoubtedly negative.

"Sam. Sir. I do love you. And I want to be with you. But I'm worried." I watched Sam's eyes narrow, and decided to continue before Sam could interrupt, or before my courage in transmitting my message flagged.

"I know that you *can* be a 'switch' ... but I also know that you're mainly turned-on by being the 'top'. And, I think I've come to the conclusion that I am also turned-on by being the top. When you spank me, I may get turned on, but most likely it will be because I'm thinking of spanking *you*. The idea of *you* being *my* sex slave has become an incredible turn-on for me. But I know that you would want it the other way around ... if you were being honest with me. It's great that we're so compatible, but I'm not sure that I'll ever be the 'sex slave' you want me to be."

I was nonplussed. I sat back in the chair, my eyes glazing over as I contemplated how to respond to Kelly's concern. The problem was, I didn't know what I really wanted. Of course, I had pictured myself as the 'top', introducing young women to all sorts of fetishes. But I had also been turned-on by allowing Kelly to punish me. In the way she wanted.

It wasn't a surprise: I knew that Kelly got turned-on by being dominant – or at least fantasizing about it. We were both, I realized, in a state of flux, our turn-ons evolving along with the experiences that we were having with each other.

"Kelly, I don't know what to say. Because, I'm really not sure how I feel. You're correct that I've usually fantasized about being the top ... but I've also gotten very turned-on when you spanked me. I had assumed that if I were sub, I would do just as you described: Imagine myself as the top, giving the spanking. But, when you have actually spanked me – or just now, when you were *about* to spank me – I got turned on by the expectation of a sore bottom; of giving myself to you. Yes, of *submitting* to you."

I stopped, and took a couple of deep breaths. I was getting worked-up; I, too, was worried about our relationship, two individuals, both strong and intelligent, both craving submission ... by the other.

I continued, "I think our interests and outlooks are still evolving. And, I think that – perhaps – we're both worrying too much about the far future."

I took a sip of wine and smiled, "You know, before I could ever be your 'sex slave', you would need to be trained as a domme. That entails a period where *you* would need to submit as the sex slave; you would need to both know the feeling of trust, and command the strength it takes to submit unquestioningly. You would need to not only feel all of the implements, but live the lifestyle long enough that you could appreciate what your sub is feeling, how he needs to be nurtured and protected, and how emotional someone can feel in that position."

Kelly nodded, "I understand that, Sir. But I also want to make you as happy as possible. I'm OK with submitting to you – or having us switch off – but I don't think I'm going to be turned on just by getting spanked; I will always be thinking about myself as top."

Now, I nodded, "That's OK. People think about all kinds of things during sex, that their partners aren't aware of. I don't care what you're thinking about … as long as it gets you off." I thought about it, and volunteered, "If you want, we can agree to *not* discuss what we were thinking about during sex, even while we're open about what turns us on, our detailed fantasies." I looked down into my lap, wondering whether and how my fantasies were evolving, and realized that the room was totally silent.

I looked up at Kelly, and said, "Our fantasies may still be aligned – or perhaps they're both wandering, and crossing paths many times. You were unexpectedly turned-on by being the top, and I have been surprised how turned-on I've gotten being the bottom. Let's not overthink this, or try to crystal-ball the future too much."

Kelly was deep in thought when a buzzer harshly interrupted our discussion. I jumped up and ran into the kitchen, turning off the timer on the way to the stove. I turned off the pasta, tested a strand – it was *al dente*, and then poured the pasta into a colander in the sink. I shook the colander several times, and then several times more, to get the pasta as dry as possible, before dumping it into the pot with the sauce.

I tossed everything, and stirred in some finely chopped Italian parsley. I then served two plates, and decorated them with a fresh basil sprig, and grated some strong Romano cheese over the top of the pasta. I wiped the rims of the plates, and then sprinkled a little more of the parsley over the pasta and around the edges.

As I carried the plates of steaming, and very aromatic, pasta into the dining room, I said to Kelly, "Next time, I can cook something a little fancier for you. I wanted to keep it simple this time, so we could spend more time together."

Kelly looked at the plate in front of her, and exclaimed, "This looks great! I love pasta, and it smells so good." Without further ado, Kelly picked up her fork, and began eating, having to blow on the pasta to cool it down sufficiently. "Yum! You really know how to cook."

Kelly laughed, and I was about to mention that most great chefs have historically been men (although this may be because most people in every profession were men), but Kelly spoke up quickly. "You really *will* make a good sex slave, servant, and cook. I would make you bathe me, and dress me ..." Now, Kelly was starting to get carried away, but in a way that didn't bother me at all.

We finished our dinner with relatively little further conversation, although I did ask Kelly about her ethnic/cultural background. Sure enough, her birth mother's and father's parents had been Irish. I learned that 'Kelly' meant strife, and that if her parents had produced a son, he probably would have been named 'Killian', which also meant strife. It wasn't clear why 'strife' – whether it had been in her parents' relationship, or some other hardship.

I washed the dishes, and Kelly put them in the dishwasher. We put away the leftover pasta, and cleared the dining room table, except for the tablecloth and candleholder. I blew out the candles.

Kelly suggested that we sit outside for a while, as the temperature was perfect, and the backyard was lit invitingly. I prepared small dessert plates with the cannoli, some whipped cream (also not home-made) on the side, with a sprig of mint from my garden. I also made espresso for us, sweetened with a splash of Kahlua, and Kelly carried the demi tasse cups to the patio table.

We sat there, under a canopy of brilliant stars, savoring the cannoli and espresso. And each other. When we were done, I carried the plates back into the kitchen, quickly washing them and putting them into the dishwasher.

When I returned to the backyard, Kelly was not in her chair ... but her clothing was. I saw Kelly floating near the deep end of the pool, her eyes closed, and her curvaceous body silhouetted by the dancing blue light.

I sat at the patio table for several minutes, watching Kelly drift around the pool; she seemed as comfortable in the water as she had been lying on the bed after her needle play experience. Her head came up, and she treaded water, while smiling at me. "Do you want to join me, mister?"

I slowly got up and undressed: I took off the apron. Suddenly, I started laughing uncontrollably; I hadn't even realized that I was essentially undressed, already. I dropped the apron onto the table, and walked to the edge of the pool, dipping my foot in the water. "It feels a little cool. Maybe, I'll go in the jacuzzi."

Kelly laughed as she swam up to me, and hopped out of the pool, putting her arms around me, thereby forcing me to feel the cool water. I flinched.

"What a baby! I thought you would want to connect in the 'deep end', in a manner of speaking." We both laughed, and I gave her a quick kiss on the mouth before walking over to the jacuzzi, and lowering myself into the hot water.

I suddenly remembered, "Kelly, would you mind flipping those two end switches by the sliding door?" Kelly did so, and the pool was suddenly black, the only light now coming from the green landscape lights that illuminated some of the trees, and the tiny white dots that lit the meandering path around the pool, through the grass area, and along the flowerbeds.

Kelly got into the jacuzzi with me, and we held each other, a couple isolated, out in the blackness of space, with just a few lights of nearby and far-off stars dotting the vacuum around them. We swayed in the water, and Kelly got onto my lap, straddling me, as I supported her by holding her luscious bottom.

Our eyes were now dark-adapted, and I pointed out several constellations and the Milky Way – our home galaxy – high above us. A thin crescent moon was rising in the East, above the house behind us. Fireflies flickered, and a few crickets chirped, but the world was otherwise still and quiet. Kelly pulled herself toward me, squashing her breasts against my chest, and burying her face in the crook of my neck. We were both getting tired.

A few minutes later, Kelly asked, "So, do you want to do it in the pool, mister?" She stifled a yawn.

I realized that despite our close body contact, and slight rocking and swaying in the water, I was not at all turned-on. Well, mentally, maybe. But the wine, dinner, and relaxation from the energetics of the day were not conducive to me 'getting it up' anytime soon. I kissed Kelly, and said, "Can I please take a 'rain check' on that, Miss?"

Kelly laughed, "Sure." Then she gave me a curious look.

"Yes, Kelly, I'm getting a little tired. And, it can be challenging to do it in the water, unless you're very well lubricated." I looked at her.

"Oh, that won't be a problem." She smiled. "But – actually – I'm getting tired, too."

"Then let's get out of the jacuzzi and go downstairs." She floated off my lap, and we got out of the jacuzzi. Fortunately, I had left the pool room sliding door unlocked, so dashed in and brought us two big, fluffy towels from the half bath. We dried off and wrapped ourselves in the towels. Kelly grabbed her clothes, and we made our way downstairs.

"Shall we take a quick shower?" I asked. I wasn't sure what else we would be 'up' for this evening, but a shower was a good start.

We dropped our towels on the chaises across from the shower, and got under the rain jet. We bathed each other silently, even shampooing each other's hair. "Do you want to go in the sauna, too?" I asked, although I was already feeling pretty relaxed.

"No, Sir." Kelly responded. "I'm sorry for being a party pooper ... but can we just go to bed?"

I laughed, glad that I wasn't the only one who was tired. It wasn't my age. It had been an energetic and somewhat stressful day. I sat Kelly down on the chaise and combed out her hair again, leaving it long, straight, and shimmering. We walked into the office, Kelly carrying her clothes. As she kneeled down to open her rolling suitcase, I asked, "Would you mind modeling those underwear you were wearing? I never got to see them."

Kelly smiled and stood up, dropping the dress and bra, and slipping on the bikini panties. They were 'nude' color, with a white lace waistband. Kelly turned a few times and, after seeing me nod, she slipped off the underwear and continued rummaging through her suitcase.

Finally, she pulled out a silk negligee – very simple, with virtually no lace, but nearly transparent. She slipped it over her head, and let it fall along the contours of her lithe body. They were 'baby doll' style, barely coming down far enough to cover her (formerly) private parts. She turned around quickly, and the nightgown flew up, alternately exposing her dark triangle and her rounded bottom, before it fell back to its full length.

I retrieved a couple of bottles of water from the bar fridge, and brought them with us to the bed, putting one on each dresser. I pulled back the satin sheets, and we climbed in. Using the computerized remote, I turned off most of the lights in the room, leaving a few dim ones on near the desk. The candles – now burned down to their stumps, still flickered, but would be out soon.

Kelly and I snuggled with each other, and kissed, long and languidly. I turned her around, and spooned her, my slightly hardened shaft against Kelly's lower back. Without turning around, Kelly said, "Ummm! Would you like to make love, before we go to sleep?"

I don't remember exactly what happened, but I think I had said 'Umm hmm' ... just before I fell asleep.

At some point in the night, I woke, briefly wondering where I was. Kelly was lying on her back, and my arm was around her waist. I quietly got up – both to pee, and to take a couple of aspirin, lest I wake up hung over and not able to take advantage of the day I had planned.

On the way back to bed, I turned off the rest of the lights; only the nightlight in the bathroom was now lit, casting an eerie green glow in the playroom doorway. I climbed into bed, and lay against Kelly, putting my hand over her waist, as it had been. I was asleep again instantly.

I woke another couple of times during the night, realizing that I had been dreaming. In the fog of near-sleep, I remembered parts of the dreams: Running in flowered mountainsides holding hands with Kelly, who was wearing the summer dress she had worn at dinner.

I realized that this was some combination of Kelly on the patio after dinner, the *'Planet Earth'* scenes of mountain flower fields, and a certain mountain scene from *'The Sound of Music'*. When I finally lifted my head, I realized that Kelly was not in bed with me.

I lay there a few more minutes, getting my bearings, and then got out of bed and ambled to the bathroom, where I put on a robe from the closet. I walked up the stairs, and my mind cleared, as I smelled fresh coffee. I found Kelly at the kitchen table, a mug in her hand, still wearing the baby doll nightgown, but now also wearing the underwear she had worn last night.

"Good morning, sleepyhead!" she exclaimed with a broad smile, her trademark hazel eyes sparkling. She looked good enough to eat. Oh, we had already done that!

"Good morning, Kelly. Looks like you got an early start. Are you feeling OK, this morning?" I realized that the aspirin must have worked, as my head was doing fine.

"Oh, yes, Sir! I feel fine. I wanted to let you sleep a while longer, as I know you were very tired last night." She smiled, and I knew what she was thinking.

"It must have been the alcohol. Sorry Kelly. I had planned at least one more wild and passionate lovemaking experience before we retired for the night. I guess even the espresso didn't help."

Kelly laughed, "That's OK, Sir. Maybe we can do some 'wild and passionate' lovemaking this morning?"

Now *that* sounded good. But not until I had taken care of some 'business', that was quickly becoming more urgent. "I just need to spend some time in the bathroom, and then I'll be ready for you."

Kelly cocked her head and gave me an enigmatic smile. "That's OK. I'll keep you company." She started to get up.

"Kelly ..." I stammered. I was an open person, but this was something for which I wanted privacy. Needed privacy.

Kelly just looked at me. "What?"

"May I please have some privacy? I really would not be comfortable with you in the room."

Kelly just stared at me. "What, the guru of total openness can't poop in front of someone?"

I stammered again, "Kelly ..."

Laughing, Kelly gave me a break. "OK. You may have your privacy this time. But if you were my sex slave, you would not have a choice but to do whatever I demanded. And, I guarantee, that would include total openness with me." Again, I wondered what kind of monster I had unleashed.

Kelly continued, a smile on her face, "Well, if you want your privacy now, you'll have to let me give you some enemas later. Just like you did with me."

I groaned, realizing what this would mean. I was going to be open one way or another. I had planned for Kelly to give me a mock-medical examination later this morning, so the enemas would not be such a bad idea, making any rectal insertions a bit nicer for Kelly. "OK, Kelly, you can give me an enema or two later."

Fortunately, Kelly agreed, and I rushed upstairs to the master bath for a little private time.

CHAPTER 9: KAMA SUTRA

When I returned to the playroom, Kelly was sitting on the bed, talking into her cellphone. I heard her confirm a 2PM visit with her friends; when she looked up and saw me, she said goodbye, and turned off the phone. Kelly bounced off the bed, and ran into my arms. I lifted her gently, and set her back on her feet, giving her another good-morning kiss.

"Shall we take a quick shower, first?" I asked. We sure did take a lot of showers, but I always enjoyed seeing – and feeling – Kelly's body. We had learned each other's preferences in bathing; for example, Kelly liked to wash her own hair, and I liked to wash my own face. I had also learned which parts of Kelly's anatomy were most sensitive to the alkalinity of soap.

Kelly thought a moment, and said, "I think I should administer your first enema, before we get in the shower."

I groaned again, not really looking forward to *any* enemas, let alone my 'first'. I had actually only had one enema before in my life ... which I had given myself a couple of years ago, just to have the experience, after I had seen some enema websites. "Kelly, I just got up," making an excuse that sounded lame, even to me.

"Well, I didn't; I've been up for a couple of hours, just waiting for you to get your beauty rest. Anyway, it seems like it would be easier for you to get one now, and the others later, rather then taking three or four in a row."

Nurse Kelly gave me a wicked smile, and I was simultaneously excited and afraid.

"Three or four? I'm not sure I'm going to let you do that." Our relationship was now confused, with each of us assuming the dominant role variously and randomly.

"I want you cleaned out, mister. Probably 8 quarts will do." I gulped, as Kelly continued, "We can start with a big one, and see if we can get a clear return after only two or three."

"I guess we can do that, Kelly. I'm not too excited about it, though."

"Well, I am!" Kelly exclaimed. "Shall we do it on the exam table?"

I reluctantly pressed the numeric keypad on the exam room door, and turned on the lights as I entered. I guess I would have to teach Kelly how to make and administer an enema, now. I grabbed the enema set and the container of table salt. We would do a cleansing enema for the second one.

I adjusted the sink faucet for lukewarm water, and mixed up 4 quarts with a couple of tablespoons of salt, swirling the mixture until the salt was fully dissolved. I then hung the enema bag on the IV pole, and connected the tubing and valve.

With Kelly watching intently, I selected the stainless steel 'bullet' nozzle, connecting that to the tubing, and lubricating it with a thin coat of KY. I released the valve for a moment, allowing the water to flow through, priming the tubing. Then I got up on the table, lying on my back, and holding my legs to my chest.

Nurse Kelly picked up the heavy nozzle and moved the tip around and through my anus. I relaxed my muscles, enabling Kelly to slowly advance the nozzle, until – like a butt plug – it was fully inside my rectum, the thin neck held in place by my anal muscles. I then lowered my legs, so that I was lying flat on my back, with the enema tubing emerging between my legs.

Kelly smiled at me, and rolled the valve slightly, starting the flow of warm saltwater into me. Only ten minutes ago, I was ready to make love to Kelly, and now I was on the exam table, with Nurse Kelly fully in control. The water didn't feel bad at first, but after a few minutes, I began to cramp. Kelly slowed the flow, and gently massaged my abdomen.

The cramp passed, and the water continued to flow into me. I was starting to feel full, and glanced up at the bag, surprised to see that three quarts had already been administered. I tried to relax, but it became more uncomfortable, as I felt that I needed to use the toilet urgently – the water pressure stretching my rectal muscles, signaling my brain that something needed to come out.

Finally, Kelly said, "That's a good boy! You've taken the entire 4-quart enema. Now, let's let it do its job for a while."

A 'while'? I wanted to get to the bathroom sooner rather than later, and told Kelly so. "Just relax, young man. I'll take the nozzle out of you, but you'll have to hold the enema in for a while longer."

I groaned and lifted my legs, enabling Kelly to remove the enema nozzle, disconnecting it from the hose and washing it in the sink. I closed my eyes and tried to relax, but my bowels were not happy. Finally, Kelly offered to let me use the toilet, and I gratefully accepted. Kelly helped me off the exam table, and we walked across to the bathroom, where I sat on the toilet.

Kelly quickly said, "You know what I'm going to do. Don't you dare release that enema until I give you permission! Do you understand, young man?"

Once again I groaned, "Yes, Miss, I understand." Just then, I had another cramp, and was sure some of the enema would be expelled. But I managed to relax and hold it in. My thoughts ran to the punishment that Kelly would have given me, had I expelled the enema without her permission.

In a role reversal from what had done during her prior visit, Kelly straddled me, sitting on my lap. Her weight wasn't uncomfortable, but it certainly locked me into position on the toilet. As Kelly had found earlier this morning, I wasn't entirely comfortable with sharing this bodily function, although I enjoyed the feeling of prostate stimulation during rectal insertions.

As I sat there, awaiting permission from Kelly, I realized how open – brave – Kelly had been the last time she was here. I could feel another cramp coming ...

"OK, young man, you may expel that enema, now." Kelly looked into my eyes, which I kept diverting from hers, as I felt the swell of the ocean rise inside me, finally breaking through the anal dam, a flood of water gushing forth from me. I closed my eyes, and tried to control my breathing. The water came out in floods, over and over, as Kelly sat on my lap, watching – and hearing – me experience my first large enema.

Kelly reached over and flushed the toilet, but continued sitting on my lap, as the floods continued. When I opened my eyes, she was looking into them, her face only inches from mine. Her eyes softened, and she held my head and kissed me ... as still another flood exited my rear.

Finally, Kelly got off me, and stood at the sink washing her hands, while I wiped. When I was off the toilet, we got into the shower, bathing each other as though we had been doing this for decades.

"Do you feel cleaned-out, now, young man? You're halfway through your enema series, and you took that very well."

I sniggered, "I feel OK. But it wasn't much fun." Kelly just smiled; I'm sure she was satisfied that I knew what she had been feeling, when I administered *her* enemas.

We took fresh towels to dry off, and went back into the playroom. I made a quick detour to the desk, taking a book from the credenza, and meeting Kelly at the bed. We folded the covers back several times, and smoothed the satin bottom sheet. Then, we got up onto the bed, and sat next to each other, cross-legged. I turned the book so that Kelly could see the cover, and heard a quiet gasp, as Kelly read the title: 'The '*Kama Sutra of Vatsyayana*'."

"The Kama Sutra, written in India sometime between 200-400 BC, was not just a sex manual. It was the teaching of a way of life, for success and happiness, which included 'desire', which is one of the four Hindu goals in life."

I thumbed through the text of the book. "The Kama Sutra includes advice on acquiring a wife, how a wife should live, the wives of other people, and how to meet a woman, how to gain her confidence, and how to court a woman. It also provides detailed advice to prostitutes ('courtesans'), and how to deal with love quarrels."

I looked at Kelly, "The Kama Sutra also provides advice for embracing, kissing, biting and nail scratching, a woman on top, oral sex, and 'striking' – and the sounds that go with it. And, yes – the part most people have heard about, it diagrams and describes a multitude of sexual positions." Kelly nodded, as we turned the pages and looked at the illustrations in this translated version.

"In addition to some of the positions – at least a few are possible, without being a gymnast – we could try some specific things: churning, piercing, rubbing, pressing, the blow of a bull, the sporting of a sparrow ... and, especially, the pair of tongs, the top and the swing."

Kelly yawned, "This is getting too technical. Can't we just try a few of the positions?" Kelly looked at me with all seriousness, "Or we could just finish your next few enemas."

I got the point, and pulled her down with me to the sheet. We kissed, and I moved my erection over Kelly's trimmed pubic hair. She took me in her hand and guided me into her, and then pulled me to her in a close embrace. We would only be able to last few a few thrusts in each position, so I moved slowly.

Kelly squeezed her vaginal muscles, grabbing me, and sucking me further into her – precisely the description of the 'pair of tongs'. I wondered if she had done this before. I asked her, "So what positions have you tried before?"

Kelly laughed, while at the same time thrusting herself against my motions. "Well, I tried a few of the Kama Sutra positions with one of my first boyfriends in college. But he didn't last long enough to get very far. And he would just fall asleep afterward."

Kelly lay back, and I asked her to straighten her legs. I put my left leg outside her right leg, and then rolled us over ¾ of the way. I pulled Kelly's bottom toward me, and she thrusted in perfect synchrony. She was literally dripping wet, and I was grateful that the resistance would be lower for ease of getting into her in some strange positions, and in reducing the sensation, so that I could last longer. Of course, I realized that we would need to 're-start' several times this morning.

We then rolled a bit further, so that Kelly was on top. She smiled and, after a couple of thrusts, sat up, riding me like taming a stallion, fully in control, knowing exactly what she wanted, and taking it.

Kelly stopped moving, and carefully swung herself to the right. I think she wanted to pivot, while I was in her, but this wasn't feasible – at least not without a lot more practice. Which would be fun. She lifted up, taking me in hand, as she straddled me, her back now to me, and slipped me back into her. She rocked fore-and-aft, although there was a limit that my curved, hard shaft invoked.

I then started laughing, and Kelly stopped the rocking, sat up on me, and turned her head to me. "Sorry, Kelly. I just had a sudden memory of a 'reality' TV program where people went to the ER due to sex. And when a girl jumped into bed on her boyfriend, she – literally – broke his penis. It's not really funny ..." Kelly giggled, but didn't comment. She lifted off of me, and assumed a knee-chest position on the bed.

I entered her from behind, facilitated by Kelly widening her knees and getting lower to the bed. I held Kelly's hips, as we rutted, my front rounded forward so that we were joined from knees to mid-back. I decided on a near-term action plan, and surprised Kelly by coming out of her.

I went to the dresser and grabbed something, and stood by the corner of the bed. I also dragged a pillow down to the corner of the bed, and folded it over. Kelly smiled, and got off the bed, and I guided her into position, her chest on the pillow, and her legs straddling the corner of the bed positioning her rear perfectly. I entered Kelly, and asked, "Kelly, would a little pain be OK?"

Kelly said instantly, "Yes, Sir. I was wondering when you would think of that. Sir." We both laughed, and I popped her twice on the left buttock, and then twice on the right. Kelly was still laughing, and I was still moving slowly, entering her fully on each stroke. Then, I quickly tore open a package, and swabbed her upper right derriere with one wipe, and then uncapped the needle and plunged it into her. Kelly was silent.

I repeated the same thing on her left side, and again, she didn't make a sound. We were still moving slowly against each other. I held Kelly's hips, as I stared down at the two needle hubs in her bottom, mesmerized by the rippling tissues of the strong woman below.

Kelly's right hand pushed underneath her, and I felt her fingertips, as she massaged her own clit. My hands moved up to her breasts, pushing down on the pillow and sliding my hands under, holding her breasts, which more than filled each of my hands. Suddenly, Kelly's hand stopped moving, her head flew up, and a primal sound came from somewhere deep within her.

I stopped moving, and pulled both needles out of her, sticking them into the side of the bed – as nurses used to do in the 'old' days. Kelly's hand was squeezing her vulva, and her fingertips were against me, as I started slowly moving, but staying deep inside her. Kelly convulsed several times, and was now panting loudly.

I bent forward, so that our bodies were in close contact, my hands still holding her breasts, and Kelly now relaxed, sinking into the pillow. My eyes closed, I could *feel* this woman; my love. I moved faster and harder, my front now slamming into Kelly's rear. My brain was not too far gone to notice that Kelly was rubbing herself again.

Then, my male reflexes took over, and my brain became a jumble of visions – of Kelly. I was barely conscious when my orgasm exploded into her, the pounding continuing, as I filled her with my hot fluid. Kelly was throbbing, or convulsing, and I realized that she'd come again. She was now nearly flat on the pillow, and I was bent far over her, my face in her freshly shampooed hair.

As our breathing slowed, my senses became hyperaware: The acidity of the citrus aroma from the shampoo mixed with the pungent musk of sex; the involuntary throbbing of my wilting erection inside Kelly, and her occasional pelvic squeezes; the sound of the air conditioning coming on, and feeling overheated.

We stayed in that position until I slipped out of her. I pulled the needles out of the side of the bed, depositing them in the sharps container on my credenza before going into the bathroom and wetting two hand towels with warm water. I cleaned myself, and brought the other towel to Kelly, who was still in position over the corner of the bed. She turned her head toward me as I approached, and smiled.

We looked through the book, and picked a few positions to try – when I was ready again. I was wondering how we should spend the time, and the things we could do that would turn me on the most, when Kelly snapped the book shut, and looked at me. "It's time for your next enema, young man."

I couldn't help it: I groaned again. But within a few seconds, I realized that I would cooperate, and – looking down at the bed – said, "Yes, Miss. I'm ready for my next enema."

Kelly laughed, and crawled off the bed, "Then come along, young man. Don't make me wait." She laughed all the way to the exam room. I followed her, but wasn't laughing.

I sighed, and grabbed the box of Fleet cleansing enema powder, which I mixed with three quarts of warm water. If I ever had to go through this again (which I was sure would happen), I would have to try some of the more exotic solutions – coffee, green tea, or various herbs. I dissolved the powder, and hung the enema bag. I then made a mistake: I asked Kelly, "What type of nozzle would you like to use, this time?" I realized my error, almost as soon as the words came out of my mouth.

Kelly's eyes lit up and she smiled broadly. "Let's use the one you put in me, that you had to pump up to stay in position?"

She was, of course, referring to the Bardex double-balloon system. I had never felt that; in fact, nobody had ever given me an enema before. I hesitated, knowing that I could overrule Kelly, but resigned myself to submit. What I would do for this woman!

I reached into the cabinet, and handed Kelly the strange-looking contraption. I pointed to the folded balloon at the tip, and said, "This needs to be lubricated, then you can squish it inside me. You'll know when it's fully in – if you pull back very gently, you'll feel it resist coming back out of my anus.

"This bulb needs to be squeezed very carefully, as it could be dangerous to over-inflate the balloon inside me. I'm sure I'll let you know when to stop squeezing. Then, you can squeeze the other bulb, and the outside balloon will fill. You should be able to slightly move the device in and out of me, held between the two balloons. I'll get in a knee chest position, so you'll have the best access and view."

With that, I climbed onto the exam table, and got into a knee-chest position. I closed my eyes, trying not to hear Kelly lubing the balloon. Soon enough, I felt the cold against my anus, Kelly applying pressure and squeezing the folded balloon into me. She slid the catheter in and out, and I don't know if she felt the deflated balloon hit the inside of my anus, but *I* certainly did!

I then simultaneously heard a puff of air, and felt the balloon greatly increase in size inside me. "Whoa! That might be enough."

Kelly laughed, and said, "That was hardly one squeeze! You don't seem to be in any pain." With that, she squeezed again, and the balloon filled my rectum. I was startled, and somewhat tense, but when I relaxed, I realized that my prostate was also being stimulated; so it wasn't too bad.

Kelly then inflated the outside balloon and, as I had suggested, she moved the device slightly in and out of me. There was no question it was locked in place.

I tried to relax, as Kelly started the flow of the enema solution. It didn't feel so bad, now that I was getting used to it, but I would have to consciously keep myself relaxed. "Kelly, would it be OK if I lay down on my stomach, now?"

Kelly said, "Sure, that will be fine." I could hear something in the tone of her voice – excitement, authority, power, and perhaps fear. It was a strange combination of feelings and emotions that had transformed her.

I put my arms around the pillow, and closed my eyes, as the water endlessly flowed into me. This time, I didn't get any cramps, but I felt overly filled. It became increasingly uncomfortable, and I asked Kelly, "Do you think this is about enough, for one enema?" My eyes were still closed, and I had no idea how much I had taken, except that it was enough.

Kelly rolled the valve closed, and slapped me on the bottom. "You did very well, young man. You took more than two quarts. I won't make you take more this time, but we'll have some fun, next time."

I groaned again – this was becoming a habit. What did she mean, 'some fun, next time'? Wasn't she having fun this time? At my expense? Then I relaxed. I was happy to 'spare no expense' to make Kelly happy. I guess that was the true test of submission. Or love. My brain was confused.

Finally, I felt Kelly deflating the balloons, and slowly pulling the catheter out of me. I hoped that I didn't leak on the exam table, as Kelly hadn't put any pads under me. I swung around on my stomach, until my legs came off the side of the table, and I lowered myself to the floor gingerly. I walked into the bathroom, Kelly following. I wondered if she would want to sit on my lap again.

But Kelly just stood in the doorway, as I sat down on the toilet. I looked at her, "May I, Miss?"

Kelly smiled, and nodded, "Yes, young man, you may."

I relaxed my anal muscles and released the enema. The first wave of floods poured from my body. I really didn't like the feeling; it wasn't a turn-on for me to be on the receiving end of this experience. I looked up, and saw Kelly across the hall, washing the Bardex in the exam room sink. She looked up and smiled at me.

I looked over at Sam, sitting on the toilet, another flood coming out of him. As I thought about it, I realized that the idea of getting or giving an enema is not a turn-on by itself. But I knew that Sam didn't like getting enemas, nor sitting on the toilet in front of me. As open as he professed to be, Sam was still hung up about a few things. So, it was his submission, his willingness to be uncomfortable – just because I wanted it – that was turning me on.

Whether it was his love for me, or maybe the turn-on of submitting to me – for whatever reason, he was demonstrating his ability to accept my command. It really *was* a feeling of power, of control. I finished cleaning up the exam room, and washed my hands again.

Sticking my head in the bathroom door, I told Sam, "Meet me back at the bed, when you're ready." Sam just nodded. He didn't look too happy, but I would fix that in just a few minutes. We had a lot more positions to try, and I had to make sure that Sam was 'up' to the task. I sat on the bed, and read through some random pages of the Kama Sutra.

A few minutes later, Sam had finished, and he was back on the bed facing me. Without warning, I pushed his chest, and he fell back, his head landing perfectly on one of the pillows. Before he could lift his head, my mouth was on his other head, licking, sucking, and swirling my tongue over him.

I put his frenulum between my teeth, and shifted them back-and-forth, like a cow chewing its cud; then, I put it between my lips, and squeezed them together as hard as I could, while moving my closed lips back and forth.

Sam moaned (at least this time, I knew it was a 'moan', not a 'groan'). As he became stiffer, I sucked more of his length, until my mouth was taking in its fill, my tongue licking and lapping the underside of his cock.

I chuckled, as I thought how I needed some of that gooey caramel syrup, right now. Sam reacted to the chuckle, his dick jerking, and a soft 'Mmmmm' coming from deep in his throat. He was now deep in my throat, and I began to hum; I don't know why, but the tune was 'Yankee Doodle Dandy'.

Sam was 'Oooing', 'Aaahing', and starting to laugh, and my humming became more laughing, my mouth full of him, tasting his sweet pre-cum. He was ready for the next Kama Sutra positions. That didn't take long!

I slid my mouth off Sam, and reached over for the towel that he had brought to me. I gently cleaned him, and announced, "I've been doing some research, Sir. And I think we should try the 'Wide Open' position, next." I saw Sam's head jerk up, and a smile appear on his face. He sat up and shrugged his shoulders. I moved his legs slightly apart, and lay down with my bottom touching Sam's feet.

I then scooted my way towards Sam, putting my legs around his waist. Sam got the idea, and pulled me up to him, and inserted his now-thick cock into me. As Sam held my hips, I lay back fully and arched my back, bringing my pelvis up, and then down, his erection pressing in just the right way, as he moved slowly inside my cunt. I realized that Sam was controlling the back-and-forth, and I was controlling the up-and-down. It felt really good.

Evidently, Sam thought so, too: He was now purring like a kitten; actually, more like a lion cub, cute and gentle ... until it gets excited and wild. As I concentrated on the feeling of him inside me, Sam rocked forward, sliding his arms up my body and over my breasts. He pinched my hardened nipples, and rolled my breasts in his hands. His rocking motion kept him inside me.

I smiled at Sam, and said, "Now, we'll do the 'Indrani' position." I pulled my knees to my chest, and told Sam, "Get up on your knees. You can pull me towards you, or lean over me a little until you're in me." Sam obediently did as I had asked, and after a couple of minutes of fumbling, we were in position, with my bottom nestled in Sam's groin, his legs squeezing in on my hips.

Sam leaned forward – a more comfortable position, considering the curve-of-the-cock, and he lowered himself as much as my legs would allow. We were face-to-face, and Sam was deep inside me; in fact, deeper than I thought he had ever been. I was sure that he was hitting my cervix on each stroke, but there was no pain, only a fullness — a feeling that I had craved for a long time. I smiled at Sam, but his eyes were closed.

I hadn't taken a yoga class for more than a year, but thought I could still get into the Lotus position, for the eponymous Kama Sutra positions. I gently pushed Sam away, and he opened his eyes and nodded. He sat back, sliding out of me, and I crossed my legs into the Lotus position, and pulled them to my chest.

Sam's eyes lit up, and he backed up, and got down on all fours, then crawled up to me, lowering himself, and entering me, as he continued to pull himself closer, until my crossed legs were against his stomach, and mine. It was a little uncomfortable for me, but a unique feeling, when Sam entered me fully. Again, it felt as if he was reaching the 'end of the line' inside me.

Sam could sense my discomfort, and pulled out of me, giving me a 'now what?' look. I told him, "Sit on your knees again, with your heels under your bottom." As Sam did this, I raised my left foot in the air, and straightened my right foot, laying it next to him. Again some fumbling, Sam managed to enter me, massaging my upright leg, as he rocked forward and back.

After a few thrusts, and with Sam still in me, I lowered my left leg and raised my right. Sam continued rocking, and massaged my other leg. Just about 24 hours ago, Sam had been giving me a wonderful full-body massage. "Sam, next time we try this, let's both get oiled-up. We can massage each other, and slide around into the different positions."

Sam chuckled and nodded, "Why didn't I think of that?" After a few moments, Sam stopped moving, and asked, "Do you think I might be allowed to come pretty soon, Miss?"

I knew that neither of us would hold out for much longer. We would have to try some of the more energetic positions another time. But there was one position in the book that Sam had mentioned, and I had later seen: The Suspended Scissors. I wasn't sure if I had the strength or stamina for it, but wanted to surprise Sam with something different.

I didn't think Sam had tried many of these positions either – and for a good reason: They didn't look very comfortable, and many were virtually impossible, unless you were double-jointed. Well, I guess some of the Indian yogis were. But Sam had serious control – none of my other partners would have made it this far, or been able to try so many positions without coming.

"Sam, I saw a position in the book that I think we should try ... as a sort of 'finale'. I don't think I'm going to have the stamina for much more, today." I thought for a moment, and decided on the open and honest approach. "Also, I'm getting a little sore, down there."

Sam smiled, "I think you've had great stamina. We can quit now, if you want. That will give us a lot of possibilities for future exploration."

It was a trade-off. But, as Sam was still turned-on, I wanted to try. "I would like us to try a position that looks interesting: The 'Suspended Scissors'. We'll need some energy and balance ... but I'd like to see if it is even possible."

Sam stereotypically scratched his head, "I remember the name, but I don't think I understood the brief explanation ..."

"Let's try it." I wasn't sure of the best way to do this, but slithered on my stomach across the bed, and then off it, my upper body hanging down towards the floor. I pushed myself a little farther, and reached out with my left hand, which rested on the floor. I was already tired.

I alternately pushed with my feet, and then pushed off the floor and reached one more hand-length, until I was mostly suspended off the bed, only my ankles and feet still supported by it. I should have tied my hair: It was falling around my head down to the floor, leaving me in a dark, strangely isolated place.

I called to Sam, "Now – please be careful! – lift my right leg, and step over my left leg. Then, we'll see if you can get in me." As an afterthought, I added, "If you're still turned-on enough."

I felt Sam's footsteps, and then his strong hands, lifting my leg, and then stepping over me, straddling my left leg. He stepped away from the bed, further towards my head, until his cock was against my perineum. He lifted it, and moved still closer, holding himself against me with his hand – as he held my right leg up with his other hand. I realized that he was going to have to get turned on again, as I had suspected.

Sam is a strong guy with good stamina ... but he's not a superman. My arm started getting tired, as Sam slid himself against me for what seemed like several minutes. Finally, I felt him slide down me, his hand pressing the head of his cock against me. I still wasn't sure it was going to work.

Suddenly, Sam was in me, pushing as deep as he could in this strange, sideways position. Just when I thought my arm would give out, Sam reached under my left arm and tried to lift me. It didn't quite work – I didn't get off the ground (that would have been a great, sexy gymnastics act) – but he lightened the load on my arm. Sam felt thick, but moved easily in and out of my wet cunt.

Now, Sam was pounding even harder and, before I thought it remotely possible, he detonated inside me: One powerful thrust and spurt ... and he was still. My arm couldn't hold myself up any longer. "Sam, you have to get out of me. My arm's giving out."

Sam slid out of me, and quickly laid my right leg on the bed; then, he reached around and, with both hands, lowered me to the floor. I pulled with my arms, and my legs fell from the bed.

Sam lay next to me on the carpet, looking up at the ceiling and panting; tiny beads of sweat glistened his forehead, and his face was dark red. My mind went, unbidden, into forbidden territory, and I hoped that my energy wouldn't be cause for this guy to have a heart attack!

But that wasn't fair. Sam was only fiftyish, was fit and had never smoked. The Suspended Scissors had been as difficult as it looked, but at least one of us got off. I was happy that we had tried, and that Sam had been successful. Last week, I was lamenting that Sam and I had done so much together, yet never made love. Now, I was sated and sore; and looking forward to whatever else Sam had planned for the weekend.

CHAPTER 10: AL FRESCO LUNCH

I finally caught my breath after our Kama Sutra antics. While I was in pretty good shape, I knew I would need to do better to keep up with Kelly. Although, now that I thought about it, winded and delirious on the playroom floor, if Kelly were the domme, and I the sub, I wouldn't *have* to keep up with her; just keep 'up'. I started to chuckle, but ended-up choking, and rolled over onto my stomach. Kelly was on the carpet beside me, her eyes closed, and her breathing ragged. She was beautiful.

Kelly had also been adventurous, suggesting the positions, and she had demonstrated amazingly strength, holding her body in the Suspended Scissors position. I hadn't realized how much effort she was expending, until I got tired, myself.

She was right, that we'd had enough Kama Sutra for the day; maybe longer. It was fun, but it took quite an effort, leaving less focus on everything else. I lay back and closed my eyes, and a few moments later, Kelly asked, "Are you OK, Sam?"

I opened one eye at her. "I'm fine. That was a strenuous way to have sex." It had been sex, not lovemaking, much as I would have wanted it to be. We got up and staggered toward the bathroom. I turned on the shower, and closed my eyes under a cool rain. Kelly joined me a few minutes later, and began soaping me up.

I felt spent, and let her do the 'dirty work', washing every millimeter of my body, which she did very well. When she got to my bottom, she inserted a finger and massaged my prostate. It felt good, but had no effect – I was not going to get turned on again anytime soon.

I asked Kelly if she wanted to go into the sauna, but she suggested the pool, instead. We took the towels we had used earlier from the chaises, and went upstairs and out into the beautiful day. It was too bad we had stayed in, and it was a great idea of Kelly's to take a break outside.

Kelly slipped into the pool, and I followed her – the water cool, but refreshing after our enervating sex experience. Kelly swam gracefully around the perimeter of the pool, taking long strokes and gliding effortlessly. She was a natural; at so many things.

I sat on the edge of the pool and, as Kelly swam near, I asked her if she was hungry. Kelly propelled herself to me with one strong kick, grabbing my legs, and nearly pulling me back into the water. She looked up at me, "Yeah, I'm starting to get hungry. I guess it's the fresh air. I didn't have much breakfast, except a couple of pieces of that yummy banana nut bread that you put out yesterday."

It was more than the fresh air, and I realized that I hadn't eaten anything yet this morning. I asked Kelly, "What do you feel like eating?"

Kelly gave me a mischievous smile, and said, "You. Maybe we could use that caramel sauce."

We laughed, both knowing well that Kelly's dessert would have to wait. "I'll see what I can rustle up." As I walked back to the kitchen, Kelly pushed off the edge of the pool, and floated, her breasts bobbing, nipples just above the water, and her long hair floating on the surface of the water, in a radial pattern around her head.

I had bought some freshly-made wild mushroom soup from our specialty market, thinking it might be the first course for our dinner tonight, and decided to heat that for a quick lunch, along with a seeded baguette that I cut in diagonal slices, buttered, and put into the broiler until the butter was brown and bubbly. It took less than 10 minutes, and I carried everything out to the patio table, and set the places for an *al fresco* lunch. The patio and pool were getting more use than they had in years.

Kelly climbed out of the pool and picked up the large towel, drying her face and hair. I had expected Kelly to wrap herself in the towel (mine was around my waist), but she folded it carefully, and put it on the seat of the chair, then sat down, her nude body still glistening with droplets of water. Her eyes had an almost feral intensity, and her youthful energy was evident, even as she sat down at the table. I had put out glasses of ice water with a slice of lime, opting against wine, as I remembered how much we had indulged last night.

I watched Kelly taste the soup, as she sat in the bright sunlight, totally comfortable with her nudity. Again, my mind wandered to Kelly's upcoming birthday party; I hoped that the weather would be nice, and that four comely females would be sitting here with me. One of the party favors I had bought would come in handy when we sat down to eat, here on the patio.

Kelly was engrossed in her soup, obviously hungry from our workout ... or the fresh air. I picked up a piece of the baguette with brown butter bubbled on top, and bit into the crunchy combination of seeds, crust, and buttery richness.

Glancing over at the clock on the wall just outside the kitchen, I was surprised to see that it was nearly 1PM, already. Kelly's friends would be arriving in an hour. There were no further preparations necessary, as we would just be having a get-to-know-each-other conversation. And, at least one bare-bottom spanking. I hoped.

We finished our lunch, and Kelly decided to do a little sunbathing on one of the chaises around the pool. As I looked at the full roundness of her bottom and the sensual curves of her lower back, I again imagined all four friends lying on chaises next to each other, their bottoms lined up, glistening with oil.

I went into the kitchen to wash the lunch plates, and brought a few snacks – the banana nut bread and yogurt-covered pretzels – down to the playroom coffee table. While I was downstairs, I prepared a few things ... just in case Linda or Julie wanted a better demonstration of submission than Linda's birthday spanking. I wondered whether Kelly would volunteer for such a demonstration, but I wasn't going to push her. At least, not today. I went back upstairs, and set out a bowl of Macadamia nuts on the patio table.

Kelly was lying on her back now, her eyes closed; she was the perfect image of relaxation. I walked over to her, bent down, and kissed her lightly on the lips. Kelly smiled, her eyes still closed. I told her, "I'm going to take a quick shower and get dressed; your friends will be arriving in a little while. You can stay out here as long as you like."

Then another fantasy entered my brain. "If you want, you can stay as you are, and I'll bring your friends out here when they arrive. Maybe they'll want to join you in some sunbathing and swimming?"

Kelly's eyes flashed open, and she slowly shook her head. "I don't think so. Let's have them meet you first under more normal circumstances. They'll be skinny-dipping at my birthday party." I got the message, and headed into the house. Well, it would have been a fun idea.

I took a shower downstairs – wondering whether Kelly would join me (she didn't). Then, I went up to the master bedroom, where I selected a pair of Khaki shorts and a Hawaiian shirt with muted colors.

When I went back downstairs, I found Kelly standing in front of the bathroom mirror, in a simple white bra and bikini panties, doing her hair. She looked over at me and smiled. "I think I'll put on a shift." I smiled but didn't ask if she was thinking that might give me better access, in case we gave her friends a demonstration. I felt a stirring below, and realized that I had fully recovered from the morning's Kama Sutra workout.

I made the bed in the playroom, and then lowered the projection screen, so that end of the room was hidden. I put on some soft jazz, and adjusted the lighting, with the focus on the couch and coffee table area. Then, I tried a piece of the banana nut bread – it was really good.

I was sitting at my desk as Kelly walked into the room, smiling at me. She rummaged around in her suitcase, and pulled out a summer shift, slipping it over her head and letting it fall down her body. It was sleeveless and short, with a scoop neck, and a bright green tropical foliage pattern. I walked over and hugged her, then gave her a little pop on the behind.

Kelly looked at me, starting to say something, then shook her head. "What is it?" I inquired.

"Sam, I know you're getting excited by the possibilities with my friends. But, please try to behave yourself." I gave her a funny look, knowing full well what she meant, but she continued. "I'm not worried about being embarrassed, but they're my friends and I really hope they will like you. But don't push them. I think you shocked them enough in the restaurant."

I gave Kelly a 'who, me?' look, and we chuckled. "If you're not worried about being embarrassed, does that mean you'll give them a demonstration of submission?" I held my breath, as I knew I was pushing Kelly, perhaps farther than she was ready to go today.

She gave me a 'look', and said, "We'll see."

That was a better response than I had expected. There was hope. And, I now realized, Kelly's special birthday party surprise would happen, just as I had planned.

CHAPTER 11: FRIENDS VISIT

The doorbell rang a little after 2PM, and Kelly opened it to find her friends laughing, nearly effervescent. The girls hugged, and Kelly brought them into the house. Linda was remarking that they had never known anyone in this part of town – near the outskirts, with large lots, mature landscaping, and custom homes. I said hello, and gave them each a quick hug. Their eyes were roaming around the living room, but Kelly dragged them through the kitchen and directly out to the backyard.

"Wow!" Julie exclaimed, as she got the full impact of the pool area, grass area, large trees, and flowers.

Linda nodded, "Yeah, this is pretty nice. No wonder you want to have your birthday party here."

The pool waterfall was babbling, and the water in the black-bottom pool and jacuzzi sparkled, reflecting the strong sunlight. Kelly took her friends on a stroll along the meandering path and, for a moment, I was worried that they would continue around to the garage, where Kelly would see the partially completed construction that would be a centerpiece of her birthday party experience.

But the girls walked off the path, along the line of boulders that bordered the grass. I had big plans – well, at least fantasies – involving these girls and those boulders. But I would have to be patient, as Kelly had wisely suggested.

After completing the backyard circuit, Kelly and her friends sat at the patio table, and I brought the pitcher of iced tea and some cups out to them, taking the last chair. I made a mental note that we would need one more chair for Kelly's birthday party. And I realized that I still hadn't put the birthday cake on my to-do list. I poured the tea, and listened as the girls chatted about their summer plans.

Julie was taller than Kelly, and quite cute, with a slim figure and self-confident air. Her chestnut hair was parted in the middle, and hung straight on both sides of her head, while a bang was combed from the left side, and fell to her eyes, covering most of her forehead.

Those eyes were amazing – large, and brown, with thin eyebrows and long lashes; she probably didn't look like this when she got out of bed in the morning. Her jaw was straight, but her full cheeks and dimple near the left side of her mouth softened the look. Julie's hips were not wide, but her bottom was nicely rounded. She wore short, stylishly-tattered cut-off shorts, and a white blouse. Between the makeup and attire, Julie looked older than her years.

Linda was a contrast to Julie: She was shorter than Kelly, and somewhat heavier – a solid physique, with large breasts, and wide hips, with only a slightly narrower waist. Her hair was black, and flipped inward at the bottom, just below her shoulders. I couldn't determine Linda's eye color, as they looked black from where I sat. She had a beautiful, oval-shaped face, her skin perfect, and it appeared that she was wearing very little makeup.

Along with her wide hips was a big butt – perhaps the perfect spanking bottom, assuming she was the 'bottom'. As I looked at her, Linda smiled at me – a nice smile, but closed-mouth, and somewhat unfathomable; quite different than Julie's large casual smile, dimple, and gleaming teeth. Linda wore a strapless sundress with a white bandeau top and colorful diamond pattern below.

There was an interesting dynamic in the conversation between the three friends: Julie was outgoing, while Linda was much more reserved. Kelly seemed to hold the conversation together, but I could see how Julie could drag both Linda and Kelly into situations where they might otherwise be uncomfortable. I remembered that Kelly had said that Julie was the gang-leader, outgoing and wild (at least a big talker), while Kathy – whom I had yet to meet – was really the 'open' (and perhaps even wilder) one of the group.

Julie turned to me and, with a smirk on her face, said, "So, Kelly tells us that you like to spank her." What an opening remark! I was stunned.

All faces at the table turned, and Kelly screamed, "Julie!" Linda covered her face with her hands, and I had no doubt that it was turning red as we spoke.

I laughed. Julie was really a character. But, then, I realized, so was I. "Well, I like a lot of things. I like openness and honesty. And, I'm turned-on by the idea of submission."

Julie chuckled, "Just the *idea*?"

I wasn't sure how to broach the subject, but Kelly had fortunately already done the more difficult job of introducing them to some of my ideas. I had been so confident, fantasizing about meeting her friends today, but now I wasn't so sure. Kelly and I had been – to a large extent – living in a dream world; now, under the harsh sunlight of the real world, I faced her friends, wondering where I should begin.

"I've always thought people should be open and honest with one another – especially if they're more than casual friends. Kelly may have told you that my wife and I had an 'open' marriage years ago. She was not threatened by my desire to have female friends – especially when they would do things with me that she wasn't fond of."

"*Do* things?" Julie questioned.

"Yeah. Like playing tennis, going for bike rides, hiking, and trail running." I looked at Julie, but she just stared at me, obviously wanting to hear more details. "Then, maybe, taking a shower together. And, for example, taking people to a nude beach – especially for their first time. I love to see their reactions, how open they are, and how they cope with the new experience."

My wife and I first went to a nude beach, in France, during our honeymoon, nearly three decades ago. We went to nude beaches often, after we returned home, and introduced many of our friends to the experience. Almost all of them had fun, and the openness translated into other things that we did with our friends."

Julie said, huffily, "We've all been to nude beaches. That's not a big deal."

I nodded, "I agree. But it's still a hang-up for many people. Those of us who grew up in the American-Victorian tradition of modesty, innocence, and abstinence may require some time to get used to the idea, but fundamentally, there is nothing wrong with nudity, and there should be nothing wrong with sexual (or at least *sensual)* play between consenting adults – even married ones, if limits are set and adhered-to." Julie and Linda were now nodding.

"I was delighted to be allowed to have such relationships. A friend. A playmate. A way to have 'sex' without commitment, danger, or expectation. Having fun, and perhaps some new experiences for each of the partners. Does that sound bad?" I didn't get a response from Julie or Linda, but they seemed to be thinking deeply about what I had said.

"So, my wife didn't think anything of my friends changing in front of me, or" and I looked into Julie's brown eyes, "even taking a shower together. As my wife and I were totally open with each other, she knew about everything that happened, so it was never thought-of as an 'affair'.

"And while our 'open' marriage did include a few sexual experiences with other couples, that ended when the AIDS epidemic hit: It just wasn't worth it to risk an incurable, deadly disease in order to have a few moments of release with another person."

As I said this, I realized that the four young women had been born after AIDS had become a big deal. They had lived their entire lives in a world that was full of sexually transmitted diseases, HPV (human papilloma virus) and herpes among them.

Nearly half of all sexually active adults might be diagnosed with HPV, although there were now some vaccines that would hopefully reduce the incidence in the future, including one that my research group had developed, nearly ten years ago.

Julie was still staring at me, so I continued. "But there are a lot of fun things that people can do with each other that don't require sexual contact. Over the years, I've grown to understand that there's nothing wrong with having a close relationship with someone, even an intimate one, if there is no sex involved."

Julie bellowed, "But you just said that your concept was a 'way to have sex', without commitment or danger." I could see that she was now thoroughly confused.

Kelly explained to her friends, "Sam has a different concept of what 'sex' is. It is both more freeing and more restrictive than the rules by which most other people live."

Julie took the bait. "So how do you define 'sex'?"

I briefly considered avoiding this discussion, but felt that Julie deserved a thoughtful answer, one that she could relate to. I glanced at Kelly, and she gave an almost imperceptible shrug. OK. Let's see how this goes.

"The only really safe way to prevent STD's is by eliminating all possibility of fluid contact – via mucous membranes, semen, and even saliva."

Julie rolled her eyes, "So you're one of those people who believes in abstinence?"

"No, not abstinence. My definition of sex is quite precise: body fluid contact. By my definition, even kissing would be considered 'sex'. In fact, by my definition, even eating or drinking after each other would be considered sex!"

Linda piped up, "That's ridiculous! Julie and I eat after each other all the time, but were not lesbians; we certainly aren't having sex with each other." Julie gave Linda a curious look, and I wondered whether she had ever tried making out with Linda or another female partner.

I laughed, "'Body fluid contact' may be too strict a definition for some people, but it is entirely practical and, when you think about it, allows everything else to be a possibility! There are a lot of things that two people can do to have fun together that don't involve fluid contact." This discussion had become a 'déjà vu' of the conversation Sarah and I had had with our Dutch friends, Henk and Zöe.

It is very interesting to discuss this subject with people who are not entirely open. They may profess to be liberal, but often their lack of life experience hinders their conception of the possibilities. I thought I would engage Julie in a mock conversation, to see how far she would go.

"Julie, I want you to pretend that you're happily married, and let's see how you respond to my 'advances'." The girls giggled, but Julie nodded, 'OK'.

I asked, "If we all saw each other at a nude beach, would that be OK?"

"Well, yes, of course. I've gone to nude beaches! And, Linda and I agreed to come to Kelly's skinny-dipping birthday party, and we hadn't even met you."

"Good. If just you and I met on a nude beach, after the birthday party, without your husband, would that be OK (I mean 'allowed', or 'acceptable')?"

"Sure – we would know each other. That wouldn't be a big deal."

"Great. What if I invited you over to go skinny-dipping in the pool some night, when Kelly was at school studying?" I glanced at Kelly, and saw a frown on her face, but she was slowly nodding.

"Well, being a good wife, I'd have to talk to my husband ... and Kelly, but I guess that might be OK. Of course, I wouldn't want you to think that I was a 'loose woman', or anything ... but if we knew each other, I think we could probably do that."

"Wonderful! (I'll invite you over soon!)

"So, let's say we get out of the jacuzzi, wrap up in towels, and go inside. We're all dried off, and in the living room. Would you have a problem sitting there nude (and me, too), while we talked?"

"I guess not ..."

"OK, what if you felt horny – perhaps I'm telling you a sexy story. And I'm daring you to be open with me. Do you think you could masturbate in front of me?"

"Well ... now that's getting pretty personal!"

I exclaimed, "Of course! That's the whole idea. Would you trust me to stay on my side of the room, and watch quietly, while you masturbated?"

"I don't think I could do that ... I don't know ... it might get me excited, to have you watching ..."

I continued, "OK! So, if I were to masturbate in front of you, while you're masturbating in front of me, that would be OK, too?"

"I guess. I mean, I would probably be more embarrassed than you, to see you with an erection ..."

I chuckled, "Would you? Do you think I would look much different than your husband (or, in real life, your boyfriends)?"

"Well, no – I guess not."

I was finally getting somewhere. "Then, what if we were lying on a bed, next to each other? Not touching, but each masturbating. Not even looking at each other, just having our own fantasies, beside each other"

Julie suddenly erupted, "I don't think I would get into bed with you! That's getting too dangerous."

She was becoming excited, so I had to make the point clearly. "You mean, you wouldn't trust me to not attack you? To not rape you? To not stop, when you said 'stop'? If so, I would be really saddened that our relationship was so shallow that you had no real trust in me."

Nonplussed, she said, "I would probably trust you. I guess it's just that we've always been taught not to incite men to sex ... unless, of course, we want to have sex!"

Very true. "OK – let's say we're still on the living room couch, not in bed. Next to each other, but not lying down, masturbating to our own fantasies?"

She thought a moment, and replied, "If you put it that way, I could imagine it might be possible ..." Looking out the corner of my eye, I saw Kelly's mouth drop open. Linda had her hands over her face again, her eyes peeking out over her fingers, looking alternately at Julie and I.

I had to push it further. "Let's take another tack for a minute", I suggested. "When we dried off after the jacuzzi, and before we wrapped the towels around us, would it have been OK for me to give you a hug ... with both of us nude?"

Julie replied immediately, "If it was just friendly, and you weren't turned on or anything, and it was quick ..."

Now, let's see what happens. "What if I wanted to take a shower with you after the jacuzzi? Could we get into the shower together?"

"What, for some 'good, clean fun'?" The girls laughed, hesitantly.

At least they had a sense of humor! "Let's start with us each taking our own shower, not touching each other. Would that be OK?"

Julie reasoned, "I guess. We would have already been nude in the pool together, and stood in front of each other drying off. So I guess getting in the shower together wouldn't be a big deal."

"OK. Now for the 'good, clean, fun': Would you be willing to bathe me? Wash my entire body with your hands?"

I held my breath, while Julie pondered the question. "I could wash your back ... and, I guess your chest and legs, and maybe even your butt ... but I'm not sure I would touch you 'down there'."

Now, we were getting somewhere. "Even if I wasn't in the slightest turned-on? This is just a shower after the jacuzzi."

"Well, I wouldn't want you to make me do it, but if you were relaxed, and I was washing you, I might wash you there. After all, I've taken showers with plenty of guys, so it wouldn't be anything new."

Finally, some rationality. "Great. Now, what about me bathing you, after you're done with me?"

Julie had to think about this. "I don't know ... I guess the same thing: you could wash most of me, but I would be uncomfortable with you touching my genitals."

This was the crux of the issue. "Why?"

She replied, automatically, "Well, it's just not right!"

Now I was on a roll. "According to whom? I doubt you're religious, or a prude."

She was getting upset, "A prude? Nobody would call me that! I guess if you washed me clinically, without getting turned on or lingering over my private parts, I might be OK with that."

I laughed, and summarized the discussion ... taking it to the next step. "So now, we have established that we could see each other nude. Touch each other's bodies. And watch each other masturbate. Would it be that much of a leap to help each other masturbate? Is that shocking to you?"

Now, Julie smiled. She seemed more amused by this hypothetical situation than upset by it. "It would be pretty shocking. I don't think my imaginary 'husband' would like it."

Now, I had her. "We would, of course, ask the partners ahead of time. It would not be an 'affair', if we were honest about it, and everyone was OK with the relationship. And, it would be agreed that we would not make love – just help each other with our hands (our mouths can't assist without exposing each other to the possibility of contracting a deadly disease – not that I think you're infected, or anything.)"

"What? I should hope not. Well, if my 'husband' actually agreed to something like that ... it might be exciting, just knowing that he's aware that we were doing it. Actually, the more I think about it, it would be really exciting ... but I just don't know if it would be a smart idea to do something like that ... when it could get 'out of hand'."

We all laughed, "Ha! That's pretty good. But, again, it comes down to a matter of *trust*. That is the essential issue. Let me ask you this: If you absolutely knew that you could trust me to not take it beyond using my hand to get you off, would you consider doing it?"

She looked confused, "Uh ... well, that isn't a real scenario. I guess I might do it, if I had a guarantee that nothing else would happen."

I looked at Julie and then Linda. "Do you see what I'm talking about? There are a lot of things two people can do, without transferring bodily fluids."

Linda looked at Kelly, and said, "He really is a strange one, isn't he?"

Kelly nodded and, under her breath, said, "You have no idea."

I drank some iced tea, and decided that I should be asking some questions. "Do you guys have boyfriends? Lovers? Just hook-ups?"

Linda laughed, "Yeah, we have guys we go out with. I'm still looking for 'Mr. Right'; I don't know exactly what I'm looking for, but I think I'll recognize it when I meet him."

Julie said, "We have guys who we do certain things with. One guy for going to the theater, another to come over and fix our computer, and others who are there for a hot date, and maybe some quick sex." Linda put her hands over her face again.

I laughed, "How about a quick date, and maybe some hot sex?"

Julie nodded, "That too." We were all loosening up, and I don't think the girls were too intimidated by me. But we hadn't yet gotten to the subject of spankings and submission.

I looked over at Kelly, who was keeping very quiet this afternoon. "Should I ask them to describe their fantasies?" I laughed, and now Kelly had her hands over her face, and was shaking her head. I said, "OK, I'll go first." There was silence around the table for the first time since Kelly's friends had arrived.

"I'm turned on by people being open – for example, you guys coming over to skinny-dip with us. I'm also turned on when people place their trust in me. I'm a very trustworthy person! And, I'm turned-on by someone submitting to something they may not enjoy, just because I asked them to. That could include bringing them to a nude beach, cooking some exotic meal for them, or accepting something that might be painful or embarrassing to them."

I got up quickly, and said, "Just a minute ...", leaving the friends staring at my back, as I ran inside and downstairs. I grabbed what I needed, and ran back upstairs and out to the patio.

"Kelly, may I please show your friends one of the pictures we took yesterday?"

Kelly gulped, and I saw panic on her face. She glanced at Linda and then at Julie, and swallowed hard again. She was clearly conflicted, probably wanting to share this with her friends, but unsure of where the limits of her openness should be. She looked into my eyes, and said, "Yes, Sir. Just one picture would be OK."

I smiled, pleased that Kelly would 'submit', but hoping that she really wanted to do this herself, and not under pressure from me. I would have to take her at her word. I selected one of the pictures on the camera, and it was displayed on the LCD screen – a little small, and washed out by the sun, but still viewable.

"Have you guys heard of 'needle play'?" I looked at Linda and then Julie, while Kelly slunk down in her chair and closed her eyes. Both girls shrugged, and slowly nodded 'No'. They stared at the camera I was holding, and avoided looking into my eyes. "It is an example of body modification, needles as artwork." That drew blank stares.

I continued, "Actually, some people consider this part of the BDSM scene, but the slight pain of the needles is usually offset by the flood of endorphins into your bloodstream. It can be a turn-on, both to the person making the art, and the person acting as the 'canvas'." I handed Julie the camera with the image of my needle-play artwork on Kelly's bottom, hip and legs.

Julie squinted, and I stood up and leaned over her shoulder, showing her how to zoom in and out of the image. As I zoomed in, and Julie understood what she was seeing, she gasped, "My God. Are all those really needles? That looks painful. I don't think I would lie down and take that." She handed the camera to Linda, who silently scrolled and zoomed the image, her eyes becoming wide, and her mouth dropping open.

"I asked Kelly yesterday if she would try something new, involving needles. I even demonstrated, sticking a few needles through the skin of my own thigh. She knew what was involved, that it would probably be painful. But, she also trusted me – both to do it safely, and to respect her limits.

"The 'bottom line' (Ha!) was that she allowed me to make a decorative needle 'sculpture' on her backside. In the picture you're looking at, Kelly has 80 needles in her. But I don't think there's a mark left, 24 hours later."

Kelly opened her eyes, and shrugged. She stood up, turned her back to us, and lifted the back of her shift to her waist. She then pulled up one side of her underwear, and then the other, so that we could all judge for ourselves whether there were any lasting marks. There weren't. Kelly dropped her dress, and sat back down at the table.

I looked at Kelly and asked, "And how did you feel about the needle play art, when we were finished, and you were lying on the bed with all those needles in you?"

Kelly shrugged again. "It hurt a little when the needles went in ... but I got used to it. They didn't hurt that bad. And I was a little tipsy with Champagne, which helped me relax. When Sam showed me that picture, I realized what an incredible experience it had been. And, I was pretty turned-on."

Kelly looked down at her lap, "Actually most of these experiences – like spankings – have not excited me while they were happening, but at the end, realizing that I had bent over and taken what Sam wanted to give me, I was wet almost every time." I wondered whether Kelly would tell her friends some of the ways I had made her come ... but she didn't, and I wasn't going to suggest it.

I decided to expand on our discussion, and let her friends know that Kelly wasn't 'just' being submissive. "Kelly and I have only had a few days of experiences in submission, but I've already learned many things about her." Kelly looked up at me, unsure of what I was about to tell Julie and Linda. But I was confident that she would be OK with what I had to say.

"First, I learned that Kelly is an incredibly strong, intelligent, courageous, and adventurous person. Being a submissive is not for someone weak: One must be very self-confident, trusting, and gutsy to even try the experience, let alone get through it successfully."

I saw Julie slightly nodding her head in understanding. Linda just stared at me with a glassy gaze. I wondered whether she was recalling some of her own experiences, perhaps with the school paddle.

"Second, I learned that Kelly is a very sensual person, who – at some point – can get turned-on by the pain." I saw Kelly shake her head, and quickly corrected myself, "Or by her submission. Or – and this leads to the third point – by imagining herself as the 'top', and spanking me. I learned that Kelly is probably really a 'top', and part of her turn-on may have been putting herself in that role, even though I was the one doing most of the spanking."

Linda remarked, "Kelly told us that you let her spank you, also."

I nodded, "Yes. I made some mistakes and deserved to be punished, and felt it was only fair that I allow Kelly to make me 'pay' for my mistakes. I hadn't planned on it – or even imagined it – but as Kelly was spanking me, it was clear that this was a huge turn-on for her." I looked at Kelly, who had a blank expression.

"As you might imagine, letting me tell you all this stuff is a challenge for Kelly. She was very concerned that you guys would ridicule or tease her; but I asked if she would 'submit' to my desire to share this – especially after she had lunch with you and thought you could understand the scene, at least somewhat.

"And, whether it turns her on or not, she has submitted, and allowed me to share some of these things with you; even though she knows she'll have to face you in the future. This is a great example of openness and submission, not involving physical, but rather psychological 'pain'."

I had been talking a long time, and finished the glass of iced tea in front of me. But I was compelled to make one more point, to ensure that Julie and Linda didn't leave with a big misunderstanding about me. "I want you guys to know that I respect Kelly immensely, and that I would never want to really hurt her. I am not a sadist: I do not enjoy seeing people in pain. Just in submission, even if that involves some pain."

I continued my long-winded exposition. "If you guys read a little about this subject on the 'net, you'll learn that the 'top' has a great responsibility – to bring the 'bottom' (the submissive, or 'sub') close to his or her limits of pain, without causing any damage or exceeding those limits. Kelly has a safeword that she can use at any time to stop a scene."

I continued, "My entire turn-on is about her *voluntarily* submitting – not being forced. Not being tied up. So, I'm not really interested in bondage, or sadism, or masochism. Discipline does turn me on – like schoolgirl paddlings or canings. And submission to things other than spankings, like the needle play experience." I really wanted to keep my interest in medical fetishes a secret or, if Julie and Linda were game, a surprise.

Looking around the table, I saw three young women who weren't quite sure what to make of what I had said. Kelly, of course, understood well, but even she was nervous about having this discussion with her friends. It was hot in the direct sunlight, and all the ice had melted in what was left of the iced tea.

"How about I show you guys the rest of the house. And, then maybe Linda would allow me to give her a birthday spanking?" Kelly and Julie laughed, and looked at Linda, who now had a terrified look on her face. But she wasn't immediately rejecting the idea.

Instead of taking them through the kitchen again, I slid open a sliding glass door to the pool room, and the girls walked in. The massage table was still against the other sliding door, and I now realized that I had forgotten to put away the supplies and equipment. I saw Julie's eyes focus on the rolling tray with the stimulation unit, but if she wasn't going to ask about it, I wasn't going to offer an explanation.

Linda saw the bathroom, and said, "I think I better use the bathroom, now." I laughed. It was a good idea for her to pee before taking her spanking. I wondered whether she had thought about that, or just had to go.

As I considered whether I should share how this room would be used during Kelly's birthday party, we heard Linda peeing, the sound coming through the louvered door. Julie asked if I brought in a masseuse, and I told her that I had been casually trained by a friend, and had just given Kelly a massage yesterday morning. Julie's eyes lit up, and said, "I would let you give *me* a massage. If you need the practice."

Again, I was happily surprised. I realized that it would be no big deal, especially after Julie had spent Kelly's birthday here, with all of us nude. But it was promising that Julie was looking for ways to connect with me, and I certainly wouldn't disappoint her. "I would love to give you a massage, sometime. If Kelly's OK with it." I looked at Kelly, and she just shrugged.

Linda came out of the bathroom, and we continued our tour of the house. At least, certain parts of the house – the upstairs being boring, and the exam room off-limits for the time being. We went down the stairs and, before taking them into the playroom, we walked into the bathroom, where I showed Linda and Julie the large shower area with all the jets, and – at the end of the room – the sauna.

Linda squealed, "Oh! I love saunas." Then, she giggled, and said, "Maybe I can use the sauna while you're massaging Julie?" We all laughed. I had no doubt that by the time Linda used the sauna, she would be completely comfortable being nude with me.

We then entered the playroom, and both Julie and Linda 'Oooh'ed' and 'Aaah'ed' upon seeing the large video screen at the far end of the room. I probably should have had the curtain pulled, but as far as they could tell, the screen was at the 'end' of the room.

I pointed out my office area, and we all sat down on the couch and loveseat. "Would either of you like some wine? I have some nice reds, and also bottles of white and rosé already cooled." It was Linda, already eating a piece of banana nut bread, who spoke up. "I'd love some wine. And rosé sounds perfect for the hot afternoon."

I wasn't sure whether she was referring to the weather, or the conversation ... or whether she just needed a little fortification before submitting to a spanking.

I took the bottle out of the bar fridge, and uncorked it, handing it over the couch to Kelly, while I grabbed four crystal glasses, which I put on the coffee table. Kelly poured the wine, and everyone picked up a glass and took a taste. It was very light, as I had expected, but it was a good quality rosé, had a floral nose, and left complex tones on the back of the tongue after swallowing.

Linda finished half her wine before I had finished the first taste of mine. She looked around the room and exclaimed, "That's a really big screen!"

I nodded, and said, "Yes, I'm into audio and video, and like my gadgets." I walked over to the desk, and tapped a couple of commands on the keyboard. As the video I had played for Kelly was still cued-up, I started it playing, its sound track, coming softly through the hidden speakers behind the screen, and several along the side walls.

When the 18-foot diagonal image appeared on the screen, both Linda and Julie gasped. I had recently upgraded to a '4K' system, and the high-definition projector did a great job with both the sharpness, and bright colors. Scenes of mountains, lakes, and flowered valleys moved slowly across the screen, as I sat back down on the loveseat next to Kelly.

I briefly thought of the video that my system had captured during Kelly's 'first experience', and wondered how she would react if an edited version of that video were to appear on the screen. But I had promised her that the video would not be shared, and I certainly wouldn't have done so, without first securing Kelly's permission.

I thought about retrieving some 'wine crackers' from behind the bar, but decided that everyone was doing fine with the pretzels and banana bread. We sipped our wine, and watched portions of the video on the large screen, before I turned it off.

Linda put down her empty wine glass, and cleared her throat. "I guess you'd like to spank me, now?" We all looked at her with amazement, and I saw Kelly's mouth fall open. For the third time today, I was stunned: Linda had actually *requested* her spanking, not waiting until I had brought up the subject.

Perhaps she just wanted to get it over with … but somehow I sensed that she was – or would be – turned on by the experience. I was certain, now, that Linda had worn a dress specifically to give me easy spanking access; she had decided long before she arrived here that she would submit to the spanking from an older guy.

I put down my wine glass on the coffee table as far from the loveseat as I could reach, and also moved Kelly's glass further from the edge of the table. I smiled at Kelly, and she moved over to the couch, leaving the loveseat to me; and, soon, Linda.

Looking across the coffee table, I addressed Linda. "I would love to give you a sample spanking, Linda, and I think it might be interesting for you. But I won't force you. We've joked about this since the restaurant, but if you decide to do it, I want you to know it will be real: You'll only get 25 spanks ... plus 3 extras for good luck, health, and wealth ... and they will be given quickly. The actual spanking won't take more than a minute, or so."

I saw a surprised expression on Linda's face, and added, "But I'll spank you hard, and your bottom will hurt. At least for a few minutes." Linda nodded impassively.

"If you're ready, you may come over here now," I told Linda. I watched her carefully, as she stood up, a little unsteady, and walked between the couch and the coffee table to where I was sitting. I stood up. "I would like to hug you now, and after your spanking. If that's OK with you." Linda just nodded. I took her in my arms, and gave her a big birthday hug. Then I kissed her on her forehead, and said, "Happy birthday, Linda."

She put her arms around me, but didn't hug me; she stood silent and rigid near the corner of the couch and loveseat. I pulled her closer to me, and put my mouth near her ear.

"Thank you, Linda. I hope it will be at least a little interesting for you. Please try to relax. It's not going to be that bad." I looked into Linda's eyes, and she blinked; her face was ruddy and clouded, similar to what I had observed when I had reviewed the spanking agreement with Kelly. That seemed like months ago, but it hadn't even been two weeks.

I sat in the middle of the loveseat, taking Linda by the hand, and pulling her down. She positioned herself across my lap. I was going to make this easier for her by not requiring that she go over my knee, nor would she receive any 'corrective' punishment, or a corner time.

Linda was finally in position and stilled herself, but I saw her back rise and fall, as she took deep breaths. I smoothed down her dress, running my hand over her ample bottom. Linda took in a quick breath as I positioned my hand in the middle of her bottom, over her dress. I glanced up, and both Julie and Kelly were sitting on the edge of the couch, totally silent, and staring at Linda's bottom.

"Linda, it is my belief that all spankings should be administered on the bare bottom." She gasped again, but didn't say a word. "Because you're cooperating so well, I'll give you the option of the 25 (plus three) spanks on the bare, or double that on your underwear."

It hit me that she might be wearing a thong, which would make the underwear option moot. But she quickly responded, "I guess I'll let you do it on the bare, Sir." I smiled. This was getting better and better!

I lifted the hem of Linda's dress with both hands, folding it onto her back, exposing her from the waist down. She was wearing cotton bikini panties, covered with tiny purple, red, and yellow flowers, and violet waist- and leg-bands. I read 'Victoria's Secret' on the waistband.

I used both hands to lower the underwear, taking hold of both sides, and slowly lowering the back until half of her bottom was exposed. Linda surprised me again, when she lifted her middle slightly, allowing me to lower the underwear, until they were holding her legs together at mid-thigh. I gazed down at Linda's big, beautiful bottom, and realized that there were no tan lines; perhaps we had all misjudged Linda's comfort with nudity?

I slid my right hand over her fleshy globes, giving each one a little pat. My left hand rested on Linda's lower back – ready to hold her in position, if that were necessary. I glanced up, and saw that Julie and Kelly were both mesmerized by the scene unfolding in front of them.

Leaning over towards Linda's head, I whispered, "I'm going to give you the first few slowly, so that you'll know what to expect. Then, the rest will be given quickly. I need you to stay in position. I suggest you take a few deep breaths, and then you can let me know when you're ready." I put my right hand on Linda's right buttock, which was wobbling before I had even begun her spanking.

I felt, and heard, Linda's breathing and then – more quickly than I had expected – she said softly, "I'm ready."

Very quietly, I said, "OK, here we go." I gave Linda a hard spank on her right side, and watched as a white handprint appeared on Linda's pink bottom. Then, I gave her a hard spank on the left side. I had expected Linda to rear up and shriek when she felt the first couple of spanks but, unbelievably, Linda not only remained in position, but she didn't make a sound.

After a few seconds, I proceeded with her spanking, giving her a medium or hard spank about once per second or two. I alternated sides, and her bottom was now reddening quickly. Linda kicked her feet a few times, but was otherwise perfect in the role of 'bottom'. The 25 spanks were finished quickly, and I rubbed her bottom, my hand going in circles, starting at the center of each buttock and spiraling out.

"Kelly, what were the extra spanks for, again? You can call them out, one at a time." Kelly smiled at me and nodded, 'getting it' instantly.

"One for good health." And I spanked Linda as hard as I could on her right side. 'CRACK!' The sound echoed in the otherwise-quiet room.

A loud "Ow!" came from Linda, but she held her position admirably.

Kelly continued, "One for good wealth." My hand came down with a loud 'SMACK!' on her left side. Another 'Ow!' from Linda. I looked up at Kelly.

She said, much louder now, "And one for long life!" And I gave Linda another hard swat on her right side. There was no exclamation, but I heard, and felt, Linda breathing heavily.

Linda had bounced after each of the three hard spanks, but kept herself in position. I was amazed. I heard her sniffle a little, but then she turned her head and looked up at me. "Thank you, Sir, for my birthday spanking." Incredible!

I looked over at Kelly, and asked, "Should we give her a 'corner time'?"

Kelly was emphatic, "No! She's done very well. Don't push it."

A few seconds later, Linda sniffed again, and said, "I'll stand in the corner, if you want me to." Kelly and I laughed. Linda had no idea that in our terminology, corner time meant five minutes with a rectal insertion. I had only planned to use the thermometer, and had even prepared it when I came down earlier. Kelly would just need to pick it up from the desk and hand it to me. But I agreed with Kelly: Linda had done fabulously well. She didn't deserve to suffer any more.

I lowered Linda's dress again, leaving her panties around her thighs, and asked, "Linda, please stand up, now, and I'll give you another hug."

Linda stood, as I had requested, her dress covering her as usual, but with her underwear now showing below her hemline. I stood up next to her, in the narrow lane between the loveseat and coffee table, and gave her a big hug. As I hugged her, my hands went down and cupped her buttocks.

For the benefit of Julie and Kelly (OK, and me, too), I lifted the back of Linda's dress with my left hand, and vigorously rubbed her bottom with my right hand. When I dropped her dress, I realized that Linda was hugging me, her head on my chest.

I had planned to allow Linda to raise her own panties, but impulsively decided to lift them myself. I did this by feel only, my eyes looking up at Linda's face, as I reached down, taking the waistbands at each side, and inching the fabric up and over her bottom, my hands under her dress. I slid my hands around the waistband, making sure it was smooth, and then removed my hands and let her dress fall into place again.

I hugged Linda again, and gave her a peck on each cheek (the ones on her face). "Thank you, Linda. You did great. I am very impressed by your ability to control yourself. And, that you were open enough to go through with the spanking, at all."

I took my arms from around Linda, and sat back down on the couch. Both of Linda's hands went to her bottom, and she rubbed herself through her dress and underwear. She looked down, and gave me an inscrutable smile.

But not that inscrutable: At that moment, I knew that she had enjoyed the experience. And probably would come back for more. Linda made her way back to the other end of the couch, and sat down next to Julie, who had a dazed expression on her face.

I reached for my wine, and took a sip, looking up at the threesome on the couch. "Well, what do you think?" I focused on Julie.

Her mouth opened and closed again, reminding me of the 'fish' look on Kelly, when I had first told her about corner time and corrective punishment. Julie picked up her glass, and finished the wine in one gulp. Finally, Julie looked at Kelly and then me, and said, "That was really *hot*. I don't know how Linda felt, but I wish one of my boyfriends would take me over his lap."

This was really a day of surprises. I nearly choked, trying to respond to Julie, and eventually offered, "Well, if you'd like a sample, I would be happy to indulge you. As long as we're all set-up in here."

Could I really expect Julie to spontaneously submit, after watching Linda's spanking? And, would a short spanking be sufficient to give Julie a taste of what a real punishment would be like? My mind was a whirl, and I don't think it was just the wine. The three beautiful women, two of whom had now submitted to me, were intoxicating; no wine required.

Julie stood up, and said, "I guess if Linda can do it, then I can." I almost fell over on the loveseat. Kelly was looking up at Julie, with her mouth open again. She may have expected Linda to agree to a birthday spanking, but I'm sure she had no inkling that Julie would want to participate, also. Neither did I.

Julie slowly walked toward me. Kelly was now sitting cross-legged, the hem of her dress almost to her waist, her hands in her lap. Julie stood next to me, looking down at me with glazed eyes, and undid her belt. She unbuttoned her shorts, and pulled them down, first one side, and then the other, as she wriggled out of them. They dropped to the floor. Julie wore a simple black thong, her hands taking the thin waistband at each side. "Do I need to pull my underwear down, too?"

I could see the smile breaking through her mock-seriousness. I nodded, "Linda had to, so it's only fair." This was just too good!

Julie pushed her thong down, and let it drop; it caught around her knees. Her private parts were at my eye-level, and I couldn't help take in the view. Julie was completely hairless – probably a Brazilian wax, or it could be a 'Hollywood' wax. In any case, I would find out in a few minutes. I was obviously staring at her bare pubes; looking up to Julies eyes, I said, "Very nice. Now, let's get you across my lap, young lady."

Julie giggled, and – somewhat clumsily – laid herself across my lap. I now realized that I was getting hard, so I quickly adjusted myself, pulling Julie closer so that my erection was pressed between my stomach and her hip.

She didn't comment, and I was glad. While Kelly knew that I would get turned-on by this type of spanking experience, I didn't want to make a spectacle of myself, having just met these young women. And it was to be a sensual, not sexual experience. I rested my right hand on Julie's bottom, and she flinched slightly when my palm cupped and squeezed her cheeks.

I looked at Kelly, and asked, "Should we give Julie a few samples with some implements? And, of course, she'll need to take a corner time."

Kelly started to crack up, but kept her face serious, as she made eye-contact with Julie, and quickly looked back at me. "What did you have in mind?"

That was an incredible response from Kelly; we were obviously on the same wavelength. "Nothing too severe – no hairbrush, tawse, switch or cane. The slipper would work – Oh! You haven't tasted that, yet." I laughed. This was so much fun: The scenario, the girls, the conversation that I'm sure was still mysterious to Julie, and the expansive view of Julie's bottom.

I now realized that she was infinitesimally rocking from side to side ... and I had thought she was already well positioned. No. This wasn't possible. Could Julie be that open – and wild – to masturbate on my leg, while I spanked her? Of course, that would be fine with me. But something like this on a first meeting was shocking – even to me. Maybe I really was old-fashioned.

Looking for Kelly's concurrence, and her understanding of my code, I suggested, "How about 50 OTK, then 10 with the smooth, then one or two on each side with the textured? The 'therm' is ready. Maybe the thin black – if she needs corrective? Everything is on the credenza behind the desk." I was hopefully anticipating ...

Kelly smiled, and I thought maybe she really did want to 'get back' at Julie. Or just give her a challenge. If Julie refuses, then she's chickened out, and not so wild. If she agrees, then she will learn that we're not playing around. Well, OK, I guess we *were* playing around. My head was spinning.

"Sir, I agree with your plan, but one good one with the texture on each side will be enough. I guess it'll be a Level-5, plus the two zingers at the end."

Now, Julie turned herself and, looking back at Kelly and asked, "What are you guy's babbling about? Is he afraid to do it?"

What a taunt! Julie would find out what she was asking for. Then, it hit me: Maybe she was into the scene? Maybe she was even a domme, playing us, having never let her friends know: Julie, coming out of the 'closet' today. I doubted that. But it sure would be interesting: She could train *us*. Kelly returned from the desk with the various items, and I asked Julie, in my most severe tone, "Are you ready for a Level-7 punishment, young lady?"

Julie put her head down on the loveseat, turned to face the coffee table. "I don't know what that means, but I'm ready for whatever you want to give me."

That was pretty brazen. Julie had me convinced that she really *was* a wild person, even if she wasn't a domme. What was she really into? Perhaps we would find out at Kelly's birthday party.

"Julie, your responsibility is to keep yourself in position, and *never* put your hands behind you! Do you understand?" She may have thought I was hamming it up, but I was quite serious.

"Yes, Sir," Julie replied weakly.

"First you will receive 50 hand spanks. I should be wearing a leather glove, as my hand will be as sore as your bottom by the time I finish."

Without further ado, and surprising Julie with my swiftness, I began spanking her. My open hand swung from low to high, as it impacted her rump. Left, right, double on the left, right, left, double on the right … and repeating this pattern until fifty spanks had been delivered.

Julie hadn't moved, but was clutching the loveseat cushion, her upper body tense. Her bottom was a nice shade of red, but it hadn't been as intense as a much longer OTK (over-the-knee) spanking. This was only a demonstration.

As I rubbed her rubicund bottom with my right hand, I reached under Julie's blouse with my left, my hand passing over her bra strap, and massaging her upper back and shoulders. This caused me to lean over her, which dragged my hardening member across her hip. "Please try to relax, Julie. Your spanking will hurt more, if you're tense."

I withdrew my hand, and straightened her top. Kelly handed me the smooth Ping Pong paddle. With my left hand firmly pressing down on the small of Julie's back, I positioned the paddle over her left buttock. "Are you ready for a taste of the smooth Ping Pong paddle, now, young lady?"

Julie took a few breaths, and said, "Yes, Sir."

That's what I wanted to hear. I gave her medium swats with this relatively tame implement, alternating sides, about one swat coming every five seconds. It would only take a minute, but Julie's bottom would sting for a while. The paddle resonated off Julie's bottom with a loud 'POP!' every time it met her now-rippling tissues.

Julie groaned (or moaned?) a few times and, finally, she let out a few squeals and yelps when I gave her the last few swats, which connected with each buttock solidly.

"Julie, that was the easy paddle – thin wood, and smooth surface. And that was just a taste. But we'll finish now with a small sample of the textured paddle. I think you'll notice the difference."

I looked down at Julie, her hair frazzled, and her bottom still quivering. She was breathing hard, but had held herself in position commendably. Kelly and I switched paddles, and I looked at the fine rubber points that rose from the textured paddle's surface. Those really stung! Per Kelly's instructions I would not make Julie hold still for two or more swats on each side; one would be sufficient.

"Julie, I want you to say 'ready', and then I'll give you one swat. Then, you can give me the count and a 'thank you, Sir'. Then we'll repeat it on the other side. Do you understand?" Julie nodded. I didn't penalize her for not answering verbally.

I raised the paddle over Julie's bright red bottom, and waited. A few seconds later, Julie said, "Ready!" The paddle came down with force on Julie's right side, making a 'SPLAT!' that reverberated in the utterly quiet room, followed by an 'Ugggh' from Julie. I watched, as her tissues rippled out, like a tidal wave about to inundate her core.

I realized that Julie was rocking again. She stopped suddenly, and I heard 'One, thank you, Sir', and then, within seconds, another 'Ready!' Again, I brought the paddle down, this time on her left side, again with a startlingly loud 'WHAP!' This time, Julie let out a loud 'Ooowwwww!' But she kept her hands in front of her. I gave the paddle back to Kelly, and began rubbing Julie's bottom. There were 'Oooh's' and 'Aaah's' coming from somewhere under the hair to my left. Finally, Julie remembered. "Two, thank you, Sir."

Stopping suddenly, I took my hand off Julie's behind, and announced, "And now, young lady, you will take your 'corner time'." Julie started to get up, and I pushed her lower back down and held it there. "Oh, no. We do a special 'corner time' around here. It's much faster, only 5 minutes. And it has the same purpose: To display your red bottom to others in the room, feel some embarrassment, and think about your bad behavior."

I was almost laughing, and Kelly knew it. There was a broad smile on her face, as she handed me the already-lubed rectal thermometer.

"As you only received a Level-7 punishment, your corner time will be 5 minutes with the rectal thermometer inserted into you. I'll play with it, just to keep you awake. If Kelly feels it's necessary, you may receive some additional corner time."

Julie tried to push herself up again. "A rectal thermometer? No! That's not nice. Please just let me stand in the corner."

I laughed, "No way, Julie. This is how we do it." I looked over at Kelly. "But I do think you'll probably get a second corner time, just to make sure you remember this punishment." Kelly was miming a hysterical laugh, rolling back into the couch, and bringing her legs to her chest. It was a nice view.

Now, Linda – whose mouth had been open for the past few minutes – became hysterical, also. I started laughing, which had the effect of moving my front against Julie, and I started getting turned-on again.

I got serious, and explained, "Julie, I'm going to insert the thermometer now." With my left hand, I separated her buttocks, her rosebud fully on display, and with my right, I touched her with the thermometer, waited for her flinch, and then smoothly inserted the glass tube, until there was only an inch sticking out of her. I kept her buttocks separated, and began moving the thermometer around – in and out, back and forth, around in circles, and twirled it in my fingers.

Initially, Julie whined a little, and I heard a few 'Noooo!'s' and 'Oooh's', but she quieted down nicely. I looked at Kelly, but she just gave me an inquisitive look and shrugged her shoulders. Perhaps I would be blowing it, by involving 'sex' – at least what Julie would probably consider it – but Julie had been rocking and now, unmistakably, I felt a wetness on my thigh. It was so unbelievable that any of this had happened, that I couldn't guess what response I would get from Julie. Or, from Kelly.

"Julie, you took your punishment very well. It was only a taste, but you demonstrated that you can control your body, take some pain, and," Did I dare? "maybe even enjoyed it." I thought of asking Kelly and Linda to leave the room, but that wouldn't have been fair. To any of us. I looked at Kelly, and quickly looked back toward Julie's head.

"Julie, it appears that you have gotten a little turned-on. I think that's great." I continued moving the thermometer in and out of her. "And, after behaving so well during a punishment (and since you were taking it voluntarily, not for a real misdeed), we often help the 'bottom' get-off." Julie didn't try to get up, but she was suddenly stock-still.

I continued, "So, you may do yourself, if you would like, while I finish your corner time. If you would prefer ... we've only met, but I guess we've done a lot of things together, already ... I could help you masturbate." I laughed, "I'm glad you're in this position, so you can't slap me. I'll certainly understand if that would be too embarrassing for you." Now, I was taunting *her*.

We had already had the conversation by the pool – the 'mock' portion now potentially becoming real. We had talked about it. I'm sure Julie wanted it; but, probably not in front of her friends. Or me. Everyone around the coffee table was silent, awaiting the verdict from Julie's deliberation.

Julie released her stranglehold on the loveseat cushion, and brought her right hand down, and under her, sliding it into position. I could have slid my own hand under her and assisted, but she hadn't asked me to, and it appeared that she was doing very well on her own. We had to leave *something* for the future!

Then I realized that I was flaccid again. That was probably a good thing. My mind was muddled with an embarrassment of riches ... of the sensual kind.

As Julie began working on herself in earnest, I took out the thermometer, and Kelly handed me the small black butt plug. I hoped that this would help, not hurt, Julie's chances of coming. I held her buttocks apart even further, and placed the rounded tip of the butt plug against Julie's anus. She clenched, and then, slowly, relaxed her muscles. I did a few short in's and out's with the butt plug, and then carefully inserted it fully, the thin portion sucking it into her, only a two-dimensional round spot of black showing between her still-red mounds.

I released her buttocks and used both hands to massage and knead Julie's bottom and, as her efforts intensified, I stopped my motion, and held my hands firmly on her buttocks, pressing down and holding a small portion of our bodies in close contact.

We watched, as Julie's body contorted, her back coming up, cat-like as she reached down even further, accelerating her motions and, within a few more seconds, her movements became merely a vibration. There was a wave of convulsions of her entire body over my lap. Then we heard a high-pitched other-worldly squeal, that involuntarily emerged from Julie's throat, growing suddenly lower in intensity and lower in pitch, becoming a purr. No: It was a primal *growl*.

I looked up, and saw that Linda's mouth had dropped open again, and her eyes were incredibly wide. She hadn't put her hands in front of her face, this time, or closed her eyes, and I gave her credit for that. I looked at Kelly, and her hand was inside her underwear, working herself into a sweat, as she watched Julie's incredible performance.

As Julie calmed, I lightly stroked her lower back with my left hand, and her bottom with my right, gliding down her upper thigh, and then back up. We were all quiet again. Except, Kelly, who was panting, and clearly close to her own release. I separated Julie's buttocks and grabbed the disc of the butt plug.

I whispered to Julie, "Give a little push," and she did, the plug coming smoothly out of her. Kelly, interrupting her own genital maneuvers, reached over and took it with a wad of tissue. It was nice to have a helper!

At that moment, I knew that my prospects would multiply threefold ... and maybe fourfold! Whole new ranges of fantasies swirled through my mind, but I knew that I wouldn't be able to understand them until later. Tonight. Kelly and I would need to discuss this unexpected experience, analyze it, and make some conscious decisions on how to proceed. The possibilities were astounding!

I patted Julie's bottom, and said, "Please stand up, now, young lady." *Now* is when I heard a whine from Julie! But she slowly got herself off me, and stood up in front of me – I was again eye-level with her smooth mons. When I had separated her buttocks, I looked for hairs, but Julie had been thoroughly waxed. That, in itself, was a demonstration of accepting pain voluntarily.

I stood up, close to Julie, and hugged her. Fortunately, I was completely flaccid, so didn't need to worry about pressing against her. I put my cheek to hers, and held her tight. Finally, I lowered my hands, holding her bottom, and asked, "So, how was it?"

Suddenly, the mood lightened in the room, everyone laughing, as I gave Julie a couple more pats on the behind. I kissed her cheek, and said, "Thank you. But I think you enjoyed it, as much as I did!"

Julie suddenly reached up, held my cheeks with both hands, and gave me a quick peck on the lips. Oh, my. We had discussed what I considered 'sex', but either Julie had forgotten, or ... I gently pushed away from Julie, and looked at Kelly. She had a stern-looking countenance, but suddenly gave me a little smile, and a shrug.

I refrained from telling Julie that I now considered us to have had sex. That would be very confusing, having ALSO just helped her to masturbate – which I did not consider sex, as there was no transfer of body fluids. I would propose to Kelly that we re-define sex to *not* include saliva contact – kissing or eating/drinking after someone. This was getting complicated.

I told Julie that she could get dressed, and she stood next to me, casually pulling up and adjusting her thong, and then her shorts. I looked at Linda and Kelly, and started clapping. They followed, and we gave Julie the round of applause that she deserved. She didn't take a bow. Her face was flushed, and she sat down next to me on the loveseat and whispered, "Thank you."

Linda was slowly shaking her head, amazed at what she'd seen her friend do – a friend, who she had thought she knew 'intimately'. Kelly got up, dropped the paddles on the desk, and walked to the bathroom to wash the thermometer and butt plug. She was shaking her head, also.

I took the opportunity to chat privately with Linda and Julie. "You guys both surprised me. Kelly had said you weren't shocked by some of our play activities, but I didn't expect both of you to be so open, or so interested in our submissive scenes. I think we're going to have some fun at Kelly's party: I have quite a few surprises for her, and for at least one of them, I'll need your help.

"I'll let you know what you need to do when you arrive for the party, but let's just say it involves keeping your distance, while we role-play one of Kelly's special fantasies. I think with Julie having broken the ice, and with only the three of you coming, Kelly should be OK with what we're going to do. And I don't think you guys will be too shocked." Julie and Linda exchanged glances and shrugged.

As Kelly walked back into the playroom, I turned to Julie, "I really like the clean waxed look. I was suggesting to Kelly that maybe she should go farther than her extended bikini wax. I'd love to see her with just a 'landing strip': I think that looks neat, and is practical." I didn't explain what I meant, but probably didn't have to. I added, "And, I'd love to watch the process, and Kelly's acceptance of the openness and pain required to finish the job."

Kelly sat down on the couch, and looked at Julie. "I don't mind waxing as Sam wants, but I'm a little afraid, and I'm not sure who I would let do that." Julie was surprised, "Kelly! You know I work at a salon, and we have a couple of waxing experts. I can take you to the shop to meet them, if you like."

After listening to this exchange, I wondered whether the process could be accelerated. And, provide one more 'submission' experience as a challenge for Kelly's long weekend with me.

"Julie, do you think that we could get one of those experts to come here to wax Kelly? I would like to observe the process, and it might be nicer for Kelly to get it done here than in the salon. In fact, Kelly could stay here through Monday, and someone could be scheduled for Monday morning – if you can get hold of them, and they're not already booked."

Julie listened, and grinned as I laid out my suggestion. She replied, "Actually, our best esthetician is a close friend of mine ... Well, not quite as close as *we* were today! ... but, anyway, she doesn't usually work on Mondays. I could call her and see if she could come over here on Monday morning, as a special favor, so we can work on Kelly."

Kelly coughed, and asked, "We?"

Julie laughed, and said, "You don't think I'd send someone over and not supervise her, do you?" We all laughed, but Julie was serious. "Kelly, I'd like to be here with you guys, if you will let me. I can hold your hand, and may have some tips – you'll need to make a few decisions on how it will be done."

Kelly looked down, apparently not too happy with the quick flow of things. Then she looked at me, and asked, "Sam, is this what you really want?"

That surprised me. I wanted Kelly to do this for herself, not for me, although I thought it a good idea, for many reasons. "Kelly, I won't pressure you on this. It's your body, and I think it looks great as it is. I just thought it might be a 'new look' for you, and provide another interesting experience."

Kelly said, "Well, most of *me* has already been waxed. Let's have Julie's friend come on Monday and wax *your* private parts!" The girls laughed, but I didn't think it was so funny.

The thought of Kelly being my domme flashed through my brain, and I realized that some day I might *have* to submit to being waxed. I wasn't too happy about the prospect, and understood Kelly's hesitation and fear – her having already felt the waxing process on some slightly less-sensitive areas.

Kelly looked at Julie, then at me, and made her decision: "OK, I guess we can do it, if Julie's friend is available." Then she looked at me, and said, in no joking tone, "But I insist on being able to use my safeword, if I decide it will be too much for me, or want to delay until some other time."

I nodded; that was fair. I poured another round of the rosé, and we toasted to Kelly's upcoming 'hairdo', Julie's incredible masturbation scene, and – the least of it –

Linda's birthday spanking. It had been a fun afternoon, and I really liked these women. They were more open than I could have imagined, and I was now confident that we would celebrate an epic birthday party in three weeks.

Linda looked at her watch, and announced that they would need to leave, as they had to get ready for a 'clubbing' Saturday night out. We all rose, and made our way upstairs and to the front door, the girls chatting the whole time about what they would wear tonight, and to Kelly's party. One of my surprise party favors would give them another sartorial option.

We all hugged, and I thanked Linda and Julie for coming over, and Julie for coming. Well, actually, I thanked them for their openness and acceptance of some of my kinks and fetishes. Although they had yet to learn of my medical interests, and a few other of my fantasies, which they still might consider 'bizarre'.

CHAPTER 12: NURSE KELLY

After her friends left, Kelly and I went back downstairs and sat on the couch. Kelly sat cross-legged, and I decided to lie down with my head in her lap. I looked up at her, and stated the obvious, "That was an interesting experience with your friends. Julie's 'wilder' than I even expected ... although perhaps 'wild' isn't the right word. But they were both far more open, accepting, and even enthusiastic about our ideas of discipline and submission than I could have imagined."

Kelly looked down at me, her hair falling across my face, and into my mouth. She looked to her left, and then forcefully shook her head once to the right, and the hair flew off me. "Yes, that was really surprising. First, Linda got across your lap, and even let you pull down her underwear. You spanked her pretty hard, but I didn't hear a peep from her. Based on what she had told me when we had lunch, she was probably getting turned-on, also."

I laughed, "Maybe she would have enjoyed exactly what I did to Julie? And maybe Julie would have gotten into the chair position, and allowed me to strap her, and provide more of an aggressive sensual experience. Maybe with the anal beads; or both anal and vaginal beads at the same time?" My mind was still a blur with new fantasies, mixed together with our actual experiences over the past couple of hours.

Kelly laughed too, bouncing my head up and down in her lap. I lifted my head, and kissed her, savoring the taste of her, and swirling my tongue, like sampling a fine wine. Kelly not-so-casually put her hand on my pants, cupping me, and holding me, as we continued to talk. She said, "I think the experience was perfect for both of them. I'm glad you didn't masturbate Julie."

Now, I was concerned, and I looked up at Kelly. "Would that have bothered you? I would hope that you would have spoken up, before I did something that upset you." I reminisced what had happened in that minute or two, when I decided to offer Julie release, and when she decided to masturbate in front of us.

"It seemed incredible that we had just discussed this scenario – my masturbating her – out by the pool, and she had finally agreed that it might not be a big deal ... and a few minutes later, we'd had the opportunity to do the same thing in reality. At least I think it was real."

Before Kelly could speak, I interjected, "And I thought it would be great for her to masturbate. I'm not sure I could have done that, in front of someone else. So, it was an incredible display of openness. Actually, much more than that: Exhibitionism."

Kelly was nodding, and pulled me up. I got out of her lap, and sat cross-legged, and then lifted Kelly into my lap, her feet wrapped around my waist. We loosely held each other around the shoulders, as Kelly excitedly agreed. "Yes! I hadn't categorized her that way, but you're right: Julie is an exhibitionist." Kelly was suddenly almost out of breath.

"In our distant past, when my dad caught us skinny-dipping in our pool, I remember that he told us to get out and get 'decent'. At lunch, the other day, Julie commented that my lecherous father stood there, watching us get out of the pool." Kelly got even more excited.

"And Linda reminded us that we'd gone to the nude beach with Kathy's family (years ago), so her dad had also seen all of us nude." I wasn't sure what she was trying to say, so sat quietly, our bodies joined at the hips.

"Anyway, now I'm remembering more of that night. My dad was going to go back inside, but Julie hopped out of the pool, and started walking toward him. She was nude, unafraid, and the aggressor. My dad was transfixed, flustered, and had never been controlled so completely by a female.

When she was almost up to him, she reached out ... then turned, and dived back into the pool. I remember my father just shaking his head, and going back inside, while we swam a while longer, then got out, and – wrapped in our towels – went up to my bedroom for a 'slumber party'."

Kelly looked into my eyes. "I'm now seeing an entirely different perspective on what was really happening back then." She looked past me, her eyes glassy, her face suddenly clouding over. She vaguely shook her head, but I had no idea what was going on inside. I knew that she was trying to work something out, and it would clarify itself best without additional pressure from me.

Then, I started thinking about our plans and how the day was going. I had planned to give Kelly the rest of her Level-100 punishment this afternoon. It wasn't many levels, but she would need to be warmed up, and then feel the sting, the bite, of the most severe implements.

Now, I realized, we should put that off until tomorrow. Sunday. My thoughts rambled from Sunday, to picnic, to countryside, to the pond where Liz and I had spent many summer days. It was an idyllic setting, and I decided that we should pack a picnic and relax. After I had given Kelly a serious spanking experience.

I remembered – how could I forget? – I'd already been cleaned out, and Kelly had asked to give me a medical exam, as I had done with her. I really didn't want her to repeat the enemas tomorrow – or any time soon – so I decided to let Nurse Kelly examine me today. "Kelly, when you're ready, I will report for my medical examination. As you've already prepared me, I'd like to get that over with, so we can have a nice evening."

Kelly pushed my chest, and I fell backward onto the couch, as she extricated herself from me, and stood up. Before I could get back up, Kelly had lifted her dress over her head, and was walking toward her rolling case by the desk. I shook my head, and got up from the couch, picking up the half-empty wine bottle and glasses, and putting them on the bar counter. I walked over to see what Kelly was doing.

Kelly was still wearing the rather plain, white bra and panties, but was now rolling white nylons up her left leg, raised by a foot she had placed on the seat of one of the desk chairs. She twisted and rolled her hair, and pinned it, so that it all sat atop her head, with portions sagging over her ears on both sides. I sat in the other chair, and watched, silently.

Kelly put on the other nylon, and adjusted the tops, that were at mid-thigh. She rummaged in her case, and pulled out an old-fashioned garter belt. Or maybe it was new-fashioned, from a sex shop? She took off her underwear, and put on the garter, clipping her nylons with the straps that hung down from the bizarre piece of clothing. It was sexy! She stood up and smiled at me.

I decided at that moment that our next get-together would be a photo shoot. Kelly was certainly model material, and her natural sensuality – in addition to her knockout body – would produce some fantastic images. And, what clothing and props we had to work with! With the modern camera and lighting equipment available today, it would be easy to capture incredible shots; I just had to put Kelly in front of the camera.

My vision returned to what was in front of me: Kelly took off her bra, and stepped into some kind of outfit – it was zipped at the bottom. She pulled it up, put her arms through, and zipped up the front, and then unzipped it partially, exposing some great cleavage. The dress was white, with a red cross over her heart, and red trim on the edges of the short sleeves.

It was a 'naughty nurse' outfit, made even more outrageous with an old-fashioned white nurses hat, which sported another red cross. She reached into her case, and pulled out some red high-heeled shoes, and put them on. The transformation was complete, and Kelly stood before me, modeling the outfit. I clapped, and whistled my approval.

Kelly said, "I know you asked me to bring a schoolgirl outfit, and I put something together that I can wear for you tomorrow. But I saw this outfit in a costume shop, and decided I had to wear it for you this weekend. Do you like it?"

Was she kidding? "Of course, I like it. I love it." I would have said, 'Now, you just need a large syringe in your hand', but I decided better of it, lest I give Kelly any more ideas than she already had.

Kelly announced, "I'm ready for my next patient, now." I smiled, and haltingly raised my hand, "Present." We walked to the exam room, where Kelly promptly told me to undress. I was only wearing shorts, underwear and a shirt, so it took almost no time. I hopped up on the table. I was already starting to get turned-on, and hoped that Kelly would provide some prostate stimulation. But I had no idea what she was planning.

"OK, young man," she said. "We're going to need to do some rectal dilations and examinations," Where had she gotten all this? From me, of course! "but first, you'll need at least one more enema."

I groaned, loudly. "Kelly ..."

"What, young man? Shall we do two more?" I just looked down at my now-flagging penis. This experience would be a turn-on for Kelly, alone. I watched as Kelly took a plastic bucket from under the sink, and poured a few tablespoons of salt into it. Then, she ran the water until it was warm, and filled the bucket, stirring with a glass rod that was on the sink. She then asked me, "Where is the large enema syringe?"

My stomach was already churning, as I pointed to one of the drawers below the counter across from the exam table. Kelly said, "Get in a knee-chest position. Now." I complied, and could do nothing but wait for Kelly's rude intrusion into a usually private body cavity.

Kelly found the KY on the counter, and lubed the tip of the syringe, then smiled, and walked behind me. I buried my head in the pillow, and closed my eyes. I heard Kelly drawing the enema solution into the syringe and, I guessed, emptying it – watching the pressure of the stream, as she pushed the plunger. Soon enough, I felt the tip against my anus, and I concentrated on relaxing. Suddenly, a jet of water was being infused into my rear. The tip came out, and Kelly re-loaded the syringe.

As Kelly injected syringe-after-syringe of saltwater into me, my mind's eye saw Linda over my lap, with her dress folded back. My taking down her panties. Her telling me that she was ready for her spanking; and thanking me afterward.

Kelly was injecting another syringe of water – probably the fifth or sixth – and it was getting uncomfortable. I would have asked her to slow down, but wanted to get it over with. And I hadn't had a cramp, yet.

My mind drifted again to Linda. An interesting woman: Apparently more conservative than her friends, but obviously having a deep sexual need, and being much more open – with a strange, older guy, no less – than I could have imagined, given her general demeanor.

I had no doubt that Linda would have accepted the insertion of a rectal thermometer. I wondered, now, how she would have reacted, had I slipped my hand under her, and begun to masturbate her. Somehow, I knew that she probably would have been OK with it ... except for her friends watching. Perhaps, we *had* gone as far as feasible, under the circumstances.

I felt Kelly inject another syringe of water into me. I wanted this to be over. But, I would allow Kelly to have her way with me. At least, for the next hour, or so.

I filled the syringe again, and daubed some more KY on the tip. Placing the tip inside Sam's anal passage, I used both hands to squeeze the syringe, which emptied nearly six ounces of warm saltwater into Sam. He was taking it well, so far, although I knew that he would balk at taking another enema. I might have given him a break.

But *I* needed a break: To finish what I had started on the couch, as I watched Julie's incredible performance. I knew instinctively it wasn't an act: Julie had truly gotten herself off, after being spanked, and with Sam sticking things up her butt. The syringe had been emptied, but I held it against Sam's butthole, as I realized how turned-on I had become by *watching* Julie. I wondered if I were a voyeur.

Sam was groaning now, and I realized I had lost count of the number of syringes I had emptied into him. It had to be close to ten – nearly two quarts. "Sam, you've been a good boy. So I'll only give you two more syringes." I laughed, as Sam predictably groaned again. I was now anxious to get back into the playroom, so hurried the injection of another ten ounces of water into Sam's rear.

I helped Sam off the table, and walked him toward the bathroom. But I stopped him in the hall, and commanded, "Standing position, young man. Now!" Sam gave me a 'look', but complied.

Of all the things he had done to me last time, there was one thing that I still considered over-the-top: Making me do jumping jacks with anal or vaginal beads inside me. Sam now had nearly three quarts of water in him that would slosh around – giving him a good clean out. I think he may be catching on to the fact that I'm a 'quick study'.

"OK, young man, give me 25 jumping jacks." Sam didn't immediately move; he just stood there looking at me.

"OK," I said in a disgusted tone, "go and fetch the tawse. I can see that you require more training." I said it without cracking up, but before I had uttered the last sentence, Sam was already doing jumping jacks, counting them out in-between grunts and groans. I crossed my arms under my breasts, and stood there. Watching him.

When he finished, Sam was holding his stomach. He looked at me, and put his hands on his head, but his feet were stepping back-and-forth, and I knew that there would be a mess if I didn't let him get to the toilet. "You may use the bathroom, now, young man. And you will stay in there until I come back and get you. Do you understand?"

As Sam walked into the bathroom, he nodded, and whispered "Yes, Miss." He sat on the toilet, and there was an immediate flood coming out of him. I hurried into the playroom, and made myself comfortable on the couch. I could still detect the aroma of Julie's shampoo.

I lay back, my head on the side-cushion, my feet on the couch; I pulled up my outfit a few inches, and let my legs fall apart as far as they would go. My hands went down, and unconsciously moved in a slow, circular pattern around my clit, as I re-imagined Sam spanking Julie, and Julie getting herself off. I was turned on by that sight and, I now realized, I would be turned on being the one spanking her, *and* bringing her to an orgasm.

My hand stopped. I had shocked myself. Despite Sam's comments about my possible unease with men, I *loved* men. I wasn't a lesbian. Although, I now considered, I had never actually tried being with another woman that way. My mind had expanded, and now I looked at sexual preferences in a different way. Maybe I *could* make out with another woman. I closed my eyes, and attended to myself, imagining that the hand belonged to another woman. Julie.

That thought caused me to stop again. I couldn't really do it with a *friend*, could I? Unless they initiated it; allowing me to submit, but not show my own tendencies. My thoughts were running in an unexpected direction, so I concentrated, and envisaged Julie again, her hand underneath, her entire body flexing and writhing, Sam's hands on her bum. And the butt plug up her ass.

I came without realizing that I was ready. With each spasm, I visualized the progression of Julie's heat, finally culminating with that unnerving shriek. I came again, my legs suddenly straightening, and my entire body tensing, before I collapsed back onto the couch, lying there breathing heavily, and unable to get those images out of my head. I pondered whether I would remember in the morning the dreams that I would undoubtedly have tonight.

I got up from the couch and smoothed down the nurse uniform. Next time, I would probably dispense with the garter belt, and fold the nylons down below the hem of the dress. I walked slowly to the bathroom to check on Sam.

"How are you doing, young man? Are you ready for your last enema, now?" I knew how Sam would react, and I didn't blame him. He had been a trouper so far.

Sam bellowed, "Oh my God." I thought he would cry. He was finished, but still sitting on the toilet, as I had instructed.

I walked over and straddled him, taking his head in my hands tenderly. "OK, Sam. I'm just teasing you. We won't do another enema. But, at least, you know how I feel when you want to clean *me* out."

Sam smiled weakly, and asked, "May I please get up now, Nurse Kelly?" I backed off of him, and allowed him to get up. We both washed our hands at the sink, and then went back into the exam room. Sam got up on the table again, and I helped him lie down on his back. I reached over him, and grabbed the stethoscope that was hanging on the wall. I put in the earpieces, and held the other end to Sam's chest. I immediately heard his heartbeat.

I moved the sensor around, and heard slightly different sounds. I had no idea what to listen for, but I think I looked professional, checking Sam out with the stethoscope. Then, I pictured my attire: Nylons and garter with no underwear. OK, not so professional. I took the earpieces out, and hung the stethoscope around my neck.

I asked Sam, "Can you please show me your vasectomy scar?"

Sam looked surprised, but propped himself up on his elbows, and reached down, laying his dick on his stomach, and stretching the skin between his balls. He said, "I can't see it from here, but there should be a small round white mark, near the midline."

I looked more closely, and held Sam's scrotal skin in my fingers, moving it like going down a grocery list, until I found it: A single spot, about an eighth of an inch in diameter. I asked him, "Was that hard for you? I know you've never been in the hospital."

Sam shook his head. "Not that difficult. I drank several martinis before I went to the clinic. They informed me afterward that alcohol had been a bad idea, as I could bleed more. But it was a pretty quick procedure, and I talked with the doctor the whole time."

I handled his genitals, gently rolling his balls in my hands, and examining his cock. I pulled the fold of skin near the head – the 'frenula' I had just learned on the Internet – and told Sam, "I understand this is your most sensitive tissue. Down here." Sam nodded, and smiled, undoubtedly expecting me to 'do' him. I would, but not for a while. I watched Sam, as I said, "Let's see how it feels to have a needle pushed through this skin. It might be fun to try some needle play – maybe eight or ten needles lined up along your dick. I'll help you get hard, first."

Sam bellowed, "Kelly, please ..." He stopped, and then, more calmly, explained, "It's really going to hurt, and there could be a lot of bleeding. Can we please do that another time?" Sam was pleading with me, his eyes now locked on mine, willing me to let him off the 'hook' (in a manner of speaking).

I smiled, as I instantly knew what Sam would propose, if the roles were reversed. "OK, Sam. I'll give you a choice." He groaned, and hadn't even heard the choices, yet.

"Don't be a baby! Either you can let me insert two or three needles on the underside of your dick right now ... or, you can let me give you two big shots in your bottom." Before Sam could answer, I added, "And, you'll have to promise that I can insert the needles in your dick another time."

Sam scrunched his face, but answered, as I had expected. "Please, Nurse Kelly, I'd rather take the shots in my butt, than have you 'stick my dick'."

We laughed, and I nodded, turning to the counter, and looking around for the supplies. "I guess all the stuff is here, someplace?"

Sam looked over, and pointed at a drawer. "The alcohol swabs and gauze pads are in there. The syringes, needles, and saline should be in boxes on the counter. I'll walk you through the preparations."

I looked over at Sam, and said, "I'll put the syringe and needle together, swab the top of the saline bottle, draw 6 cc of air into the syringe, and inject it into the bottle above the saline. And then draw 6 cc of saline and clear the bubbles. Did I forget anything?"

Sam groaned, and shook his head. "No, Kelly, that's about it. Just don't stick yourself. If you do, please discard the needle and take a new one."

I prepared two shots, and set them on the counter where Sam could see them. "We need to dilate you now. Do you want your legs up, or do this in the knee-chest position?"

Sam replied, "I'm comfortable lying here. I'll put my legs up." I folded up the stirrups, and helped Sam get his legs up onto them. Sam scooted down to the end of the table, which had the effect of separating his buttocks, and positioning his butthole for easy access.

I put on an exam glove, and felt even more like Nurse Kelly; maybe, 'Evil Nurse Kelly'. I smiled, and lubed my middle finger. When the tip of my finger contacted Sam's anus, he quickly relaxed his muscles, and my finger entered him as far as it could go my knuckles against Sam's bum. I twisted my finger back and forth, and then pressed 'up' and found his prostate.

Sam closed his eyes, as I massaged his prostate, taking his hardening cock in my other hand. I didn't want Sam to come – I was going to tease and torment him. So I held him tightly, but did not rub him. My middle finger slid in and out of him easily, so I took off the glove, and found the bumpy glass butt plug in one of the cabinets. I lubed it, and pushed it against Sam's anus. It slowly advanced, each sphere of glass entering him, and the device holding itself in position anywhere along its length.

When the butt plug was fully in, I asked Sam, "Are you ready for your shots, now?"

Once again, Sam groaned. I could see that he was going to require a lot of training, if he were to become my sex slave. But I understood, as Sam had explained, that I would first need to submit to his training, so that I would be a safe 'top'. I could do that.

Sam had asked me to do many things, but most of them weren't that bad. And he had given me breaks many times; he was really a weak dom. Not that I knew much about all this, yet. I just knew that I would be stricter with him than he had been with me. I wondered whether Sam could submit to me; on a longer-term basis.

Sam finally answered, "I guess you can give me the shots now, Nurse Kelly."

I smiled. I liked this persona; probably more than the schoolgirl that I would be tomorrow. I helped Sam get his legs out of the stirrups, and back on the table, and he turned over onto his stomach, the ring of the glass butt plug sticking out between his buttocks. I picked up one of the shots, and opened an alcohol swab. "Where would you like the first one?"

From deep in the pillow, Sam replied, "On the right side, Nurse Kelly."

I picked a location as Sam had taught me, and then moved the position an inch higher and an inch farther to the right. I quickly swabbed Sam's butt, and uncapped the needle. I warned him, "A little stick, now." And I thrust the needle through his skin. It slipped easily into him, until only the hub was showing, as well as the huge syringe that was more than half filled with Sam's 'medicine'. I checked that the needle wasn't in a blood vessel, and then left the syringe standing on his right bum.

I wanted to surprise Sam, so I picked up the other shot and swab, and quickly swiped the same approximate location on Sam's left hip, and inserted the needle before Sam realized what was happening. I checked for blood again, and stepped back, surveying the muscular man lying on the table with two big syringes coming out of him.

I took my time giving the shots, injecting 2cc on one side, and then on the other, alternating sides, until the full 6cc was now somewhere in his fat and muscle tissue, nearly two inches under the skin. I left the needles in, and bent down, putting my chin on the exam table, looking directly into Sam's eyes. I ran my hand through his hair, and asked, "How are you doing, Sam?"

"It hurts," was his curt reply.

Sam was cooperating nicely, but I left the needles in for another minute, before I removed the shots, and dropped them into the sharps container on the wall. I took a gauze pad, and held pressure on the injection sites that were each marked by a tiny dot of blood.

"Let's get you into a knee-chest position, and we'll dilate your anus a little more."

Sam complied, and I lubed the large glass butt plug; it was more than an inch in diameter, and would prepare Sam for the mean-looking steel 'scope that Sam had used to look inside me.

When Sam was in position, I slowly inserted the large butt plug. Sam took it in very well, and I decided it was time to reward him. I had him lower himself to the table, and then lie on his left side near the edge of the table nearest me. He was watching me closely, wondering, I'm sure, what was to come next.

I announced, "I'm going to take a semen sample, now." There was a delayed reaction before Sam's eyes opened wide. I took his cock in my hands; it was only slightly hard. I flipped it onto his stomach, and used the palm of my hand to stroke him slowly, while my left hand pushed between his legs, and grabbed his balls.

Continuing like this, it didn't take long for Sam to harden sufficiently for me to put him into my mouth. I slid him into my throat and back out in long strokes, for the first time trying a 'deep throat' technique, and struggling not to gag. I tasted some pre-cum, and knew that Sam was almost there.

"Are you ready to give me some semen, now, young man?" Sam nodded, his eyes closed, and his breathing ragged. I set about my task again, and it took only a few more strokes before I felt his hot liquid jetting against the back of my throat.

I almost did gag, but managed to swallow his cum without even tasting it. I took a paper towel from above the sink, and dipped the edge under a drip of warm water. I cleaned Sam, and helped him get back into a knee-chest position.

"Ok, Sam. You can teach me how to use that long metal tube that you used to look inside me." Sam groaned again. This time I got upset. "Sam, I don't want to hear any more groans from you. The next time you complain, I'm going to take the tawse to your bottom." Sam was silent. "You may explain, now."

Sam turned his head toward the counter, and said, "Take the scope, and make sure the obturator is pushed all the way into it – that's the part that slides in and out, with the rounded tip. Then, you can lube the scope – most of the length, up to the last inch or two. Next to the scope is a small light source that you can stick down the scope; there's a switch on the end to turn it on. When you're ready, you can insert the scope. But be careful: If it doesn't slide in easily, please be gentle. It can be dangerous, if you're too rough, or push too hard."

I stepped to the foot of the exam table, put the tip of the scope on Sam's anus, and began the insertion. It went in easily, until there was only a couple inches of the shiny tube outside him. I guessed that the tip was six or seven inches inside him.

I held the scope in place, as I pulled out the 'obturator', and then turned on the light source, and stuck it partway down the scope. I could see the pink tissue of Sam's rectum through the scope. Moving it very slightly one way or the other allowed me to see pretty well inside him; but there wasn't much to see.

Sam was in the knee-chest position, with several inches of gleaming stainless steel sticking out of his butt. His eyes were closed. I was getting pretty bored, so I extracted the scope, and set it carefully in the sink. "I think that's all the exam we have time for, today, young man. Report back to me in a week, and I'll give you your final round of shots."

Sam wiggled his bottom, and said brightly, "Yes, Nurse Kelly," before lowering himself, and slipping ungracefully off the exam table.

As Sam reached for his underwear, I asked, "Sam, can we go back in the pool and jacuzzi one more time? Then, we can take a shower and get dressed for dinner." I had no idea what we would be doing.

Sam dropped his clothes back on the exam room chair, and went into the bathroom. I washed the scope, and put it in the flat round dish where I had found it in the cabinet. I heard the toilet flush; Sam stood by the exam room door, until I had finished cleaning up.

He was about to hand me a towel, when he suddenly pulled it back, and smiled at me. "That outfit is going to have to come off. And, I'm just the one to take it off you." I smiled, and we walked back into the office corner in the playroom.

Sam first bent me over, and lifted the back of the outfit. "Oh! I should have given you the semen sample back here!" Sam put his hand under me; he reached up, and flicked my clit a few times. Then I heard him sigh. "OK, I guess we can go in the pool now. And make love before we take our shower."

Sam pulled down the hem of my outfit, and I stood up, in the 'standing' position. Sam unzipped the front of my outfit slowly, the zipper clicking as it went down, and down still further, until the outfit was completely unzipped. Sam took it off my shoulders, and I lowered my arms so that he could remove it.

I now stood there wearing only a garter belt and stockings. I felt sexy. Next time, we would have to play more with me wearing this outfit; maybe with Sam spanking the errant Nurse Kelly? Sam kneeled down, and carefully unclipped the garters, but I pushed him away, and took the belt and stockings off myself. I took the towel, and wrapped it around my waist.

We walked upstairs, and out to the pool. I dropped my towel on the deck, and hopped into the jacuzzi, and Sam followed me. Sam hit the air switch, and the jets came alive, bubbles rising around and under us, tickling my legs, and making me think back – it was just yesterday! – to the electrical stimulation experience. At one point, that had felt like bubbles breaking over my skin.

I heard Sam say 'Shit!' under his breath. I looked at him to see what was wrong. He shrugged, and explained, "I had hoped that we would make love in the jacuzzi the next time we got in ... but I forgot to bring some KY up here. Well, I don't think I'll be ready again for a while, anyway. You've tired me out today!"

And then Sam looked at me with a grin, and said, "But I can *do* you! There are some fun things we can do with the jets."

Sam didn't know that I had masturbated in the playroom. "Sam, I'm a little tired, too. And I'm still sore down there. Maybe we can just wait until we go to bed tonight to make love?"

Sam began to laugh, and it turned into a roar. "Not even married, yet! Only your second time over to my house! And, you're already coming up with excuses. Do you have a headache, too?"

Fortunately, I knew Sam was teasing me, and fortunately, he knew that I knew. He started tickling me, and then put his arms around me, and we kissed enthusiastically. The exercise and tension of the day was sapping us, and the jacuzzi was making us even more tired.

I sat on the rock ledge, dangling my feet in the water, and letting the cooler air caress my skin. "Maybe, we should take a nap?"

Sam laughed, and we got out of the jacuzzi and, wrapped again in our towels, went back downstairs and got in the shower. Sam bathed me. And himself. I realized that I was wiped out. It was only a little after five o'clock, but we slipped under the satin covers of the playroom bed, and drifted off to a deep sleep.

CHAPTER 13: EVENING AT HOME

Kelly had immediately fallen asleep after the jacuzzi and shower, and I had crawled into bed with her. But my brain wouldn't stop, it wouldn't even slow down. Instead of sleeping, I became more awake, and the fantasies rolling through my head re-awakened my sexual desire.

Suddenly, I sat up, realizing that I had forgotten something: Had I been recording the action in the playroom, when Kelly's friends had been here? I realized that I hadn't triggered the recorders. We would just have to play the scenes over in our minds. Probably just as well. I would not have recorded Julie and Linda without their permission ... or at least their knowledge.

Getting out of bed, I grabbed the large towel that I had been wrapped in earlier. I spread the towel on the playroom couch, and lay down, closing my eyes and re-imagining the scene of Linda hesitantly walking toward me, ready for her birthday spanking. Lying across my lap. Lifting her middle, as I lowered her underwear.

I was now in a full state of arousal, my erection pressing into my stomach, as I stroked myself with an open palm. I never made it through Linda's spanking, my orgasm exploding, spouting across my stomach and up to my chest. I was spent.

I must have dozed for a while, as I awakened with viscous fluid coating a line from my navel nearly to my neck. I got up from the couch, taking the towel into the shower room, where I cleaned up quickly under a heavy stream of scalding water. I went up to the master bedroom, where I dressed in casual slacks and a polo shirt, and slipped on a pair of sandals.

Exiting the walk-in closet and passing through the bathroom, I glanced in the mirror. I felt different, but could not detect any change in my reflection. The experiences with Julie and Linda today – with Kelly's assistance – dominated my mind, and it felt like a new world had opened itself to me. It was a world that I had imagined, and re-imagined ... but I never really would have imagined that it could become real.

I went down to the kitchen, and grabbed an IPA, my favorite type of beer, from the fridge. Taking a swig, the hops burst on my tongue in a combination of bitterness and exotic flavors. India pale ale had been created during Britain's imperial era, extra hops being added to the beer in order to preserve it during the long sailing voyage to India.

I started for the door to the patio, and suddenly remembered; I put the beer on the kitchen counter, and ran down to the playroom, settling into my executive chair, and opening a file on my computer: The 'to-do' list for Kelly's birthday party. I added 'CAKE' in capital letters to the top of the list, and sat back, thinking what else I should add. Oh, yes – another patio chair.

In fantasizing about Kelly's friends and some birthday 'games' we could play, I had envisioned a large 'lazy Susan' – a circular platform on which the girls could position themselves, preferably in a knee-chest position, their bottoms facing outward.

In my mind's eye, I watched the girls playing a game – perhaps a card game – and then spinning them around to reward, or punish, each of them, depending on the results of the game. Perverted, I know. But I had already bought the plywood, and had already found a large ball-bearing 'turntable' on which I could mount the platform.

At that time, I hadn't held much hope for the girls actually doing something like that. I had set that project aside, as Kelly's fantasy role-play took precedence, and required some designing and building that I had only begun. I pictured the girls in a knee-chest position on the platform, and realized that I would need to make some measurements.

I pulled a tape measure from one of my desk drawers, and got down on the floor in a knee-chest position, my hands in front of me. I realized that the platform would need to be eight feet in diameter, requiring two 4x8-foot plywood sheets, somehow joined, and then cut into a circular pattern. It would take up most of the pool room.

I sat at my computer, and added a few items to the to-do list: Velcro, playing cards and poker chips (which I was sure were in the house somewhere, I just had to find them), and thick foam rubber. Or, perhaps knee pads. I visualized the contraption, and made a few sketches.

I would still need to decide which 'game' the girls would play – the result, of course, being spanks, needles, or rectal insertions, depending on who won and what the score had been. The idea of betting, and increasing the bets (more spanks, or whatever) came to me, and I thought about a 'different' kind of poker. Not exactly strip poker, as the girls would already be undressed; but perhaps 'spank poker'.

The main party favors had already been purchased, but I still needed to visit an Internet sex shop, in order to find another 'favor' that I thought the girls would appreciate. And, I still needed to visit the costume shop, or perhaps a second-hand store that had some Victorian clothing.

Kelly's birthday was three weeks from today, so I should easily be able to finish all the projects. Whether Kelly would be 'ready' for the experience – psychologically and socially – was another question. But the openness and enthusiasm of her friends today portended a positive outlook, and hopefully acceptance of being the starlet of a role-play experience in front of her friends.

I had forgotten my beer upstairs, and made my way back to the kitchen to retrieve it, turning on lights inside and outside, as the sun was now low on the Western horizon, the sky streaked with red, violet, lavender, and plum-colored clouds, as twilight descended. The beer wasn't as cold as it should be, but I brought it downstairs to my desk and continued working on the to-do list, and the design of a few special 'props' and gadgets.

I still wasn't sure that the girls would go for my game idea, but I wanted to be prepared; they had already surprised me today with their interest in, and capacity to take, spankings. I made a mental note to open a discussion with them on their fantasies and sexual interests ... although that might have to be done individually, and not in a group setting.

Then it hit me that a modified version of 'Truth or Dare' might be fun, *and* elicit the answers that I sought. The possibilities were mind boggling, and I realized that one 'party' would not be enough to expose the girls to my myriad fantasies ... assuming Kelly would also be interested in expanding our 'play' to other people. I began pondering what other 'experiences' Kelly and I could share with her friends. That is, *if* they responded positively to our games at Kelly's birthday party.

I heard Kelly stir, and glanced at the clock behind my desk. It was already 7:30PM, and I hoped that the evening would be more than a somnolent bridge to the day I had planned for tomorrow. I no longer felt tired. But Kelly and I had done a lot today – and yesterday – and I contemplated whether a simple 'evening at home' might be the best option. But I had not planned to cook, and it was now too late to start marketing.

I walked over to the bed. Kelly's eyes flickered open, and she yawned, as her hands stretched behind her to the headboard. I smiled at her, "Good morning, sleepyhead!" I leaned over and kissed her full on her moist, warm, and very inviting lips.

Kelly's eyes flew open, and she started to sit up. "What time is it?" She lifted her head, and looked around the room, which was now in a subdued light, except for the desk area. "Boy, I must have been tired! How long did we sleep?" Kelly was not yet awake enough to realize that I had already gotten showered and dressed.

I chuckled, "You slept soundly for a couple of hours. A nice catnap." Kelly's head plopped back on the pillow, and I sat down on the edge of the bed, next to her. "What would you like to do for dinner, Kelly?" I asked. It was Saturday night, and if we wanted to eat out, I would need to make reservations.

Kelly yawned again, causing me to yawn, also, despite feeling wide awake. She looked at me thoughtfully, and suddenly blurted, "Let's get Chinese take-out. We can eat by the pool, or in the dining room, and then I'd like some dessert."

I wasn't sure what Kelly meant, so asked her. "Dessert? What did you have in mind?" I was trying to remember if I had ice cream in the freezer.

She replied, "I'm thinking of caramel sauce," then reached down and grasped my manhood through my slacks. We laughed, but I thought it was a pretty good idea.

"That sounds good. What kinds of Chinese dishes do you like?" I didn't think she was going to sit with me and peruse the take-out menu, and I wanted to order things that she really liked.

Kelly sat up, the sheets falling into her lap, and her long hair cascading down around her, now glittering with specks of gold glints from the lights above. The compound curves of her firm breasts thrust them out aggressively and, as many times as I'd seen them, still caused an awakening down below. The vision before me once again provided motivation to grab my camera, but I had now decided that our next 'lunch' get-together would be a formal photo shoot. Well, not *that* formal.

My mind returned to the here-and-now, as Kelly announced, "You pick it. I like everything." I was just thinking about giving Kelly 'everything', when she slid out of bed, stretched her long legs, torso, and arms, and casually walked to the bathroom.

I went up to the kitchen, and found a small pamphlet with the menu of my favorite local Chinese dig, and started making checkmarks next to some of the dishes. My favorites are the spicy Szechuan creations, but I wanted to get a big enough selection that we would both be satisfied, and have some leftovers for a late-night snack, or lunch in a couple of days.

I skipped the soup, and decided on the PuPu platter, to start. I scanned the menu, and selected the Mu Shu pork, Mongolian beef, Peking duck with pancakes and plum sauce, and honey walnut shrimp, along with the Yan Chow fried rice, and garlic string beans. With all of this, there was no need to order noodles. I always ordered too much, but hoped Kelly liked at least a few of the dishes.

I looked at the desserts, and my mouth watered; I decided to skip the pineapple fritters (they would be soggy by the time we got to them) and the green tea ice cream (which I considered buying at the market), but went for two mango crèmes brulées, which would save in the fridge, if we were too full to indulge tonight. Anyway, I still had the caramel sauce, and looked forward to Kelly lapping and sucking its gooey sweetness from me.

I dialed the restaurant, and began placing the order. As I was folding the take-out menu, I saw that they delivered! I gave them my address, and they confirmed the order, and said it would be here in a little more than half an hour.

Kelly came up to the kitchen a few minutes later, looking fresh and rested, and wearing a long t-shirt with apparently only a pair of panties underneath. Her long, muscular legs, supporting her majestically, had already begun to show their summer tan. Kelly was big on top, but firm enough to get by without a bra, and I was compelled to reach out and fondle her mammary assets through the t-shirt.

Kelly giggled, and then we became serious; our bodies fused as I pressed up against her, and pulled her to me. We kissed long and vigorously, until we both had to come up for air. I gave her a pop on her behind, and Kelly jumped. I said, "I guess I'm *overdressed*, tonight." We would rectify that later, after our dinner was delivered.

"Kelly, what would you think about dinner and a movie, tonight? I thought it might be fun to eat in the playroom, while we watched a romantic old movie on the big screen." I was thinking of '*Casablanca*' or, perhaps '*Gone With the Wind*'. Or, maybe '*Dr. Zhivago*'. Or even '*West Side Story*'. "I have a collection of a few hundred movies on my server. What would you enjoy watching?"

Kelly thought a moment, and smiled, "That sounds nice. How about one of the '*Indiana Jones* movies?' Or maybe '*True Lies*'?" I coughed; I had to keep in mind that there was still an age difference, if not 'gap' between us.

"OK, whatever you want." I pulled out a couple of placemats and dinner plates, as well as two sets of silverware and a couple pairs of chopsticks, and handed everything to Kelly, suggesting that she set our places at the coffee table.

Kelly frowned, then suddenly grinned and looked up at me, "Why don't we have a 'picnic' on the bed?"

It was an interesting idea. I would have to flip the video projection, but that was only one button to push on the remote. And, it could get messy – and smelly; we might not want to sleep in the playroom, after filling it with the aroma of Chinese food. But, we could sleep upstairs.

I still thought of the master bedroom as being for my wife and I, and had not taken anybody up there for years. Except for Kelly, when I got dressed in the closet, and she had masturbated on top of me on the bed. But it was time that I jettison the last vestiges of my wife, except of course, in my memory, and recognize that Kelly was now my 'partner'. Maybe this was a good idea.

Being the obsessive-compulsive person that I am, I told Kelly I would meet her in the playroom, then I ran upstairs to the linen closet. I grabbed a king-sized sheet, and an old blanket.

Kelly and I threw the blanket over the satin sheet of the bed, and then covered it with the old sheet I had retrieved from upstairs. We tucked everything in, and Kelly set-up the place mats on top of the sheet. I would bring down a lacquered tray to hold our drinks safely, while we moved around on the bed. I cued-up '*The Temple of Doom*' – not exactly the romantic film that I had envisioned, but it would be fun. We went up to the kitchen, and I poured a beer for myself, and a Diet Coke for Kelly, and handed them to her to bring downstairs.

A few minutes later, our dinner was delivered. I grabbed a handful of napkins, and two lacquered trays, bringing them, and the bag loaded with take-out boxes of Chinese food, down to the playroom. I passed everything to Kelly, who was already sitting on the bed.

While I hoped that we wouldn't make too much of a mess with the Chinese food, I knew what Kelly had planned for dessert. So I quickly went into the bathroom, and changed into a pair of running shorts and a t-shirt. I walked to the desk, and picked up the master remote, which I brought back to the bed, climbing in carefully, so that our drinks wouldn't fall over. Kelly was already unloading boxes of food onto one of the trays. She looked cute, sitting cross-legged in her long t-shirt, which she had gathered into her lap.

Like a maestro directing his orchestra, I pushed buttons on the remote. The screen came down, the sound system and projector came on, and the room lights dimmed. I adjusted the lights over the bed a bit brighter, so that we could see our food.

We were too close to the screen, but it would envelop us in the action, and the high-def resolution would keep the video detailed – like sitting near the front of a big movie theater. One of the theater companies had the motto: 'Go big, or go home', but in this case we had gone big *at* home. (I had no doubt that *I* would be 'going big', by the time we got to dessert.) I started the movie, and adjusted the volume of the multi-channel sound system.

As the film began, Kelly and I helped ourselves to the steaming food, using both the chopsticks and forks to take portions of each of the dishes. It smelled delicious, and

Kelly enthusiastically tasted all of them. "Yum, this is good! Guess I was getting hungrier than I thought."

I realized that I had only served her soup today, plus a few snacks. We were both famished. I looked up at the screen, as one of my favorite scenes began: Indiana, Willie, and Short Round bailing from a pilotless plane in a raft ... which ends up landing in a raging river, running the whitewater rapids. It was silly, but fun to watch. Kelly was obviously enjoying both the film and our Chinese feast.

By the scene with the three of them riding elephants to Pankot palace, we were both stuffed. Kelly lay back, her head on a folded pillow, raised just enough to watch the movie; she had pulled up her t-shirt, her hands rubbing her stomach. She said, "That was great. But I don't think I can eat anymore."

I looked at her concernedly, and she quickly added, "But I'm sure I'll be hungry for 'dessert' by the time the movie is over." I laughed, and lay down next to her, my head on the same pillow, both of us engrossed in the action. It was probably good that we had finished our meal before the scene in Pankot palace, where everyone is served monkey brains!

The movie ended, and we were both still recovering from the meal. We got off the bed, and brought everything back up to the kitchen, putting the multitude of take-out boxes into the fridge, and refilling our drinks. We walked out onto the patio, and sat at the table. The pool lights were on, as were the landscape lights that illuminated the tallest trees, and the small lights along the winding path. The night was still, and the air still warm.

"Kelly, we haven't had a chance to talk much about your friends' visit. What do you think about what happened?" Of course, I was thinking of Julie's masturbation scene. But, there was also Linda's birthday spanking, and all of our discussion right here at the patio table.

Kelly pondered for a moment. "Well, I was pretty surprised ..."

I looked at her and waited. I finally asked, "About what, specifically? Which part? Who?"

Kelly laughed, and took a long swig of her Diet Coke. "First, I was surprised that you told them so much ... and that they didn't freak out. For example, your pretend-discussion with Julie, where she apparently ended-up saying that she would let you masturbate her." Kelly chuckled, and looked out at the lights and shadows of the backyard – the trees, boulders, lit path, and blackness beyond. The sky was full of summer stars.

"And then, Linda almost *asking* you to spank her. I guess she knew it was going to happen, and wanted to get it over with." Kelly looked at me, but I frowned.

I provided an alternate viewpoint. "I agree it was great that she requested her spanking – or at least volunteered for it to happen then; but I think she was looking forward to it. She probably masturbated many times, thinking about it. Wondering what would happen. In detail."

Kelly focused on something far-off, and then she looked into my eyes. "You may be right, Sam. I'm not sure. The fact she had admitted getting turned-on by her school paddlings threw me for a loop. I don't know exactly what was happening with her, this afternoon. Except that Linda certainly didn't put up a fight, cooperated well, and held still for the spanking you gave her."

Now I could see that a light had turned on in Kelly's brain. She smiled, "This wasn't the first time she's been spanked, obviously. You weren't that easy on her, but she took it as if it were nothing. As if I had been taking it." Another light turned on. "Maybe she has a boyfriend who spanks her. And she just doesn't feel comfortable opening up to us?"

I laughed. This was getting better all the time. "Kelly, I had the same thought about Julie: She took her punishment 'too well', if you know what I mean. I know she's done a lot, and is very mature ... but someone not having experienced a hard spanking – recently – probably would have made more noise, and moved more."

That got me thinking. "And, neither one of them even tried to put their hands behind them. I only warned Julie because of the paddle; I hadn't said anything to Linda."

I looked into Kelly's eyes, and shook my head, "Is it possible that they're both in the scene? While I was spanking her – given her reaction, or lack thereof – I imagined that Julie might have been a domme. I was thinking that she could probably train *us*. But now, I'm not sure, anymore."

Kelly reasoned, "We know they've both had spanking experiences in their past. So they knew what to expect, and what you expected from them. In a way, they're trained, already; maybe just not to your standards."

I shook my head again, to get the cobwebs out; my mind was boggled by the situation, and the possibilities. "If they both can see spanking as a turn-on, that bodes well for getting them to 'play' with us. We might all be very compatible. It would be amazing." My mouth fell open, and then I consciously closed it, smiling as I realized that, now, *I* was the 'fish'.

Looking at Kelly, I added, "I know. I shouldn't get my hopes up. But I was astonished by what happened today."

Kelly smiled, "It was pretty amazing. I guess, since we're being honest, I should tell you something." She turned her head to the right, looking at something in the backyard, and then immediately back to me.

"OK, what is it? I hope you're not upset with me for taking things so far?"

Kelly was shaking her head; her eyes closed for a moment. "No, not at all. I think it worked out perfectly, for both of my friends. But I was stunned, as well. Just thinking about Linda watching Julie's performance is incredible. Linda's the most conservative of the four of us."

Kelly thought a moment, and added, "I think they've been talking about this. Or, maybe they were researching it on the 'net. And, like you suggested, both of them have probably been wondering – if not fantasizing – about what would happen. I think you did a good job, under the circumstances ..."

I grinned, "Why, thank you, Miss!"

Kelly put on a solemn face, "But I'm glad my friends didn't end-up helping *you* to masturbate!"

I laughed, as that had been one of the thoughts flying through my head while Julie was doing her thing. "Why? Would that upset you?" I took a swallow of beer, and hoped I wouldn't break out in hysterics, spraying it over Kelly. That brought to mind our upcoming 'dessert'.

Kelly put her hands on her hips, still sitting in the patio chair. "Buster!" she began ... and then she softened and smiled, "Only when *I'm* there!"

Her hands came off her hips, and they waved in the air, as she softened further, nearly melting, and continued, "Well, maybe *later*, I might let them 'take care of you'. We'll have to see how things develop."

Kelly wrung her hands, more serious, now, "I don't know *what* I want. So-far, it's been fun," she smiled at me, "in a perverted sort of way." She laughed easily, and threw her hair back. "But I don't want to lose you." She pouted. "I don't mind my friends playing with us, but ..." Kelly was silent, her hands now in her lap, and her gaze on them, as she fidgeted.

I got up and pulled Kelly from her chair, putting my arms around her and giving her a big hug. Then, I released my grip, my mouth moving toward Kelly's. We kissed intensely, neither holding the other – both leaning forward, the warm, sweet wetness of our mouths, our dueling tongues, and our engorged lips in intimate contact.

I lightly ran my hands down Kelly's sides, from her shoulders to her hips. Then, they came up and grazed over her breasts, not really touching until the erect nipples outlined on her t-shirt passed under my fingers. Then, I held her firmly by the hips, both hands steadying us.

"Kelly, I don't want to lose you, either. I don't want anything – or anyone – to impede the development of our relationship."

I gazed into Kelly's hazel eyes, now nearly black, cat-like, slits of reflected lights from the backyard, sparkles of color making her look mysterious. "I just thought, if you were as turned-on as I was about how your friends reacted, then playing together might expand both of our horizons." I was hopeful. I really didn't want to jeopardize our relationship in any way.

Kelly jumped, as though an electric current had run through her. Her hair flew out, not unlike the effect of a sudden burst of static electricity. Or lightning. "Sam! That's what I wanted – needed – to tell you." Kelly sat back down, more serious now, but with an asymmetric smile. I also sat, and finished off the bottle of beer. I just listened, for a change.

I had not informed Sam, at the time: I had just left him in the bathroom, after injecting a dozen syringes of saltwater into his ass. It had been interesting, the only turn-on being Sam's acceptance, despite the fact that he clearly would have preferred it the other way around. Sam was allowing me to find my turn-ons. As he said, I was 'expanding my horizons'. I wondered where this would lead.

But, now I had to be honest. And, I wanted to hear his reaction. "Sam, I think you saw that I was getting turned-on watching Julie." Sam nodded. "I was already turned-on by watching you spank her. And then she masturbated – so naturally, so physically ... that I was drawn to do the same. I wonder what Linda must have thought – the two of us masturbating in front of her? But what Julie consummated, I didn't. I felt really horny after that."

Sam broke in, unwanted, "All you had to do was tell me. I would have taken care of it for you!" He chuckled. But this wasn't funny.

I looked at Sam seriously. "Sam, what I wanted to tell you earlier, was that when I left you in the bathroom, after your enema, I laid on the couch, looking at the loveseat, and re-imagining Julie. And, got myself off."

Sam broke out a big smile. "Is *that* all you wanted to tell me?" He laughed. "Kelly, I was ultra-turned on by the whole experience. Why shouldn't you have been?" He looked at me, "And I don't have any problem with you masturbating whenever you need it ... or feel like it. With or without me. But, of course, I would be happy to make love to you anytime ... or help get you off. Just tell me what you want, because I want to satisfy you."

Sam had a way of relaxing me. It shouldn't have been a big deal to tell him earlier. But it didn't change anything: I had been turned on, by watching another woman masturbate. It was one of the hottest things I'd ever seen. I really *didn't* know what I wanted. Only a few months ago

I had wanted nothing but to finish my degree and get a good job; nothing, particularly, turned me on.

Now, it seemed like everything turned me on. Well, not everything; but a lot of new things. I wondered whether the novelty would wear off, in time. Sam and I had only been 'together' for a month or so. At some point, he would run out of new things to share. What would he want next? And, what would *I* want?

Now, I laughed. How incredible the mind is, with associations. What do I *want*? I looked at Sam seriously, again. "Sam, I want my dessert, now! Actually, I think I'd like two desserts." Sam cracked up, and so did I.

When he calmed down, Sam asked me "Shall I bring out the crèmes brulées? Eat them under the stars?"

Sam was so romantic. When he wanted to be. I told him, "No, let's leave those for breakfast. Tonight, I want some 'caramel head'." We were both laughing. But this conversation – and a continuing train of thoughts about Julie – was making me horny again.

We got up, and brought the remains of our drinks into the kitchen. On the way downstairs, I realized that I was still sore 'down there'; maybe Sam would have to help me unselfishly. Not that he was a selfish man, as he had demonstrated many times. Sam pushed a button that raised the video screen, and I climbed onto the bed.

Sam walked around the bed and opened a dresser drawer, taking out something. When I saw the flash, I realized that he was re-lighting the candles. At least some of them: The ones that hadn't burned down all the way.

The lights were still low around the room, except for over the bed. Sam had insisted that we cover the bed with the blanket and old sheet, but I didn't see any Chinese food stains. Sam put on some soft Jazz at low volume, and finally came back to the bed.

Sam smiled, and bowed, before hopping onto the bed. "How can I do you, Miss?"

Well, he had gotten it right. "Sam, I would love to make love to you ... but it's going to have to wait. I'm still a little sore from our Kama Sutra gymnastics this morning." Sam looked at me inquiringly, but didn't say anything.

Was I going to suggest this? Somehow, I knew it was the only thing that would help, right now. "Sam, as I told you, I would like *two* desserts. In a manner of speaking." He laughed, but was all ears. "The second dessert will be the caramel sauce, and maybe some other accompaniments. Do you still have the whipped cream?"

Sam laughed, and said, "Of course. I bought two cans, and one wasn't touched." I was learning that he was always the Boy Scout.

I continued before having the chance to change my mind. I knew this would be a turn-on for Sam, too; it would get him ready for me to eat him. Sam waited patiently to hear what I would suggest; he was going to be surprised.

"Sam, for the first 'dessert', I would like us to role-play." Sam's eyes widened, as did his grin. Even if we weren't going to make love, I think I made his day. Or, at least, his evening. I outlined my plan – it was simple; I only had to blurt it out. "I would like us to re-enact the scene with Julie. I'll do myself, if you don't mind. Just like she did."

My mind continued the sentence: 'Hopefully'. I was now aching for release. I realized my bottom might be aching after the role-play, but I felt the need to re-imagine the scene – and act it out. I couldn't get the image of Julie – lying across Sam's lap, her hands moving unseen, her back arched – out of my head.

I think Sam was stunned again, for the umpteenth time today. "Kelly, that's a *great* idea! Why didn't I think of that?" And then, "I'll get everything ready, and meet you by the couch." My mind whirled. Then I thought about the scene; if we were going to do this, we should do it right.

While Sam was retrieving the thermometer and small butt plug from the bathroom, I walked to the desk, and opened my rolling case. I had thongs, and I had shorts – not denim cut-offs, like Julie's, but they would have to do. I also put on the white blouse that I had brought for tomorrow's 'schoolgirl' scene. I went over to the couch and sat down, roughly where Julie had been. And waited. Although I knew exactly what was going to happen, I was getting nervous.

Sam sat down on the loveseat, and put a small box of supplies on the coffee table: The paddles, already-lubed thermometer and butt plug. This wasn't a big deal – we had done nearly the same thing before. But my stomach fluttered. I speculated on how Julie felt, but I couldn't: We obviously didn't know the whole story – her prior experiences, her fantasies. Sam put the paddles on the loveseat next to his right hip, and looked up at me, waiting.

I made up my mind that I was going to do this. Still sitting on the couch, I put my hands on my hips, and said, indignantly, "I wish one of *my* boyfriends would take me over his lap!"

Sam smiled, "Well, if you'd like a sample, I would be happy to indulge you."

Sam obviously remembered the scene well. I had no doubt he would be thinking of it, as I sucked the caramel from his dick. Or, thinking of the re-enactment we were about to do together ...

I stood up, and said, "Well, I guess if Linda can do it, then so can I." I couldn't help but smile, as I walked slowly to Sam. I stood to the side of him, as I looked into his eyes, unfastened my shorts, and slid them down. Sam's eyes widened, as he saw that I was wearing a black thong – nearly the same as Julie's.

I stood back up, and asked him, "Do I need to pull my underwear down, too?" Sam just nodded. I was almost laughing now. I wasn't sure we could do this scene seriously. But that's what it would take for me to find my release.

I pushed my thong down, letting it drop to the floor – the thong and shorts now around my ankles. Sam looked at my triangle – which seemed much larger now than when I had gotten the waxing. It had seemed positively tiny – there had been no point in removing any more, as I could wear whatever I wanted without my hair showing.

Sam looked up at me, and said, "Very nice." Then he said in a mock-serious tone, "Now get over my lap, young lady!"

I was on autopilot, now, my mind almost a blank, as I draped my body over Sam's lap. He pulled me to him, and I felt his erection against my hip. Had Julie felt the same thing? Then I conjectured whether Julie might have gotten turned-on, at least partially, by feeling Sam's excitement. I tried to relax. Sam just sat there. Then, I remembered ...

"Are you afraid to do it?" I taunted him.

His laugh was a cackle. "Are you ready for a Level-7 punishment, young lady?"

I tried to not laugh; it would get serious soon enough. "I know what that means. And I'm ready for whatever you want to give me!" And, I was.

Sam explained, as he had with Julie, "Your responsibility is to keep yourself in position, and never put your hands behind you. Do you understand?"

"Yes Sir," I croaked. Now, I wasn't acting: The tension was almost too much.

Sam didn't delay. "Here are your 50 hand spanks." And my bum felt the sting of Sam's large hands, alternating from side-to-side, increasing in intensity, until I remembered well what a spanking felt like. Now, he was giving me double-spanks on each side, and really going for it. Sam had never spanked me this hard with his hand, before. It really smarted! I grabbed the loveseat cushion, and closed my eyes.

The spanks rained down one after the other, not giving me a chance to recover between them. It was getting challenging, but, then, Sam stopped suddenly. I hadn't been counting. Sam rubbed my bottom, and slipped his hand under my blouse, up my back, and over each shoulder, massaging my taut muscles, moving down my spine, and ending with a nice lower-back rub.

He leaned over and said, "Please try to relax, it will hurt more, if you're tense." He straightened my blouse, and sat up. "Are you ready for the smooth paddle, now?"

I swallowed hard, and replied quickly, "Yes, Sir."

Sam paddled me solidly, covering the lower parts of my bum, as well as the middle and sides. I received only ten swats, but my bottom felt like nuclear fuel, radiating heat, and exploding in pain. I guess I had forgotten.

But I hadn't forgotten that I would be getting an even more severe spanking tomorrow. I put it out of my mind, which was already overloaded with sensations. I was proud that I had held my position throughout tonight's spanking.

"That was just a taste of the smooth paddle. We'll finish with a sample of the textured paddle. I want to hear a 'Ready!' and, after each stroke, the count and a 'Thank you, Sir'."

I took a deep breath, and let it out slowly. "Ready, Sir!"

A blaze of searing heat on my already-sore bottom startled me, and I let out a cry. But I recovered quickly, and remembered to say, "One, thank you, Sir!" Sam, sympathetically, rubbed my right side.

Then, the paddle was on my left cheek. I took another breath. "Ready!" And I felt another nuclear blast. I couldn't help it. "Ooowww! Sir!" I took a deep breath. "Two, thank you, Sir."

Sam was rubbing my bum again. "Very good, young lady. Now, you will take your corner time." He reached over to the coffee table, picking up the thermometer, and – without any further discussion – separated my butt cheeks and inserted the hexagonal glass cylinder. It felt OK. I wasn't turned on by it, but didn't mind it, either. As usual, Sam was moving it around, in and out of me. Now, it would be my turn for some action.

Sam had remembered the details. "You took your punishment well ... and maybe even enjoyed it. For behaving so well during your spanking, you may do yourself, while we finish your corner time. Or, if you prefer, I could help you." Sam knew that this was going to be a solo performance.

My bottom stung, but I was starting to actually like the feel; now that the spanking was over. My hands went down, sliding over my belly, and my soon-to-be-gone triangle, arriving at their target. Sam's hands settled on my bum, slightly pushing me down into his lap, which pressed my hand more tightly against myself. I felt the thermometer slide out of me, and – a few moments later – the butt plug was against me, entering me, then fully inside me.

Sam massaged my bum, and my thoughts returned to Julie, as her experience replayed itself in my mind. Oh, my God! My eyes closed and my back arching, my hands did their job expertly. I saw Julie, writhing with energy, emotion. It was pure animal passion. She was a beautiful girl. Hands moving, clit pulsating. I was ready. I came, over and over. I squeezed out my thick secretions until my head was light, and I thought I might faint. There was no scream; I could barely catch my breath.

Sam wisely allowed me to lie there for several minutes. "Are you ready to stand up, now, young lady?" He was still rubbing my bottom, and now also my lower back. It felt good. I wasn't sure I could get up, or that I wanted to. Now, I remembered Julie's whine: As enervated as the experience had made us, we could probably have fallen asleep across Sam's lap.

Finally, I slid off Sam, and stood up, assuming the standing position. Sam got up and hugged me. As Julie had done – yes I remembered this well – I reached up and held Sam's face, and began to give him the peck that Julie had. But my tongue forced our mouths to open, and we kissed hungrily, desperately. I held Sam close, knowing now that this was what I wanted: Certainly Sam … and these experiences, in some form.

Sam asked, "So how was it?"

I reversed the roles slightly, and said, "Great. Thank you. But I think you enjoyed it as much as I did!" I laughed, and Sam glowered, sardonically. I pulled up my thong, and then my shorts, zipping them, but not bothering with buttons or belt.

Sam smiled, and said, "Yes, it was enjoyable. I think that was a pretty good recreation of the experience that we gave Julie. I don't think I enjoyed it quite as much as you did," he smirked, and added, "but I'm sure I'll enjoy the second dessert!" We hugged again, and I told Sam to fetch the dessert fixings; in the way that I would command a dog. Then I imagined a leather collar around Sam's neck.

As he went upstairs, I stepped into the bathroom.

When I returned to the playroom, carrying a large tray with dessert 'supplies', Kelly was waiting for me on the bed. As I approached, Kelly got into a knee-chest position. "What do you think?" she asked.

I wasn't sure what she was asking. "You have a beautiful bottom, Kelly."

Kelly giggled, and clarified, "I was asking how red my bum is – if it looks like Julie's, after you finished with her."

It sounded like there might be some competition between the girls. That would play into my plans for Kelly's birthday party very well. I put the tray with the caramel, whipped cream, and some other dessert items on the bed, and climbed up, then inspected Kelly's bottom. "It looks suitably red, for a sample spanking. But just wait until tomorrow, young lady!"

Kelly crawled over and sat down next to me on the old sheet that was ready, just in case our dessert got messy. I hoped that Kelly wouldn't take it as an indication of my age or how tired I was, but I suggested, "I'm looking 'a-head' to this, and I'll have to get a shower anyway, but could I suggest that we don't engage in a full food orgy tonight? I'm hoping we could do that as another lunch experience sometime. Maybe you could keep the mess localized, tonight?"

Kelly was nonplussed. "Sure, Sam. Whatever you want."

"Since you didn't get to actually taste much last time, I brought a selection; you can consider it foreplay." I couldn't resist, "And then, we'll get to the foreskin play." Kelly laughed, and I picked a first sampler selection. "This is the Kahlua, that was so delicious, drunk from your body." I handed the miniature bottle of thick, syrupy liqueur to her, and she tasted it. I now visualized drinking it from her well, using a straw.

"And these are the Florentine cookies." She tried those.

"Yum. But I'm getting pretty full. Just enough room left to eat you. And you're lower-calorie." I wasn't so sure about that, when the caramel sauce and whipped cream were taken into account. But Kelly didn't have to worry about her weight; her figure perfect as it was.

I picked a grape off the bunch, held it up, and popped it into her mouth. "Oh, I forgot." I dropped a few grapes into a small glass of Grand Marnier, and then pulled one out for Kelly.

She exclaimed, "Oh! That's pretty strong. I'm surprised it didn't burn more."

I laughed, and explained, "I dried-off the grapes, before putting them in you. I was hoping the alcohol would be a good preventive measure. I'm glad you didn't get a urinary tract infection. Or, a yeast infection!" Kelly frowned.

Then, Kelly brightened, "Let's get to the good stuff!" She reached over and picked up the can of whipped cream, shaking it, and pulling off the seal. I thought she was going to disregard my request and spray me with it, but she waited until I could lie in a convenient position, with her between my legs.

I closed my eyes, and visualized the role-play that Kelly and I had just completed. It was amazing. But the original experience with Julie had turned us both on incredibly, even more than Kelly's role-play of the scene.

Kelly sprayed whipped cream in a cone, covering my still-flaccid penis. Then, she started eating.

I visualized Julie, over my lap, masturbating, as I inserted the butt plug. And visualized the corresponding scene with Kelly. They were both passionate, and both had resulted in great orgasms – from what I could tell. But Julie's emotions were feral, savage, displaying raw hunger and lust. I had never seen anything quite like it.

I was getting harder, and bigger, by the second. Kelly had stopped sucking, licking, and lapping the whipped cream, and I now felt the cold gooeyness of the caramel sauce.

I saw Linda in my mind's eye, as she lay across my lap, and I folded back her dress. She had been resigned to the spanking, and I had initially thought that she might just be doing it to maintain the wild image that Julie always tried to create for herself and her friends. But Linda was very different from Julie, much more cerebral, quiet, reserved. That was why *her* performance here today was so astounding.

Kelly had me in her mouth, now. She had coated me entirely with the caramel sauce. She held me tightly, her fingers wrapped around the base, and moved her lips from the tip, over the head, and down the shaft, moving her tongue around, and sucking the caramel sauce off of me. The combination of those feelings was amazing.

My mind's eye saw Linda cooperatively lifting her middle, to allow me to lower her underwear. Not a flinch, as I put my hand on her bottom. Holding still for her spanking. I wasn't being that easy on her. Not a peep. And, a 'thank you, Sir' at the end. Without being told. Then, Linda thanking me again, after we had stood up. And hugging me.

My pelvic muscles squeezed convulsively, relieving the pressure in my prostate, as my semen gushed. It felt so good. I was lightheaded. Then, my mind returned – somewhat – to reality, and I realized that I was in Kelly's mouth. She had expertly brought me to the height of ecstasy.

I opened my eyes, and Kelly smiled at me, looking up from her ongoing task. She gave one last suck, and slid her lips off my length. Then, she lapped me, like licking the drips from an ice cream cone. She leaned forward, and fell on top of me, pressing me into the bed, her breasts squashed against my chest. We held each other for a long time.

Eventually we got up, and I carried the tray back to the kitchen. I met Kelly in the shower, and we did a quick 'once-over' of each other, Kelly spending substantial extra time on my sticky parts. We dried each other and dropped our towels in the hamper, walking, nude, back into the playroom.

I grabbed a couple of bottles of water from the fridge, and looked over at the bed. We would need to remove the sheet and blanket, and the room still smelled like Chinese food – a great smell when you're hungry, but not so great, when you want to sleep. I blew out all the candles, and turned off the electronics. Taking Kelly by the hand, I led her upstairs, and upstairs again, to the master bedroom. I threw the decorative pillows on the floor, and we climbed into bed. It felt soft, and enveloping.

I asked, softly, "Are you as tired as I am?" Kelly didn't answer, but just rolled onto her side. I spooned her, my arm wrapping around her body, and under her breasts, our bodies in contact from upper backs down to our knees. I heard Kelly snore. That's all I remember, before falling into a deep, contented sleep.

CHAPTER 14: TASTE OF HEAVIER IMPLEMENTS

We woke around 8AM, both of us having been exhausted by yesterday's experiences. I spooned Kelly, as I had done last night and, after a few minutes, Kelly rolled over and on top of me. I supported her entire weight, as she kissed me lightly on the lips, and then worked her way down; down my chest, down my stomach, and down to my waiting manhood. She kissed me there, and then used her hands masterfully, until I was fully erect. Kelly slid herself up my body, and put my length inside her. We moved slowly, purposefully, taking our time. It felt great: The sex, and being in love.

Continuing our movements slightly more forcefully, we looked into each other's eyes. Kelly clenched her pelvic muscles, drawing me further into her, and holding me with a grip that would prevent me from escaping. But I had no intention of 'escaping' – except into my fantasies.

Even that didn't happen. Our long, slow, wordless coupling had excited both of us and ... suddenly, Kelly closed her eyes, and her body shook, as I felt her muscles contract around me, enveloping me in her hot secretions. A few moments later, my own body responded, fully aroused, and – as Kelly opened her mouth to mine, I came, thrusting into her, and holding myself deep within her. Kelly lifted her head, and we smiled at each other.

I realized, then, that I had not been fantasizing, just looking into Kelly's eyes, feeling the warmth of her body, and her hot wetness below. Our orgasms had resulted from a slow-motion union that seemed to naturally grow in intensity and emotion. Kelly put her head on my chest, and I stroked her back tenderly, my hands eventually cupping her bottom, and pulling her closer, so that I could stay inside her as long as possible.

After our morning ablutions, we met in the kitchen, where I made espresso, and took out the crèmes brulées. We brought everything out to the patio table, and ate our Sunday-morning breakfast, enjoying the start of another blue-sky day. There were a few small clouds drifting by, and it was already warm. It would probably be a scorcher this afternoon – perfect for frolicking in the pond. We listened to the birds chirp, and watched a squirrel run down the side of a tree.

We spent the next hour tidying the house – running the dishwasher, re-making the playroom bed and the bed upstairs, and packing a picnic basket that would be bungeed to my bicycle.

Kelly moved her rolling case into the bathroom, and I collected a king-size sheet on which we could have our picnic, and a couple of towels for drying off after a dip in the pond. I hoped that we would find the pond unpopulated, but I would bring a bathing suit, just in case. Then I sat down at my desk to work out a punishment plan for Kelly.

It occurred to me that my abilities as a dom might be limited, as I had mixed feelings about causing Kelly pain. The fact that she wanted to experience this comforted me somewhat, but I wondered whether I could provide suitable 'sex slave' training over a longer period. This bothered me, as I had always envisioned being Kelly's 'master', punishing her for any misbehavior, and taking her to her limits regarding pain.

Even our experiences so far had been rather a cop-out, from the perspective of a professional dom/domme: I had been overly careful to respect Kelly's limits, and probably had not brought her to the edge of her capabilities. Today's punishment – using the heavier implements – would push Kelly further, so that we could assess both her tolerance, and her interest in feeling pain at a level that she had yet to experience.

Kelly, still in her long t-shirt, sat down in one of the desk chairs across from me watching, as I added-up her punishments from the last time she was here – a level-75 in total. I made a few notes, and then looked up at Kelly. "It looks like it will take another level-25 to complete your original level-100 punishment experience. But I think you'll need some warm-up, before we try the heavier implements."

I looked down at the sheet in front of me. "First, we can do a level-10 OTK spanking, as a warm-up. Then, I'll give you a level-5 slippering." Kelly looked at me quizzically. "We'll use one of my flip-flops, the rubber sandals that I usually wear during the summer." Kelly nodded.

"Then, you'll get a taste of the flogger, which has a tail consisting of nearly two dozen ½"-wide, 18"-long straps of elk-hide. It can start out mild, but I think you'll feel the sting as the flogging continues. We'll also try it between your legs." At that, Kelly's eyes widened, and her mouth dropped open.

I was glad that after all our varied experiences, I could still surprise – and perhaps shock – her. I opened the credenza and found the flogger I would use, handing it to Kelly. The tails were black, and the handle braided with black and red hides. This implement could provide a wide range of stimulation, from light to heavy, depending on the strength of the blows, and the location on her body where they were applied.

I took another implement from the credenza, and held it up, smiling. "And this is the riding crop." Kelly put the flogger in her lap, and stared at the long, thin device in my hands, which terminated in a small, leather 'paddle', about 2"x4" in size.

I handed it to Kelly, and she slid her fingers slowly over the leather-wrapped handle, and down the long, thin shaft. That was hot! She held the crop halfway down on the shaft, and flicked the leather on her upper thigh. "Ow!! That really stings! How many strokes of this will I be getting?"

I smiled, and said, "It's a pretty severe implement, but doesn't cover very much of your bottom. I think a level-5 should be 18 strokes." Kelly winced. I continued, "The level-5 slippering, level-5 flogging, and level-5 cropping should prepare your bottom for the last punishment: A level-10 caning. That will consist of a dozen strokes of the 'school cane'. It will be a severe punishment, and undoubtedly your most challenging, yet."

Kelly looked down at the flogger and crop in her lap, and nodded impassively. She handed me the implements and, before she sat back down, her hands went to her bottom, rubbing, reflexively.

It was now just after 11AM, and I informed Kelly, "You will report here at Noon, for your schoolgirl punishment. Please dress in your official school clothing. I want to find you in the standing position, ready to take your punishment, when I return."

Kelly cocked her head, and I explained, "I'm going up to the garage to get the bikes ready." I added, "You won't be getting a 'corner time'. Let's shower together after your punishment. You may sit here," I rose from the executive chair, "and watch a few videos of slipperings, canings, etc. from the 'net. I have a bunch of sites specializing in schoolgirl punishments bookmarked." With that, I smiled at her, and walked out of the playroom.

Sam had surprised me by walking out of the room. I had more than half an hour to dress as a schoolgirl and present myself for punishment, so I took Sam's suggestion, and surfed a few Internet sites that Sam had bookmarked.

The outfit I had brought to wear was a mishmash of different items of clothing that I happened to have, but – judging from the girls on the websites – it appeared that I would be dressed quite appropriately to report to the headmaster for my punishment. I sighed, got up from the executive chair and walked into the bathroom, where I began unpacking the needed items from my rolling case.

I took off my t-shirt and bikini underwear, and donned a pair of full-cut microfiber briefs. I had considered buying heavy cotton underwear, but decided that what I already had in my drawers would have to do.

After peeing, washing my face, and brushing my teeth again, I put on a simple white bra, and the white blouse I had worn last night. Then, I pulled out a short skirt, dark blue with a green plaid pattern, stepping into it, pulling it to my waist, and zipping and buttoning the side. I twirled around, and thought the outfit looked pretty good, already.

Standing at the mirror, I fumbled with tying a solid dark-green tie – the best I could come up with, stuffing the end of the tie between the buttons and under my blouse. It wasn't perfect, but would have to do.

Finally, I pulled out a grey jacket that I had carefully folded at the bottom of my rolling case. There were a few creases but, overall, it lent the proper formalism for a boarding school (or reform school) uniform. I took the jacket off, and hung it on the back of the bathroom door.

I swung the door mostly closed, and looked at the image of a schoolgirl staring back at me. I turned my back to the mirror and bent over, looking between my legs at the reflection of my lower body. I could see the crotch of my underwear below the short skirt – from this angle – but my underwear probably wouldn't show from a normal perspective, even if I bent over. Of course, that wouldn't be a consideration during my spanking, today. I wondered how long Sam would allow me to keep these clothes on.

Thinking back to my first punishment – was that only a week ago!?!?! – I thought I should invent a scenario for being punished. What had I done wrong? I decided to make it simple: I was smoking. I chuckled, thinking that I wouldn't specify *what* I had been smoking.

I would be coming back the third time, for a school offense, having been given a choice between being expelled, and taking whatever punishment the headmaster would dole out – which I knew would include a caning. I had never been caned, before – either in my fantasies or in real life.

I thought back to last night – across Sam's lap – masturbating, as I fantasized that I was Julie, taking her first punishment. Well, at least her first punishment from Sam. I closed the toilet, and sat down on the cover, as my mind was deluged with images of Julie. She had always been wild (or at least wanted to be thought-of that way), and she was outgoing and uninhibited.

But I had never seen her – or even imagined her – demonstrating a pure, natural, personal emotional response. She had always been joking, trying to shock people, *acting*. What we had seen last night had been part of Julie's core. And that had been a brave but fragile, tough but emotional, and taunting but tender soul. Again, opposites that can, somehow, exist in the same person. Qualities that balanced, like a seesaw – or perhaps she was bipolar, yet it was so unexpected.

I put on white knee socks, and slipped into a pair of black, low-heel, patent leather pumps. I couldn't remember when I had bought these, or for what occasion, but they had been in the back of my closet, unworn, for many years. I got up and grabbed my jacket, putting it on and stuffing more of the tie inside my blouse, as I walked into the playroom.

I moved the desk chairs to each side, and took my position, about a foot from the desk. I separated my legs to a little more than shoulder-width, and looked down to make sure that everything was in place. I quickly reached behind and put my hands under my skirt to smooth the leg bands of my underwear, and then quickly rubbed my bottom.

It was probably the last time my bottom wouldn't be sore for the rest of the day. I hoped it would be worth it. Pleasing Sam. Satisfying my curiosity. Melding with my sexual desires. I thought briefly of the pirate fantasy. And then, with Sam, me being the 'top', Sam submitting to *me*. I enjoyed seeing *him* in pain. Perhaps I had a sadistic streak ...

I heard Sam walking into the playroom! My hands soared to my head, clasping my fingers on the top of my skull, wiggling my hips as I steadied myself. Sam was walking up behind me. My stomach turned over, and I thought I might throw up. I had to calm myself! I closed my eyes, my body rigid, in the expected position.

I entered Sam's brain and saw myself, wearing grey jacket and plaid skirt, in the standing position at the desk. The image was in slow motion, as Sam walked from behind me, then saw me from the side, and then from the front: A schoolgirl, come to the headmasters office for her punishment.

I snapped out of my thoughts, and out of Sam's head, when I heard a loud, "Kelly!" My eyes opened, and I saw Sam standing there ... in an old-fashioned black graduation gown, a mortarboard on his head. I smiled at him, and almost laughed, not expecting him to be costumed for the role.

"Do you find this funny, young lady?" With that, he snapped a ruler on the desk, and I jumped. Sam really knew how to instill fear and build tension!

"No Sir," I replied. I tried to remove the smile from my face.

Sam looked at me, radiating seriousness. My knees became weak. Sam snapped the ruler on the desk again, and said, in a loud and harsh tone, "Do you know why you're here, young lady? Kelly, is it?"

I was glad that I had prepared an answer, but my throat was so dry I wasn't sure I could get it out. "Yes Sir," I said softly.

Then, my courage returned, and I stood straight, and announced, "I was caught again smoking ... for the third time. I was told that I could choose: Either be expelled from the school, or take whatever punishment you saw fit," I swallowed. This was really hard, even though it was supposed to be role-play. But I knew well that the punishment would be hard, and very real. I finished my answer, "including a caning."

Sam smiled, and became serious again. "That's correct, Miss Kelly, this is your last chance. I don't think you want to be sent home to your parents, do you? Or sent to a State reform school?"

"No, Sir." I swallowed again, and choked out, "I've decided to take the punishment, Sir. I know it will hurt, but I really do want to stay here. Please, Sir, I'll take whatever you give me, in order to put this behind us ... and not upset my parents."

"That's a fine decision, young lady. Your education is important. And it's vital for you to understand how dangerous smoking is to your health." Sam looked at me sternly. "Are you prepared to cooperate throughout your punishment? To demonstrate your desire to improve, and be allowed to stay enrolled here at the school, you will need to cooperate fully, and immediately. Do you understand, girl?"

"Yes, Sir," was all I could muster. Sam may never have made-it as an actor, but he was sure convincing in this role. My stomach was doing cartwheels.

"Leave your jacket here, please." I took off the jacket and laid it over one of the desk chairs. Sam came around the desk, and walked across the playroom, pulling the straight-backed chair from the wall

Sam sat down and, without being asked, I walked up to him, and promptly placed myself over his knee, my toes just touching the ground, and my hands supporting my upper body. It wasn't a very comfortable position. My hair was a curtain around my face, trapping me in a claustrophobic space, as I awaited Sam's hand. It would come soon enough.

Sam flipped my skirt onto my back, and smoothed my underwear. Without further ado, Sam spanked me hard and fast. I don't know how many spanks I received, as I was trying to concentrate on staying in position.

Sam stopped, and I felt him grab the waistband of my underwear and pull them down. I raised my middle slightly, and the panties were pushed down to just above my knees. Sam adjusted his position and, without warning, I felt a sting, as his hand impacted my butt. Now, Sam was spanking my bare bum, faster and longer than he had ever done before.

The spanks smarted, initially, but didn't feel much different than I had experienced last night. But the longer the spanking continued, the more painful it was. It felt like my bottom must be raw, already, and this was just the warm-up!

It went on and on; I was sure that Sam counted out the 200 spanks, but it seemed like it lasted for a very long time. By the end, I found it difficult to hold still. I knew my legs were kicking, and my upper body was now hanging limply from Sam's thigh. Hair caught in my mouth, and I realized that I was whimpering. My bottom was on fire.

The sound died out, and I realized that Sam had stopped spanking me. He did not rub my bottom but, as I calmed, he instructed, "Get up, girl!" I slid off him, and got in the standing position in front of him.

Sam reached over and pulled my underwear down the rest of the way, and I stepped out of them. Then he rose, and led me by the hand to the loveseat, where he had me kneel at one end, and drop my upper body over the edge, holding myself up with my hands on the carpet. My bottom was high in the air – positioned just how Sam wanted it.

Sam paced around my head, and I saw him folding the flip-flop in his hands. He positioned himself and I felt the rubber tread extending across my bottom. Then it left me, and … 'THWAP!!'

Landing in the middle of my bottom, and including both left and right cheeks, I was pushed forward, my stomach on the curved arm of the loveseat, and my arms straining to hold myself up. It was several more seconds before I felt the next stroke. 'THWAP!!!' "Ooooww!! Sir!"

"Stay still, girl! We're just getting started!" Sam didn't delay, and another 'THWAP!!' landed; my bottom was *really* on fire, now!

After the third stroke, I broke down in tears. There was no way that I could take much more of the slipper. And I still had to face (or, at least, my bottom had to face) the flogger, crop ... and the cane. I tried to collect myself, as my bottom became one mass of pain.

Sam waited about 10 seconds between each stroke – just long enough for the pain to evolve, but not decay before the next stroke. The additional strokes hurt, but I was starting to mentally 'zone out'. It was a good thing that my hands were on the ground, and there was no possibility of lifting them; I would have gladly taken additional strokes for the chance to rub my bum right now.

Finally, the slippering was over, and I relaxed – dropping further down, with my forearms on the ground, and my thighs on the arm of the loveseat. I was sobbing softly, and panting, as my bum burned. I now felt a tension deep within me, and realized that I was also getting hot down below; or, as I was currently positioned, somewhere above.

Sam bellowed, "Get up, young lady. We have a lot more work here today before you've learned your lesson." I groaned, but got up, as instructed. Sam walked me to the office area, and positioned me over the side of the desk, with my legs outside each of its legs, my chest flat on the cool wooden surface. At least this position required less strength.

But my comfort was short-lived, as I saw Sam pick up the flogger and take his position behind me. He folded my blouse onto my back, so that I was exposed from the waist down. I then felt the first licks of the flogger, whipping left, and then right across my already-flaming bum. I could swear that I felt all two dozen elk-hide strands, as they pelted my bare skin. Sam slowed the swinging of the flogger, but increased the intensity. Now, my ass was stinging like Hell.

Tears came to my eyes again, but I tried to control my response: I failed. I whimpered, then sobbed as the flogger reddened my hips and upper thighs, stinging like a thousand bees, as it swept left, then right, then left again across my lower body. The tears flowed, and now I was crying in earnest.

I heard Sam say, "You've received 60 strokes sideways; now, we'll try 40 more strokes up and down." I couldn't process what he was saying, but I made an effort to stay in position, despite my blustering breath, and burning bottom. My ass had to be cherry-red by now, or perhaps purple. We were less than halfway through the punishment – the easy half – and I guessed that my bum would be black-and-blue by the end of the session.

I felt the flogger strike in an upward direction, lighting my inner thighs on fire, and providing a surprising sting on my sensitive parts. Sam was rotating the flogger in a circular pattern, with the tails coming up from under me on each pass. Then, he did the same coming downward, the upper part of my buns getting thrashed.

I wasn't sure which was worse. Then I found out: The tails of the flogger came whipping up from under me, and I felt a searing heat between my legs. 'THWACK!!!' "Aiyeeee!" I let out involuntarily. Oh, my God! I don't know how much more of this I can take.

Sam suddenly commanded, "Stand up, and turn around!" My bottom was so sore! I stood up, and turned around, in the standing position, with my legs as wide apart as they had been around the desk legs. Sam smiled, and started rotating the flogger again, bringing it up under me, along my upper thighs, and across my pubes. I closed my eyes, but that didn't stop a flood of tears from flowing down my cheeks.

Sam finished by flogging my hips – first the left, and then the right. I instinctively knew that I was red from my upper thighs to my waist, all the way around my body. My labia stung from the few direct strikes of the flogger there, and my lower body radiated heat.

I opened my eyes, and watched Sam put the flogger on the desk and pick up the riding crop. More tears flowed. I knew that I could use my safeword – 'HORSERADISH' – at any time to end the scene. But I didn't want to.

Sam led me across the playroom, and positioned me over the foot of the bed, my upper body supported on the covers, my legs extending diagonally to the floor, and my toes just touching the carpet. He sat next to me, and – finally – spent some time rubbing my bottom. And my hips. And thighs. And between my legs.

My whimpering subsided, as the pain fused, diminishing the sting, instead creating a dull soreness around the entire lower portion of my body. Sam got up, and pulled a pillow over to me. My arms went around it, my head buried deep in its folds.

Sam's words were gentler, now. "You've behaved well, young lady. We'll just make sure you've learned your lesson thoroughly ... and *then* you will receive your caning." I took some deep breaths, but the pillow restricted the airflow; it once again felt claustrophobic.

I heard Sam take his position behind me, and I tried to relax my bottom. It was still burning. I flinched when the leather of the crop was placed against my bum, and dragged across it, then down my butt crack. I felt the leather of the crop under me briefly, and then it was in the middle of my left buttock. Then, it was gone. I waited.

'SWOOSH!' 'CRACK!!!' And, a white-hot rectangle was seared into my bottom. I was panting into the pillow, tears flowing again. The pain was intense. 'SWOOSH!' 'SMACK!!' A fraction of a second later, I felt another rectangle of blazing pain. Again, and again, the leather tongue of the crop burned into my flesh.

The full 18 strokes took five minutes, but it felt like an hour. I was sobbing into the pillow, not believing how much more intense this experience was, compared to my 'first experience'.

Finally, it was over. Sam put the crop on the bed in front of the pillow, and rubbed my bottom. He then pulled me up from the bed, and hugged me. I leaned against him, my arms draped over his shoulders, and my head on his chest.

We stood there, holding each other, my bottom still ablaze. Sam said quietly, tenderly, "We need to complete your punishment now. You will be receiving 'twelve of the best' with the school cane." I shuddered. Sam had previously explained what a serious implement this was – something to be feared. And I was afraid.

Sam took my arm, and walked me back to the desk. "You will now remove the remainder of your clothing, young lady. You will be fully bared to take the cane."

"Yes, Sir," I croaked. I undid the top few buttons of my blouse, and pulled the tie out, unknotting it, and laying it on one of the desk chairs. I finished unbuttoning my blouse, and took it off, laying it over the back of the chair.

I reached behind with both hands, and unfastened my bra, sliding it off over my arms, and dropping it onto the chair. I got into the standing position, now completely nude. Sam sat at his desk, and typed something into the computer.

A minute later, he swiveled his executive chair, and opened the credenza, pulling several canes from the lower shelf. He examined each one, and I wasn't sure I wanted to see this. I closed my eyes. Sam swished two or three of the canes through the air, and my eyes popped open again. He selected one of the canes – not the thickest, but it looked like a serious instrument of pain. Which it was.

"Are you ready for your caning, young lady? Let's get this over with." Of course, I would *never* be ready for the caning – at least, that's how I felt standing here, my bottom burning. But, if I had said 'No' – or almost anything else, for that matter – I would surely receive additional punishment. My mouth was dry, and I rasped, "Yes, Sir." Sam smiled. I took advantage of this brief moment of compassion, and asked, "Sir?"

Sam looked surprised, but asked, "Yes, young lady?"

My confidence grew. "Could I please have a drink of water, before my caning?" I would use any excuse to delay the inevitable, but I really was thirsty. My throat was parched. Sam went behind the bar, and poured a glass of ice water, which I finished within seconds after he had brought it to me. I would have asked for more, but didn't want my bladder too full during the caning.

Sam took my empty glass, and set it on the bar, then led me over to the straight-backed chair, which he turned around. He had me bend over the back of the chair, and hold the seat. The chair was low, and I positioned myself with my breasts just over the back, and my feet on either side of the chair's legs.

I felt faint. This was not acting: My bottom was already very sore, and now I was to receive 12 strokes of this mean implement. I watched, as Sam stood by the side table, and retrieved an alcohol swab from the drawer, which he used to wipe-down the cane. Then, he swished it through the air a few times. My knees felt weak, and I wasn't sure I could survive the finale of my punishment. Sam strode around the room, swishing the cane, only intensifying my psychological discomfort. Finally, I heard him behind me, and felt the cane placed across my poor, sore, bum.

"Ready, girl?" Sam tapped the cane against my bum.

"Yes, Sir." I heard myself saying it, but was sure my brain hadn't consciously instructed my mouth to utter those words. I took a deep breath, and let it out slowly.

'SWISH!' 'CRAAACK!!' My senses overloaded, as my nerves transmitted their signals, and my brain interpreted them as intense pain. "Aiiyeeee!" I panted. "Oh, God, that hurts! Sir."

I heard no response, but when I was fully over the chair again, the cane tapped my bottom. Then, the cane left me, a moment later swishing down with another 'CRAAAAACK!!!' And I felt a second white-hot line burning across my bum. I considered using my safeword. But I held my position.

Sam walked around the room, and then stepped behind me, and rubbed the lines of fire, where the cane had landed, with his hand. I couldn't believe that my skin wasn't broken; my entire bottom felt raw.

Sam took his position again, and I held tightly onto the seat of the chair. 'SWISH!' 'CRAAAAAACK!!!!' "Ow!!! Ooooww!! Ooooww!" Oh, God. I don't think I can take it. Sam waited. I breathed heavily, and then spat out, "Sorry,

Sir." And, then – for good measure, "You may continue, now." At this point, I just wanted it to be over.

Sam took his time, sliding the cane back-and-forth across my sore rear, finding the right spot. There could be no right spot – my entire bottom was throbbing. The cane swung back, and then forward, with a loud SWISH! CRAAACK!!! Again, a hot knife melted a line into my rear.

This time, my body flew up, and I hopped around ... but was careful not to let my hands go behind me – which is what they were yearning to do. The tears started flowing again, as I bent over the chair, getting back into position for the next stroke.

My mind was now a blank, off in some other dimension, still able to feel the pain, but no longer registering what was happening around me. There were many more strokes, scorching pain, and hopping around. But every time, I got back into position, mechanically, rather than with reasoned forethought.

I don't know how I did it – actually, I don't remember the last half of it – but I completed the caning, my bottom feeling like a bloody pulp, although I assumed – hoped – that Sam had taken care not to damage me too badly. Although I hadn't tried sitting, yet, I could now certainly understand the phrase 'not being able to sit down for a week'.

Sam told me I could stand and rub my bottom, which I did, vigorously, dulling the pain, but not reducing it much. We walked over to the desk, and I got into the standing position again. Sam hugged me – a little more intimately than how a headmaster would console a student. I sobbed a while longer, then Sam handed me some tissues, which I used to blow my nose, and wipe my eyes. Sam sat at the desk, beaming at me.

"Kelly, you have just taken a hard caning, completing your level-100 punishment. Actually, with your warm-up, you received a level-35 today; but it was a very intense level-35. There are many more implements used for spanking, but you've now experienced a range of possibilities. How does your bottom feel?"

I laughed sarcastically, "It hurts, Sir, of course. How do you think it feels?" Sam looked at me solemnly, but then I saw his face soften. Before he could comment on my statement, I added, "Sorry, Sir. But my bottom feels like it's a mass of raw flesh. I'd really like to see how it looks."

Sam smiled, and said, "You may run to the bathroom and look, but come back here quickly." I ran to the bathroom, and swung the door mostly closed, then stood with my back to the mirror. Looking over my shoulder, I saw that my entire bottom was a deep red, with multiple thin white lines – actually, raised welts – cutting across it. I slid my hand over the welts, feeling their roughness.

Then, I bent over, as I had done earlier, and looked between my legs at the mirror. Everything was a deep red – including the insides of my thighs and the sides of my hips; they were sensitive to the slightest touch. I swung the door back open, and quickly washed my face before returning to the playroom.

When I returned to the desk, Sam told me to get dressed. I slowly picked up my clothes, stepping into the underwear, and sliding them up my legs and over my bottom. It hurt. Then, I put my bra around me, upside-down, fastened the clasp, and then rotated it until the cups were in front. I lifted the straps, and put my arms through, bending forward to adjust my breasts. I picked up the blouse, and put it on, and then stepped into the skirt, pulling it up, tucking in the blouse, and then zipping and buttoning the side.

Sam nodded, and said, "You don't have to put on the jacket, yet. He grabbed his camera, and took some pictures of me standing there; from the front, and from the back. Then, he asked me to lower my underwear again, and lift my skirt, and he snapped some shots of my thrashed bottom. Finally, he told me to pull up the underwear, which I did, dropping the skirt. I put on my jacket, and Sam took a few more shots – of me standing next to the desk, bending over it, and bending over one of the desk chairs.

Sam brought me a Diet Coke with ice in a crystal glass from the bar. We went over to the couch and sat down. "Ow!" *Tried* to sit down. Sam smiled, as I finally sat on my knees. I sipped my Coke.

"Kelly, I am very proud of you. Seeing what you went through today, I'm glad that we didn't try to finish your level-100 last time; I don't think you would have ever come back." We both chuckled. But he was probably right. He continued, "I almost reduced your caning to six strokes ... but wasn't sure if – or when – we would ever do this again, and wanted you to experience the full effect of a severe caning."

I didn't mention it to Sam, but I hadn't really been 'conscious' during the last few strokes. The combination of endorphins and psychological defense mechanisms had allowed me to withstand the caning to the end, but I was now certainly feeling the 'full effect'. I knew Sam would debrief me later, but now I felt like getting out of this room.

CHAPTER 15: COUNTRY PICNIC

"Sam, can we please go in the pool for a few minutes? I think the cool water may be the only thing that will soothe my bottom."

Sam laughed, "Sure. Let's do that, and finish with a cool shower. Then, we can dress for the picnic. I think everything else is ready."

"I'm not so sure that I can sit on the ground and have a picnic." I giggled, but was serious.

Sam replied, "There's a nice cool pond that we can soak in, which I'm sure will feel good to your bottom." Well, that sounded all right.

Now that I had just dressed, I removed my clothes again, bringing them into the bathroom, where I dropped them on top of my rolling case. Sam took off his shorts and tank top, and dropped them on the small table between the chaises in the shower area. We walked upstairs, and out into the bright day.

It was now getting quite warm outside, and the pool felt good, as I slipped into the refreshing water, and pushed off from the side. Sam got in, and followed me around the pool, as I floated on my back, watching small clouds drifting through the sky high above us. I glided over to the waterfall, and put my head on the lowest rock, the rest of my body floating diagonally into the pool. I closed my eyes.

As the water gurgled, flowing around my head, thoughts flowed through my brain, becoming turbulent, creating vortices. My body felt strange – not just my sore bum, but my entire being: It was tingling, reverberating, in a different 'space'. But I hadn't gotten turned-on by this spanking experience. Perhaps it was too real.

My fantasies were evolving rapidly, as I once again thought of Julie masturbating, over Sam's lap, on the playroom loveseat. I pushed off from the waterfall, shaking my head. Sam was sitting on the edge of the pool, watching me. I swam over to him, and held onto his legs.

"Shall we get ready for our picnic?" Sam inquired, cautiously, as he knew I needed time to come down from the spanking experience.

"I guess so. The pool feels really good. I think I'll be able to sit down again in a week or two." Sam laughed, but I was serious.

We went downstairs, and started the shower. Sam set the lower jets for cool, and aimed the top row at the height of my bottom. The jet of water against my tender tissues hurt at first, but the coolness was soothing. Sam bathed me, caringly, lovingly. Then I bathed him. Interestingly, he wasn't turned on, either. At least, he didn't have an erection. I wondered why.

We exited the shower, and dried ourselves with large, fresh towels. Sam put on his running shorts and tank, and I took fresh underwear, shorts, and a sleeveless top from my rolling case. Sam opened the medicine cabinet, and took out a tube of soothing lotion, which – while I stood there – he proceeded to smear on my bottom, around my hips and upper thighs, and on the insides of my legs. It felt good.

I dressed carefully, slowly raising the underwear over my sore bum. Sam watched and chuckled, and then I saw a brief flash of panic in his eyes. "What is it?" I asked, worried that it might be something serious.

Sam said, slowly, "Well, I just realized. You might have a difficult time riding the bike: It has a gel seat, but your bottom may still complain." He laughed, but I didn't think it was very funny.

I finished dressing and, per Sam's suggestion, grabbed a string bikini to wear, in case other people had the same idea about going to the pond today. It might be a little risqué, but with no back, my bottom would be much more comfortable. I combed out my hair, but that was the only nod to fixing myself to go out.

Sam grabbed the cooler as we passed through the kitchen to the garage. There was the van in which we had spent a memorable afternoon in the park. Sam had cleaned the bicycles, pumped up the tires, and fastened the picnic basket to the frame of one bike. Now, he added the cooler. He held up two helmets.

"We can use these, if you would feel more comfortable; but we won't need to ride on any roads, just the trail that starts behind the house." I declined the helmet, and we walked the bikes along the property line at the side of the house to the trail in back. There seemed to be some wood and junk on the side of Sam's house, which seemed vaguely inconsistent with his compulsive neatness everywhere else. But I didn't think too hard about it.

I couldn't believe it: After hiding it so well, and after the close call when Kelly had taken her friends on a tour of the backyard, I had walked Kelly right past the construction project for her birthday party. I looked the other way, and we kept walking the bikes; Kelly hadn't asked about it, and I wasn't about to tell her. It was to be a big surprise, hopefully one she would appreciate.

We turned our bikes onto the trail, and mounted them. Well, I mounted mine. Kelly was still struggling with putting her sore bottom on the small seat. Kelly tried riding the bike standing up on the pedals, but didn't get very far that way. Eventually, she settled herself on the seat, and we followed the trail into the forest.

The trail narrowed, and became bumpy with the gravel giving way to a dirt path with small rocks embedded into it. Kelly rode ahead of me, and I heard a string of 'Ow!'s', as her bike bounced along, and Kelly's rear bounced on the seat.

It had been a long time since Liz and I had ridden to the pond, and I hoped that I would remember where to take the path across the stream. Soon, I recognized the area where we had parked our bikes; there was a small pile of three stones indicating where to cross the stream. That hadn't been there before, and I wondered whether our 'private' pond had become a popular swimming hole.

We carried the picnic basket and cooler across the stream, walking through the very cool ankle-deep flow of water, and continued onto the narrow walking path.

Kelly was ahead of me, and I watched her rear sway with each step; I was reminded of Liz again, but there was no comparing their bodies: Liz had short blond hair and was small on top, while Kelly had long dark auburn hair, and was relatively big on top. Both women had narrow waists and generous hips, their bottoms presenting an inviting spanking target.

Liz had been in pretty good shape, for her late-30's age; but Kelly was an athlete, her muscles well defined, her strength obvious. And, Liz had been a housewife and part-time masseuse, while Kelly had written a Master's thesis, and was going for a Ph.D.

We came out into the clearing by the pond, and Kelly gasped, "This is really beautiful!" The setting was as perfect as I had remembered, the willow tree hanging down gracefully over the pond, the boulders still in their places, and the stream still gurgling, emptying over a rocky waterfall into the pond. It was an idyllic spot, and – as I had hoped – we had it all to ourselves.

We laid out the large sheet, holding the corners down with small stones from the edge of the pond. Our picnic basket and cooler sat on the edge of the sheet farthest from the pond, and Kelly and I sat on the near-edge of the sheet – Kelly on her knees, mesmerized by the flow of the water and sounds of birds chirping in the forest around us.

I opened the cooler and took out a bottle of Gewürztraminer, which I thought would be refreshing on such a warm day. As the cork came out with a resonant 'pop', the aroma of lychee and some other fruit reached my nostrils; perhaps it was apricot, or peach, but I couldn't tell. I poured a taste for Kelly and I into plastic cups, and we toasted to the beautiful day, and our idyllic private setting.

As I started unloading the picnic basket, Kelly decided to try the water. She stood up on the sheet, and removed her blouse and bra, then unbuttoned her shorts and pushed them down, along with her underwear, and off her long legs.

Kelly stood there, casually separating her shorts and underwear, dropping both on the sheet, as I examined the condition of her spanked and caned rear. Most of her bottom was still a deep red, and the cane marks were clearly visible as white lines that crossed both of her buttocks horizontally. I slid my hand over them, and Kelly flinched a little. No skin had been broken, and the welts were already not as raised as they had been an hour ago.

I sipped the crisp, clear wine, as Kelly walked slowly into the water, finally lowering herself fully into the pond, and pushing off from one of the rocks. I smiled, and watched Kelly move around the pool, exploring the waterfall, the lush vegetation, and surrounding boulders. She yelled, "The water's great! Come in with me."

I quickly removed my shorts and tank, and walked to the edge of the pond, sitting down on a boulder, then sliding into the water. It was refreshingly cool, but no longer shockingly cold, as the warm summer weather had heated the shallow stream.

We cavorted in the pond, the shade of the trees protecting us from the baking sun. Leaves rustled in the soft breeze, and light filtered through the canopy of branches, illuminating the pond and clearing in thousands of continuously moving flecks of light. We stood, waist-deep at one edge of the pond, and hugged each other. It was truly a romantic setting, and I envisioned us making love – on the sheet, or possibly with Kelly bent over one of the boulders.

It was already mid-afternoon, and I was getting hungry. Making my way to the edge of the pond, I climbed up the rocks, and walked to the sheet, picking up one of the towels we had brought. I stood there, drying my face and hair, when I heard Kelly shout, "Sam!" I hung the towel around my neck, and waved to her, but Kelly gave me a surprised look and pointed toward the path we had taken earlier.

Turning to look, I was shocked to suddenly see two women approaching us. They appeared shocked, also, seeing me standing there nude, but they continued their approach. I casually pulled the towel from my neck, and wrapped it around my waist.

The women came into the clearing, taking off their backpacks and dropping them on the boulders at the edge of the pond, no more than a dozen feet from our king size sheet. They looked up and smiled at me, and I offered a cheerie 'Hi!' as I sat down on the sheet, wondering how this would play out.

The women were evidently in their late 30s, both fit, but looking very different from one another. Both were good-looking, one with dark hair – I saw now, in the dapples of light coming through the trees, that it was brown, with lighter streaks, and fell over her shoulders; and the other with light red hair, almost a cross between blonde and orange, parted in the middle, and hanging wildly to the middle of her back.

'Dark hair' was full-figured, with more of a pear-shaped than hourglass body type. 'Orange hair' was slender and well proportioned; she had a straighter body, with only a slightly hourglass shape. They smiled at Kelly, and then at me, and 'orange hair' returned my 'Hi', and added, "It's a beautiful day here, isn't it?"

I nodded, "Great day for a picnic," (I pointed to the basket), "and some skinny-dipping." The women smiled.

'Dark hair' unfastened her belt, unzipped her pants, and removed them, then pulled her t-shirt over her head. She wore a sexy, but elegant, bikini bathing suit – very dark blue in color, tiny bottoms, held around the waist with multiple strings. The suit had a halter-top, connected at the center with a circular metallic ring, multiple strings passing around her neck to hold it up. It displayed her assets well.

'Orange hair' smiled at her friend and then, facing me, pulled her top over her head, her shapely B-cup breasts on display. I saw a glint, and realized that she wore a gold ring through her left nipple. She tugged down her shorts, putting them in her backpack. She wore a low-cut bikini bottom, sand- or tan-colored, with a thin, dark belt-like band around the waist. It was cute. When she turned to talk to her friend, I saw that the back was cut diagonally, exposing virtually all of her bottom – perhaps a 'Y' shape, instead of the 'T' of a thong. The women slipped into the water.

As I poured another glass of wine, and looked in the basket for the grapes, my mind's eye saw a painting by Delacroix: A handsome man stood at the edge of a pond, filled with beautiful nymphs. I couldn't recall the name, or details exactly, but imagined that the nymphs had the orange-blond hair I saw in the pond before me.

The women drifted over to Kelly, and I saw them talking. I couldn't make out the words, as the waterfall sound masked their voices. They were smiling and nodding. Kelly pointed to me, and they laughed. I couldn't imagine what they were saying. What an enjoyable way to spend a Sunday afternoon!

The cool water of the pond felt great. Sam and I were in a dream world again, another unbelievably romantic setting. I drifted around the edge of the pond, moving hand-over-hand along the rocks, looking up at the trees. My bottom was feeling a little better. As I held on to a rock at the edge of the small waterfall, my eyes scanned across the clearing.

Sam was vigorously toweling off his hair; he looked every bit the fit man that he was. My eyes caught a movement on the trail, and two women unexpectedly appeared in the clearing. My head swung to Sam, who was standing there nude, and I called to him. He put the towel over his neck, smiled at me, and waved. Unbelievable. Finally, he saw me pointing, and saw the women. He quickly put the towel around his waist, and greeted them with a friendly 'Hi'.

I pushed off, and treaded water near the center of the pond, as I watched the women undress. The one with the ginger hair color was cute, with a petite body and small breasts, but still with the curves of femininity. She looked younger than the one in the navy bikini, and had a bubbly, perky character. They got into the water, and eventually drifted over to me. I smiled at them, "Hi. Welcome to the pond." I'm not sure why I said that, as this was the first time I had been here, myself.

The women introduced themselves – Alex, short for Alexandra, with the dark hair; and Fiona, with the ginger hair and, I now saw, some light freckles on her face. Alex lived not far from Sam, and Fiona was visiting from Toronto, Canada.

I pointed to Sam, and introduced him, saying that he was a very interesting and intelligent person ... that we had been together for a couple of months, and that I was learning a lot from him. Boy, if they only knew! I invited the women to come sit and talk with us. As an inducement, I mentioned that Sam had brought some nice wine. They agreed to come over and visit.

My skin was shriveling, and I swam across the small pond, and climbed out on the rocks. I had walked less than halfway to our sheet, when I realized that I was nude. It had been so natural, I had forgotten. That wasn't important – I'm sure the women could see through the pond water that I was going 'au naturel'.

But now I realized that my spanked and caned bottom was on display! Oh, my God! How would we explain this?

Alex and Fiona would think that Sam was beating me. Or worse!

I turned and gave a small wave to the women, as they stared. Then, I walked back to the sheet, picked up a towel, and dried off, wrapping the towel around my waist, but remaining 'top-free'. I sat down on the sheet, gingerly, as I realized that my bottom was still sore. Sam leaned over, and gave me a nice kiss.

As he filled my glass of wine, I looked at him gravely: "Those women just got a good look at my behind. My caned ass, with the welts across it." I couldn't help but smile. But I didn't want Sam turned-in as a ... what? Woman beater? He was the farthest from that!

I told Sam, "Somehow, we're going to have to explain." I couldn't begin to imagine what we would say. I wasn't embarrassed; it wasn't that big of a deal, as we didn't even know these women. But I thought again of what might happen, if they decided that Sam was doing something to me against my will.

I thought about some of the websites I had surfed. Then, an idea struck me. "Sam! Let's tell them that you're a film producer, or director." Sam looked at me, his eyes full of curiosity. I explained, "You make spanking movies for your BDSM website! I acted in one of your movies, and we fell in love." I put my hands out with my palms up, as though I had just solved a riddle

Sam smiled and answered, "Why don't we just tell them the truth: That I'm a dom, and training you as my sub? They will either be shocked, or will understand. I'm not sure it makes a difference."

I said, "OK. And, if they respond positively, I could explain that I'm now turned-on by the prospect – and the reality – of being spanked. And that we hoped they didn't feel uncomfortable with us telling them all this, as we're really nice people, otherwise." We started laughing, and I noticed that Alex and Fiona were climbing out of the water near their backpacks.

It was funny. Well, probably not for Kelly. But she was correct, that we would need to explain, somehow, to those women. I started unloading the food from our basket, including sandwiches that I had made on pita bread this morning, and most of the leftover snacks from the past few days – banana bread, yogurt-covered pretzels, a couple of apples, a few hunks of nice cheeses, crackers, some salami, the jalapeno jelly, almonds, and I wasn't quite sure what else.

We set everything out, and I found another couple of plastic wine glasses in our well-stocked picnic basket. Kelly put out the silverware, including spoons for the jelly, and a knife to cut the cheeses. The women were now approaching us, smiling. They both still wore their bathing suits, and orange hair had a towel around her neck that hung down far enough to cover her breasts.

Kelly smiled, and invited them to sit with us on the sheet. She turned to me, "This," pointing at 'orange hair', "is Fiona. She's visiting from Canada. And this," pointing to 'brown hair', "is Alex. She's a neighbor of yours."

I reached over and shook their hands. "Pleased to meet you. I'm Sam." Kelly, Alex, and Fiona laughed, as Kelly had already introduced me, from the pond. "We've put out a few things. Please help yourselves." Picking up the bottle of wine, and a plastic cup, I asked, "Would you like some wine?" Both women smiled and nodded.

As I poured the wine, Alex asked, "So how did you guys meet?"

Kelly answered, "Sam and his wife were friends of my parents, and his sons were on the soccer team with my older brothers. Sam lost his wife in a terrible car accident. We re-met recently, when my parents had a party. Sam is providing guidance on my career. Once we started talking, we realized how many interests we had in common, and ..."

Kelly glanced up at me, "I guess we fell for each other. We've only been together a couple of months, but it's become more than a casual hook-up." I didn't think that Kelly had needed to offer so much information, but all of it was essentially true.

I handed the cups of wine to Alex and Fiona, then toasted everyone, "Here's to a beautiful summer Sunday at the pond." As they tasted the wine, I couldn't help but add, quietly, "With beautiful women." I looked at Alex, and she smiled pleasantly back at me.

"What do you do, Sam?" Alex asked. Kelly looked up at me brightly, awaiting my decision of how I would frame the story.

I was glad that this question was asked about me, before Kelly had to provide an explanation of why her bottom had been thrashed. I decided on the course I would take. I prefer honesty, whenever possible – which is just about always. But, I also felt like having a little fun with these women.

"I retired from a career in pharmaceutical research," I glanced at Kelly, and she was frowning, "and then decided to 'get a life'. Now, I produce fetish movies for the Internet." Alex's mouth dropped open, and Fiona looked like she was about to laugh. "And, I train young women to be submissives." I realized that this would need further explanation.

Alex was tongue-tied, and just said, "Oh?"

Quickly continuing, I explained that submission is a sexual turn-on to some people, just as domination and control is to others. That didn't mean that a submissive was a weak person: To the contrary, the sub must be very strong, able to control his/her emotions. And must be willing to accept some pain, in order to find sexual release.

I continued, "It's not for everyone." I took a sip of wine, and looked at Kelly. "Kelly is learning the role of sub, but we're finding that it may not suit her. I think she's really a dominatrix in sheep's clothing." I laughed, looking at Kelly, "Well, sometimes in no clothing." Everyone laughed, albeit somewhat nervously.

Fiona was quick to ask for details. Kelly answered, "Sam has been very nice to me, maybe too gentle. I told him that I wanted to role-play, and learn what it feels like to receive a serious spanking. This morning, we role-played a 'schoolgirl spanking' fantasy; actually, more than spanking."

Kelly looked up at me, perhaps for approval, and continued, "I experienced my first caning today. It was pretty intense. Sam brought me here to cool my butt in the pond," everyone laughed, and Kelly added, "and for a nice picnic to celebrate my submission to this new experience."

Now, Kelly looked at the two women seriously, "I found that I could get turned-on, but Sam's right: I don't think I'm cut-out to be a submissive. It isn't the pain, or giving up control; I just think I'd be more turned-on being the 'top' – the one *giving* the spanking, not the one receiving it."

Kelly sipped some wine, and looked thoughtful. "But I think Sam and I have learned that we're each a 'switch' – we can take the top role or the bottom role, and still get excited." Kelly looked at me, "Nevertheless, I think I prefer to be excited without my bum being sore." Everyone laughed again, this time more easily, as Kelly reached back and rubbed her bottom.

Alex sipped her wine quietly. I had been brave to share something like this with one of my neighbors; especially, one who I hadn't even met before. Or, maybe it had been foolish, and we should have kept our mouths shut. But we had needed to give *some* explanation for Kelly's bottom.

Fiona was getting more animated. "Kelly, can we take a closer look at your bottom?" Alex gave her a dirty look, then turned to me and shrugged, a thin smile etched on her face.

This time, Kelly didn't seek approval from me. She stood up, and turned around, dropping the towel. The women gasped, and Kelly looked over her shoulder, trying to see her bottom. She explained, "Sam spanked me with his hand, then with a slipper, and gave me a taste of the riding crop." I heard another gasp from Alex. "Then, I bent over a chair, and Sam caned me."

Kelly felt compelled to explain further. "Sam has spanked me before, and I've gotten turned-on by it." Kelly smiled, looking down, and added, "And he is always such a gentleman, giving me a 'happy ending' after most of my spankings." Alex's mouth fell open, and she looked away. Kelly sat down, cross-legged, and pulled the towel into her lap.

I jumped in. "Dominance and submission are a type of sex play for consenting adults. Part of the BDSM scene – that also includes bondage (tying people up with ropes), sadism, and masochism. I think Kelly will confirm that I'm not a sadist, and it's clear that she's not a masochist. My turn-on comes from someone willingly submitting, not being tied up, or forced. Kelly has been wonderful, and very open, in allowing us to experiment with many new things – for both of us." I didn't know what else I could say. We had laid it out, and now had to await the response of the women sitting with us on the picnic sheet.

Fiona nodded, "I think that's pretty hot. I once had a boyfriend who spanked me. He really got off every time we did it."

I turned to her and asked, "And, did you 'get off', also?"

Fiona's eyes glazed over momentarily before they focused on the scene in front of her. "Not really. My boyfriend just used his hand, and after a few spanks was ready for sex. Which usually involved me sucking his dick."

Alex choked on the last swallow of her wine. I opened the cooler, and offered her a bottle of water, but she pointed at the wine, and I re-filled her cup. Alex accepted it gratefully, taking a couple of swallows, and croaking out a 'thank you'. Fiona took a slice of banana nut bread.

"Alex, forgetting about spanking – if you can, what do you think about our openness? In terms of our conversation with you guys, and with our being nude?"

She reached for a small bunch of grapes. "Well, as far as nudity, I don't mind it at all. And, I think it's great that you can tell us about your sexual interests. But I don't think I could be quite that open – at least not with people I had never met before."

I smiled, "If you don't mind nudity 'at all', why don't we *all* go skinny-dipping after lunch?" Now, Kelly gave me a dirty look. I was pushing too hard, again.

But Alex responded well. "I might be OK with that."

Fiona got more excited, "Alex, that's great! I told you we didn't have to worry about bathing suits, if this pond was as private as you said." She looked at us, "I'm a lot more open about these things than Alex. She hasn't even been to a nude beach! Can you believe that?" I didn't know if Fiona was that much younger than Alex chronologically, but she certainly seemed to be much more of a free spirit.

We ate our picnic lunch, finished-off the bottle of wine, and marveled at the beautiful surroundings – still private, except for the four of us. We learned that Alex lived a few blocks from my house, was divorced, and was involved in sponsoring local arts, her husband having left her a considerable fortune, before gallivanting off with his new lover.

Alex had traveled extensively, and we found that she was quite liberal and open – in spirit. But she'd had little experience being open in 'real life'. She was clearly heterosexual, but seemed to have lost interest in sex and close relationships.

Fiona ate one more Florentine cookie, and then abruptly stood up, pushed her bikini down, letting it fall to the sheet, and stepped out of it. I noticed that she had a small butterfly tattooed on her right hip. She exclaimed, "Well, I don't know about everyone else, but this heat is getting to me. I have to get in the pond to cool off."

With that, she walked the few steps to the pond, onto a rock, and let herself fall forward into the cool water. Just like Liz had done when we first came to this beautiful spot a couple of years ago. We watched Fiona splash in the water.

Kelly looked at me and smiled, taking the towel out of her lap and setting it aside. She jumped up, and walked to the pond, slipping into the sparkling water, and swimming over to Fiona, who was now studying the waterfall.

Alex looked at me. "Kelly seems like a nice girl. I like her." Her use of the term 'girl' was not lost on me.

I looked at Alex, unsure of how to proceed. "Yes, Kelly is very special. She's getting her Master's degree, and is a very intelligent and strong woman – both physically and psychologically. I had mentioned to her my interest making spanking films, and our discussion of dominance and submission peaked her curiosity. This resulted in her offer to experience the scene in the role of a sub and, eventually, requested that I train her. We've grown closer, and have fun playing together."

Then, I explained further, "Kelly is a very open person, but doesn't really know what she's looking for – in life, in a partner, or in sexual turn-ons. I've been trying to expand her perspective on some of the possibilities. She's finding herself, as I'm sure are many, if not most, women in their twenties."

Alex nodded, "I understand. Fiona is still finding herself, also, although she's now in her thirties." I gave a questioning look, and Alex continued. "Fiona is my niece – my sister's daughter. My sister is ten years older than me, and Fiona is ten years younger. What a difference a decade makes! Whenever Fiona visits, she tries to get her 'auntie' to do something on the wilder side – like picking up someone at a club, and having a fling. I just tell her that I'm 'all fling-ed out', but she still pushes me to 'get it on' with someone."

I watched Kelly and Fiona frolic in the pond; they seemed to be hitting it off. Now it made more sense: Alex must be in her mid-40s, and Fiona was in her mid-30s. Not that much older than Kelly. I remarked, "Fiona's cute, and has a lot of energy. She seems pretty relaxed about nudity."

Alex replied, "Yeah. I guess the 'younger generation' is more open about these things. Although she's only half a generation younger than me." And, I thought, half a generation older than Kelly.

I stood, holding my towel in front of me. "Well, my wife and I frequented nude beaches all over the world for 20 years. In my opinion, there's no reason for a mature adult to be upset by nudity – theirs, or someone else's. I hope you're not too uncomfortable, but I'm going to join the girls in the pond."

With that, I dropped the towel, and walked towards the pond. When I got to the water, I glanced back at Alex. She was staring at me blankly; when I caught her eyes, she smiled at me. I lowered myself into the water, and floated in the coolness, gazing up at the leaves above us, fragments of deep blue sky showing through the canopy of trees.

As I approached Kelly and Fiona, they smiled at me. Kelly announced, "Fiona and I have been talking about you 'older guys'." I winced, and she laughed. "She said that you act a lot younger than Alex, even though you're about the same age. And I was answering some of her questions about spanking and submission." That was interesting.

Now Fiona squealed, and pointed, "She's actually going to do it!"

Kelly and I looked across the pond, and saw Alex removing her top and, after glancing at us and shaking her head, pushing down her bikini bottom. She had a beautiful body, the relative narrowness of her upper body accentuating her full breasts. Her pubic hair was dark, and trimmed in a rectangular patch.

She daintily stepped on a submerged rock, lowering herself, and finally leaned forward, and entered the water with a splash. She side-stroked gracefully over to us, a big grin on her face. "That feels good! I was getting hot, even sitting in the shade."

I didn't know whether she meant the weather or the discussion, but guessed that she was probably referring to both. Alex kept most of her body under the water, but I could see her breasts projecting out from her torso, bobbing around in the flow of water entering the pond from the waterfall.

Fiona hopped up onto one of the rock ledges bordering the waterfall. Her head of orange hair illuminated her freckled face, while down below, she was entirely hairless and smooth. Fiona's small breasts were pert and, with her animated style, she seemed younger than Kelly. Her nipple ring was small, proportioned to the size of her breasts, and there was a gold ball on the lower portion of the ring. I pushed off the rocks, and floated in the middle of the pond. What an enjoyable day!

A while later, I heard some splashing, and turned to see Fiona and Kelly exiting the pond and walking up to our sheet. Alex was swimming back to where their packs sat on the rocks. I made my way across the pond, and climbed out, sitting down on the sheet, next to Kelly and Fiona, who were still chatting, oblivious to their nudity. Alex walked over, drying herself with a towel, then wrapping it around her body. She smiled at me, transmitting genuine warmth.

"Fiona, we should get going." Then, looking at Kelly and I, "That was really nice. It was great meeting you two."

We all stood, three of us still quite nude, and I hugged Alex, kissing her lightly on the cheek, before I released her. Kelly and Fiona hugged, and then we swapped 'partners'. Fiona and I hugged each other, our naked bodies in close contact, but only briefly. Fiona smiled, and agreed, "Yeah. This was really fun. Maybe we can get together again, before I fly back home." She was now looking at Kelly, who nodded enthusiastically.

Fiona picked up her bikini bottom, and put it back on, casually. Kelly and I sat down on the sheet, as Alex and Fiona walked to their packs. We watched, as Fiona put on the t-shirt and shorts she had worn earlier.

Alex unwrapped herself and folded the towel, then slipped a t-shirt over her head. She pulled a pair of panties from her pack, and slipped them on, then re-donned her shorts. She stuffed the wet bathing suit into her pack, and lifted the pack to her shoulder. Alex and Fiona smiled at us, and waved, before turning, and walking back the way they had come, down the trail.

I looked at Kelly, "Well, that was interesting!"

Kelly looked over to the now-unpopulated pond, and back at me. "I thought so. Fiona's really nice; I enjoyed talking with her. She works at an ad agency in Toronto, and visits her aunt every summer. She thinks her boyfriend will be proposing to her, when she gets back home."

I listened, wondering how much of their conversation Kelly would share. Kelly went on, "Fiona thinks her aunt is too staid, so she tries to shock her, and get her to be more receptive to things – men, in particular. Alex was divorced many years ago and, according to Fiona, doesn't get turned-on by much, anymore."

I commented, "Alex never told me what she does. I mean, for work."

Kelly frowned, "I don't think she works anymore, but Fiona said she collects art, and is involved in some community projects. She seemed nice, for an older woman." I couldn't help but wince, again, but Kelly didn't seem to notice. "You guys would make a nice couple." Kelly smiled, and looked down to her lap.

I was feigned indignation. "Are you trying to get rid of me, already?" We laughed, but I wasn't sure it was so funny. Was Kelly trying to tell me something?

"No, silly. But both of you seem to have a similar background – living in the same neighborhood, being used to high standards, having traveled internationally."

We didn't really know what Alex's 'standards' were. I was glad that Kelly hadn't added, 'and you're about the same age'. Then, I had an inspiration. "Maybe, we should have invited them to your birthday party?" But that would inhibit some of our plans; some of *my* plans; especially, if Alex also came over.

Kelly laughed, "Actually, I invited Fiona. But she's flying back to Toronto on Saturday. And, Alex will be leaving on a trip to Europe." I relaxed. It *would* have been interesting ...

I grabbed a couple of Diet Cokes from the cooler, and handed one to Kelly. It was now sweltering, even in the shade. We ate a few more of the snacks, and I started packing everything back into the picnic basket. Kelly stood, and walked across the clearing, and a few feet into the forest, where she squatted, and smiled at me, as she peed. That was a good idea. I walked over next to her, and peed against a tree.

We finished packing up, shaking out the large sheet, and folding it. I hugged Kelly, and we got dressed, having never even taken out our bathing suits. Taking one last look at the tranquil pond and clearing, we started down the trail, carrying the cooler and picnic basket, and quickly arrived back at our bikes.

The ride home was uneventful; except for some daydreams: Of Fiona at the birthday party, in a circle with Kelly and her friends; on the Lazy Susan, playing spank-poker. Her bottom in the air, her anus relaxed; as I inserted a thermometer.

Before my thoughts could wander further, I realized that we were nearing my house. I got off the bike, and Kelly followed, as I led her on the other side of a hedge along my side yard – away from the construction project that I hoped she hadn't already noticed. We put the bikes in the garage, and carried the picnic basket and cooler into the kitchen. I was shocked to see that it was nearly 5PM.

Kelly walked out to the patio and, by the time I had followed her out, she had removed her shorts and t-shirt, and slipped into the pool. As I joined her, she remarked, "It's even hotter now than it was before. I guess summer is really here." We lolled in the pool, the water enveloping us in coolness, although it was at least ten degrees warmer than the pond water. Kelly swam up to me, and said, "That was a beautiful picnic spot. Thank you." I kissed her fervidly.

"Thank *you*! I enjoyed it, too." Then, I asked, "You didn't seem too bothered by Alex and Fiona seeing your caned bottom."

Kelly thought a moment, and responded, "I was a little embarrassed at first. And, I was worried that they would get the wrong idea; I had a vision of you being carted off by the police for being a wife-beater." She smiled, and corrected herself, "A girlfriend-beater." We laughed. "But I think they understood. More-or-less."

I had to ask, "Do you think Fiona would have 'played' with us, at an appropriate time and place?" As I finished the sentence in my head: 'Like your birthday party'.

Kelly quickly said, "Maybe. Probably. But she said that she hadn't gotten turned-on by her boyfriend spanking her." Kelly pushed off, propelling herself backward through the water, away from me. "She was a pretty outgoing person. I can imagine her trying some things with us." Now, I felt a stirring below. And realized that we had not made love at the pond, as I had envisioned.

"I was planning on making love to you at the pond ... but I guess we were interrupted."

Kelly swam back to me, and kissed me long and hard. Now, I was getting hard. We got out of the pool, grabbing our clothes, and walked downstairs, my erection bouncing with each step I took. I led Kelly into the playroom, and over to the bed. We had made the bed from last night, and I decided on the expedient approach, gently bending Kelly over the corner of the bed. She reached under, and took me in her hand, sliding me into her hot, musty, wetness.

I moved smoothly within her, as I reached forward and held her breasts from underneath. My body met the contour of Kelly's, and I kissed her lightly all around her back. Wordlessly, we moved together, and Kelly's hand slid under us, grasping my balls.

Again, a stream of images flooded my brain – Fiona's orange hair, Alex pushing down her bikini bottom. But, most of all, I saw Kelly's poise, her openness, and her comfort – even with our unanticipated visitors – at the pond. I came quickly, and unexpectedly, too soon – I knew – for Kelly's arousal to develop fully. I leaned over her, and kissed her neck.

When I had calmed, we stood and walked into the bathroom, and I took a couple of towels from the shelf next to the shower. "If you like, I can go down on you in the sauna? You seemed to enjoy that, last time."

Kelly chuckled, and said, "No – it's too hot for that." Then, she pondered the options, and said, "How about right here?" I wasn't sure what she meant, but found out quickly, when she spread the towel on one of the chaises and lay back, bringing her knees up, and letting them flop outward, in the butterfly position.

I smiled, and took my position, straddling the foot of the chaise, and going down on her, as I had offered. I was a little off-put by the thin rivulet of semen leaking out of her, but focused on her clit, thinking that now *I* could use the caramel sauce to advantage. My head went down, and my tongue did its job.

Kelly was, as usual, very responsive, and began thrusting herself against my mouth, as I fluttered her engorged knob with my tongue. I realized that I hadn't shaved this morning, and the stubble of my beard provided a texture that could be interesting for Kelly. I was certain that she would let me know, if it was over-stimulating her sensitive tissues.

I rested my chin on Kelly's upper labia, very slowly sliding it upward, until it lifted Kelly's hood, the short hairs now directly stimulating Kelly's clit. I had to be careful not to overdo it, so I let my chin rest there, not really moving it, just letting it rock slightly, applying pressure to one side, then the other, of Kelly's sensitive prominence.

It didn't take long: Kelly thrust against me once, twice, and then, with convulsions that bounced my chin off of her, and with a clipped squeal, her craving was fulfilled. I put my palm over her, pressing down gently, as Kelly continued to thrust against it, until she finally relaxed, her body melting into the chaise. I held her hips, laying my head against her dark triangle, which I realized would no longer be there, 24 hours from now.

After an unknown amount of time, we rose, and stepped into the shower, the large rain-like drops deluging us, as we held each other. Finally, we bathed each other, soapsuds dripping down both our bodies, hands gliding over each other with familiarity. In the short time we had been together, Kelly and I had probably taken more showers than my wife and I had over two decades. Good, clean fun. But it had become more than 'fun'. For both of us.

We dried off and, before getting dressed, I led Kelly across the hall to the exam room, and asked her to lie face down on the table. She gave me a 'look', but did as I asked. I inspected her bottom – now six hours after her slippering, flogging, cropping, and caning. The redness was now gone, only the stripes from her caning still showing, mean darkened lines crisscrossing her soft skin horizontally.

The welts had gone down, but I opened a tube of soothing cream, and smeared it on her. Looking almost like icing, I thought of 'hot cross buns'. I rubbed the lotion into her skin, and Kelly didn't flinch; the effect of the severe spanking had already diminished substantially.

As Kelly was dressing, I sat at my desk and checked e-mails. Julie had confirmed that she and the esthetician – Barbara – would be over around 10AM. I smiled, and wondered how Kelly would react to the process. She'd already had a waxing experience, but tomorrow would involve much more sensitive parts of her anatomy.

Kelly was very comfortable with her body, and I didn't think that she would be too bothered by embarrassment, after the initial 'opening' of herself to the esthetician. Julie had also included a list of suggestions on how to prepare for the waxing.

I drove us to a local haunt that had the best burgers in town. We ate most of our dinner in silence. As we finished the last few fries, I asked Kelly, "Are you nervous about your waxing tomorrow morning? Julie confirmed that they would come over at 10AM."

Kelly held a half-eaten French fry in front of her, "Oh. Now that I know it's really going to happen ... I guess I am a little nervous." I looked at her, and she added, "Not really about the pain – I got a pretty good 'feeling' for what waxing is like during my bikini wax. But I'm nervous about exposing myself like that to a strange woman. And Julie. And you." She looked up, and gave me a half-smile.

I offered, "Well, if you really want, I could leave you girls alone; although I hoped you would let me observe."

Kelly was shaking her head. "It's not really you; I'm OK with you watching. It just seems like I'll be on display. And, I will be embarrassed if I scream, or have to cry. Hopefully, the pain won't be that bad."

I nodded, "One of the things Julie suggested is taking a couple of Tylenol around 9AM. That should help."

Kelly and I finished eating, and we drove back home. We were both tired from the day, and our long weekend was not yet over. We went into the downstairs bathroom, and got undressed, Kelly donning her silk nightgown over the Jockey cotton bikinis that she had been wearing, as I slipped on a robe.

We sat down on the couch, and I lowered the video screen and fired-up the projector, selecting the computer as input. I printed the e-mail from Julie and handed it to Kelly, along with a Bluetooth keyboard. "You may want to do some research on Brazilian waxes, in preparation for tomorrow morning. You can also take a look at some of the styles, and decide if you would like to leave a 'landing strip'."

While Kelly was busily searching the 'net, I stepped behind the bar, and prepared a nightcap for us: Zinfandel port and small squares of 70% dark chocolate. When I returned to the couch, Kelly scrolled through a few images on a 'pubic hair style' website.

Not only were there waxing styles, but we also saw brightly colored hair (in fluorescent greens, purples, and blues), shaped hair (hearts, butterflies, and crosses), and even 'vajazzled' styles, with designs in crystals and jewels. We laughed at most of the exotic, but not necessarily erotic, pubes, but there were a few that looked nice, and not too over-the-top.

We consumed our port and chocolate, and finally turned off the computer and the video. I asked Kelly, "Do you want to sleep down here, or upstairs, tonight?"

She shrugged, "Either. I'm getting used to the bed down here, but the one upstairs is really comfortable." We decided to go upstairs, and crawled into bed. We held each other close and, before we had even considered making love, I realized that Kelly was snoring softly, her arm still across my chest. Just like last night.

I closed my eyes, recalling parts of Kelly's punishment experience this morning, and our pond experience in the afternoon ... and drifted off into a sound sleep.

CHAPTER 16: WAXING & WANING

When I woke, Kelly was not in the bed. I put on my robe, and went downstairs, finding her on the patio drinking a cup of coffee. She was still in her nightgown, and looked as radiant as ever, even before she'd had a chance to wash her face and brush her hair.

I sat down next to her, and gazed out at another beautiful day in the making. "Good morning, Sunshine!" I leaned over and gave her a peck on the lips. Kelly smiled brightly, her eyes now a dazzling green with flecks of gold, her long hair seemingly a shade lighter than I had remembered. She was still a knockout, as my manhood began to confirm, under my robe.

A few minutes later, Kelly had finished her coffee, and we walked downstairs together. "Would you like to make love, this morning?" I asked, admiring the curves under the thin silk that fell over her breasts, and down around her hips.

Kelly gave me a pained smile, and said, "I'd rather not." I remembered that it would be time for her waxing appointment in a little under two hours.

Trying to offer a suggestion, while not pushing, I offered, "You could always douche afterward."

She smiled at me, and said, "I let you douche me in the van, but my doctor said douching isn't a very good idea, as it can change the acidity inside me, and potentially cause a yeast infection." That was news to me. Then she added,

"But we can take a shower together ... and I'll be happy to give you a blow-job, if you want." Kelly batted her eyes at me.

"A 'blow-job'? That doesn't sound very romantic." Of course, I was only half-serious, as what man – including me – wouldn't want to receive oral sex from an enthusiastic partner?

Kelly chuckled, "I don't feel very romantic at the moment." She looked into my eyes and swallowed hard, "I guess I'm more nervous now about the waxing."

I hugged her, and said, "I understand." Again, I thought how brave this young woman was, and how glad I was that it wasn't me getting waxed today.

We walked into the bathroom, and Kelly pulled the nightgown over her head, and stepped out of her underwear, as I hung the robe. "Why don't you lie on the chaise, like I did yesterday? Then, I'll take care of you."

Who was I to argue? We went into the shower room, and I lay back on the chaise, my legs straddling the lower portion, and Kelly sat facing me, also straddling the chaise. I was only slightly hard, and Kelly flipped my penis onto my stomach, and began stroking it with her open hand. It didn't take long for me to 'rise to the occasion', and she circled her fingers around the base, and put me into her warm, wet mouth.

Kelly was very good at this and, creatively tried new approaches, this time keeping her tongue against the underside of my erection, as she slid me deeply into her mouth, her wet lips contracting onto its thickness with each stroke. I opened my eyes and, glancing down, saw only a wall of beautiful hair, swaying back and forth, and tickling my stomach. I closed my eyes again, and savored the feeling of being inside Kelly – still a warm, dark, moist cave, but at the other end of her body. Moments later, I came in her mouth, as her lips continued to move over me.

Kelly sat up, and smiled demurely, and then pulled me into a sitting position. She put her lips to mine, and kissed me, her mouth opening against mine, the salty hot liquid coating both of our tongues.

I was a little squeamish about this, but it seemed only fair that if Kelly could accept my cum in her mouth, then so should I. I tried not to think about what it was, as our tongues did their dance inside our conjoined mouths. We had come (cum?) a long way, since our first experience, when sharing of bodily fluids had been off-limits.

We got into a warm shower, and bathed each other caressingly. I spent time washing Kelly's vaginal and anal regions, and then she washed herself again. We dried off, and got dressed. I put on a pair of shorts and a Hawaiian shirt, while Kelly put on a bra and t-shirt, and then borrowed a pair of my running shorts, which she pulled on without underwear.

I walked across the hall, into the exam room, and cleaned the counters, leaving no medical instruments, syringes or needles in sight. I walked out, leaving the lights on, but closing the exam room door. It wasn't clear whether we would do the waxing here, or possibly upstairs on the massage table.

Kelly and I went upstairs, and out to the patio to relax until Julie and Barbara arrived. I realized it was after 9AM already, and ran back into the kitchen to fetch two Tylenol and a glass of ice water for Kelly. She was still nervous, and I engaged her in conversation to take her mind off the impending waxing. "Shall we keep our Thursday lunch dates this week and next?"

Kelly seemed taken aback, "Do I really have to leave today?" She frowned, and displayed her faux pout. Maybe it wasn't 'faux'. But I knew that if I booted her out of the house, she would certainly consider it *my* 'faux'.

I laughed, and told her, "I have to get a few things ready around here for your birthday party."

Kelly looked at me like I was crazy. Maybe, I was. What heterosexual male would make this beautiful woman leave? "Sam, the party's not for another two weeks. There can't be that much to do." Little did she know.

I still had a long list of to-do items, some of them involving construction that I wasn't sure how I was going to design. The party favors had been ordered from an Internet store, but I had to visit the local costume shop, the tailor, and – next week – plan the menu and market for the food I would be cooking. And, order the cake. I couldn't remember what else was on the list, but it was nearly a full typed page.

But I would also miss Kelly. She brightened my life in a way that I was getting used to, and at some point would not want to live without. "There's more than you think. I do have a few surprises in store for you, that I have to prepare."

Kelly stared at me, cracking a big smile. "I had a feeling you would surprise me with something. But I still have no idea what it might be." I thought, 'And that's just the way I want it'.

The time had passed quickly, and we heard the doorbell ring. Kelly and I went back into the house, and met Julie and the esthetician, Barbara, at the front door. Barbara was carrying a small case, and asked where we would be doing the waxing. I looked at Kelly, "The massage table is a little wider, but the exam room has the best lighting. I think we should do it down there, if that's OK with you." Kelly just shrugged and nodded.

Barbara suggested we sit down to discuss the waxing plan, and I brought everyone down to the playroom, where we sat on the couch. Julie wore shorts and t-shirt, but Barbara wore khakis, and a light blue short-sleeved blouse. Barbara sat on one side of Kelly, and I on the other, and Julie took the loveseat. Turning to Kelly, Barbara asked, "So what is it, exactly, that you're looking for?"

Kelly shrugged her shoulders, and answered, "I already have an extended bikini wax, but I think I want a Brazilian. Sam suggested a 'Hollywood' wax, whatever that is. I thought as long as we're doing it, I should go all the way, and take it all off, but Sam likes the idea of a 'landing strip'. What do you suggest?"

Barbara explained that at her salon, a Hollywood style removes all hair – in other words, no landing strip in front, and all hair removed between the buttocks, while a Brazilian is basically the same, but leaving a landing strip, or some small design. We laughed, and told her about the heart and butterfly designs we had seen on the 'net; neither of us was into that.

Barbara pulled out a cardboard sheet with dozens of designs abstractly drawn, with the name of each style below the illustration. "If you want to do it in steps, you might try the flame or teardrop design first. You're going to need to get waxed monthly, as maintenance, so it might be a good idea to leave more hair this time, and go for a thin landing strip," she pointed at the 'pencil' design, "next time. Then you can decide whether you want it all removed the following month." We nodded. Barbara then asked Kelly, "Where are you in your cycle?"

Kelly smiled, and said, "I should be getting my period in about a week."

Barbara nodded, and said, "That's good. Your genitals are more sensitive around your period, so waxing then could be a little more painful, so we try to do the waxing at least a few days before it starts, or after it ends. A week before is perfect." Then, Barbara inquired, "What type of wax was used for your extended bikini?"

Kelly shrugged, "I'm not sure. It was in small heated container, and was applied using a wooden stick – like a tongue depressor. Then, a small strip of cloth was put on top, pressed into the wax, and then ripped off of me. It hurt."

Barbara nodded, "We're going to do something different today: I use a sugaring paste."

Kelly frowned, "What is that? And why would you use that, instead of the other type?"

"Good questions," Barbara replied. "The paste is made very simply, and you can even do it at home – if you're brave enough to wax yourself. Basically, you boil sugar, water and a little lemon juice, until it caramelizes, and then put it in a jar and let it cool. There are a lot of advantages to sugaring. First, it is all natural, while hot waxes have resins and other chemicals. Second, it cleans up easily with water, and doesn't leave you sticky. Third, it sticks to your hairs, but not to your skin, so it should be less painful."

At this, Kelly asked, "But there's still pain?"

Barbara smiled and nodded, "Yes, it can still hurt, depending on exactly what part of your anatomy is being waxed. But there are techniques that minimize the pain. I'll explain that as I'm working on you." Kelly just nodded. She still looked nervous.

Barbara continued with her explanation. "One of the biggest advantages of sugaring is safety: I will probably use a single glob of the paste for your entire procedure. With hot wax, it's necessary to dip a stick into the pot, increasing the chances of contamination, although professionals should use a new stick for each dip."

Barbara stopped and thought a moment. "And, finally, sugaring takes the hairs out intact, without breaking them. So it takes longer for the hairs to regrow. You'll see that your hairs grow in thinner and softer each time. While your hairs need to be at least a quarter inch long to do a hot waxing, they only have to be a sixteenth inch long for a sugaring, so we can take them out earlier. After a few treatments, many of the hair follicles actually come out, so the result lasts longer, and there are fewer hairs each time that have to be removed."

Julie piped up, "Barbara has done sugaring waxes on me for several months, and I can attest to how well it works. I think it's less painful than hot waxing."

Barbara added, "And sugaring is much simpler to do when I'm going to someone's home, as we don't have to set-up the heated pot. It's a lot less messy." She looked around the room, noticing the bed at the other end. "Where do you want us to do this?"

I spoke up, "We have a massage table upstairs, but I also have a medical exam room that's well-lit, so I thought that might be most convenient." I saw Julie give Kelly a probing look, but Kelly didn't comment.

Barbara stood, and we all got up; I led everyone to the exam room, pushing the numbers into the electronic lock, and swinging the door open. Julie entered the room first, and gasped. Kelly whispered, "I'll explain later."

Barbara stood in the doorway, and said, "This will work fine." Looking at Julie and I, she asked, "Are you guys going to stay in here?" We nodded, and Barbara looked at Kelly to confirm it was OK with her. Kelly shrugged and nodded.

Looking back at us, Barbara suggested, "Why don't you to go around to the other side of the table, and I'll work on this side. We did as she asked, squeezing into the tight space between the exam table and the wall. Barbara set her case on the countertop, and unloaded a few supplies, including a jar of dark brown sugaring paste, some 4x4" gauze pads, latex-free gloves, a bottle of talcum powder, and a few spray bottles.

Kelly was still standing in the doorway. Under her breath, she muttered, "I guess we're going to do this." She took a step into the room, and removed her running shorts (actually *my* running shorts), putting them on the chair. Then, she hopped up on the table, and lay down, her head on the pillow, and her legs straight. She looked tense, her body stiff. Maybe, I should have offered her some wine before we got started?

Barbara went to the sink and washed her hands. Then, she opened the packages of gloves, and pulled them on. They were baby blue. She gently pulled Kelly's left knee out, and moved her left foot up, so that it was against Kelly's right knee. I guess it might be called a 'half-butterfly' position.

Barbara then took a pair of small scissors, and began trimming Kelly's hair, starting with the hairs on each side of her labia, and moving up to her already short-haired triangle. Kelly giggled, and Barbara explained, "I'm going to trim you, so that there will be less pulling." We watched her carefully work and, several minutes later, Kelly's hair was much shorter than before.

Opening a 4x4, Barbara sprayed it with a disinfectant from one of the bottles, and began to wipe Kelly's left groin, starting a few inches down her leg, and working up to the top of her triangle. Then she dusted Kelly with talc, rubbing it onto her with a gloved hand.

Barbara turned to the counter, and opened the jar; she tipped it, so that we could all see the dark brown paste inside. Sticking her fingers into the jar, she pulled out a glob of the viscous stuff, rolling it in her fingers. She stuck the glob onto Kelly's leg, several inches below the area to be waxed, and slowly pulled it along Kelly's skin, until there was a swath of paste an inch wide and several inches long. Kelly's eyes were closed, and we could hear her breathing deeply.

Barbara said, "I'm letting your body heat warm up the paste. This is much easier than wondering whether the hot wax is cool enough to apply without burning you." Barbara quickly pulled the wax off, and reapplied it a little lower on Kelly's leg. "That didn't hurt, did it?"

Kelly chuckled, her eyes still closed. "No, but you weren't pulling out any hairs, were you?"

Barbara agreed, "There weren't many hairs there. But I think you'll find that this will go much easier than your bikini wax." She quickly pulled the paste off Kelly again, and rolled it in her fingers; it was getting noticeably thinner, but not runny.

"OK, we'll get started now." She pushed the ball of paste onto Kelly's leg, a couple of inches below her genitals, and pulled it very slowly several inches diagonally up, towards her hip. She patted it down, waited a few moments, then peeled the top back a little.

Barbara pressed the paste blob in her hand to the edge of the strip of sugar and, suddenly, she ripped the strip of paste from top to bottom off of Kelly, who let out a breath. Barbara immediately applied pressure to the area with her gloved hand.

"Oh! I thought you would let me know when you were going to pull it."

Barbara smiled, and said, "It's much easier on you, if it's a surprise. Did that hurt?"

Kelly opened her eyes briefly, "I guess it wasn't too bad." Then she closed her eyes, and rested her left arm across them.

Barbara repeated the process on an adjacent strip of skin. When the wax was pulled off, Kelly emitted a short 'Ow!'.

The next strip was close to Kelly's left lower labium. Barbara put the side of her hand at the edge of the flap of tissue, pressed down, and moved it to Kelly's right slightly, so that it stretched her skin. Placing the glob of paste against Kelly, Barbara pulled extremely slowly, taking half a minute to spread the paste a couple of inches. Then, she picked up the remainder of the glob, and went over the same swath, sugar on sugar, thickly.

Barbara patted it down, and commented, "The paste is always applied opposite to the direction of the hairs, and drawn past the area of hairs, so that the top portion," she now picked at the edge of the sugar paste, and pulled it back, so that she could grab the end, "can be lifted, without pulling any hairs."

Again, Barbara stuck the blob of paste in her hand onto the edge of the sugared area, and ripped the strip of paste off Kelly, who let out an "Aaahhh! That hurt." Her hand was still across her eyes, and she looked more pained than she sounded. Only about half the strip of paste had come off, and Barbara pressed the glob in her fingers onto the remaining paste, lifting and ripping again, taking the remainder of the paste off. She again pressed the area with her gloved hand.

Barbara now commented, "You're sweating a bit now, so I'll dust you again with the talc. It's normal to sweat, but we need the hairs to be dry, so the paste sticks to them." She sprinkled some powder on Kelly, and rubbed it around the area. We could already see that the portion of

Kelly's skin already waxed was entirely hair-free and smooth. Julie took Kelly's right hand and held it.

I felt guilty that I hadn't thought of this, but I was entirely absorbed in watching the slow and methodical process. It was clear that this was an 'art', and would require substantial training and practice to do properly, and with minimal pain.

The next strip of paste that Barbara applied started at the bottom of Kelly's left labium, and was slowly pulled upward, along its entire edge. Barbara left her hand over the area, and told Kelly in a soft voice, "This area is more sensitive, so it might hurt a little." With that, she quickly pulled at the edge of the paste, and about half the length of the strip came off. Kelly bit on her lip. Barbara stuck the glob to the remaining paste, and pulled again, and the rest was removed.

"Aiyeee!" Kelly shouted. "Maybe I should have taken more Tylenol." We all wanted to laugh, but it wasn't funny, so we restrained ourselves. Kelly held her body still, and it seemed to be a real challenge of 'submission' to lie there, knowing that there would be many more pulls of the paste that would hurt. Kelly hadn't seemed bothered to lie there, letting this woman she had never met work around her genitals; and, allowing Julie and I to watch all this happen.

Barbara continued the sugaring, working excruciatingly slowly. Kelly's already-waxed areas were sugared quickly, there being few hairs there. Barbara molded the paste near Kelly's centerline, curving it outward, to leave a convex edge of pubic hair.

Kelly was sweating, and Barbara sprinkled talc and rubbed it in. "Kelly, do you want to take a break for a few minutes? It might help for you to relax, before we do the other side."

Kelly took her arm from across her eyes, and glanced up at Barbara, "That sounds like a good idea. As much as I want to get this over with, I could use the break."

I asked, "Kelly, do you want me to bring a towel to cover you?"

Kelly laughed, "Don't bother. You guys have seen everything already, so there's no point." Then she lifted her head, "Maybe a glass of wine would help relax me." I laughed, and squeezed past the corner of the exam table.

"Does everyone want some wine?"

Julie smiled, and nodded, while Barbara shook her head, "No thanks. It's too early in the morning, and I need my coordination to do this properly."

I opened a white zinfandel, and poured three glasses, balancing them precariously, as I walked back to the exam room. Barbara was in the bathroom, and Kelly was sitting up on the table. She reached for the wine, and gulped most of it down, before I had handed a glass to Julie. I laughed, and gave Kelly my glass, taking hers back to the bar to refill it for myself. As often as I had seen Kelly in pain, I found it tough to watch this sugaring procedure.

When Barbara returned, she said that we should switch positions, so Julie and I went around the table to Kelly's left side, as Barbara squeezed around the table on Kelly's right side. I took the empty wine glass from Kelly, and set it on the counter, along with Julie's glass, and mine – putting Julie's glass to one side, so that we wouldn't get them mixed up, this time.

Kelly and I had already agreed that saliva should not be considered one of the body fluids not to be transferred with others, but I still preferred not to eat or drink after others; at least those with whom I didn't have an intimate relationship.

Barbara lifted Kelly's left leg and straightened it, and adjusted her right leg so that Kelly's right knee was off the table, her right foot against her left knee. Barbara started working again, this time on Kelly's right side. The sugaring proceeded as before, working from Kelly's leg up to the top of her half-triangle.

After nearly every rip of the sugar, Barbara sprinkled talc on Kelly and rubbed it in. "You're still sweating quite a bit, which makes the sugar stick to your skin. Try to relax, as much as you can." Kelly stared at the ceiling and chuckled.

Finally, Kelly's right side was mostly bare, and Barbara carefully molded the sugar in another convex path around Kelly's centerline, leaving a leaf- or flame-shaped hair pattern. Barbara pushed the paste ball against Kelly wherever bits of the sugar were left, and quickly pulled up, removing them. Kelly's pubic area was now bare, save for the 'flame' of hair that Barbara had left – roughly an inch at the widest point, and a couple of inches in length.

Barbara smiled at Kelly, and announced, "Your front is done. You did very well." Then, she added, "About a third of the hair will grow back in 3-4 weeks, so if you maintain this every month, the waxing will go a lot easier, only having to remove a small portion of the hair we removed today."

Barbara straightened Kelly's right leg, and came around to our side of the exam table. "Kelly, we need to do your backside now."

Kelly groaned. "You can roll onto your right side, with your left leg bent, knee pulled up to your chest; but you'll have to hold your left buttock and pull it up, so that I have access. Or, if you're comfortable with it, you can get into a knee-chest position. That would be easier, if you don't mind being a little more exposed."

Kelly shrugged, and flipped over onto her stomach, and then pushed herself into the knee-chest position on the exam table. Barbara then took the glob of paste and slowly pulled it a couple of inches from just above Kelly's anus upward, along her butt crack. Waiting a few moments, Barbara stuck the glob of wax in her hand to the swath between Kelly's cheeks, and quickly pulled upward, ripping the wax – and Kelly's hairs – from her.

"Ooowww!" Kelly exclaimed. She put her face into the pillow.

A couple of shakes of powder, and another three strips of the sugar paste, and Kelly's backside was hairless. Almost. Barbara instructed, "Please stay in this position. I will need to tweeze the remaining hairs." Kelly groaned again, although this time it was muted, coming from somewhere within the pillow.

Barbara took her time, closely examining Kelly's rear, and plucking the few remaining hairs. She then sprayed some distilled water on a 4x4" gauze pad, and wiped Kelly down. All the remaining bits of wax and powder were cleaned off. Kelly's bottom looked great.

Barbara changed into a new pair of gloves, put some aloe ointment on a 4x4, and wiped the area from the top of her butt crack down to her anus. Then, she instructed Kelly to turn over and lie down, and Barbara wiped down her front with distilled water, and then the aloe lotion.

"You're done, dear," Barbara announced. Kelly let out an exaggerated breath, and lifted her head to see her almost-bare mons. Nearly 45 minutes had elapsed since we had first entered the exam room.

As Kelly sat up, and swung her legs off the exam table, Barbara instructed her on post-waxing care. "Kelly, there are a few steps you can take to minimize irritation and the possibility of infection over the next 48 hours. I'll leave a list for you. First, please wear loose clothing – no underwear, if possible. Second, a cool shower, or cold cloth will help, but please don't get in a hot bath, jacuzzi, or sauna. You also shouldn't go into a swimming pool or any water, other than tap water for the next couple of days." Kelly looked at me, and shrugged.

Barbara continued, "Tonight, please use Neosporin cream on the entire waxed area, and starting tomorrow, for a few days, keep your skin moisturized, or use aloe vera gel to sooth it. Starting in 3 days – that's Thursday – you should exfoliate your skin, and repeat that every three days for at least a couple of weeks. Tylenol may help, if you're still feeling pain in the waxed areas." Barbara glanced at me, and then at Kelly, "And, finally, please refrain from sex for the next couple of days."

Kelly said she understood, and hopped off the exam table, putting back on the running shorts I had lent her. Barbara packed her supplies, and we walked her upstairs, and thanked her for making the 'house call' on such short notice. I paid her, and she and Julie departed. I had hoped to speak with Julie privately for a few minutes, but that would have to wait.

Kelly and I went back downstairs, and she immediately went into the bathroom, swinging the door mostly closed, and dropping her shorts so that she could take a look at the results of the waxing. I stood next to her, and we marveled at the result – her pubes were smooth and shiny, except for the small 'flame' of short-cropped hair rising above her genitals.

I told her: "That really looks hot!" Of course, I was referring to Kelly's 'clean' look, not to the redness and irritation of her skin due to the waxing.

Kelly smiled, and nodded. Then, she turned around, bent over and, pulling her butt cheeks apart with her hands, examined her backside. Finally, she stood and pulled up her shorts. "I like it." She smiled at me, and then added, "But I'm not sure I want to go through this every month." I hugged her, and we walked back into the playroom.

CHAPTER 17: PLAY IT AGAIN, SAM

Looking at myself in the mirror, I was glad that I had gone through with it. The waxing was not at all enjoyable, and there was some pain. But now that it was done, I realized it hadn't been that bad. I hoped that future waxings wouldn't be as painful, as Barbara had promised. Although there was clearly an art to it, and it would take practice, I realized that it might not be that difficult waxing myself. Or, letting Sam do it. He would love that.

I pulled up my shorts, and we walked into the playroom, Sam fetching the half bottle of wine that was left, and taking a couple of fresh glasses to the coffee table. We sat on the couch, and toasted to my new hairstyle, and to our weekend together. In his analytical manner, Sam asked if I had enjoyed our long weekend. I had to think – it was mind-boggling.

The pool and jacuzzi, massage and electrical stimulation, needle play and hot wax, Kama Sutra positions, giving Sam a mock medical exam, getting a severe spanking, and then having a picnic in the idyllic setting by the pond. Eating our Chinese dinner in bed while watching the movie, and – of course – our incredible first lovemaking, with rose petals, candles, and champagne. Sam is a very romantic man – *my* very romantic man.

Then, I remembered the unexpected afternoon with Julie and Linda. I was not being spanked, or spanking anyone else, but what a turn-on it had been, watching Linda volunteer to go over Sam's lap. And, it had been even more of a turn-on watching Julie take a hard spanking, and then masturbate with animal passion in front of us. And, later, our re-enactment of Julie's experience. Truly mind-boggling!

"Sam, I don't know where to begin. I'm exhausted, and excited. It was really a weekend packed with adventures and surprises." I looked into Sam's blue eyes, "And making love with you." I swirled the wine in my glass. "I don't really want to leave. Again."

Sam took my glass and put it on the coffee table, then scooted over next to me, and kissed me sweetly. And then we kissed passionately, holding each other, grasping desperately. I didn't want to let go of Sam.

The next thing I knew, Sam had pulled me sideways, falling on top of him on the couch. He smiled, held my cheeks in his hands, and turning my head slightly back and forth, as we rubbed noses. Then, I held *his* face, and his hands slid around me and down to my bum, pulling me to him, as our mouths opened, and we shared each other's sweet wetness. Our energy spent, I slipped between Sam and the couch back, lying sideways, my arm across Sam's chest.

"I love you, Kelly, and I'm here for you. But you've got to take care of your new 'do', and I've got errands to do for a couple of days. Let's have lunch again on Thursday – this time, you can come here; I would really like to photograph you. And, you can plan to come over Thursday next week. And the week after." Sam tilted his head to me, "And then, we'll celebrate your birthday! A quarter of a century old!"

I pretended to be outraged, and said, "I may need to spank you for that, young man!" I knew he had been joking ... but he had still said it. And he knew that I was joking, but I would still do it.

We were both laughing, and I was about to ask Sam if I could come over next weekend, but he surprised me when he was suddenly still and silent. Then, there was an earthquake on the couch, as he got up and stood – in the 'standing position', between the couch and coffee table, in front of me. I couldn't believe it. Actually, I could believe it: Sam was again willing to submit to me.

Sam stood there, obediently. I sat up and swung around, sitting in the middle of the couch with my feet on the ground. Sam began to get over my lap. My mind was awash with images from our weekend.

I decided to surprise Sam, since he liked surprises, so much. "No, young man. Go fetch a hand towel. And the smooth paddle! And lube the small vibrator." He seemed startled, "Kelly ..." He knew better than that!

I gave him a dissatisfied look, and he immediately headed for the bathroom. I turned and barked, "And come back here without your clothes!" Then, "And you should pee, if you need to." Now *this* was a role I could enjoy.

As Sam got himself ready, I realized that my post-waxing instructions would not allow most of the things we enjoyed here – the pool, jacuzzi, sauna, taking hot showers, making love ... It was funny: Spanking was just about the only thing we *could* do together; at least for the next couple of days.

Sam returned, nude, and handed me the small towel, Ping Pong paddle, and vibrator. I widened my legs, and lay the towel across my lap. Then, I gave Sam the 'come here' signal with my right pointer finger. I saw a quick smile cross his face, and then he looked serious; I couldn't tell if it was an act, but I suspected it was. Sam took his position across my lap, over the towel, putting his head in his arms that were folded on the seat of the couch. He had a cute bottom – one that I had gotten to know pretty well. I put my left hand on the small of his back, and my right hand on his bum; just as he had done with Julie.

"You'll receive 50 hand spanks, and then 20 swats with the paddle."

Sam turned his head, and howled, "Twenty?!?" Now, he had given me more excuses – to stay a while longer, and give him some of his own medicine.

"You'll take whatever I decide to give you, young man! Yell out the count every 10 spanks." With that I began spanking him, alternating sides, at first giving only medium swats, but after half a dozen, I was trying to spank him as hard as I could. As he had said, it was *only* a hand spanking. How bad, could that be?

Sam's bum wiggled and jiggled, and I knew that he had to make a conscious effort to hold himself in place. I heard '10', and spanked faster. Sam's bottom was getting red, now, and he was rocking from side-to-side. I was glad I didn't have to count, and more images of Julie passed in front of me. I heard, '20', and '30', and '40', then snapped out of my daydreams and spanked Sam as hard as I could for the last few strokes. He was breathing hard. Sam turned his head to me, and said, "Thank you for the spanking, Miss."

I laughed, "That's only the warm-up. Prepare for your paddling! This time, you can count by 5's." I picked up the paddle, and placed it against Sam's left butt cheek.

Then, I heard "Ready!"

I was having a blast. And so would Sam's bottom in a moment. I heard the pops of the paddle against Sam's bottom before I realized that I was the one spanking him. Again, my thoughts drifted to Julie's spanking; and her masturbation scene. Sam counted the strokes, and I increased the intensity of the last five swats, Sam's feet kicking, and his mouth emitting muffled sounds. That was tiring! But it was good arm exercise. I realized that I should practice spanking in both directions, to strengthen both arms. Again, I heard a 'thank you, Miss' from Sam. Now, he was ready for the next phase.

"OK, you may masturbate, now, and I'll play with the vibrator." Sam's hands slid down, and he had to lift himself to get his arms past my left leg. As he lowered himself again, I separated his buttocks, and pressed the tip of the vibrator against his anus. A few seconds later, he relaxed his muscles, I pushed a little harder, and the vibrator slid into him. With an inch or two sticking out, I moved the end of the vibrator around in widening circles, and moved it in and out an inch or so.

Sam's hands got to work, isolated underneath him, somewhere in my lap, as his arms were pinned between his body and my leg. I moved the vibrator, and Sam moved his hands. It seemed like it was taking a long time.

I held the vibrator with my left hand, as my right slipped between his legs and my right leg, and gently grabbed his balls, holding them firmly. I continued to move the vibrator around. Sam's breathing got ragged, and I wiggled the vibrator, and pulled it all the way out, before plunging it back in. At the same time, my right hand held his balls tightly.

Sam's body tensed, and I heard a long 'Aaaaaaahhh', as Sam came, into the towel, under me. He continued to pump, his body rising and falling with each stroke, finally relaxing completely onto my lap. I removed the vibrator, and wrapped it back in the tissue in which Sam had brought it. I rubbed Sam's bottom, and let him relax for a minute. Lull him, until the next surprise.

After things were quiet for a minute or two, I said sternly, "Get up, young man!" After a brief delay, Sam struggled to get off my lap and stand up. I stood, also, and said, "Follow me!" I led him to the exam room, and sat on the chair.

Sam looked at me, innocently. "I'm sure you know why we're here, young man. You talked back to me. Twice! You know better than that, and such action requires corrective punishment." I was laughing inside, as Sam's mouth fell open. "Please make up a 6cc shot. I'll give you half on each side, for your transgressions."

Sam walked past me, shaking his head, but he stood at the counter, assembling the syringe and needle, filling it, and putting a couple of alcohol swabs on the counter. All the while, I watched his penis bounce – he was not yet flaccid again – against the cabinet under the counter.

Sam hopped up on the exam table, and turned over, lying on his stomach. I opened a swab, and picked up the syringe. Sam's bottom was red in the middle, but giving him the shot in his upper hip – where it should go – would avoid his spanked areas. I swabbed him, uncapped the needle, and inserted it swiftly. Sam was silent.

I was getting pretty good at this, but Sam had reminded me that I hadn't undergone his formal 'shot training' – whatever that entailed. I injected 3cc, taking my time, before pulling the needle out. I reached over him, and swabbed his left side, and gave him his second shot. Then, I dropped the syringe into the sharps container, and told Sam to lie there for another five minutes. Then, he could get dressed, and come into the playroom.

I went into the bathroom and sat on the toilet, carefully pulling aside the crotch of the running shorts, so that I could pee without irritating the waxed areas. Then, I packed my rolling suitcase. I couldn't recall if I had left anything in the playroom, or the master bedroom but, if so, I could retrieve it next time.

I put the rolling case outside the bathroom door, looking into the exam room: Sam was lying quietly on the exam table. I walked to the couch, sat down, and finished my glass of wine. There was not much pain from the waxing, but I knew that my skin would be irritated for at least a couple of days.

I heard Sam walking across to the bathroom and dressing. He walked to the couch, and sat next to me. He reached for his wine glass, but it was empty. "Kelly, I'm sorry. I think you know that I was just teasing you. But I probably deserved that punishment."

"Well, thank you for letting me punish you. It gave me some shot practice. And, I'm sure it will fuel a few fantasies, after I get home." I stood, and walked to my rolling case. I guess Sam hadn't expected such a sudden departure, but if I was going to go, I wanted to get home. Sam carried the suitcase to the front door, and we hugged and kissed again, before we walked out to my car. Just as last time, Sam waved, as I departed.

Looking in the rearview mirror, I saw Sam standing there. My Sam, the dom. My Sam, the sub. My Sam, the lover. As I turned the corner, my thoughts flowed from Linda, to Julie, to Alex, to Fiona ... and back to Julie.

I couldn't imagine what surprise Sam was planning for my birthday party, and I couldn't wait to find out. But with Julie, Linda and Kathy there, I could imagine some things that could surprise me. And turn me on. I sighed. Oh, the possibilities!

###

Thank you for reading Book 3 of the Experiences series. If you enjoyed it, please take a moment to leave a review at your favorite retailer. And, if you liked this story, you'll LOVE the continuation in Book 4: Birthday Experience!
- Simone Freier

Discover other titles by Simone Freier:

Experiences Series Book 1: Origins of a Fetish

Experiences Series Book 2: First Experience

Experiences Series Book 3: Weekend Experience

Experiences Series Book 4: Birthday Experience

Experiences Series Book 5: European Experience

Experiences Series Book 6: Friends' Experience

Experiences Series Book 7: Island Experience

Experiences Series Book 8: Domme Experience

Connect with the Author:

Follow me on Twitter: http://twitter.com/SimoneFreier

Friend me on Facebook: http://facebook.com/SimoneFreierAuthor

Visit my Website: http://SimoneFreier.com

Favorite me at Smashwords: http://smashwords.com/SimoneFreier

www.ingramcontent.com/pod-product-compliance
Lightning Source LLC
Chambersburg PA
CBHW021301250626
47155CB00002B/335